BET YOUR LIFE

A former champion jockey, Richard Pitman is now a leading journalist and TV racing presenter.

Ex-stable lad and former marketing manager for the Grand National, Joe McNally is founder and managing director of lazybet.com.

Also by Richard Pitman with Joe McNally

Joseph's Mansions

BY RICHARD PITMAN

Warned Off
Hunted
Running Scared
The Third Degree
Blood Ties

RICHARD PITMAN
with JOE McNALLY

Bet Your Life

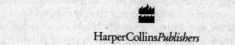

HarperCollins*Publishers*

HarperCollins*Publishers*
77–85 Fulham Palace Road,
Hammersmith, London W6 8JB

www.harpercollins.co.uk

This paperback edition 2005

First published by HarperCollins*Publishers* 2004
1

Copyright © Richard Pitman and Joe McNally 2004

Richard Pitman and Joe McNally assert the moral right to
be identified as the authors of this work

A catalogue record for this book
is available from the British Library

ISBN 0 00 651451 0

Typeset in Sabon by
Palimpsest Book Production Limited, Polmont, Stirlingshire

Printed and bound in Great Britain by
Clays Ltd, St Ives plc

*To the loyal band of readers who have
collected our novels. May you think the
teamwork between our first hero,
Eddie Malloy, and our latest,
Frankie Houlihan, works for you.*

For my wife, Margy, with love. Joe

ONE

Eddie Malloy stood in the wings of the stage of the Makalu Conference Center in San Francisco. He watched Keelor in the spotlight, winding his people up to give Malloy a storming welcome. The talk Malloy was about to give was one he knew by heart. It had earned him almost $700,000. It was the story, Keelor was now saying, of a man who died and rose again; whose survival instinct was so powerful, so deeply rooted in his core, that it dragged him back into the world of the living.

Malloy swallowed. There were three thousand people out there. All of them worked for Keelor and his Makalu Corporation, a global conglomerate selling everything from razor blades to holidays. Malloy was the star speaker at the annual conference and only he and Keelor knew they had a surprise coming after the talk.

He concentrated on trying to calm his nerves, thinking back to when he used to get a mild flutter in his gut before going out to ride in a big race.

1

After they'd effectively kicked him out of the racing game he'd sought his buzz in the mountains and the nervousness then had been of a different kind, less stressful. There were no people to let down as he started up a rock face or strapped on crampons at high altitude. It was just Malloy and the mountain. No punters cheering him on or cursing him, no audiences sitting waiting to be entertained. Just him and a challenge. The way it had been all his life.

Now his nerves were shredded, his bowels empty. He never enjoyed this but he'd become good at it and he wanted the money. He consoled himself with the knowledge that this would be his last tour for quite a while given the announcement Keelor had to make in about an hour's time.

Keelor finally got to the end of his spiel and Malloy checked his fly with his one remaining hand, wiped the moist palm on his trousers and turned as Keelor said, 'Now give a proper Makalu welcome to Eddie Malloy, the hero who came back from the dead!'

Normally, so focused on getting started, Malloy would only be aware of applause at the periphery of his mind as he walked on stage. But this time the wave of sound which hit him as he emerged into the lights dealt him an almost physical blow and he thought briefly of Devon Loch and its mysterious fall yards from the post in the 1956 Grand National. Some had said the volume of cheering had shocked the horse into collapse.

Malloy smiled in bewilderment as he reached for Keelor's outstretched hand and they turned to face this amphitheatre of three thousand clapping, stamping, whooping Americans. Keelor pumped his hand and reached to clasp Malloy's shoulder, staying with him to milk the applause, smiling at Malloy, gazing at him with proprietorial pride. Malloy spotted the nuance in the look and it unsettled him for a moment.

After almost two minutes the noise receded and the sound of chairs being sat on heralded an expectant silence. Keelor left him alone. Malloy smiled out into the darkness beyond the stage lights, reminding himself not to squint to try and see these people. As he stepped onto the podium and into the single spotlight he gave those curious about his scarred face the time to look at it in silence, then bowed his head for a few seconds. When he raised it his smile had been replaced with what Malloy hoped was a look of modest sincerity.

He said, 'Before I begin, I'd like to say that I've been doing these talks for almost two years now and I've been all around the world.' He paused. 'I have never had a welcome that came remotely close to yours. It means a lot to me. Thank you.'

They were cheering again before he finished speaking.

When they settled, Malloy began. He dropped his voice a tone to compensate for the pinch the nervousness would put on his vocal cords until he had warmed up.

'On May tenth, 1996, the best day in the lives of dozens of people turned to the worst. For nine of them it was to be their last day on earth. I lay with some of those corpses. I was found by rescuers but judged so close to death they left me there, convinced I wouldn't see out the hour let alone the terrible storm. The storm that took everyone by surprise. The storm that defied the predictions of millions of dollars' worth of weather-forecasting equipment and the best analysts money can buy. The storm that descended in minutes from a blue sky to remind a bunch of proud, selfish human beings how laughably fragile we are as it scoured and blasted us from the flanks of the highest mountain on earth.

'Statistic. For every seven people who reach the top of Everest, one dies. Remember, when you reach the top of a mountain, any mountain, you're only halfway finished. The trick is to get back down safely. One in seven. Not good odds. So why do people do it? I can tell you why *I* started climbing. No big philosophical reason. I needed the challenge. I needed to be good at something again.

'When I was twenty-one I was the champion steeplechase jockey in Great Britain.' Malloy put his hands on his hips and spread his legs. 'And boy was I a cocky kid!' They laughed on cue. 'I'd ride half a ton of solid muscle at big black fences at thirty miles an hour, practically yelling at the other jocks to come and get me. Sometimes they did. Sometimes they didn't. I won a lot of races, loved the thrill of winning, courted the danger. A jump jockey can expect to take a fall every ten rides or so. Most are soft ones. Some will break bones. The very occasional one will kill you . . . Addictive adrenaline rush. Sky-high libido. Stratospheric insurance premiums.'

Another laugh.

'Anyway, the Jockey Club, which is full of people who talk and act exactly the way you guys believe upper-class Brits do, decided they didn't like the company I was keeping. I was too full of myself to recognise that not all of my newfound friends were there because they loved me. One of them managed to inject dope into some of the horses I rode then framed me for it, and I lost my riding licence. Back then, seventeen years ago, it felt like they'd taken away my reason for living.

'It took me five years to clear my name and get my jockey's licence back, and I'll tell you, that's not just a long time, that is an eternity in the racing world. You can go from hero to zero in racing if you're not around for five months, never mind five years. There's always a line of guys waiting to take your place. Break a leg and someone else rides the good horse you should have been riding. He wins on it. The owner's reluctant to take him off next time it runs. Enough of those and a man has to start again at the bottom. I did that. I started again. But I never made it back to the top.

'So I packed up my boots and saddle for the last time, started having more than one meal a day, and set out to find something to – as I said to a friend at the time – stop me sitting at home climbing the walls. He said, "Why don't you try climbing the walls outside?" And he took me to Scotland for a month and taught me to climb.'

Over the next ten minutes Malloy took the crowd, amusingly, through some of his adventures on the rock face and his progression to high-altitude climbing. 'Altitude was a fresh challenge. I knew I could climb rock, figure out the moves one by one, hang by my fingertips if I had to, stay cool, measure the risk. But altitude takes no account of climbing skill or strength, or courage. Either you can hack altitude climbing or you can't. It's a physiological lucky dip. Those that come up short will get mountain sickness, eventually, no matter how long they spend acclimatising. Now mountain sickness doesn't sound too serious. Makes you think of throwing up then maybe taking some paracetamol and pressing on. The medical terms don't sound quite so cosy: HAPE and HACE. The first one is High Altitude Pulmonary Edema. That's the one that floods your lungs, drowns you. Then there is High Altitude Cerebral Edema. That one swells the lining of your brain till you die. The only cure is descent and you need to be fit enough to make the right decision and to get yourself down. Or you need to rely on others. And if you decide to go into the mountains, you should never rely on others. Never. You, your life, your survival, is your responsibility, nobody else's.

Some of the people who left Everest Base Camp in early May 1996 didn't quite understand that.

'Even those lucky enough to have the physical make-up to handle altitude suffer badly above twenty-six thousand feet. That's when you enter what doctors call the death zone. You're moving close to the height jet liners cruise at. How would you feel if you looked out of your aircraft window almost thirty thousand feet up and saw someone out for a walk? Albeit a very slow walk. Climbing at altitude, even with supplemental oxygen, is like running full pelt on a treadmill while trying to breathe through a straw. Without bottled oxygen you take one step, ten breaths, one step, ten breaths. The final climb from the South Col to the summit of Everest took most of our party fourteen hours. It's less than one thousand metres in distance.

'And while you're doing it, you're dying. You've had no appetite for days and very little sleep. You need energy and your body starts consuming itself to get it. Weight loss of twenty pounds or more over a few days isn't unusual and that's from a person already very lean.' Malloy paused and sipped some water. 'Now I want to tell you about the worst twenty-two hours of my life.'

When he finished, the applause built smoothly to a crescendo. It was different from the way they'd welcomed him. The gung-ho ambience had changed to one of thoughtfulness, of respect. There was no wild whooping, just clapping and the sound of seats flipping back as, steadily, the whole audience got up. Before joining Malloy, Keelor signalled for lights on in the auditorium and Malloy found himself almost mesmerised by the gradual illumination of all those people who'd been nothing to him but a presence in the darkness. All standing now, three thousand of them, looking at him; some smiling, many with tears in their eyes.

Drained, he bowed his head.

He felt Keelor's arm around his shoulder, smelled the freshness of cologne, felt warm and sweaty himself, in need of a shower and a cold beer. Keelor gave him a one-armed hug and Eddie felt him recoil momentarily as Keelor clasped the hinged prosthetic. Keelor recovered quickly and spoke to his people. 'Well, what did you think of that?' The applause swelled again. Keelor smiled wide. 'Eddie kind of glossed over the fact that he saved the lives of three people that night. Didn't spend too much time on the fact that it cost him his arm, did he? What a guy!' More noise. The whooping was back now that the boss was on stage again.

Keelor raised a hand. 'Listen,' he said, and they obeyed. 'Sit back down. I've got something to tell you.' They sat. He said, 'You all know we have a new venture, our first in the UK. We reckon the global betting and gaming market is going to be an unbeatable investment over the next ten years and the UK is one of the most respected centres in the world. It's the home of horseracing as we know it and we, my friends, are gonna get a piece of the action.' More whoops and cheers. 'There are fifty-nine racecourses on that little island and we want as many of them as we can get. It'll be a tough acquisition programme. Eddie told you something about the attitudes of the authorities over there. Getting where we want to go is going to be a huge challenge for whoever heads up our operation over there.' Keelor put his finger to his nose, cradled his elbow and adopted a quizzical expression. 'Now, would you happen to know an individual who loves a real challenge, who's got guts and leadership qualities way beyond the norm? Preferably someone who's got great inside knowledge of the racing game in England and good contacts?'

The buzz started in the auditorium and grew quickly, sparking applause which swelled as people rose again, cheering and whooping and chanting 'Eddie! Eddie! Eddie!'

Keelor turned to face Eddie Malloy and said, 'Welcome to team Makalu.' Malloy took a deep breath, slowly raised his hand and waved. Keelor hadn't touched on the real reason Malloy had agreed to become Chief Operating Officer of Makalu Racing UK Ltd because Keelor didn't know what that reason was. Keelor thought money was the key. For Malloy it was the power. There were scores to settle. A dish of revenge to be consumed; one that had taken years to grow cold. Malloy, hunkering on stage, confronting a sea of reaching hands, savoured the thought.

TWO

Vaughn Keelor's Makalu brand was one of the best known in America. His logo, the M in the name formed from two snow-capped mountain peaks (reproduced in 3D on company signs), had a public awareness score behind only Coca Cola and McDonalds. The Makalu name sat on aircraft, trains, fast-food outlets, theme parks, construction companies, banks, soft drinks, travel agents, health-food stores, gymnasiums, walking boots, outdoor clothing, tents, alternative medicine outlets, bicycles, private hospitals, drugs companies, retail pharmacists and casinos. The two products that had got Keelor started in business still featured proudly in his portfolio – spectacles and disposable razor blades.

As a seventeen-year-old in his hometown of Chicago, Keelor, who'd worn specs since childhood, was frustrated at how much it cost for a fashionable pair of glasses. Anxious for adulthood in the hope that it would be a great improvement

on having to rely on his father and mother to provide everything he wanted, Keelor had begun
shaving at fifteen after being told it would hasten
beard growth. Now he felt that razor blades and
nice glasses ate up too big a slice of his earnings
from the three jobs he had going. Against the
other fashion items he spent on – clothes and
shoes – the razors and glasses didn't pull their
weight with the girls.

Keelor had a reputation to uphold as the coolest
kid in his little world. If you saw Vaughn Keelor
wearing something new, you could bet it had
recently hit the shops or was just about to. Keelor
was the fashion touchstone for his age group. But
he knew he'd got himself to the lead in a race he
couldn't win unless he got a fourth job or took
up crime.

Or, he got himself a piece of the markets he spent
so much money in. 'What's so expensive in sticking
two pieces of glass into a wire frame?' he'd ask
himself, 'Or wrapping an inch of sharp metal in
an ounce of plastic?' Keelor was convinced there
were huge profit margins in glasses and razors but
he had no way in to suppliers, nor any real idea
of how business worked. One day, tired, wet, and
stinking of automobile wax, he took a coffee break
from his job in the car wash and picked up a week-
old copy of *Exchange & Mart* that someone had
left lying around. Leafing through, he found a section on Business Opportunities.

Those two words were enough to make Keelor

sit upright and put his coffee down. Both hands on the magazine now, he quickly scanned the small paragraphs and box ads. 'Consignment of reading glasses, 1000 pairs, assorted frames, bankrupt stock – $250.'

Twenty-five cents a pair. He'd paid more than twenty-five dollars for the pair he was now wearing. Okay, they were prescription glasses, but the frames were the thing. A lot of the kids who knew him had taken to wearing frames with plain glass in, just to be with the in-crowd.

Keelor took the magazine and went outside, past the row of queuing cars, exhausts pumping fumes from engines kept running to keep the aircon going in the July heat. He hurried to the edge of the woods, into the tree-shade and sat on 'his' log. He'd taken an interest in the outdoors after seeing a magazine piece about skiers in Aspen and how easy it was to get girls if you could ski like Klammer. The colourful suits and darkened goggles appealed to him and he wondered if the goggles came in prescription issue. He'd added a visit to Aspen to his list of dreams.

Keeping his finger on the page in *E&M* he opened it again and started developing the idea that had come to him in the shed. Kids copied him, right? His clothes, his hairstyle, his glasses? So why wouldn't they do so no matter what he wore? If he could raise the $250 to buy this stock, get prescription lenses put in one pair and plain glass in twenty similar frames, he could make a fortune selling them at twenty-five dollars a hit. This was it. He shifted on the log, away from the traffic hum on the interstate to gaze into the cool darkness of the woods. He smiled as he saw Aspen looming much larger than it had of late.

Keelor's begging and borrowing over the next twenty-four hours got him seventy-two dollars. The consignment owner sold him 250 pairs of glasses for his cash and promised to hold the remainder for him. Within three weeks Keelor was back for the rest and had plenty of money to spare. He was on his way.

He'd given himself a target of one hundred pairs to sell at twenty-five bucks each. As soon as he reached it he kept his promise to himself and quit his three jobs to work solely for himself. Within six months he had taken the lease of one thousand square feet of retail space in an upmarket Chicago suburb, the shop now a tourist destination, famous in its own right as the first to bear the Makalu name and the famous mountain logo.

Keelor had been taking skiing lessons at weekends on a dry slope. He could have afforded a trip to learn on some real snow but he'd promised himself the first time he'd ski on snow would be in Aspen, and he'd be skiing as well as any of the other guys on the slopes when he first stepped out of that cable car.

His research on skiing had developed into a deeper interest in mountains in general and at first he'd wanted to name his company after Everest.

But plenty of other businesses had used some version of that name. The name of the second highest mountain on earth, K2, didn't quite have the resonance he wanted. Besides, with its thirty-three per cent death rate of those trying to climb it, the PR connotations weren't good. The fifth highest peak, just fourteen miles east of Everest, interested him. At 27,765 feet it was less than 1500 feet shorter than Everest and, appealingly for Keelor, its name, Makalu, meant 'the supreme challenge'. Its shape was a perfect pyramid and two images of it made an equally perfect M.

By the time he was twenty, Keelor was a millionaire with a string of opticians and a mail-order business in disposable razors and blades at half the price other retailers demanded. His youth, success and flair for PR brought regular and consistent media coverage and, despite his lack of a business education, he featured regularly in the business press, mostly in a positive light.

At twenty-three, Keelor made the cover of *Time* and *Newsweek* as America's youngest billionaire. Four of his twelve businesses featured in the top fifty on Wall Street and his face was one of the best known in the country. He owned the biggest house in Aspen and as a skier could hold his place with professionals. He'd sailed his yacht in the round the world race, climbed on Yosemite's big walls and had declared an intention to be the first space tourist. He was also planning to climb Makalu, with the intention of summiting on his twenty-fifth birthday. Preparations were already in place for the mammoth media circus that would tag on to the Himalayan trip.

Keelor's taste for adventure was a double-edged sword for those investing in his company. The pension-fund managers, the big brokers in the city got very nervous each time Keelor announced what they believed was a daredevil stunt. On one hand, it brought another surge of publicity forcing Keelor and the Makalu brand higher in the perception of consumers and adding value to Makalu shares. On the other, it placed Keelor in danger of injury or death. These guys had bought millions of shares in Makalu Inc., shares they were relying on to continually increase in value to fund the pensions of employees, to bring in profits for their own companies, to bankroll investment in other business ventures. Keelor's key strength was also a huge weakness in business terms. Keelor *was* the Makalu brand. If anything happened to him, there was no way of predicting the behaviour of consumers. Would they stay loyal to the brand? Keep buying Makalu merchandise? There had to be doubts, and on the stock market doubts translated into plunging share prices and billions being wiped off investments in minutes. To his shareholders, Vaughn Keelor was more important than the President and deserved at least twice the protection.

But Keelor wouldn't have it. No bodyguards, no twenty-four-hour medical experts following him around. He already used the best people and the best equipment on any adventure and the risks he took were calculated to the nth degree. He was ultra confident in his own judgement and abilities, whether on a treacherous mountain or deciding what business to go into next. He had never made a significant mistake. Some investors, playing the law of averages that he had to mess up soon in a big way, had tried to second-guess the market and sold Makalu stock only to see it go even higher afterwards. That made others very reluctant to expose themselves to the same fate, so, tense as it was at times, they sat nervously on their invest-ments and prayed for the continued well-being of Vaughn Keelor.

They weren't the only ones hoping Keelor would continue making money. There were plenty of women whose image of Mr Right fitted Keelor exactly: young, handsome, athletic, resourceful, charming, and very, very rich. But no one was more aware of how valuable a catch he was than the man himself, and he used that for his own PR purposes as much as he did his adventure outings. Keelor was as likely to be photographed with a beautiful foreign royal on his yacht as with a shaggy yak and a team of Sherpas.

But by the time he met Eddie Malloy on Everest, Keelor was forty and had been married for twelve years, the last ten of those very unhappily. Finally bored of the beauty queens and supermodels he'd decided he wanted to be respected for more than his money. Keelor reckoned his intellect had never been properly recognised and that the years of being photographed with eye-candy hadn't helped on that front. He had started looking around for an intellectual woman and hit upon Sandra Beckinsford, the youngest ever advisor to the president. Sandra's childhood interest in biology, fed by her high IQ rather than any steely ambition, had led her to the White House as a specialist on biological warfare. She too had featured in the gossip columns and on magazine covers (although she resented the attention) and this PR value ratcheted Keelor's interest a few notches higher. A wife like that could help on the political front too.

So Keelor invested time, money and patience in the pursuit of Sandra Beckinsford. Fourteen months after they met, they married. Sandra's first achievement was persuading Keelor that a low-key wedding would gain them much more respect than renting half of California and flying in a thousand celebs.

And Keelor's craving for respect was the weapon his wife used from then on, sometimes cutting him lightly, at other times bludgeoning him. Two years into the marriage Keelor realised he'd made a serious mistake and one that could only be put right by damaging his image, and therefore his business. There'd be too much collateral damage to his empire if he was seen as a failed husband. So he lived with it.

Had Makalu shareholders known how close Keelor had come to dying on the mountain that

May day, a messy divorce would have seemed a glittering alternative. Keelor had lived through the storm, as had Eddie Malloy, although they'd been in different expeditions. Both emerged heroes. Malloy through what others said about him; Keelor from his own lips as the sole survivor of team Makalu's summit party.

Before leaving America for London, Malloy set up several meetings with people in racing. Weeks before, when Keelor had first mentioned the job offer, Malloy had made astute use of some reliable contacts he still had in the industry. He'd been aware of racing gossip only on the fringes of the sport and wasn't up-to-date on the politics. In recent years there had been huge changes to the way the sport was run and he needed a thorough briefing on where the power and influence now lay. He knew that the BHB, the British Horseracing Board, had a new chairman, Simon Bonnaventure, who was very ambitious, well-connected and, by all accounts, ruthless – not a quality usually found in men who run racing. And Malloy already had good cause to remember Simon Bonnaventure.

From 1752 until 1993, when the BHB was founded, racing had been managed by the Jockey Club. Now the Club had a much-reduced role, although they were still responsible for security. Malloy had had plenty of experience of their security department, which he believed had wrongly instigated the case against him that had resulted in his warning off – one of the draconian powers of the Jockey Club, unchallengeable in court. A warned-off person was not allowed anywhere on premises licensed by the Jockey Club – a considerable drawback when those premises are all racecourses and training stables and you earn your living as a jockey.

Malloy had no quarrel with the security department itself; it was under-resourced, always had been. He liked a lot of the guys who'd worked there in his time, the foot soldiers. His quest to clear his name had not only gained him respect among the security team on the ground, it had helped them greatly by landing some of the biggest villains in prison. After getting his licence back, Malloy had gone on to help them solve a number of cases.

Despite this, some of the people at the top, the stewards of the Jockey Club, had kept twisting the knife in him, even after his comeback when he'd proved himself innocent. Many Jockey Club members owned racehorses and had great influence with trainers and other owners, the people jockeys relied on for rides. Malloy was certain they had planted and nurtured sufficient rumours about his honesty to ensure almost all sources of rides eventually dried up. He could have carried on trying to make small money from riding bad horses, poor jumpers, but he had ridden the best, had been the top man, champion jockey. He couldn't stomach the prospect of being a nobody in the sport and one cold and wet November day at Kelso he took off his boots and colours for the last time and drove away from the course as the last race was being run. He had never been on a racecourse since.

But there was one man Malloy trusted completely and knew well, a man who owned a string of more than twenty horses, all jumpers. His name was Bobby Cranfield. He'd been one of the few owners who'd stood by Malloy till the end and the first man Malloy had called when he got home from Kelso that day. Back then Cranfield was the owner of a big PR and advertising agency. After a hunting accident left him wheelchair-bound, Cranfield sold his agency and accepted an offer from the Jockey Club to become its PR Director. Who better, then, to bring Malloy up-to-speed on the state of racing?

They met at Cranfield's home in the Cotswolds where Malloy watched him do his party trick of launching himself from his wheelchair into the swimming pool. Daily exercise and weight training kept Cranfield strong enough to get himself in and out of his Olympic-size pool although his lower limbs were useless. He still swam a mile every day. Malloy detached his prosthetic, exposing the stump of his left elbow, and joined Cranfield for the first five hundred metres then sat by the side of the pool listening to Cranfield's voice echo off the blue tiles.

Malloy left the meeting with a bound document containing most of what Bobby had told him but leaving out the most important part. Cranfield had told him something that could not be committed to paper, and had said that if it leaked out he would deny they'd ever met. Malloy assured him there'd be no leak. He drove away knowing he couldn't even tell Keelor. Still, it would be all the sweeter if things panned out. It would blow Keelor, and the racing world, away.

THREE

Malloy worked through spring and summer and come December he'd taken over two racecourses and finalised deals on three more. His time as a jockey had left him with the conviction that most racecourses were badly run. It was well-known that few made a true commercial profit, maybe only a dozen out of the fifty-nine. The others survived on subsidies paid from High Street bookmakers.

Malloy was convinced that courses could be run in a much more businesslike way. His detailed examination of the businesses he'd acquired for Makalu led to considerable nervousness among employees who had to find answers to tough questions, and it wasn't long before a whispering campaign started, branding Eddie Malloy a traitor to racing tradition, an ex-jockey turned heartless businessman.

Bobby Cranfield called him to arrange another meeting at his home. They agreed to do it that same evening, Sunday, the only time Malloy had to spare in the next three weeks. Cranfield suggested they had dinner.

Cranfield ended the call then rang Frankie Houlihan who, indirectly, worked for him as a Jockey Club Security Department Investigator. 'Can you come and see me tomorrow morning? At home?'

Houlihan had only ever been at Cranfield's home with Kathy when she was alive. He considered Cranfield a friend but thought this an odd request. They spoke regularly but it was always at Jockey Club HQ in London or on the racecourse. 'Is everything okay with you?' Houlihan asked.

'Everything's fine. Don't worry. I just need to talk to you before I discuss something with Sam. Can you make it?'

'Sure I can.'

'See you at nine.'

Houlihan ended the call and laid his mobile on the kitchen table. He filled the kettle and wondered what Bobby Cranfield had to tell him that he couldn't mention first to Sam Hooper, head of security, Houlihan's boss. Usually it was the other way round, organ-grinder before monkey. Still, he mused, maybe they'd decided he wasn't cut out for the job after all, although he was certain that if that were the case, Hooper wouldn't have passed up the delight of breaking the news himself.

He made coffee and drank it in the silent house, looking out at the grey Sunday morning; Cranfield out of his thoughts now, replaced by Kathy and reminders to buy flowers before reaching the cemetery.

Houlihan stood beside Kathy's grave, her engraved name bringing, as always, the memory of seeing it printed in the racecard the day she died. The day he'd watched through binoculars as his wife had been thrown from a runaway racehorse. Shivering, he relived again that long, lung-bursting run from the stands out on to the course, feeling as though he was moving in glue, never getting there. Then, standing over her, seeing her neck at that crazy, impossible angle and knowing she was gone.

Huge storm clouds darkened the morning. Leaves swirled and rattled against the tombstones. He'd been here in every type of weather now. This was his second winter. One spring, one summer, one autumn behind him. And one Christmas, with the next one two weeks away. Houlihan had made his mind accept she was dead, but his heart still couldn't believe it. He blushed with embarrassment as he recalled the craziness of his trip there on Easter Sunday when he'd waited from dawn till darkness, sitting by the graveside, trying to make himself truly believe that God would raise her up.

Madness.

Yet still he came, sometimes every Sunday. He knew she wasn't there below him. Her spirit was gone. But bereft of any other comfort including that of prayer, which he'd denied himself in an effort to save his lacerated conscience the added burden of hypocrisy, he was drawn back again and again to where her body lay.

He lingered a while, talking to her, seeing her laughing face, recalling scenes from their life together, before saying goodbye and walking the red shale paths of the cemetery till the clouds burst and flooded them, leaving him floundering in a rusty river, smiling oddly as he marvelled at the deluge.

Dawn was breaking when Houlihan left his home in Lambourn to drive to Cranfield's place. He'd tried hard to stay on at the cottage he and Kathy had bought when they'd married but the memories had been too painful. He'd moved to Lambourn mostly because he needed an air of optimism around him and the business of Lambourn people was racing. Many of the top steeplechasers in Britain were trained there, and where there are racing people you find hope and dreams. Houlihan's dreams had died with Kathy but he'd settle for a bit of hope that some day the misery would lift and the grieving would ease. It was cold and wet as he left the village but he rolled his window down to listen to the sounds of stable yards coming to life on a new morning.

Bobby Cranfield's CCTV camera picked Houlihan up after he'd driven through the gates, and Cranfield was waiting at the door, waving as Houlihan swung into a parking place. 'Good morning!' Cranfield called in his usual cheery manner and Houlihan smiled as he climbed the steps and shook hands.

'Good morning to you. You look well.'

'Never better.' Cranfield turned his wheelchair, preceding Houlihan into the big hall and talking as he went. 'Had breakfast?'

'No.'

'Want some?'

'That's why I waited. I've heard about Myra's breakfasts.'

Cranfield turned his head to look up at Houlihan. 'It's her day off.'

'You're kidding!'

'Yes, I am. Can't you smell the bacon?'

Over the meal they talked about things in general. Cranfield had known Kathy. It was through that friendship Houlihan had met him. After Kathy died it was Cranfield who'd offered him this job. Only after taking it did Houlihan realise how many strings Cranfield must have had to pull to get him, an ex-priest, a job as a Jockey Club Security Department Investigator.

Cranfield had done it out of pity, but also out of friendship. And maybe guilt had played a part. It was Cranfield who had introduced Kathy to race riding, before Houlihan had met her.

Houlihan thought back to the meeting at which Cranfield had asked him to apply for the job, saying, 'Well, you're used to hearing confessions, aren't you?' Houlihan's only experience in police work had come from a posting to the RUC as chaplain. That had been more political than pastoral but at least he'd gone through some basic training. And he had known, as Cranfield had, that he couldn't continue wading in grief. A return to the priesthood was out and he was not qualified for any other work. He loved racing and, with Cranfield as his sponsor, he'd got the job in the security department, knowing he mustn't let Cranfield down.

Still, he'd cracked his first big case, nailing a kidnapper of top-class horses earlier in the year, easing the pressure on both of them and earning Houlihan a lot of respect in the industry.

Myra came and refilled the coffee cups and took away the dishes. Cranfield gazed out of the big window as the morning brightened over his estate. 'What are they betting on a white Christmas?' he asked.

'I think you can still get five-to-one.'

'Might be worth a bet.'

'December's only averaged snow on two days a year for the past ten years. Skinny-enough odds when you think that one of those days would need to be the twenty-fifth.'

Cranfield smiled. 'You've been doing your research.'

'Heard it on the radio.'

'A useful piece of trivia for a change.'

Houlihan nodded, trying not to look impatient.

Cranfield said, 'You're curious.'

'I am. Put me out of my misery.'

Cranfield spun the chair slightly so he could rest his elbows on the white tablecloth. 'Do you know Eddie Malloy?'

'I know of him. Ex-champion jockey, Everest hero, now in charge of Makalu.'

'That's him. Nice fellow. He was sitting in that chair at dinner last night.'

Houlihan nodded.

Cranfield said, 'Malloy's beginning to get himself a few enemies in racing. Some people don't like the way he operates.'

'I've heard.'

'What have you heard?'

'That he's throwing people out of houses, demolishing "traditional" buildings, asking people who've been there ages to reapply for their own jobs, winding trainers up by charging them if they want to work their horses on course. That sort of stuff.'

'That's just one side of the story. Malloy's a fair man. I've known him for many years. He's got a long history. Was a great jockey.'

Houlihan held his hands up. 'I'm not attacking him, Bobby, just answering your question. I read all about him in the papers. Seems to me he's had a tough deal from racing in the past. It looks like our department wasn't blameless in a lot of the man's troubles.'

'You're right. It was before your time and mine, and those responsible have gone, but the department owes him for what it did to him, and for his help with later cases. He was no mean investigator himself, was Malloy, especially when his back was to the wall.'

'I read about that too. A tough guy. Maybe people shouldn't have been so surprised at what he did on Everest.'

Cranfield nodded, then gazed out of the window again for a while before turning back to Houlihan. 'There's a campaign building against Malloy and Makalu. I understand there'll be an ad in tomorrow's *Racing News* trying to rally support against the company's acquisition policy.'

'Support from whom?'

'Racing in general. And this is where it gets complicated for the Jockey Club. We're in the middle of trying to do a deal with Makalu to sell all thirteen of our courses.'

Houlihan tried to hide his surprise. The Jockey Club, through a subsidiary company called Race-course Holdings Trust, owned some of the top courses in Britain: Aintree, home of the Grand National; Epsom, which hosted the Derby; Kempton; Sandown; Cheltenham; and Newmarket, among others.

Cranfield continued, 'You know we've been under increasing pressure recently to concentrate on our core responsibilities: licensing, security and disciplinary matters. Well, you'll be pleased to know that your department is going to be the main beneficiary if this sale goes through. There'll be a massive investment in security, funded by some of the proceeds.'

'And if it doesn't?'

'If it doesn't then I'd say the future of the Jockey Club looks bleak, Frankie. The BHB is where all the power is now and Bonnaventure's working hard to kill us off. We've always handled the security side. He wants it. We haven't done as well on it as we should have in the past because it's been poorly resourced. We reckon the RHT sale could bring us close to one hundred and fifty million pounds. Wise investment of that sort of capital could fund the best racing-security operation in the world. Nobody would be able to match it, let alone Bonnaventure, so it would ensure the survival of the Jockey Club.'

'Is there anyone else in the running as a buyer?'

'Inkerman's group are the only ones other than Makalu who could raise that kind of money, and they're the last people we want. Makalu are committed to investing in the courses they buy, to run them as commercial propositions. Vaughn Keelor, the man at the top, believes that betting and media rights worldwide over the next ten years will grow enormously in value. Inkerman, although he'll never say it, takes the opposite view. He thinks the global betting market is limited and that it's very difficult to convert non-players to players. Inkerman's a property man through and through. We're convinced that when land values hit the right level he'll close the courses he has and start building.'

'Maybe with some of the ones he has now, but one hundred and fifty million pounds would take some recouping through selling houses, assuming he could get the planning permission.'

Cranfield sipped coffee and wiped his lips with a napkin. 'You say that, Frankie, but the average house price in London is now around two hundred and fifty thousand pounds. The average. Think how many houses you could build on the land at Sandown, Epsom and Kempton alone. And how much would they go for?'

Houlihan shrugged. 'Fair point.'

'Our commitment as owner of these courses is to reinvest profits in them for the good of racing. And while Makalu won't be quite so altruistic, at least they'll make sure racing continues.'

Houlihan nodded. Cranfield looked at him and said, 'You're one of the few people who know about this. When Hooper briefs you later he'll ask you to pass your current caseload to Geoff Stonebanks and try to find out who's really behind the campaign against Makalu. The *Racing News* ad will be placed by Bert Jacobsen who's fronting things.'

'The fella who's being thrown out of his house?'

'That's his story. Eddie Malloy discovered he's been defrauding the racecourse for years.'

'So why doesn't he just sack him?'

'Jacobsen claims it was all down to faulty paperwork by the accounts manager who died last year. Malloy doesn't have the time at the moment to spend on a court case and Jacobsen's due for retirement next year. But he's a handy fellow for evoking sympathy and stoking up bad feeling against Makalu, which is something the company can't afford. Keelor, the big boss, has made his name as a man of the people. Negative publicity scares the hell out of him.'

'And Keelor's bankrolling the RHT purchase so the department wants to help preserve the good name of Makalu?'

'That's pretty much it, Frankie. I'm telling you the details because it's important to get your commitment, important that you know how vital this is to the department's future.'

Not to mention the Jockey Club's, thought Houlihan.

Cranfield went on, 'And because I know Hooper won't tell you anything except get on with the job.'

'You're right about that,' Houlihan said. 'So, how do you want me to handle the report side – direct to Hooper?'

Cranfield leaned forward slightly, lowering his voice. 'Could you make sure I see everything first?'

Half an hour into Houlihan's return journey, Sam Hooper called him and told him to get into the office for two o'clock. A few minutes after that call came another, from Elaine, the receptionist at Jockey Club HQ. 'Frankie, your brother just rang. Pat?'

'Yes.' Houlihan tried not to sound as surprised as he felt.

32

'He left a number, asked if you could call.'

Houlihan pulled into a lay-by and dialled, not knowing what to expect. The family rift caused by him leaving the priesthood had seemed irreparable. He hadn't spoken to Pat in almost two years but he recognised the strain in his voice – tight, edgy. 'Pat . . .'

'Frankie. How are ye?'

'I'm well. You?'

'I'm all right, but Ma's very ill.'

'What? What's wrong?'

'She's just going downhill, Frankie, with this depression. She took to her bed the day you walked out and has barely risen from it since. She says she'll not see Christmas.'

Houlihan wanted to say, 'Pat, you know what she's like. She'll see plenty more Christmasses if she'd stop drowning in self-pity,' and other things that would have angered him. But Pat had made this contact and maybe it was time to start trying to build some bridges.

'Is our Theresa still looking after her?' Houlihan asked. Theresa, the youngest, was the only one still living at home and the only one who'd never turned against Houlihan. He loved her for that as much as for her overall sweetness. She was guile-free, Theresa. Childlike at twenty-two. Pat, Margaret and the others had left her to run around after Ma, who would wear her down physically, mentally and emotionally.

'Theresa's not been so good either,' Pat said.

'Margaret's been there quite a bit, helping out. She left her job she was so concerned.'

'What's wrong with Theresa?'

'She just needs a rest . . . we all do.'

Houlihan let that one go.

Pat said, 'We're calling a family conference.'

Conference? They'd all gone up in the world, thought Houlihan.

'To try and work out what to do,' Pat added.

And you've now decided to include me, thought Houlihan. After twenty-one months of no contact?

'We'd like you to be there.'

His tone told Houlihan that had been hard to say. Houlihan could almost see him cringing and then realised that his brother had drawn the short straw. There had evidently already been one family 'conference' and Pat had lost out; he'd been nominated to make 'the dreaded call'. And Houlihan also knew they wouldn't 'like' him to be there. It meant they wanted something from him.

He suppressed the anger. 'When is it?'

'Christmas Eve at the Drumroan Hotel.'

'What is it then, a dinner as well?'

'Not at all. No, we've hired a meeting room.'

Houlihan's mouth opened. Nothing came out.

'For four o'clock,' Pat said.

'You've hired a meeting room. For four o'clock. Is there an agenda? Will a flip chart be provided? Do I need to do a presentation?'

'Frankie . . . come on.'

'Frankie come on, nothing, Pat, for God's sake!

I haven't seen any of you for nearly two years and you're asking me back on Christmas Eve to some bloody antiseptic meeting room in a hotel? What is it, the prodigal son or the bloody Nuremberg Trials? Can't one of you have the decency to open the damn door of your own home to me? Shove your conference!'

Houlihan hung up, sweating and shaky, upset and surprised that it had all gushed out. He rubbed his eyes and went into his usual self-analysis. So where, he asked himself, is this episode going to figure on the recovery graph, if it ever happens that I get my life back together?

Later that day, in the office he shared with Geoff Stonebanks at Portman Square, Houlihan waited for the summons from the boss. Hooper had been in the job less than six months and no one in the department was anywhere near being able to read him. Ex-cop, Chief Inspector, the only thing Houlihan could reliably gauge from his behaviour was that he thought he'd been cast into a pit full of amateurs blundering around with little direction, poor resources and zero ambition.

Houlihan heard his name being shouted and he went into Hooper's office and sat down. Hooper, frowning, businesslike, shifting papers on the desktop, not looking at Houlihan, eventually said, 'Thanks for coming in. What are you working on just now?' He was still pushing stuff into drawers as he spoke. Houlihan said, 'The Irish passports scam and the money laundering through betting exchanges.'

'Where are you with them?' Hooper's concentration was suddenly and fully on Houlihan now, his almost black eyes unblinking as he waited for an answer. It was a tactic Houlihan had seen him use a number of times before but for some reason it still unnerved him. And so he shifted, involuntarily, in his seat.

'Making steady progress through surveillance on the Irish job and waiting for some info from a contact on the exchanges.'

'So it would be easy to brief another investigator and pass the work over?'

Houlihan, playing the part as Cranfield had asked, looked puzzled. He shrugged and said uncertainly, 'I suppose so. Why?'

Hooper didn't answer at the demand of subordinates. He said, 'Pass those cases to Stonebanks. Today.'

Houlihan held his gaze for a few moments then asked, 'Am I out?'

'You're out of these cases. You're still in the department. I want you to concentrate on one matter until I tell you to stop.' Houlihan didn't respond. Hooper said, 'Someone's out to get Makalu and Eddie Malloy. I want you to find out who.'

'Get them?'

'Blacken the Makalu name. Discredit them. Discourage people from doing business with them.

Someone's putting money behind a campaign to drive them out.'

'Their problem, surely,' Houlihan said, knowing how much it would irritate his boss.

'Whose problem, surely?' barked Hooper.

'Makalu's. They've got plenty of money, let them employ a PR man and fight their own battles.'

'Never mind a bloody PR man! I'm telling you to do it!'

These were the times when Houlihan luxuriated in the fact that he did this job because he liked it and he wanted to be busy, to keep his mind occupied. He didn't need the money. Kathy's insurance settlement had left him very comfortably off. He said, 'Why? Geoff's got plenty to do without taking on my work as well, especially when Makalu can easily afford to sort this out themselves.'

Hooper's eyes were wide. He leaned across the desk. 'Houlihan, Makalu is the biggest investor racing has ever had. We have got a duty to offer them some protection. You have got a duty to do as I damn well tell you. Now get your arse back to Lambourn and tell Stonebanks to get off his and get some bloody work done. And don't tell him what you're going to be working on, just tell him you're on standby to go undercover and that you don't know yet what the case is.'

Houlihan folded his arms and said, 'Well, if you insist, Mr Hooper.' He got up and pushed the chair back in. 'But I'm warning you, Geoff will not like this one little bit. Double his workload and, as far as he's concerned, I'm twiddling my thumbs.'

Hooper glared at him and shouted, 'Houlihan!'

Houlihan raised both hands. 'I'm going. I'm going.'

He swapped conspiratorial smiles with Elaine as he passed her desk. She said, 'Did you reach your brother?'

'I did. Thanks.' And that worry now moved to the top of the pile in his mind.

Geoff Stonebanks was glad to see Houlihan but not so happy to hear the news. On the desk in his small office at home, wire baskets and plastic trays were weighed down with paper. Bulging cardboard files rested against the legs of his desk, some spilling under it. Houlihan watched the big man put his hands over his eyes and sigh heavily as he passed on Hooper's orders. 'Who does he think I am, for God's sake? He won't even pay for a secretary. Joan's got to help me with all this.' He opened his arms to try and encompass the work that lay before him then threw his head back as though crucified and made a strangulated moaning noise, which got steadily louder till Houlihan started laughing.

'You're crazy,' he said.

'Hooper's driving me bloody crazy.' Stonebanks leaned forward conspiratorially, looked right and left, then, knitting his brows, he nodded at Houlihan to move closer. Houlihan dragged his chair forward. Stonebanks said in a low voice,

'Did he mention anything about the straw as well, Frankie, did he?'

Houlihan stared in puzzlement.

Stonebanks said, 'You know, along with the work you've got to give me, did he say anything at all about the straw?'

'What straw?' asked Houlihan, as though his friend were going mad.

'You know, the straw that broke the camel's back?'

Houlihan laughed again, then said, 'The only body part he mentioned was arse, as in, tell Stonebanks to get off his.'

The big man sat bolt upright. 'Houlihan! That's the first time I've ever heard you say arse!' He went into an imaginary swoon. 'Ask nurse to bring the smelling salts!' he cried.

'You should be on the stage,' said Houlihan. It hadn't taken him long to adjust to the earthiness of the racing world. When he'd been a priest he had gone racing as often as he could and was well used to hearing the curses as the favourite fell or was beaten in a photo finish. And he'd witnessed a few X-rated racecourse scenes fuelled by alcohol, hot days, tight skirts and loose morals. Yet when he started with the Jockey Club many treated him as though he must be protected from all signs of sin. Sometimes he played along; sometimes he'd say, 'Stop worrying. I've heard enough outside of racing to write a book.' Still, he couldn't quite bring himself to use 'proper' swear words, and hearing the Lord's name taken in vain rankled with him as much as it had always done.

Stonebanks got up and made coffee for them and asked Houlihan to brief him on his cases. Houlihan did, but told him that until he had any definite instructions from Hooper he would stay on them. Stonebanks was relieved. 'That'll give me a chance to clear my desk.'

Houlihan smiled, shaking his head. 'I've helped you clear it twice before. Don't waste your time. It's in your character to surround yourself with paper. Live with it.'

Stonebanks shrugged and sipped coffee. 'It sort of sneaks up on me when I'm not looking. I'm sure it breeds.'

FOUR

A smile spread slowly across Eddie Malloy's face, wrinkling the frostbite scarring on his left cheek. He read the ad's headline again. '*Homeless? Jobless? Penniless? Where will Makalu leave you?*' Below it was a picture of Bert Jacobsen and an open letter from him. '*After 37 years as groundsman at Badbury racecourse and just weeks away from retirement, Makalu Racing UK Ltd are throwing my sick wife and me out on the street. Despite a promise from Lord Melchett, the former owner, that we could live here for the rest of our lives, Makalu are evicting us from the only home we've ever really known.*'

Jacobsen's letter went on to list the other apparent 'savage cuts' made by the company and appealed for other racecourses to hold out against their 'ruthless acquisition plan'. He announced a pressure group he had set up called RACE – Racing Against Corporate Exploitation – and appealed for '*all who love the sport of racing*' to complete the slip below and return it to him.

Malloy checked his watch. Keelor wouldn't be awake for a few hours yet. He switched on his PC microphone and dictated an email, watching as the words appeared on screen a second after he spoke them. He'd tried to adjust to using what he called his 'rubber fingers' on the keyboard and the prosthesis reacted well to the muscle signals from what remained of his forearm, but it was just too slow. And one-handed typing made him self-conscious about his disability.

He sent the email to Keelor, telling him to have a look at the *Racing News* website for the full text of the ad and the follow-up article which quoted Malloy's response to Bert Jacobsen's claims: *'There are issues concerning Mr Jacobsen's employment which I'm not at liberty to go into at present. When all the facts are known, I doubt that any fair-minded person would consider him badly treated. The ground on which Mr Jacobsen's cottage stands will be covered by part of the new grandstand. Mr Jacobsen will carry on living there until his retirement. As far as the establishment of RACE is concerned, Makalu Racing UK has only one objective – to see all of its racecourses operate as successfully as they possibly can – and happy and efficient staff are, of course, vital to its success.'*

The email receipt came back stamped 2.02 a.m. New York time – 7.02 a.m. UK time. Malloy knew Keelor was getting nervous at the way things were going and he wondered how long he'd hold his nerve.

* * *

Hyde Park lay just across a road that was already busy with traffic this gloomy December morning. He got up and went to change into his running gear, hoping that the weather would improve when the sun rose. A three-mile run through the park would give him a chance to clear his mind, to sort the day's work out. He cursed while trying to tie his laces and once again wondered why he could ever have taken the easy accomplishment of such a task for granted. Since Everest he often told himself that fingers were wonderful things.

On the pavement, in the rain, waiting for a chance to cross the road, Malloy looked around at the Christmas lights in the windows and felt a momentary sadness. He wasn't far off forty. He had more money than he'd ever dreamed he'd have and a job that gave him a chance to right some bitter wrongs. But he had no real friends. As a twenty-one-year-old champion jockey he'd been surrounded by people he considered true friends. When one of them framed him and the others deserted him, Malloy decided he'd make do with 'acquaintances' for the rest of his life. He set aside space for one exception – the right woman – and when he'd met Laura he felt unshackled, finally free to be himself. He started seeing life in the daylight rather than the darkness he'd grown used to. So he opened up again. He kept just one thing from her for fear of it lessening her love. And he'd often wondered if that was what had killed the marriage, that single thing from long ago, the event that had staked his soul and fixed him, leaking misery into him over the years like rust.

His parents, hard as they'd been on him, were long dead. His remaining brother hustled off to Australia by his foster family. He had no one.

The next evening, as Malloy was immersed in paperwork, a brick came through his window. It bounced on the desk he sat at. The boom and shattering glass sent him diving to the wooden floor, covering his head with his false arm, reasoning quickly that it afforded potentially less painful protection than his good one. A diamond-shaped glass shard spun into the lamp bulb, popping it, releasing a puff of light smoke in the cold air and leaving the room dark. Malloy lay still for a minute then rose to his knees and peered carefully over the debris to the street outside. He could see no one. Staying out of view he scrambled across the floor and into the hall. A few minutes later he edged back in, still not switching on the main light. The brick lay in the centre of the room, wrapped in a clear plastic bag. He retrieved it and took it into the windowless gym at the rear. There was a note in the bag too. He read the large block capitals: 'GET OUT WHILE YOU STILL HAVE ONE GOOD ARM'.

Malloy thought about calling the police but quickly decided against it. He knew the odds were a million to one against catching the culprit, and he didn't want to be seen to overreact to what was obviously a clumsy attempt by one of the RACE supporters to intimidate him. That brought a smile as he recalled some of the agonies he'd been through. He decided he wouldn't even tell Keelor as he reached for the phone book and riffled through to 'Glaziers'.

FIVE

The Christmas Eve flight to Dublin was packed. Everybody seemed excited; laughing easily, talking too loud. Except Frankie Houlihan. He felt his stomach descend with the plane as the city lights grew bigger and brighter. The family had relented and agreed to hold the meeting at Margaret's. Although that had been the sticking point for Houlihan the first time Pat called, he'd been sorry to see it conceded. He just didn't want to be there.

Dublin he didn't mind. In fact, he loved the city. It held lots of good memories, especially from childhood when the family had been united. But the Houlihans, with the exception of Theresa, had effectively banished him from the fold, and coming back to Dublin would never be quite the same.

Pat met him at the airport, three-piece suit, polished shoes and silver BMW showroom-shiny as ever. They shook hands. Pat took his overnight bag and opened the passenger door. On the road the small talk lasted for maybe five minutes.

Houlihan got the impression Pat was under instructions not to discuss anything meaningful until everyone was present. They settled into an uncomfortable silence.

Margaret greeted Houlihan with a strained smile. She touched his arm, kissed him lightly on the cheek. 'Come in, Frankie. It's good to see you.'

In the hall with the light on her, he thought how much like Ma she looked, caught himself staring too long because of it. 'Are you all right?' she asked.

'Fine,' he said.

'We're in here. There's tea and sandwiches. A drop of whiskey or sherry if you fancy.'

He followed her into a large drawing room lined with filled bookcases. There was an open hearth with a log fire and a five-foot-high picture above it showing a hunting scene. Margaret had moved here just over a year ago, Pat had told him. Her husband Ferdy wanted to be closer to the solicitors' practice he was now a partner in.

Cornelius and Thomas got up from their chairs at the dining table. They were smiling as they came towards him. Thomas hugged him with what seemed real warmth. Cornelius smiled and shook his hand, touching his arm gently with his other hand as he did so. They both seemed genuinely pleased to see him.

Everyone sat down at the heavy polished table and there was more small talk about flights and travelling at Christmas as Margaret poured tea and pushed it towards Houlihan. She settled herself at the end of the table, the head of it. Still self-appointed matriarch then, Houlihan thought. She said, 'Should we start?' The others mumbled and nodded their agreement.

Houlihan said, 'Where's Theresa?'

Margaret said, 'She's at home with Mother.'

'I thought it was a family meeting?'

'She really wouldn't have that much to contribute.'

'Says who?' asked Houlihan.

'Frankie, come on, you know what she's like.'

When Theresa had been about six or seven, their mother had decided she was 'backward', not developing properly, and had sent her for all sorts of medical tests, none of which proved Ma right. But she'd clung to the belief ever since that Theresa wasn't 'normal'.

Houlihan knew Theresa was simply gentle and kind, without a bad word for anyone. A bit of a dreamer, not much interested in boys but with a brilliant brain and a fantastic memory. From his viewpoint, she'd been the only one to stand by him over Kathy, the only one to call him regularly even though she knew Ma disapproved.

Houlihan said, 'She's our sister and as much a part of the family as anyone here. You can't have a family meeting without the whole family.'

Pat said sarcastically, 'So you want Ma here as well?'

'Bring her along when you're picking Theresa up. I've no problem with that.'

Pat looked sheepishly at the others knowing his bluff had been called. Margaret said, 'If Theresa comes over, there'll be nobody to look after Mother.' It was always 'Mother' since Margaret had married the solicitor. She'd been 'Ma' to all of them before that.

'Let's go there then,' Houlihan said, getting the bit between his teeth now, beginning to perk up.

They looked at each other again. Smiles were in short supply. Pat turned to Margaret. 'D'ye think Ma would be all right for an hour on her own?'

'I thought she was desperately ill?' Houlihan said. 'Wouldn't see Christmas.'

Margaret's jaw muscles flexed. 'She's picked up quite a bit in the past few days.'

'You should have called me then, saved me a trip.'

She finally blew. 'Frankie, for God's sake! You're going to have to face this sometime, you know. She's ill, very ill. It's all down to you. You need to take some responsibility!'

'For what? Her confining herself to bed with a massive attack of self-pity brought on by the embarrassment of her "pride and joy" deserting the priesthood? Her "pride and joy", of course, being the priest, and not her son, the person who actually filled the vestments.'

'She was fine till you walked out on everything!' Margaret replied.

Houlihan continued, 'She was a vain, proud woman who gloried in being able to flaunt her son, the priest, constantly in the faces of her neighbours and her cronies. She's in that bed back in Friary Road because she can't face the coven she ruled when things were going her way. She knows she won't be able to handle all the veiled taunts, the questions so carefully couched, so badly disguised as inquiries about her son's 'progress' outside the priesthood, about his marriage, about Kathy . . . all of them meant to hurt her, pay her back for years of showing off. That's why she's in bed. No affliction other than injured pride. If you can't see that, you're all kidding yourselves.'

Pat said, 'So why did you come?'

'I came to listen to what you have to say. What Ma needs is to face up to life. Anything I can do to help her do that, I will.'

Cornelius spoke softly. 'Frankie, you just said you came to listen to us, then right away you go and tell us what Ma needs. You haven't seen her for nearly two years. You don't know. Some of what you said is true right enough, but it's moved on from there. It really has.'

Thomas said, 'He's right, Frankie. You'd need to see her now and talk to her to know. Maybe you should do that.'

Their quiet manner struck Houlihan, making him regret his outbursts. He nodded. 'I'm sorry.' He looked around the faces. 'I was so wound up about coming here. It all just boiled over. I apologise.'

Margaret's expression softened. 'We were all pretty wound up too. We haven't done right by you. We know that. It seemed like we'd gone too far down the road to try and put things right, and maybe we have, but we should all try . . . see what we can rescue from it.'

He nodded. She said, 'Do you want to see Mother?'

'If she'll see me.'

'She will if you just walk in.'

'Tonight?'

'Christmas Eve. Not a bad night to do it,' she said.

Frankie smiled and shook his head slowly, not believing he'd got himself so quickly into this. Cornelius leaned over and put a hand on his shoulder. He said, 'Me, you and Thomas – three wise men from the East.'

'Not,' Houlihan said.

For Houlihan, the house he was raised in had a certain smell. He had never noticed it all the years he was living there but always did when he went back. As he walked down the hall, Theresa emerged from the bathroom, drying her hands. She saw him and her smile brought a warmth to his heart he hadn't felt since Kathy had been with him. She rushed towards him, enveloping him in her arms, in her long dark hair, soapy aroma, giggles. And she hugged him so hard she hurt his neck. 'Frankie, I was praying you'd come and see us. Thank God!'

She pulled her head away from where she'd buried it against Houlihan's neck and looked at him. Her eyes filled up. She said, 'I have missed you so much! So much!' And she kissed him on the cheek and held him tightly again. He felt his own tears rise.

Once they'd both calmed down, Theresa skipped away to put the kettle on and Margaret went into Ma's room on her own. The brothers sat in the living room as they'd done so many times over the years. The décor hadn't changed and the holy pictures, the statues, the crucifixes were where they had always been.

Margaret returned and pushed the door quietly closed behind her then stood holding the handle. Softly she said, 'She's sleeping deeply. I hadn't the heart to wake her.'

The brothers looked at Frankie. Pat said, 'Maybe you can wait awhile?'

Houlihan nodded. Thomas said, 'When are you going back, Frankie?'

'Boxing Day.'

'Then where are you spending Christmas Day?' Pat asked nervously.

'I've some business in Dublin tomorrow with old friends. I'm booked in at the Kiltullagh tonight.'

Margaret said, 'You can't spend Christmas Eve on your own, you must stay with us, we've plenty of room. And who on earth does business on Christmas Day?'

'You'd be surprised at what goes on in these big

cities on Christmas Day, our Margaret. And thank you for the offer of a bed, but I've arranged to meet some of my friends for supper at the Kiltullagh.'

Theresa brought tea and shortbread and hot scones, and she fussed around happily, handing out plates and napkins, butter and jam. When everyone was sipping and chewing, Theresa dropped a cushion on the floor by Houlihan's chair and sat down, hooking her elbow around his leg. She looked up at him and he realised how much he'd missed that smiling, open, loving face.

The coal fire had long ago been replaced with a gas one but the false flames still looked fairly convincing when Theresa decided to turn out the main light and leave just the small lamp glowing on the mantelpiece and the tree lights twinkling in the corner. In the shadowy silence Houlihan sensed the awkwardness in the room, the discomfiture, and he knew they all felt it, even Theresa. If ever his family should be comfortable together it was in this room where they had always gathered throughout their upbringing to watch TV, do homework, celebrate Christmas. Where they'd kneeled each night, led in bedtime prayers by their father whose voice Houlihan could hear now saying, 'The family that prays together stays together.'

They hadn't done that. They'd prayed together then fallen apart when he'd left the priesthood. No, Houlihan thought. They were all still together, he was the only one who'd been banished. Such thoughts usually brought anger but this time he just felt sad.

Theresa broke the silence. 'Do you remember when Da used to sit in that chair, Frankie, and try and balance me on his shins?'

Houlihan smiled sadly at her, grateful for her attempt at trying to bring some normality. He said, 'I remember it well, but I can't believe you do. You were only about two!'

'I do remember it! Honest!'

Cornelius said, 'I remember the time he was doing it and you threw up in his lap.'

Theresa brought both hands to her mouth as she recalled it. 'I do too. I remember everything stopping suddenly and me sliding off him onto the floor.'

Margaret said, 'It was his good suit too.'

Thomas added, 'It was shinier than his shoes. I'm surprised the puke didn't run right off it.'

'Oh, Thomas, that's disgusting!' Margaret said.

Gradually the others joined in, and, sitting there in the deep shadows, reliving the memories, they seemed to generate a warmth which steadily melted most of what remained of the apprehension and bitterness. More than once in the following two hours they found themselves laughing together for the first time in years.

At nine thirty, Ma was still asleep. Margaret said, 'Did you want to just look in on her, Frankie? No need to wake her.'

He hesitated then got up. 'I'll go in on my own,' he said.

She was lying on her side. There was enough light from the bedside lamp to show him her face. It looked much older and very much thinner than when last he'd seen her, the day he came to say he'd be leaving the priesthood because he loved a girl called Kathy Spencer. He sat on the chair by the bed and watched her, listened to her breathing, saw her face in its various ages over the years in all the stories he'd just been reliving. She was fifty-seven years old but could have been taken for seventy-five. Her dry, thin, wrinkled skin seemed a pale yellow.

This, he said to himself, was the woman who'd carried him in her womb, borne him, raised him healthily and happily and steered him very cunningly into fulfilling her ambition. Houlihan had never resented that until he met Kathy, never even thought about it really; but since falling in love with Kathy he'd analysed it to destruction, to the point it had bred something bordering on hatred of his own mother. And still, sitting by her side, seeing how ill she was, he couldn't quite quell that ounce of hatred. This frail, sick woman had been well enough to send him a card a few days after Kathy's death that said, 'I hope she's burning in hell.'

But before he left her side he stroked her hair.

They were all looking at him when he went back into the living room and their expressions said the same thing: 'Well?'

He said, 'She's aged twenty years.' He slumped into his chair. Theresa reached for his hand, squeezed and held it. They all sat in silence for a while then Margaret said quietly, 'Will you help, Frankie?'

'What do you want me to do?' He was prepared for requests for regular visits, phone calls, letters, a programme of reconciliation with all the work and pleading to be done on his part. And he wasn't sure if he was ready to agree to that.

He needn't have worried. The family's idea was much more radical.

Margaret said, 'We think the only thing that will help her recover fully is if you return to the priesthood.'

He looked at her, at the others, then round them all again. He realised he was smiling stupidly. 'You're kidding,' he finally managed to say.

Pat said, 'Frankie, there's nothing to stop you really, if you think about it. The only reason you left is . . . isn't here any more.'

'That person you call a "reason", Pat, was my wife. Her name was Kathy.'

He said, 'I'm sorry, Frankie, I didn't mean to offend you.' He sighed heavily. 'This is hard,' he said. 'Awful hard.'

Cornelius spoke. 'Frankie, 'twas the most terrible thing that happened to Kathy, and to you, but isn't it right that if you hadn't met Kathy you'd still be a priest?'

'Who knows? How can I say what might have

happened in the two years since then? And by the way, I still am a priest as far as the church is concerned. Your vows can never be forsaken. Tell Ma that, maybe that'll help her. Tell her I'm still the priest she made me into but I'm just not practising now. I'm just not playing the game any more.'

Nobody spoke for a while. Theresa held his hand tighter and looked up at him, her face fretful. Margaret said, 'Will you think about it?'

'No.'

'Please,' she said. 'It's not for us.'

'So it's blackmail then? I return to practice or take responsibility for what happens to her?'

Thomas sighed and rubbed his face. 'Maybe it is blackmail, Frankie, but we don't know what else to do.'

Silence again.

'Have you asked her?' Houlihan said. 'Have you asked Ma if that's what she wants?'

Cornelius said, 'We don't want to put it in her mind in case it raises her hopes. We don't think she could stand another let-down.'

Houlihan slipped his hand out of Theresa's and buried his face in both hands. Theresa moved up and put her arm across his shoulder. He turned his head to her, to the others, held out his hands to plead. 'There are a million reasons why I can't go back. Believe me.'

Thomas said, 'Have you ever considered it?'

'No. No, I haven't. It's an impossibility. It's just not done.'

Thomas continued, 'Has there been anything in you since Kathy died, any part of you that wanted to go back?'

Houlihan looked at his obviously astute younger brother in a new light then. 'I'd be lying if I said there wasn't some part of my psyche, my emotions, that has longed for the peace I used to have.'

'You *used* to have,' Margaret repeated. 'Listen to yourself. Look at yourself. How much peace have you now? How much real rest does your mind get? When were you last happy?'

'When were any of *you* last happy?' Frankie retorted defensively.

Cornelius said quietly, 'When Ma was happy.'

'So it's back round to blackmail again.'

'No blackmail, Frankie,' said Margaret. 'Nobody can make you do anything. You'll decide. There'll be no more talk on this from us after we leave here tonight. I promise you that.'

There was the matriarch again, he thought, promising on behalf of everyone else. 'Good. I'll hold you to your promise.'

'You won't need to.'

More silence, the longest yet, then Margaret said, 'I think it's time we all went home.'

'You all are home,' Theresa said innocently.

SIX

Sitting in the departure lounge on Boxing Day morning, Houlihan thought that if they'd put him on the scales instead of his luggage he'd have paid an awful lot of excess for the weight on his mind. For all his trepidation on the way to Dublin he hadn't dreamed what the family would ask of him. He was never going back to the priesthood so the onus was on him to find another way to get ma well again. The thought had filled his mind since walking out of the house and glancing back at the palest light through the curtains of Ma's room. He knew that soon he'd need to come back and see her. Just him.

The flight was on time and Houlihan made it to Kempton for the King George VI Chase. He liked to get out on the course, away from the crowds. Standing by the jumps, he relished the feel of the ground rumbling under approaching hooves, loved watching the runners in a ribbon of colour rise and flow over the fences. Out there he could listen to the very heartbeat of the sport, birch crackling, stirrups jingling, leather slapping on muscle, jockeys cursing, then everything fading so quickly as they galloped away leaving just the whisper of the commentary from the stands in the chill air.

After the race, he set off to find Geoff Stonebanks. They'd agreed to meet so Frankie could debrief him on the work he'd done so far on the passport scam.

Their meeting led Houlihan to make some calls to try and track down a couple of people he knew would be at Kempton. The delay meant it was almost dark by the time he left the weighing room.

Only half a dozen vehicles were left in the car park. Houlihan heard raised voices as he approached one car and saw three men standing by the boot. A few yards from them he smelled whiskey and heard one man say, 'Why don't you fuck off back to America?'

An English voice responded, 'I was born in Ireland my friend. Why don't you and your mate go away and sober up?'

'I was born in Ireland! I was born in Ireland!' the man mimicked. 'Then you should know fucking better how to run a racecourse. It's about horses, man, not business!'

Houlihan stopped close by and saw the smallest of the three try to move towards the driver's door, saying, 'Look, I'm late. You're blocking my car. I'm reversing in a minute so you'd better move.'

The biggest man reached in his pocket and Houlihan heard keys jangle then saw the man draw something across the car's boot. He recognised the screech of metal on metal as a scar was slashed into the paintwork. 'Reverse it with that on, Mr Malloy,' the man said then stepped back with surprising speed, avoiding Malloy's lunging kick as he yelled, 'You bastard!'

Houlihan moved forward, 'Hey, fellas, come on now!'

The big man looked at him and said, 'Fuck off. Keep walking.' Then he yelped as Eddie Malloy's fist smacked into his jaw. The other man leaped towards Malloy, trying to grab at his hair, his neck. Malloy dodged him, moved sideways and tried to kick the man on the knee but missed. The big man recovered and the two of them came at him from wide angles, swinging fists and kicking out. Houlihan took a few running steps and jumped on the big man's back, hooking an arm around his throat and hauling him backwards, trying to bring him down. The man grunted, then Malloy ran at the other man, butting him hard in the face. The man groaned and fell and Malloy kicked him in the gut then stamped hard on the side of his leg at the knee joint. The man screamed.

Houlihan was on the ground now, underneath the big man, still clinging desperately to his neck. He thought briefly that he would laugh if he wasn't so scared as the man cursed and struggled, flailing at him. Houlihan had never been in a fight in his life and simply did not know what to do next. Then he heard the man grunt as Malloy kicked him in the balls. The big man stopped struggling and rolled off him, moaning and writhing as Houlihan steadily released his grip.

Houlihan lay there looking up at Malloy, who stood over the big man as he worked his way onto his knees, then, using a car bumper and bonnet, to his feet. Malloy, still primed for fighting, moved round to face the man who lurched back to rest on the bonnet. Malloy said, 'Was it you bastards that threw the brick through my window?'

The man didn't respond, he just stood there panting, clutching his genitals. Malloy's hand arced fast and he slapped the man hard across the face. The noise echoed in the almost empty car park. Malloy leaned towards the man and said, 'If you come near me or my place again, or any of your cronies do, I'll fucking kill you!' He was shouting now and seemed on the edge of losing control.

Houlihan got to his feet and moved towards him as Malloy slapped the man again before grabbing his hair with his good hand. Houlihan reached and gripped Malloy's shoulders. 'Hey, hey! I think you've got them beat. Take it easy.'

Malloy turned towards him and Houlihan saw rage. He held Malloy's wild stare and lowered his voice, pulling slowly but with increasing pressure to get Malloy away. 'Come on. Leave it. I'll phone the police. Leave it.' A noise made them both turn and they saw the other man get up and try to limp away. Malloy released the big man, wriggled out of Houlihan's grip and ran after the other one, kicking him hard in the backside, sending him tumbling then scrambling again to get up and hurry away as best he could. Houlihan went after Malloy to try and stop him hitting the man again but Malloy was laughing now and shouting, 'Hard men? You don't know what a hard man is, you fuckwits!'

At this Houlihan turned to see the big man fleeing in the opposite direction. He thought it best not to alert Malloy who continued to curse the other man as he disappeared into the darkness. Houlihan stood behind Malloy, conscious of his breathing now in the growing silence. The world, for the past few minutes reduced to a few square yards of wet tarmac and a flurry of violence, began to open out again and he looked round, back towards the racecourse, expecting to see people running towards them to find out what was happening. But there was no one. It was just him and Malloy.

Malloy turned to him, a wildness still in his eyes, and smiled. Houlihan smiled back and they stood in silence for a few moments before Malloy stuck out his hand. 'My name's Eddie Malloy.'

Houlihan shook his hand. 'Frankie Houlihan.'

Malloy looked at him for a few seconds then said, 'Jockey Club security? Ex-priest?'

'That's me,' Houlihan said, feeling his trousers wet from rolling in a puddle and bending to peel the material away from his thigh.

'Now good Samaritan,' said Malloy.

'Now bad fighter.'

Malloy smiled, slapping him gently on the shoulder. 'You did fine. You've got guts.'

Houlihan looked at him. 'Maybe, but I like them where they are, inside my skin.'

Malloy laughed. 'I owe you a drink.' He tried to dust some of the mud off Houlihan's jacket. 'And a new suit.'

'I'll settle for the drink,' Houlihan said.

'Good. Let's go.'

'What about the Chuckle Brothers there?'

Malloy feigned surprise. 'Surely you don't expect me to buy them a drink?'

Houlihan smiled. He already liked this man. In his place, Houlihan knew he'd be shaking with fear and adrenaline. He said, 'Should we call the police?'

'If you want to wait here for another hour then listen to them say there's bugger all they can do.'

Houlihan looked at him. 'We should call them, just for the record.'

Malloy sighed. 'Okay, okay. But let's go and see them, save us hanging around.'

At the police station they gave statements and descriptions, although it was obvious to all that Malloy saw it as a pointless chore. Back outside Malloy told Houlihan he had a dinner date in Lambourn but he insisted on having a drink with Houlihan first. They both agreed it wasn't wise to be seen together in a pub full of racing people so Malloy followed Houlihan back to his house.

As they approached it, Houlihan felt glad he'd cheered the place up a bit by hanging Christmas lights and putting a tree in the window. He'd bought it a week before. He'd given the tree that Kathy had carefully packed away to a charity shop, along with all the little baubles she'd loved. Although she was on his mind every day, those physical reminders of her at such a poignant time would have shredded his heart.

They parked in the street outside his door and Malloy followed him inside. Houlihan switched the lights on and saw how dirty his clothes were. He turned to look at Malloy and said, 'Look, not a mark on you. You can tell who the amateur is.'

Malloy smiled and slapped him gently on the arm. 'You did fine. Believe me.'

Houlihan shrugged and felt awkward. 'I've never been in a fight before. Didn't know what to do. It's like having to dance without any lessons.'

Malloy chuckled and smiled warmly at him. 'Never been in a fight before? I'd have thought you'd want a black belt minimum in your job these days.'

Houlihan said, 'I'll speak to the training department. Want a drink?'

'I'd love a bloody drink! I can walk to Andrew's place from here.'

'What do you fancy?'

'What have you got?'

'You name it, I'll find some of it.'

'Whiskey.'

'Malt or blend?'

'Blend, please?'

'Scotch or Irish?'

'You're showing off now.' They both smiled. Malloy added, 'Irish.'

'Bushmills?'

'Brilliant.'

'Take your jacket off,' said Houlihan as he poured two drinks and carried them to the kitchen table. 'I'll just grab a quick shower if you don't mind. What time are you due at your friend's place?'

'Any time. Don't worry. Cheers.' They clinked glasses. Malloy said, 'To Butch Cassidy and the Sundance Kid.' Houlihan smiled, feeling childishly proud.

Hair still wet, wearing clean jeans and a tee shirt, Houlihan settled at the big pine table in the brightly lit kitchen and sipped his drink. 'You're welcome to shower if you want.'

'I'm fine,' Malloy said, unbuttoning his leather jacket. 'Any bruises?'

'Nah, I'm okay. How about you?'

Malloy smiled. 'They never landed a blow.' He raised his glass again and Houlihan saw he'd almost finished his drink. He reached for the glass. 'Refill?'

'Please.'

Houlihan brought the drink. Malloy was staring

into space. Houlihan waved the glass in front of his eyes and Malloy snapped out of it. 'Sorry.'

Houlihan sat down. 'Wondering if they'll be back for another go?' he asked.

Malloy smiled and sipped his drink. 'I was years further back than that, Frankie.' His voice was quiet, almost sad. Houlihan waited for him to say more but Malloy said, 'But they might come back. Depends who's paying them and how much. When I got to the car they sort of appeared from behind it and started mouthing off about Makalu. I thought they were drunk but now I think they'd deliberately made themselves smell of it. They both moved too quickly when the action started.'

'So you think you were set up?'

'Probably.'

'Anything to do with the ad in the *Racing News*, the RACE campaign, do you think?'

Malloy nodded then drank.

Houlihan continued, 'I heard you say to the big guy about a brick being thrown the other night. Was that at home?'

'Where I call home, in London. A sort of house-cum-office.'

'Much damage?'

'Smashed window, scratched varnish.'

'And you think it was these same guys?' Houlihan asked.

'Maybe not those two, but there was a note in the bag with the brick. It said: 'Get out while you still have one good arm'. He glanced across at

Houlihan and said, 'I lost an arm a while back. Not that you wouldn't have noticed with this bloody big rubber hand swinging from my cuff.'

Malloy held it in the air and Houlihan smiled and said, 'One of the best I've seen.'

Malloy feigned a shy smile and said, 'Go on, you don't mean it!'

Houlihan laughed.

They were quiet while they drank, then Houlihan said, 'I bet you didn't call the police for the brick either.'

Malloy said, 'Why sit up waiting for some plod to come and take a few notes and tell you he's not that hopeful of catching anybody. Then he needs to go back and write it up when he could have been helping an old lady across the road. Waste of my time and theirs.'

'Did you keep the note?'

Malloy raised an eyebrow. 'Now you're beginning to sound like a cop, Frankie. Stop it. We're here for a nice quiet drink. Don't talk shop.'

Houlihan shook his head slowly and smiled. 'Okay, but will you tell me if those guys come back for another go?'

'Ah, don't worry about them. Half-assed thickos.'

Houlihan smiled. 'Sounds like the name of a pop group; the Half-assed Thickos.'

Malloy chuckled. 'Well they didn't have any hits tonight.'

Houlihan responded to Malloy's raised glass, impressed by the man's quick mind and laid-back attitude. He'd expected a flat-out, driven businessman, humourless and stern. He admired the confident way Malloy rested his plastic arm on the table as he drank and talked. The scarring on the left side of his face looked worse than it had in the press pictures he'd seen. He noticed Malloy's left earlobe was missing and the ear itself was badly disfigured. The skin on his nose was slightly damaged and his mouth drooped on the left side but Houlihan concluded that Malloy had been quite fine-featured and had probably lost little of his appeal to women since the Everest incident. Maybe it had even added to his allure.

Mellowing visibly, Malloy looked around him. 'This is a nice little place, isn't it?'

'It's all right,' Houlihan said. 'I've not been here long.'

'Like it? Lambourn, I mean?'

'I do. I like it a lot. Plenty of optimism around.'

'Blind hope, more like,' Malloy chuckled.

'Where would we be without it?'

'Back in the ould country, cutting peat. Here's to blind hope and the P&O ferries.'

Malloy raised his glass and Houlihan acknowledged with his. 'An Irish Malloy?' Houlihan said. 'How many generations back?'

'I was born there, in Donegal. Came to England when I was five. The usual, no work, or at least not the kind my old man liked. Landed up in Cumbria working on Lord Kentmere's estate. That's where I got into the horses.'

Houlihan drank again, warming further to his companion, the only visitor he'd had – apart from Geoff Stonebanks – since moving in. They talked some more about their backgrounds but when Malloy checked his watch again Houlihan apologised for keeping him back. 'Not at all,' Malloy said. 'No worries.' He held up his glass. 'This is warming me through nicely. Time enough.'

Houlihan had been waiting for some indication that Malloy knew Hooper had asked him to take on the Makalu case, but he was pretty sure by now that Malloy hadn't been briefed. He wondered why and considered not telling him, but only for a moment. His instinct was to be dead straight with Malloy. He said, 'Do you know Sam Hooper?'

'Your boss?' Malloy asked.

Houlihan nodded.

'Met him once. Didn't take to him.'

'He called me into the office and told me to pass all my work on to another investigator and free myself to take on Makalu. To keep a watchful eye.'

Malloy smiled and raised his glass again. 'Good start then, eh?'

'I suppose you could look at it that way. Are you surprised nobody told you?'

'Good question. I don't know. D'you think Hooper put you on this off his own bat or because somebody told him to.'

'I think he was told.'

'Who gives those sorts of orders? Trevelyan?'

Kenneth Trevelyan was Chief Executive of the Jockey Club.

Houlihan shrugged. 'Maybe.'

'Is he the type to?'

'Not to my mind. Hooper intimidates him.' Houlihan was uneasy now and regretted having painted himself into this position. He was loyal to Bobby Cranfield and knew Cranfield might be the one who'd made the decision. But he still wanted to be straight with Malloy. He said, 'Could your boss have had any influence?'

'Wouldn't surprise me. He's got a finger in every other pie.'

'Well, I just thought it was time I told you I have a sort of formal interest in this, so I'll probably need to ask you some more boring questions.'

Malloy smiled. 'Well, you'd better get to it before you drink any more, Frankie boy, you're looking a bit glassy-eyed there.'

Houlihan smiled back, knowing he was being kidded. He went to the microwave and picked up a spiral notebook he'd left on top of it, extracting a pen from the coiled binding at the top. 'You said you thought the brick could be linked to the ad in the paper.'

'Seems likely.'

'Tonight's carry on as well?'

'Could be.'

'You should tell the police about the brick. And the ad.'

Malloy raised his eyebrows and Houlihan sensed

he was about to repeat his earlier views, but Malloy seemed to rein himself back. He said, 'Okay, I'll call them tomorrow.'

Houlihan nodded. 'Good. Thanks. Got a couple of minutes to tell me about the guy that placed the ad, Bert Jacobsen?'

Malloy drank. 'Jacobsen's a crook. Been stealing from the company for years before we took over. And there are a few more like him around, along with the slackers and the chancers and the leeches. Racing attracts these sorts of people. You'll know that better than anybody.'

'I haven't been around it that long.'

Malloy smiled and got to his feet. 'You've made your mark, Mr Houlihan. I'd heard about you even before tonight.'

Houlihan looked up and smiled. 'Don't believe the bad bits.'

Malloy stretched and sighed, 'Well, that's ninety per cent of it gone.'

Houlihan chuckled then said, 'You'd better get on your way or you'll miss your meal.'

'I will. What are you doing tonight?'

Houlihan shrugged. 'Probably make a few calls, see if I can find out any more about the Chuckle Brothers.'

'Save your breath. Come with me to Andrew's. There'll be plenty of grub. You know Andrew Kilroy, don't you?'

'I do know him, and it's really kind of you to ask but I'll give it a miss if you don't mind.'

Malloy held his gaze for a few moments and, despite being attuned for it, Houlihan saw no pity in them and knew Malloy had asked him to come along because he genuinely wanted him there. He was grateful for that. Houlihan said, 'Really, given that I'm supposed to be undercover helping Makalu, it might not be the best idea to burst through the saloon doors carousing with its MD.'

'Eh, Chief Operating Officer if you don't mind, Mr Houlihan!'

Houlihan smiled. 'Sorry, boss man.'

Malloy said, 'I take your point, but Andrew and his guests will be the soul of discretion, I'm sure.'

Houlihan laughed. 'You and I know there's not enough discretion in the whole of Lambourn to fill a glass. You could tie everyone here together and put them through an industrial wringer without getting a trickle of discretion.'

Malloy put his good hand on Houlihan's shoulder and conceded. 'I suppose you're right. When it's done and dusted we'll have a few nights out, eh?'

'I'll look forward to it. Will you call me if anything else happens?'

'Sure.' Malloy took a business card from his jacket. He looked at it, handed it to Houlihan and smiled. 'Business cards, eh? It doesn't seem that long ago I was living in an old caravan, stealing carrots from the horse's feed. Spent the grub money on booze. And hey, look at me now! Leather jackets; business suits. What a load of bullshit, eh?'

Houlihan smiled and got a card from his brief-case. 'Doesn't seem that long ago I was nicking the altar wine. Spent my money on slow horses.'

'Never mind. You avoided the fast women.'

Houlihan realised that Malloy knew a bit more about him than he had thought.

Malloy continued, 'I'd better get moving, get some food inside me before I drink any more. I'm riding out in the morning. First time in a long time.' He held up the plastic hand. 'Not sure I'll be able to slip the reins the way I used to but I hope to stay in the saddle at least.'

Houlihan opened the door for him, letting in a cold blast. 'Enjoy yourself.'

'Thanks. Is it okay if I leave my car there till tomorrow?'

'Of course.'

Malloy opened the boot. 'Better get my bag. My riding gear's in it.'

In the chilly grey dawn, Eddie Malloy was legged up into the saddle of a big bay gelding. He settled himself, feet quickly finding the stirrups, good hand adjusting the reins. It had been more than five years since he'd sat on a racehorse and his sudden elation was quickly followed by an unexpected tide of sadness for the loss of all this. The cama-raderie of the stable yard and the weighing room, the feel of warm power below you on a cold morning, the smell of leather and hot horse, the hope for the future. All gone. He'd had his day.

The string pulled out of the yard, steel-shod steps echoing, steamy breaths of horses and riders trailing. Malloy's mind spun back twenty years and he tasted again the ambition, the fierce dedication, the torrent of optimism; everything that had driven him to try and be the best. All he'd ever wanted to be he had been. He'd got there with no help from anyone but himself. He hadn't failed, he reminded himself for the millionth time, he'd been forced out. Unjustly. That was where the bitterness lay.

As they trotted along the road he looked at himself now; semi-crippled, getting old. The glory days would never return.

Moving up onto the gallops there was no shelter from the icy wind and his frostbite scars seemed much more sensitive to it than the rest of him. Everest came back to mind, bringing the sickly feeling it always did now, holding him again in the eye of that terrible storm. He wondered if his trip back there, due in a couple of weeks, would help lay the ghosts.

As the string reached the start of the all-weather gallop he made himself concentrate on his false arm, forcing the fingers to close slowly around the rubber-clad rein, wishing so much he could feel it.

A week later, Houlihan read the follow-up piece on Jacobsen and his RACE campaign in the *Racing News*. Jacobsen claimed to have had '*very substantial numbers of forms*' returned, although he wouldn't give a figure, which suggested to Houlihan it would be in the low hundreds at best. Jacobsen said he hoped anyone joining his campaign would protest peacefully but that no one could legislate for the anger certain individuals may feel at the way Makalu had behaved. Houlihan read this as either a veiled acknowledgement to Malloy that the brick and the car-park confrontation were linked to his campaign, and/or an incitement to supporters that violence should be considered. Houlihan reflected too on Bobby Cranfield's belief that someone more powerful and media savvy than Jacobsen was driving things.

That night, Eddie Malloy came home to find another message. Delivered conventionally through his letterbox this time, in an envelope, the note said, *'I have a matching one. If you want to complete the pair keep doing what you're doing.'* Malloy rolled the bullet in his palm until the engraving, very skilfully done, glistened beneath the overhead light. It said *'Eddie Malloy'*.

Malloy smiled and shook his head. 'How corny can you get?' he asked aloud.

SEVEN

Since Houlihan's visit to Dublin he'd called Theresa every day. She'd told him that Ma had been pleased he'd been there on Christmas Eve and that she'd been sorry she'd been asleep. But Theresa was a poor liar. Houlihan didn't question her account but he did call Thomas.

'How's Ma been?' he asked.

Thomas hesitated and Houlihan knew he was trying to choose his words. 'The truth, Thomas. That's the best way.'

Thomas cleared his throat. 'She was awful upset that you'd been back in the house.'

'Oh.' Houlihan hadn't quite expected to hear it was that bad.

Thomas said, 'She'll come round, Frankie. We're working on her. At least she showed some of her old fire, shouting at the lot of us.' His laugh was short and nervous.

'Always look on the bright side, eh?' Houlihan said.

'She's still full of spirit anyway. It was a good

sign. We'll give her some warning next time, let her know you're coming.'

'It might be a while before I can get back over. I've been given this, well, special assignment. It's going to be hard to make solid plans for a few months. I might only be able to give you a day's notice.' Houlihan was half-hoping his brother would tell him just to leave it all until after the assignment was over, but a part of him wanted to go and confront his mother as soon as possible.

Thomas said, 'We'll just need to work to that, then. Don't worry. I'll speak to the others.'

'Thanks. How is everyone else?'

'Good. Grand. No worries there.'

'And you? How are the studies going?'

'Pretty good. I even managed to stay awake in a lecture the other day.'

'Wow, I am impressed.' Houlihan smiled and sensed more warmth from Thomas. He added, 'I'll call you next week.'

'Fine. Look after yourself on your special assignment. Anything dangerous?'

Houlihan considered for a second or two then said, 'Nah, not really. Confidential stuff but pretty straightforward.'

'Good. Will I tell Ma you called?'

Houlihan hesitated. 'What do you think?'

'I think she'd like to hear that. I think it would start building bridges a little bit.'

'Then tell her.'

* * *

Negotiations between Makalu and the Jockey Club over the sale of the thirteen courses had advanced sufficiently for Keelor to make a Concorde trip to London. Malloy met him at the airport and Keelor greeted him like he was a brother. They sped out of Heathrow onto the M4 and headed west.

In a remote Welsh cottage in the shadow of the Black Mountains, Bobby Cranfield was waiting for them. Also driving west for the meeting was the Chief Executive of the Jockey Club – Kenneth Trevelyan – and a solicitor called John Taylor.

Keelor wasted little time in questioning Malloy about the RACE campaign. 'Why don't we jump on this guy Jacobsen? He's been screwing the racecourse for years, hasn't he?'

'He denies it and I don't want to waste time and energy hauling him through court. He blames it on faulty accounting by a secretary who died last year.'

'The books are the books. They tell the story, Eddie.'

'They do, but Jacobsen's only got a month left and he's gone, retired. It's not worth the hassle, believe me.'

'But we've got the brand to consider, don't forget that. Looks to me like Jacobsen's stirring up a lot of sympathy for himself, which equates to bad feeling against Makalu. I can't afford that.'

In Keelor's final sentence Malloy noticed a coldness in his voice he'd never heard before. He took a moment to consider his reply. 'Okay, Vaughn.

Let me give it some thought. Bear in mind that this campaign Jacobsen's running could backfire on him, and whoever's really behind the whole thing, he . . .'

Keelor interrupted. 'You mentioned this on the phone last time we spoke. You think Jacobsen's a front man. Why? What makes you say that?'

'Three things. Where did he get the money to pay for the ad in the paper? Who wrote the copy for it? Who wrote his follow-up statement? Spend two minutes talking to him and you'd be asking the same questions.'

'He was smart enough to pull the stunt with the false invoices.'

'It was a pretty clumsy fraud, Vaughn. We picked it up within a week of taking over. Believe me, somebody's feeding him the stuff for the paper and probably bankrolling the campaign.'

Keelor crossed his arms. 'Well, you've got me even more worried now! Thanks!'

Malloy smiled. 'Don't worry. My guess is that Bonnaventure's our man, and if I can get some proof he can say goodbye to racing.'

'The Chairman of the BHB?'

'Yes.'

Malloy, arms fully outstretched on the steering wheel, could feel Keelor staring at him. Keelor said, 'Why, because he wants his guys to take over the Jockey Club Security?'

'He wants to see the Jockey Club dead and buried completely, always has done. If we buy their courses they've got funds to run the best security operation in the world. Indefinitely.'

'They'll use their own capital for that? That's stupid.'

'They only need to do it for so long. Once they've got a top-notch operation, the industry will be about the cleanest you can make it and racing will need to start funding the whole show to make sure it stays that way. Also, I heard a rumour that Bonnaventure is involved in setting up an offshore company to start buying racecourses in the UK. The Jockey Club owns almost all the top courses. If we get them before Bonnaventure's company gets a toehold he can pack up and go home.'

Keelor mulled this over then said, 'How good is your information?'

'Pretty sound.'

'Who's your contact?'

'Sorry, Vaughn, I can't say.'

Malloy felt the look again. Keelor said quietly, although with a tinge of impatience, 'Eddie, I am not going to tell anyone.'

'That doesn't matter. I gave my word. Sorry.'

'I'm paying you a million dollar bonus on this contract. I'm entitled to know your source.'

Malloy checked his mirror and pulled onto the hard shoulder, switching on his hazard lights. When the car stopped he turned off the engine and looked at Keelor. 'Listen, Mr Keelor, I don't care how much you're paying me. You don't buy the right to have me break my word. If that's what you expect for your money then let's turn round and get you back to the airport so you can start looking for someone else to run this operation.'

Keelor watched him then his face broke into a slow smile. 'No need for you to do that, Eddie. You just passed the test. I knew when I hired you I could trust you a hundred per cent. There aren't too many men around today who can't be bought.'

Malloy didn't return the smile. He started the engine. Pulling away, he wasn't at all convinced that Keelor had been testing him, and he chided himself for not getting to know the man better before accepting this job. Still, he reminded himself not to feel too moralistic. There'd been no source, he'd made that up. His suspicion of Bonnaventure was self-generated. But he had a history with the man and it was one he didn't want Keelor to know about, not yet.

There was silence for a while, then Keelor said, 'Assuming you're right about Bonnaventure, how do we nail him?'

'I don't know yet. I'm working on it.'

Keelor went quiet again. Malloy felt there had been a noticeable change in the balance of power between them since he'd made his stand. A few minutes later Malloy said, 'Remember the brick through my window?'

'Bonnaventure?'

'Maybe. Not personally, but if he's behind this RACE thing I wouldn't put violence past him. Two nights ago I got another delivery, a bullet with my name on it along with another note.'

'Why didn't you tell me?'

'It's amateur stuff.'

'Amateur? A few days after they attack you at Kempton? What are the cops saying?'

'I haven't told them about the bullet. Or the brick. It's a waste of time.'

'So what'll make you call them, Eddie? Another bullet, aimed at you? Come on, if you're trying to build a case against Bonnaventure you need to give the cops everything as you get it. Three moves down the line you might find a bomb under your car. How serious are the cops going to treat you if you wait till then to say, "Oh yeah, I meant to mention the bullet and the time they cut through my brake cable." Come on.'

Malloy considered this and also the same advice from Houlihan. 'I'll call them when we get to Bobby's place.'

'Good. And I'll find a couple of bodyguards for you. Just to be on the safe side.'

Malloy turned quickly and glared at him. 'No way! Forget it. I'm not having a pair of gorillas shadowing me twenty-four-seven.'

Keelor laughed. 'You watch too many movies, Malloy. I'll get you two discreet, very presentable pros you'd be proud to take home to your mom.'

'No thanks. Bad idea, Vaughn.'

'Malloy, you're a major asset. You need protection.'

'And how do you think people are going to feel about doing business with me if we're worried enough to have bodyguards? Don't you think they'll maybe try someone else rather than risk finding themselves in the line of fire. And what's that going to do to your brand? "*Makalu so hated in UK that boss needs bodyguards.*" Drop the idea, Vaughn, believe me.'

He was aware of Keelor shrugging slightly before saying, 'You, Eddie Malloy, are definitely learning to press the right buttons with me. The more you talk, the more you talk me out of it.'

Malloy felt some relief but he couldn't help but wonder if Keelor was playing mind games with him.

Ninety minutes later, travelling on a quiet road in watery sunlight, Keelor looked at the soft hills and said to Malloy, 'I thought Wales had bigger mountains than this.'

'They're up north. This is sort of the halfway point of Wales. Snowdonia's where the real mountains are.'

Keelor smiled and crossed his arms. 'Snowdonia. You can tell by the name. How long to get there?'

'A couple of hours.'

'Wanna head out early tomorrow, do some climbing?'

'We've got no gear. We'd need full winter kit.'

'We'll buy some. What do you say?'

'I'd love to. I've not been out for months. What about your flight back?'

'I'll postpone it a day. We've always said we should climb together. Let's do it.'

'Fine.' Malloy held out his false arm, shaking it slightly. 'It won't quite be El Cap, but we should manage some decent scrambling.'

Keelor laughed, patted him on the shoulder and said, 'Good. Now tell me about Cranfield.'

'Genuine guy. Racing mad. Injured in a riding accident a few years back which put him in a wheelchair but he doesn't let it get him down. Made his millions in PR and believes the Jockey Club has done more for racing than anyone so he wants to keep it going in some form. Owns about twenty horses, a big estate in the Cotswolds and this cottage we're meeting at.. Got a place in New York and one in Jamaica.'

'Trevelyan?'

'Don't know much about him personally but Bobby says he's a shrewd operator. Bobby brought him in about a year ago to give the Jockey Club a bit more of a hard commercial edge. He was CEO of a big finance company for three years before that.'

'And this guy Taylor's the lawyer?'

'That's right. He works full-time for the Jockey Club as company secretary but he's a solicitor by trade. He won't say much.'

Keelor shook his head and smiled. 'If we were doing this deal in New York we'd need a full floor for the legal guys alone.'

'They'll cross their T's and dot their I's, don't

worry about that. Discretion's the big thing for them now. There's a sign in Bobby's office that says, "Three people can keep a secret, if two of them are dead."'

Keelor smiled. 'I like it.'

Given their earlier conversation on the hard shoulder, Malloy wondered if the irony of their last exchange would dawn on Keelor.

At the meeting and again at dinner that evening, Malloy noticed that Keelor made a point of deferring to him on even the smallest matters, making it clear that, in the UK, Malloy was the boss and highly valued and respected. His approach surprised Malloy and added another string of complexity to his task of trying to figure the American out. Still, he thought, maybe he'd discover some more next morning on the hill.

They left Joe Brown's shop in Llanberis carrying new boots, crampons, ice axes, down suits, rucksacks, a rope, two steel flasks which they had filled with coffee in Pete's Eats, and two packed lunches. They then drove the snaking six miles up through the pass. Excited, Keelor would point towards the snowy northern walls and ridges of the Snowdon range to their right, then spot climbers on the southern slopes of the Glyderau to their left.

Malloy shared his feelings of anticipation and warmed a bit to him. Even though they'd both climbed Everest, the dramatic Llanberis pass carved by a glacier millions of years before was a realm of shifting shadows and snow flurries with the wind for an orchestra, booming, whistling and shrieking in the gullies. This was their theatre. High above was the stage that stirred their appetites for measured danger. Although just a tenth of the height of Everest, the snow and ice would make the ridge a risky outing needing full concentration to stay alive – the key attraction for many who go into the hills. The focus required to ensure safety naturally emptied the mind of everyday worries, saturating climbers with the most primal energy and purpose. Malloy and Keelor were just two who found it had a wonderfully cleansing effect.

In the car park at Pen-y-Pass they checked the weather forecast then changed into their new gear, shivering in the wind.

Setting off along the Pyg Track they faced more than two thousand feet of ascent. The snowline began above two thousand feet and their route was along the ridge of Crib Goch, one of the three peaks that made up the Snowdon massif. The path was broad enough for most of the first 1500 feet to allow them to walk side by side, and they swapped stories of past outings in the hills.

Malloy was soon into his rhythm, breathing deeply and steadily as they gained height, luxuriating in the thick oxygen-laden air. The new boots seemed a good fit although the ice axe felt strange in his hand. As the valley floor dropped away and the Pass opened out to the twin lakes at its foot they got to talking about Everest.

Keelor said, 'You know, this is my first outing since that day.'

'Really?'

The terrible storm they'd both survived had happened two and a half years before. They'd first met on the mountain, waiting to be interviewed about the tragedy by CNN. Malloy had been back in the mountains a dozen times since. He knew he'd never have been able to stay away for more than a few months, even though he could no longer climb the faces he used to. One of the things he had loved about rock climbing at a high grade had been the marriage of athleticism with grace and balance. Balance had been one of his strengths as a jockey. Balance, rhythm, and what they called good hands. Just one good hand now, thought Malloy. And apart from the practical disadvantages of climbing with a rubber arm, the image in Malloy's mind removed all grace and saddened him.

Still, he could never imagine not coming back to the mountains, although he wouldn't judge anyone else's decision on when, if ever, to go back. Especially in Keelor's case where he'd been the sole survivor in his summit party. Malloy decided not to probe further. Some people felt better talking about their involvement in tragedies and some preferred to lock it away in their minds. It was up to Keelor if he wanted to talk it out.

Keelor didn't follow it up. Malloy said, 'It's a shame you can't make it for the school opening next week.'

'I know. Sorry, Eddie, I've got to do this conference in Sydney. You'll make an able deputy, though I'd love to see the faces of those Sherpa kids. Bring me back some pictures.'

'I will.'

'It's just a flying visit, isn't it?'

Malloy smiled. 'Yes. Don't worry, I won't be away from the office for too long.'

'No, no, don't worry about that.'

To Malloy he didn't sound convincing. But then he continued, 'And you're sure you don't mind the school having the Makalu name attached?'

'So long as Babu Topche Sherpa's alongside it in the same size letters I don't care what name's on it.'

Babu Topche Sherpa was one of the victims of the '96 storm. He'd been Sirdar, the Sherpa boss, in Malloy's party. Only thirty-four, he'd died after trying to climb back to the south summit in a blizzard to take oxygen to Bret Wain, another guide who'd got stranded and died later that night. Babu Topche's sole reason for offering his services to Everest expeditions was to earn enough money to build a new school for the Sherpa children. He had summited Everest seven times and commanded the highest fees among the Sherpas, all of whom had respected him deeply. The average earnings of Sherpas not employed by climbing parties was $160 a year. Before leaving Kathmandu, Malloy had promised Babu Topche's wife and four children that he would somehow find the money to build the school. That promise was one of the reasons he'd started working the talk circuit. He put half of his earnings towards the project.

It was also how he'd got to know Vaughn Keelor better. They'd met for the second time on a TV talk show and at the post-show party Malloy had asked Keelor if he'd make a donation to the school project.

'How much do you want?' Keelor had replied.

'Whatever you want to give,' Malloy had said.

'Well how much do you need to finish the project?'

'One hundred and twenty-five thousand dollars.'

'You got it.'

The price had been having the Makalu name alongside Babu Topche's but nobody minded. Malloy had put more than $100,000 of his own money in and now they'd have the biggest and best school in Nepal. Malloy was to officiate at the grand opening.

They walked on in silence for a while then stopped to fit crampons as they reached the snow-line at the shoulder of the pass. Malloy struggled with the straps, his false fingers failing to grasp properly. He was reluctant to ask for help. Self-reliance was the rule in the hills. He'd been taught that on the walk-in to his first hill years before – Stuart Harper, his friend, drumming into him the importance of being able to handle any situation on your own.

But Keelor saw him fiddling with the strap and bent quickly to help. 'Sorry, Eddie, I should have offered.'

'I should be able to do it myself. Just need a bit more practice.'

'Sure. Things'll get easier,' Keelor said, checking the fit of the crampons. 'How's that?'

Malloy took a few steps, the sound of crunching snow suddenly taking him back to Everest as he recalled those interminable journeys through the Khumbu Icefall. 'They're fine. Thanks.'

The sky was clear and the Crib Goch ridge glistened, daring them to climb and traverse it. Malloy had been up there twice before, in summer. What stuck in the mind of anyone who'd made a successful crossing was the section that was eighteen inches wide with a drop of three thousand feet on one side. *This*, thought Malloy, *will be interesting. Especially with a rubber arm.* He turned to Keelor. 'Ready?'

The American smiled and raised his axe. 'Lead on.'

EIGHT

Malloy had requested a seat that would put him on the starboard side of Thai Air flight 611 from Bangkok to Kathmandu. He checked his watch regularly, knowing that around two hours' flying would bring him within sight of the jagged Himalayan range. The first peak he recognised was Kanchenjunga, at 28,169 feet the third highest mountain on the planet. Fifteen minutes later he smiled as he recognised Makalu. The name had meant nothing but a mountain to him until he'd met Keelor. Then came Everest. His eyes locked on to it; sought, with a terrible involuntary fascination, the South Col, whose wind-scoured acres 27,000 feet up had claimed so many lives when last he'd been there.

He flinched as he recalled his first sight of the frostbite that had claimed his left arm and ravaged his face. He remembered the whiteness of the bloodless flesh when they'd peeled away his clothing. And as the flight path reached its nearest point to the summit, Malloy thanked God he had made the top in '96 and that he would never need to go back to finish the job. Too many of the victims in '96 had been returnees, infected by previous failures, looking for a final cure.

From Kathmandu an Mi-17 helicopter took Malloy to the village of Lukla, 9200 feet above sea level, where he was met by Mingma Gombu Sherpa, a survivor of his expedition. They embraced warmly and set off on foot for Namche Bazaar, a day's walk away. There were neither vehicles nor roads. Walking was the only way, although Keelor had offered to pay for an additional helicopter flight into Namche from Lukla airstrip to save Malloy forty-eight hours. But Malloy wanted to walk, to be back among the biggest mountains in the world, walking with a friend who had also been through the horror of '96. He needed the comparative solitude, the empathetic silences that sometimes lasted more than an hour as the pair trekked onwards towards their overnight quarters in the hamlet of Phakding.

On a bench in the smoky hut they were staying in, Mingma sipped yak-butter tea and watched his friend drink his. When he judged the time to be right, Mingma said, 'I have some news for you.'

Malloy looked at him through the steam rising from the bitter drink. Mingma's round face seemed friendly and Malloy saw in it no clue about what was coming. Mingma said, 'My cousin, Mingma Gombu, found the rucksack of Mark Duncan.'

Malloy knew the name, knew it was associated with the '96 tragedy. Mingma saw his uncertainty and said, 'He was the cameraman on the expedition where just one survived.'

Malloy nodded slowly. He hadn't known Duncan but he recalled Keelor mentioning him on the talk show they'd appeared on. Duncan had been with the Makalu film crew. 'No sign of his body?' Malloy asked.

'No,' said Mingma. 'No body.'

Malloy bowed his head. Those who die on Everest are normally left there. The air is too thin to support a helicopter and recovery by a climbing party can imperil those trying to get the corpse down. Sometimes, bodies would be pushed into a crevasse by way of a burial, but many of the corpses, clothing shredded by the fierce wind, lie exposed to the eyes of others and to the temperatures and thin air which help preserve the flesh and bones for years. Malloy knew Mark Duncan's body would not be brought back to his loved ones even if the Sherpas had found him, but the knowledge that he had been found would have been of some comfort to his family.

Malloy told Mingma he would take Mark's rucksack home with him and return it to the man's family.

A week later, back in London, Malloy made final preparations for the opening of the new grandstand at Badbury racecourse. The Princess Royal had agreed to officiate and her attendance had guaranteed a flood of requests for invites from racing and business people who considered themselves VIPs. One was from Simon Bonnaventure, Chairman of the BHB. Under normal circumstances, the BHB chairman could have expected an invitation to such an event, but Malloy, even aside from his suspicion that Bonnaventure was behind the brick and bullet, disliked the man intensely and so had vetoed it. He knew Bonnaventure felt the same about him.

Their enmity had grown steadily since an incident at Cheltenham many years before. Bonnaventure's only racing interest back then had been as an owner, although he was already making, and buying, political 'friends' in the sport. He was a busy writer of letters to the racing press, his hectoring, inflammatory style much parodied among journalists.

Bonnaventure was a poor boy made good. His millions came from the success of bands he'd managed in the pop business, a number of whom had tried subsequently in the courts to get back some of the money Bonnaventure had 'earned' from them through what he called his 'well-planned contracts'. No band had yet succeeded. Bonnaventure had also upset a few songwriters by insisting on a fifty per cent credit as co-writer having changed just a few words of the original. A writer refusing to cooperate found his song going unrecorded by the massively successful bands controlled by Bonnaventure. Obscurity was the usual outcome.

Bonnaventure brought his reputation for hard dealing into his hobby of racehorse ownership, railing constantly against the establishment for allowing bookmakers 'to milk the sport like the cash cow they know it to be'. Bonnaventure's philosophy was that if the people who ran racing were stupid enough to let the bookmakers take most of the profit while bearing few of the costs, then those people were there for the taking. He was certain that a man with his sharp brain and hard edge would soon blow most of them away, and he'd spent his eighteen months in charge of the British Horseracing Board trying to prove himself right.

His spat with Eddie Malloy had taken place in the parade ring at Cheltenham racecourse. Unknown to Bonnaventure, the regular jockey for his horse had been injured in the previous race and the trainer, James Branson, without reference to Bonnaventure, had asked Malloy to ride. Bonnaventure had hurried into the parade ring, late and flustered, to find Branson giving Malloy instructions on how best to ride the race. Ignoring Malloy he collared Branson. 'What's this? Where's Kelly?'

'Had a fall in the last. The doctor stood him down. Malloy will do just as good a job.'

Continuing to ignore Malloy who stood just a few feet away, Bonnaventure pointed an aggressive finger at his trainer and said, 'You don't book jockeys for my horses without my say-so.'

Branson's face reddened. He averted his eyes

and shuffled uncomfortably. Malloy knew how badly Branson needed the training fees for the half-dozen horses Bonnaventure had with him. He'd heard plenty of tales about Bonnaventure's arrogance and bad temper and he felt a mixture of sympathy for Branson and anger that the trainer wasn't standing up for himself.

Branson said, 'Sorry Mr Bonnaventure.'

Bonnaventure said, 'Sorry's not enough, Branson. Say out loud, "I will not book jockeys for Mr Bonnaventure's horses in future without his approval."'

Branson glanced at Bonnaventure and for a second Malloy thought he was going to rebel. 'Come on!' said Bonnaventure. Branson mumbled the words. Bonnaventure smiled slyly and raised his voice. 'I didn't hear that. Say it out loud.' Some of the others in the parade ring were watching now and Bonnaventure made Branson repeat the line twice, the second time loudly enough for a number of other owners and trainers to hear.

Bonnaventure turned to Malloy. 'Right, Malloy. You'd better ride this race straight and don't balls it up.' Malloy glanced around. Bonnaventure was still enjoying the attention of the scowling audience. Malloy spoke at the same volume as Bonnaventure. He said, 'Bonnaventure, say after me. "I'd better find myself another jockey because Eddie Malloy would sooner shovel shit than ride for a prick like me."'

It was Bonnaventure's turn to redden with rage

while those around chuckled and smiled. Bonn-aventure made the mistake of using one of his standard big-boss phrases: 'What did you just say?'

Malloy repeated it, making sure half the parade ring and the surrounding punters heard. Leaving them smiling, and Bonnaventure almost apoplectic, he walked back to the weighing room. Bonn-aventure was forced to withdraw his horse as it was too late to find a substitute jockey.

Bonnaventure reported Malloy to the stewards for refusing to ride and causing the horse to be a late withdrawal. The stewards accepted Malloy's explanation that he felt he could not ride the horse with any confidence as the owner had directly questioned his honesty in an abusive fashion. Malloy also pointed out the highly public way Bonn-aventure had expressed his feelings in the parade ring and made a counter-complaint that Bonn-aventure had brought the sport into disrepute.

At a later inquiry, the stewards of the Jockey Club found against Bonnaventure and warned him about his future conduct. That public caution had ignited Bonnaventure's desire to see an end to the Jockey Club and he'd worked towards that goal ever since. Malloy couldn't prove it but he was certain Bonnaventure had also spread malicious rumours about his integrity, harking back to his five-year warning-off and reigniting some of the doubts of old among owners and trainers. The rides had steadily dried up until Malloy could no longer make a living as a jockey. But even on the day he finally quit at Kelso, he never regretted what he'd said to Bonnaventure at Cheltenham. The memory of Bonnaventure's face that day still brought a smile to Malloy's.

Bonnaventure had made no direct request to Malloy for an invite to the Royal Box for lunch after the opening ceremony at Badbury. They both knew he'd never acknowledge that Malloy had any measure of control over what the Chairman of the BHB might be able to do on a racecourse. But Bonnaventure had let it be known that he expected to receive an invite. Malloy realised the man's position allowed him to come and go on any British racecourse, and that Bonnaventure would almost certainly expect access to the Royal Box, whether or not he'd been invited. Malloy had already drafted instructions for his head of security, emphasising the importance of close liaison with the Princess's personal security men who'd had a list of the invitees for some time, and he called him in to go over the plans again. At the meeting, Malloy did not refer specifically to Bonnaventure but made it clear that if, on the big day, anyone argued about access to the Royal Box, that he, Malloy, should be called on the radio immediately.

After the meeting, Malloy went to visit the Royal Box, greeting workmen who were putting the finishing touches to the new stand. The box itself, on the top tier of the grandstand, was ready, although the furniture was not yet in. Malloy stood looking through the glass doors as dusk fell on his racecourse. 'His' racecourse. He smiled at the thought. He was back in racing proper. For him, nothing would ever match his time as a jockey. But this – and the thought that the deal to take over the thirteen RHT courses was very close to being sealed – gave him a lot of satisfaction, not least because he'd 'shown' those who thought he was 'only' a jockey, his brain capable of nothing but pacing a race and timing a take-off. He'd shown them his brain worked in the business world too. He looked down at his false arm. He'd also shown them that he'd cared enough about other people to lose a limb in saving them. Saving men and women so they could return from Everest to their families.

His own return had been to no one. Parents dead. Marriage dead. Desire for another 'try' at a long-term relationship dead too. He had pinned all his hopes on the marriage. But the emotional baggage he'd brought with him had never been fully unpacked and it was the hidden stuff that, eventually, made him unliveable with. That's what Laura had said: 'You're unliveable with, Eddie Malloy. For anybody.'

He wondered how she'd feel in ten days' time when he'd be in charge of the biggest operation in British racing. And immediately he knew. She'd feel he'd found another vehicle to hitch his 'desperation for approval that you call ambition' to. She'd known more about him than he himself had. That had been the problem. Malloy once said to her, 'It's like living with your conscience all the time, living with you.'

He shook his head slowly, managing a smile. Maybe he was always trying to prove himself. Was that what had driven him on Everest? He liked to think it was humanity, courage, loyalty. But he wasn't certain it had been. He thought again about seeing an analyst. Wasn't that what rich people did, he asked himself mockingly. After all, he'd soon have that one-million-dollar bonus when the RHT papers were signed next week. Maybe he would see someone. Maybe.

He took a final look at the racecourse before darkness fell, recalling the day more than ten years ago when he'd 'stolen' a race on a horse called Silver Salmon by sneaking up the inside of a rival to win in a photo finish. He saw himself again in those lemon colours, head down, kicking rhythmically, two good arms pumping away. It seemed a lifetime ago.

Vaughn Keelor had wanted to fly over for the signing of the final documents on the RHT deal but he couldn't resolve the PR dilemma. The five-hour difference between London and New York meant Keelor could not attend a press conference in England and get back across the Atlantic before the news broke to hold a press conference there. He was adamant that he'd do nothing to risk alien-ating the financial press in America and asked Malloy to try and persuade the Jockey Club team to come to New York for the announcement.

But they didn't like the sound of it. 'Grand-standing', Bobby Cranfield had called it. It was news that would have an impact on British racing of Richter-scale proportions and the Jockey Club were determined the announcement would be made with as much dignity as possible. In a few years the Club had gone from being omnipotent in racing to being a supporting player condemned by many as anachronistic. The sale of these racecourses would be the breaking of their strongest remaining link with the sport, although it had to be done to keep them alive, give them a chance to rebuild substantial influence. Malloy explained to Keelor that Bobby and his colleagues saw the press conference as more akin to a wake than a celebration. They wouldn't be coming to New York.

So they agreed synchronised conferences for the following Thursday. Keelor would host the one in New York and Malloy the London one. Keelor asked Malloy to fly over after his conference for a party that evening. He said he was confident the Vice President would be there.

'Of the company?' Malloy asked.

'Of the United States of America,' Keelor replied.

And a week after that, thought Malloy, lunch with the Princess Royal. Changed days. During the time he'd been warned off he'd lived in a caravan, unable to afford anything else. A caravan close to a dung heap, breaking horses for a dealer. Funny thing, fate.

NINE

They held the press conference at Portman Square, Jockey Club Headquarters. One of the factors that made Malloy proud was that they'd kept the news from leaking. Although he'd been confident about the discretion of Bobby and the other Jockey Club people he'd been dealing with, racing was a relatively small industry where almost everyone earning a living in it knew everyone else. Keeping secrets of this magnitude was a considerable achievement, a fact mentioned with grudging admiration by more than one reporter at the conference. Malloy knew how big the news really was when he saw three of the press corps racing out of the room as soon as they had the gist of the story. They had deadlines to meet and the timing of the afternoon conference added to their pressure. Keelor's main aim with his timings had been to give the press all of Friday and Saturday to plan maximum space in the business sections of the heavy Sunday newspapers. He didn't worry too much about upsetting a few English racing journalists.

Bobby Cranfield took five times as many questions as Malloy. There was a real sense of shock in the room that the Jockey Club could agree to such a deal. Bill Cannon, the chief reporter at the *Racing News*, asked Bobby, 'What about the campaign that's been running against Makalu? What do your racecourse staff think of their skills in employee relations?'

Bobby replied, 'Our staff are being briefed as we speak. I'm sure they'll be delighted to find that they'll be working for such a go-ahead company committed to substantial investment in these racecourses.'

Cannon made notes then said, 'Do any of your racecourse staff live in tied houses?'

'Some do,' Bobby replied.

Cannon looked at Malloy. 'So will they suffer the same fate as Bert Jacobsen did at Gloucester?'

Malloy said, 'Mr Jacobsen's retired now and I think that if you go and speak to him you might find he has a different perspective on what happened.'

'Is that a yes or a no, Eddie?' Cannon asked. 'Will any RHT staff lose their job or their home?'

Malloy said, 'If anything, the investment we plan for these racecourses will lead to new jobs rather than redundancies.'

'So no job cuts and no evictions?'

'No company wants unhappy staff, Bill. We're no different.'

Cannon smiled, shaking his head. 'For an ex-jockey you make a bloody good politician, Malloy. You've come a long way.'

Malloy smiled.

Then came a string of questions on how the BHB might view the takeover. Bobby answered them all in the same vein – go and ask the BHB.

Cannon said, 'If you've done nothing else, you've spiked Simon Bonnaventure's guns for good. Do you take any pleasure in that, Bobby?'

'We take heart from the fact that the Jockey Club will now be able to invest in ensuring the security function in British racing will be the best in the world.'

'And you've stuck one up Bonnaventure at the same time?' Cannon asked.

Bobby smiled, looked at the faces around the room. 'That's not the sort of expression we hear too often under this roof, Mr Cannon.'

'Maybe not in public,' Cannon said, 'but I think I'd be safe in saying that when the cognac glasses are raised after dinner tonight, tongues might loosen a bit.'

'I'm a whiskey man myself,' Bobby said.

'What about you, Malloy?' asked Cannon. 'Champagne tonight?'

Malloy nodded, smiling. 'In New York.'

Malloy took a taxi to Heathrow for his Concorde flight. Keelor had a limousine collect him at JFK. The party was at Keelor's mansion in Westchester

County; Keelor had said the security would be easier to organise there. The party was well underway when Malloy got there and he didn't get to speak to Keelor till half an hour after he'd arrived, although a maid was standing by to show Malloy his suite. He showered and left wet prints on the white marble floor as he walked to the bedroom to put his arm back on and change into a clean shirt and suit. His suite was on the third floor and as he buttoned his shirt he wandered over to the French doors and looked across at the distant New York skyline under a watery sun. His life, again, had taken on an air of unreality, which continued that evening as Keelor led him onto a stage in a huge marquee in the garden and had all the guests, Vice President included, applaud him. Malloy was still half-stunned when he finally fell asleep that night.

Next morning things seemed on their way back to normal. All the guests had gone. It was just Malloy and his boss at the breakfast table eating scrambled eggs and bacon. Keelor looked as happy as Malloy had ever seen him. The big American kept leaning across to pat him on his good shoulder and tell him how proud he was of him, as well as himself for 'making the best recruitment decision of my life'.

Malloy tried to look suitably modest while growing increasingly uncomfortable at the over-the-top praise, which he believed was nothing more than an exaggerated management technique. Keelor prided himself on being a great manager as well as a great businessman and he believed all his staff loved him.

Malloy tried to change the subject. 'You're coming over for the big opening?'

'Of course. It's in my diary. Looking forward to meeting Her Highness.'

'I told Bobby we might manage dinner that night by way of putting a final seal on things.'

'Sorry, Ed, I need to get back here the same night. Don't worry, the deal's done. We don't have to be too nice to these guys any more.' He smiled.

Malloy looked at him. 'It's not a matter of being nice; Bobby's a friend of mine.'

'Fine!' Keelor raised an arm theatrically. 'You buy him dinner. Give him my apologies, will ya?'

'I will,' said Malloy coldly.

'Come on, Eddie! We can't all be everywhere we'd like to be. I'd have loved to have gone back to Nepal with you for the school opening. Loved to have climbed there again, you and me. It'd be great to have dinner with your friend but we've got a business to run, you know.'

Malloy remembered the rucksack Mingma gave him. He said, 'I've got something for you. Remind me to give you it when you come over.'

'What is it, a knighthood for saving British racing?' Keelor laughed, almost cackled, and Malloy wondered if he always got this manic when he pulled off a big deal.

'It's Mark Duncan's rucksack from Everest.'

Malloy would always remember thinking that if he'd punched Keelor in the face at that moment he would not have got such a shocked expression. The big man's features froze, mouth open, not even a blink, and he grew pale. Malloy asked, 'Vaughn, are you okay?'

Keelor began nodding slowly, puzzlement now creasing his face. The muffin that had been halfway to his mouth was carefully put back on the plate. 'Mark Duncan, my cameraman?'

'That's what's stencilled on the sack: M. Duncan, Makalu on Everest, '96.'

Keelor, still unblinking, looked at him. 'Was it empty?'

Malloy shook his head. 'Full.'

Keelor paused and Malloy saw him force some composure back into his manner. 'What's in it?' he asked.

'I didn't open it. I reckoned that was something for his family to do, nobody else.'

Keelor said quickly, 'You're right. You're absolutely right. God, poor Mark.' He put his head in his hands, rubbed his face then drew his fingers back through the greying hair. 'You gave me a hell of a shock when you told me that, Eddie. I'm sorry but it was the last thing I expected. He was a great guy and I miss him like hell.'

'Sorry, maybe I should have broken the news a bit more gently.'

Keelor reached over to clasp his forearm and

looked surprised again. Malloy smiled and said, 'Wrong one.' Keelor blushed and laughed nervously. Malloy was seeing a side of the man he didn't know.

'Who found it? I'll need to organise a reward,' Keelor said.

'Mingma Gombu Sherpa. Mingma Babu Sherpa's cousin.'

'I'll arrange it,' Keelor said, almost back to his businesslike self.

When Malloy arrived at his London home he smelled petrol as he approached the front door. He put it down to the heavy traffic on the road behind him. But when he opened the door the stench was so strong he paused his finger on the light switch fearing the tiniest spark could ignite the fumes. He found that carpets, furniture, curtains, beds, the clothes in the wardrobes, anything combustible had been soaked in petrol. Groaning and feeling sick he hurried to his office. There was enough light from the street to let him read the large letters painted on the wall: NEXT TIME WE LIGHT IT WITH YOU INSIDE. KILL THE DEAL BEFORE THE DEAL KILLS YOU. He tried to see if the safe had been opened. It was too dark to see with watery eyes as the fumes began to work his tear ducts. He went back outside and called the police.

Malloy waited in the cold dark garden. He hoped they'd arrive soon to give him time to get into a hotel and start arranging a clean-up. Scanning through his mobile for Keelor's number he came across Frankie Houlihan's. He remembered he'd promised Houlihan a call if anything else happened and now – semi-jetlagged, confused and slightly shocked – seemed a good time to hear a friendly voice. He'd need to take some advice from the Jockey Club people anyway. Houlihan had been right and so had Keelor. This was escalating quickly. He shouldn't have discounted the brick and the bullet. He rubbed his eyes again and thought of what could have happened if he'd switched on the light and kicked out a spark or if his mobile had gone off as he'd walked in. He looked at the dark house in front of him and pictured it in flames.

He remembered back to how he'd handled violence in the past when he'd been hunting the criminal who'd framed him, when the jockey killer was after him. And that self-preservation instinct of old, that all-or-nothing feeling he'd often tried replicating in the mountains, started seeping back into him. It was time to start fighting back.

TEN

Malloy rang Houlihan and told him what had happened. Houlihan said, 'You need to get away from the house, now.'

'I'm waiting for the cops.'

'Wait in the car. Lock it.'

Malloy smiled, surprised at how comforted he felt by his new friend's concern and stern instruction. 'I will,' he said.

'And you can come and stay here once the police have gone.'

'Is that an order?'

'Yes, it is,' said Houlihan.

'Good, because I was going to ask you to put me up for a few nights but you need to know what you might be getting into. It could be your place next if they find out I'm there.'

'I'll risk it. We need to get these people.'

'You'll find me up for that, Frankie. You'll find me well up for it.' Malloy smiled and felt confident and stronger as that self-preservation instinct continued to sharpen by the second, making him eager to go on the offensive.

Keelor's first question when Malloy rang with news of the incident was, 'Is the rucksack safe?'

Taken aback, Malloy said, 'I don't know. I didn't check. It's kind of hard to breathe in there.'

'Okay, okay. No worries. I'm sorry but it's been on my mind since the minute you told me. It seems to have brought everything back again, making me wonder if I could have done more for Mark and the rest of the team. And I know what getting the sack back will mean to Gemma and the kids. Jeez, I'm sorry, are you okay, Eddie?'

'I'm fine but things are getting serious with this guy. All the Bert Jacobsen stuff was just a front like I always said it was. Whoever's behind this doesn't want the RHT deal to go through.'

'It's gone through. Signed, sealed, delivered . . . they're ours. The guy's wasting his time, can't he tell that from the press reports?'

Malloy, tired and finding it difficult to think straight, sighed heavily. 'Vaughn, I need to go, the police have just arrived,' he lied.

'Eddie, call me right back and let me know if the rucksack is there.'

'Okay. Give me ten minutes.' Malloy returned to the house, trying to recall where he'd put the sack. In his office, he thought. Yes, he wouldn't have put it anywhere else.

He left the front door open this time and moved

through the dark rooms opening windows. Light from the street showed him enough of his office to realise the rucksack wasn't there. He swore. He crouched low and felt under the desk then around all the walls near the floor. Nothing. He went back outside and called Keelor.

'Bad news, Vaughn, Mark's rucksack's gone.' Malloy heard Keelor gasp, then silence. 'Vaughn, are you okay?'

Keelor said, 'Wait, just hold on . . .'

Silence again. Malloy was sure Keelor had covered the mouthpiece. It felt to Malloy like it was a long time before he heard Keelor's short breathing, like tiny repeating versions of the gasp he'd given when Malloy had first told him of the rucksack. Keelor eventually spoke. 'Did anyone know about the rucksack?'

'Only Mingma and whoever he told. I told nobody.'

'Did anyone follow you home from the airport?'

Malloy wondered where Keelor was going with this. He said, 'Not that I noticed.'

'Eddie, I need to get that rucksack back. I've told Mark's wife, his kids. I can't go back to them now and say I don't have it any more. That some fucker stole it!' His voice was rising, out of control. Malloy eased the phone a few inches from his ear. 'You need to get that fucking rucksack back, Eddie! This is your job now! Understand?'

Malloy said, 'Vaughn, cool it. I'm sorry about the rucksack, okay? It wasn't my fault.'

'Of course it was your fault! This guy's after you and you know it and you go and leave the rucksack in your house! In your fucking house! You can't even remember to bring it with you to New York! Your head's too full of the big time, Malloy, that's your problem! You neglect your basic fucking duties! Now get this guy and get that fucking rucksack back! You hear?'

Malloy hung up on him, put the phone on top of the wall and gave it the finger. 'Up yours, Keelor.'

He sat, brooding. Keelor was showing his other side and Malloy didn't like it. Didn't need the hassle. What the hell was the big deal with the rucksack anyway, Malloy wondered? He'd been a click away from being barbecued and all Keelor got angry about was a dead man's rucksack. He decided that when Keelor had paid him his one million dollar bonus for the RHT deal he'd quit, set up his own business, something outdoors, something in adventure.

A few minutes later, Keelor called him back, calmer now but not apologetic. 'Eddie, I've got two men flying over tomorrow to help you find this guy. I want you to meet them at Heathrow. The flight's due seven ten p.m. your time. Check in with me when they arrive and we'll take it from there. Okay?'

'I'll see how tomorrow goes. I'll call you.'

'You be there, Eddie.'

'I'll call you. Goodnight.'

Malloy hung up and switched off his phone.

Who did this guy think he was, Malloy wondered, shaking his head. He spent the next ten minutes congratulating himself that he had enough money to get by and didn't need to bow to somebody else's whims and temperament for a living.

When two uniformed constables finally turned up, Malloy had to put his hand on the arm of the first one in to stop him switching on the lights. 'Too many fumes. Light switches can spark.'

The policeman said, 'I think it'll be okay.'

Malloy looked at him, knowing that his professional pride had been hurt. Malloy said, 'You're a young man to be taking such a big risk. Haven't you got a torch?'

The policeman looked at him, even more wound up now. His colleague spoke from behind them both. 'There's one in the car, Nigel, I'll get it.'

Inside the house all three of them followed the torch beam. There seemed to be no damage except that caused by the petrol. They went from room to room. When they opened the door of the gym the first thing the beam fell on was Mark Duncan's rucksack. Malloy sighed loudly and leaned back against the wall.

Outside with the rucksack, Malloy now remembered hearing the plastic clips rattling on the wooden floor of the gym as he'd opened the door that night and slung the rucksack carelessly inside. He was about to call Keelor back to tell him but then thought he'd let Keelor sweat about his

115

precious rucksack. The more he thought about it the stranger it seemed. From the moment he'd told Keelor about the sack, the man's reactions had been way over the top. Malloy had initially accepted Keelor's explanation about the emotional side of the news and his wish to return Mark's things to his family, but his tantrum tonight told Malloy there had to be more to it.

Malloy undid the straps and opened the blue sack. Carefully, he unpacked it: spare goggles, hat and gloves, two chocolate bars, a video tape in a plastic case. Keelor had asked him first-off what was inside and had seemed pretty relieved when Malloy had told him he hadn't looked. Was this tape what Keelor really wanted? If so, what was on it?

Malloy called Keelor back. 'The rucksack just turned up.'

'Where?' Keelor was still tense.

'In the gym.'

'Empty?'

'Untouched. As far as I can tell. I haven't opened it. Do you want me to?'

'No. No. No need. Was that where you left it?'

'No. I left it in my office,' Malloy lied.

'He moved it? Did he move anything else? Anything missing?'

'Nothing.'

'I can't figure it, Malloy, can you?' Keelor's voice was returning to the friendlier tone Malloy was more used to.

'No, I can't, but the main thing is it's safe. I'll give it to your boys tomorrow night.'

'Just hold on to it, Malloy, but keep it safe. Get yourself out of that flat. Find somewhere else. And please keep that rucksack close to you until I pick it up. I don't want this bastard spoiling things for Mark's family.'

Malloy shook his head as he listened. 'So your guys won't be making the trip after all?'

'No need, is there?'

'You mean apart from helping find the guy who might be trying to kill me?'

After a moment's hesitation Keelor said, 'I'm organising some protection on your side. Don't worry.'

'What kind of protection?'

'More news tomorrow, Eddie. And I'm sorry for losing it earlier. I just couldn't have found a way to tell Gemma and the kids that their last link with Mark was gone. You understand that.'

'I understand quite a few things now, Vaughn.' Malloy thought immediately that he'd said the wrong thing. Keelor might interpret that as him having opened the rucksack. He added quickly, 'I understand that when somebody tells you one day you're the best recruitment decision they've ever made, they might not hold the same opinion of you the next day. See you next week.'

ELEVEN

'A right pair of plods,' Malloy said. He was sitting in Houlihan's house wearing one of his tracksuits. His own clothes, stinking of petrol, were bin-bagged in the boot of his car. His hair was still wet from the shower and he held a glass of Bushmills. Houlihan had one too and was leaning forward in the big armchair, listening to Malloy's story. 'So anyway, that's how serious the Met takes it.'

Houlihan said, 'What about the clean-up, have you organised anything?'

'Uncleanable, I'd think. Throw-outable, definitely. Mr Keelor will just need to pay to have the whole house refurnished.'

'And the security system upgraded.'

'At ten grand, it was a pretty good spec already. That's why I'm beginning to worry just a wee bit. I think we've got some pros involved here, don't you?'

'Sounds like it might be.'

'And they don't come cheap. And also, they

usually do a proper job, so I think there'll be another visit.'

Houlihan watched Malloy for a few seconds, trying to read his true feelings. He saw a tired face, the frostbite scars seeming more vivid than before. Houlihan asked, 'What's the plan, then?'

Malloy held the glass up to the light. 'The only plan I've got for now is to finish this and sleep for twelve hours. If you don't mind, that is.'

'Sleep away. You'll be first to use the guest bed so make the best of it.'

Malloy smiled and nodded his thanks then put his head back and sighed as he stared at the ceiling. He said, 'You know, I feel quite at home here. Felt the same first time I came.'

'Good,' said Houlihan. 'You're welcome any time.'

Malloy laughed. 'You won't be saying that if my friend pays us a visit with fifty gallons of four-star.'

'So long as we're not inside when he does.'

They talked about the RHT deal and the press conferences and Houlihan asked about the party in New York. Malloy didn't mention the Vice President and everyone applauding him in case Houlihan thought he was boasting. Houlihan poured a second drink for each of them. 'Hungry?' he asked Malloy.

'I am now you mention it.' He looked at his watch. 'Nearly midnight, bit late for a takeaway.'

'I can run to scrambled eggs on toast.'

Malloy stood up quickly. 'If you do the eggs, I'll do the toast. I'm good at toast.'

Houlihan smiled and they took their glasses and moved to the kitchen. As he stirred the warming eggs, Houlihan nodded towards the rucksack in the corner. 'Souvenir?'

Malloy told him the story, leaving out the fact he'd opened it. 'Keelor's more worried about that rucksack than he is about me,' he said. 'I'll be glad when I hand it over to him.'

'Do you think Mark Duncan's family will welcome it as much as Keelor thinks they will?'

Malloy shrugged and made a face. 'It's hard to say. He knows them, I don't. There was a lot of shit flying around after Everest with people looking to blame somebody in each party for the deaths. There's still a lot of bitterness among some of the families. Others have just accepted it and moved on.'

Houlihan spooned egg onto hot buttered toast. 'What about the people you saved, do they keep in touch?'

'Chuck Connors calls me from time to time, he was a client. Two of the others were experienced mountaineers, Bernadine Kazinsky and John Waterman. I wouldn't expect to hear from them. See, I lost an arm,' he laughed, 'if you hadn't noticed.' Houlihan smiled. 'John lost two toes and Bernadine got through in one piece. They probably feel a bit guilty that I came off worst and that makes it a bit harder to pick up the phone. But I was never looking for thanks or undying gratitude, you know. It was just one of those things you do.'

'Didn't you save the guide too?' Houlihan slid the steaming plate across as he spoke.

Greedily, Malloy took a mouthful, nodding as he chewed. 'Grant Selsden, big New Zealander, original model for your brick shithouse. I don't know to this day how I got him back to the tent; where I got the strength.' He swallowed and washed it down with whiskey then grimaced. 'Doesn't mix well.'

Houlihan smiled once more. 'The kettle's on.'

'You're a fine host, Mr Houlihan.' Malloy raised his glass, urging Houlihan to do the same then apologising, 'Sorry, I'm drunk. I shouldn't drink when I'm so tired. Hits me ten times quicker than normal.'

'I'll make some tea.'

'Good. Thanks. You've been great. I really appreciate it.'

'No problem.'

They ate quietly for a minute and Malloy reflected on how easy he was finding it to talk to Houlihan. He wondered if it was because of his awareness of Houlihan's past as a priest – was this what made him such a good listener? Malloy decided it was more than that. He'd quite simply felt comfortable with the man since they'd first met, leaving aside Houlihan's bravery in piling into that fight. In a way he was more relaxed with Houlihan than he'd ever been with his wife. Malloy smiled to himself – maybe it was the drink.

121

'So does this Grant fella keep in touch with you? He was the leader, wasn't he?'

Malloy nodded. 'It was his gig. Third time he'd summited Everest, first time he'd led clients. He was unlucky. Would probably have had a good business by now if it hadn't been for that storm. We talk now and then. I'd known Grant for a couple of years beforehand. He invited me along as a sort of back-up. I didn't have the experience to be a paid guide but it didn't cost me anything either to make the trip.'

'How much would you have had to pay as a client?'

'Grant had eight of them paying fifty thousand dollars each.'

Houlihan nodded. He remembered an article Kathy, a star journalist, had once written on the growing demand for guided trips. He said, 'Some pay more than that, don't they?'

Malloy said, 'The top guys charge up to seventy thousand dollars a head.'

'Did any of those lose people in '96?'

'Tom Hutchison lost five of his summit party, including a sixteen-year-old kid, and died himself. Keelor was the only survivor. Hutchison was supposed to be the best American guide there'd ever been. Some thought a couple of Europeans were better but Keelor wanted an American to guide his party and Hutchison had to be the choice. He'd summited twice without supplemental oxygen before he started guiding and had climbed the other thirteen eight-thousand-metre peaks in the world. A pretty exclusive club. He'd got five parties to the top of Everest in the previous eight years and, more importantly, had turned two parties back within a couple of hundred metres of the top.'

'Bad weather?'

Malloy shook his head, finished his last piece of toast and said, 'Weather was fine but they'd hit their turnaround time and Hutchison had the discipline to stick to it and the respect of his party to enforce it. Not an easy thing to do when you're effectively working for these people. They've paid you seventy thousand dollars each and they've ground out every step for days, finding strength from God only knows where to keep going. Then, two hundred metres from the top, standing there looking at it, Hutchison says, "Not today, boys, it's two o'clock. If we carry on we might not get back to Camp Four by dark. Turn round and start walking back down. It's over." How would you feel looking at your cash disappear along with your dream? But Hutchison had their respect. The top of any mountain is only halfway. The real trick's getting back down safely. That's where Hutchison won out.'

'So what happened to him in '96?'

'The same as what happened to everybody above twenty-six thousand feet. The storm.'

Houlihan noticed a subtle change in Malloy then; an unease. Houlihan said, 'Is it hard for you to talk about this?'

Malloy half-smiled. 'Your priestly precep? . . . perspec?' He laughed and held up his glass and stared at the remaining whiskey. 'I'll try again. Your priestly . . . *perceptive* . . . powers seem to be all there. I've talked about it often enough for money. You wouldn't think it would still be bothering me. I suppose telling it all on stage is a bit of a performance really. I usually manage to bring it off all right.' He smiled sadly.

Houlihan asked, 'Have you ever talked about it to anybody?'

'You mean rather than talking at somebody?'

'Yes. Just quietly with a friend.'

Malloy paused. Houlihan saw his eyes glisten. Malloy took another gulp of whiskey while he composed himself and said, 'No. I haven't.'

Houlihan's experience as a counsellor kept him silent. He just watched as Malloy stared at the wall. Then Malloy drew his legs up and swung his shoeless feet over the arm of the chair, resting his head in the corner. Still staring at the wall he started talking. 'I never needed to be near the top to be scared. I'd be in a constant state of terror in the Khumbu Icefall, at about twenty thousand feet.' He paused a few seconds then turned to Houlihan. 'Do you know much about the South Col route?'

Houlihan shook his head. 'Nothing.'

Malloy straightened now, pulling his legs round, putting his feet back on the floor, leaning forward. 'You need to cross the Khumbu Glacier, which is like a two-and-a-half-mile river of shifting ice. It's not a movement you notice but you know it's happening, the crevasses tell you that. Crevasses didn't scare me, not the ones I could see anyway. Lots of them you can just step over. Others are eighty feet wide and hundreds of feet deep. The Sherpas strap aluminium ladders together and lay them across and you do a sort of tightrope walk hoping your crampon spikes don't catch in the rungs. Even if they do and you fall, you're roped, so as long as you don't fall awkwardly you'll be okay.'

Malloy sipped more whiskey then continued. 'The glacier flows down a valley called the Western Cwm. Near the bottom of the Cwm it spills over a steep drop and its speed picks up to around three or four feet a day. The movement splinters the ice into a sort of nightmare town of massive towers, some of them ten storeys high. Seracs, they call them, and we had to weave our way through them knowing that there is one certainty in the Icefall: sooner or later, with virtually no warning, each of them will topple. Nineteen climbers had died in the Icefall by the time we made our first trip through it. Do you remember when you were a kid and you'd be leaning over a cliff or off the diving board and one of your mates would come up behind and give you that little push then grab you?'

Smiling, Houlihan nodded. Malloy said, 'That was the feeling I got in the Khumbu Icefall every time I heard a crack, and there were plenty of them.'

'Not good for the nerves,' Houlihan said.

'But it doesn't half strengthen the sphincter.' They laughed. Malloy went on. 'Anyway, I had to go through the Icefall seven times. The way it works is you move from base camp up and down the mountain. You spend a bit more time up high with each trip and you steadily become acclimatised. But I never got used to the Icefall. Come the end, what I was looking forward to most wasn't reaching the top, it was making my last trip through those seracs.'

Malloy drained his glass. Houlihan got up. 'Another one?'

'How bored are you by now?'

'Not at all. It's a privilege listening to you. Especially when I don't have to pay thirty-five dollars for a seat.' He took Malloy's glass and refilled it.

'Cheers,' Malloy said, then he looked at Houlihan. 'Are you sure you want to hear the rest?'

'Positive.'

Malloy put his glass down on the carpet and massaged his face with his good hand, rubbing his tired eyes then the back of his neck. He said, 'Looks silly that, doesn't it? Rubbing your face with one hand? It's like stretching with just one arm.' He sat forward. 'Mind if I take this off?' He nodded towards the false arm.

'Be my guest,' Houlihan said. He was trying not to laugh. Malloy spotted it and smiled. 'I know, surreal, ain't it? Bad enough having a virtual stranger stinking of petrol turning up on your door without him drinking all your whiskey then taking his arm off.'

Houlihan laughed. 'I've seen worse.'

'I hope not.' He unzipped the tracksuit top and undid the straps holding the prosthesis on. Houlihan, slightly embarrassed, didn't know which was least polite, to watch or not to watch. But Malloy seemed untroubled and lowered the arm to rest on the floor beside his whiskey glass. He called down to it, 'Hey, pass me that drink up, mate!'

Houlihan laughed and his liking for the man grew.

Malloy continued. 'Nine of us left Camp Four on the South Col at eleven thirty p.m. on May ninth. Grant led. We had two Sherpas, two veteran climbers, me who'd done enough to be classed as experienced, and three remaining clients. We'd started with eight clients but five dropped out. Exhaustion, altitude sickness, injury, you know. Anyway, it was a fairly strong party – stronger, probably, than many of the others who left the South Col for the summit that night. We reckoned there were more than sixty people camped on the Col, and when the wind finally died most of them started getting ready for the final climb.

'I know Grant was worried about that, the numbers. The toughest part ahead of us was the Hillary Step, which is like a forty-foot cliff-face. Ropes would need to be fixed on it and then just one climber at a time could be on those ropes, whether you were trying to go up or down. It was a big bottleneck. Grant had called one p.m. as the turn-around time so we had thirteen and a half hours to do that last one thousand metres.

'It was a perfect night. We didn't even need our headlamps on. I'll never forget seeing the electrical storms over the Terai swamps hundreds of miles away on the Indian border. Orange and blue lightning flashes; no thunder, too far away to hear it. Anyway, Grant and Ngawang and Ngima – the Sherpas – climbed with Chuck, Grace and Philip, the three clients. Normally the Sherpas would have gone on ahead to fix ropes where they were needed, but John, Bernadine and I had asked if we could do that. We were all feeling pretty strong although I'd had a bitch of a cough for about ten days.

'Anyway, by about three a.m. we were well ahead of the others. They were out of sight and Bernadine suggested we waited till they caught up in case Grant needed some help with them. John and I didn't think that was a great idea but Bernadine nagged us into it. She was pretty forth-right at the best of times and altitude hadn't helped calm her down. It makes a lot of people ultra-sensitive. Anyway, it was no big deal and we settled down to wait. But after twenty minutes the cold would have cracked your bones and it didn't take too much to persuade Bernadine we should get moving again.

'So we set off . . .' Malloy stopped suddenly and, looking perplexed, stared down into his whiskey glass. He resumed, fingers at his mouth, looking at Houlihan. 'Sorry, I was wondering if I was right there. Was that the time Bernadine threw the tantrum? We stopped a few times you see . . . Anyway, I think she led us away; I was behind her and John tracked me.' He paused again. 'Or did John lead? Doesn't matter I suppose.' He sighed heavily and drank more whiskey. 'Anyway, we reached the Hillary Step well before noon, probably not long after eleven actually. Three of the Indian army team were starting up the ropes. Well, two of them were, the third guy was out on his feet and it was obvious to everybody but him that he wasn't going any higher. But he wouldn't unclip from the rope, kept insisting he'd make it. Then John . . . or was it Bernadine . . .? Wait a minute, did I say the Indian army team?'

Houlihan nodded. Malloy suddenly looked very tired, smiled slowly and rubbed his eyes again. 'I'm wrong, it was the New Zealanders. The Indian team were . . .' He was silent again for what seemed a long time and then said, 'I'm really beginning to ramble now, sorry. Do you mind if we leave the rest of it till some other time?'

'Of course not. You look exhausted.'

Malloy nodded, closing his eyes. Houlihan got up. 'Come on, you can sleep till noon.'

Malloy finished his drink and, with his one hand, pushed himself wearily to his feet. Houlihan took his glass to the sink and said, 'You know where you're going, don't you?'

'Yes. Thanks. See you in the morning.'

Houlihan said, 'I'll double-lock everything.'

'You read my mind.'

Houlihan moved quietly around the house, locking up. He heard Malloy's bed creak slightly then a loud sigh of relief. He knew that emotional exhaustion had played a big part in his friend's cutting short of the story. Knowing how reliving his own tragedy in his head could affect him, he considered it a wonder that Malloy could talk so freely about his experience. Switching off the final light he silently wished his friend a good night's sleep.

TWELVE

The phone was ringing when Houlihan returned from his run the next morning. He picked it up, smearing the earpiece with sweat as he raised it. It was Bobby Cranfield. 'Houlihan?'

'Yes, hello Bobby.' He was panting

'Are you okay?'

'Fine. Just been running.'

'There was another attack on Eddie Malloy's place last night.'

'I know. He's here.' Houlihan explained what had happened.

Bobby said, 'The press have got hold of it. They're linking it to the RHT deal. I need to speak to Malloy before the press do.'

'He's knackered, Bobby, still asleep.'

'Can you wake him?'

'He wouldn't thank me for it. The guy's shattered. I'll ask him to call you.'

'Oh,' Cranfield sounded frustrated. 'I'll drive out.'

'Fine. See you when you get here.'

'Don't let him speak to anyone till I get there, Frankie. You need to start playing a bigger part in this now.' He hung up before Houlihan could respond. Houlihan felt he was being admonished. Hearing a noise behind him he turned to see Malloy coming in from the hallway, lowering his mobile phone from his ear. 'Bollocks! Twenty-one messages!' He was barefoot and naked from the waist up. Houlihan tried not to look at the stump of his left arm but he noticed the smooth pink patches on his cheek where stubble didn't grow.

Houlihan said, 'They'll be from the press. Best if you don't respond. Bobby Cranfield's on his way out to see you. He's been taking plenty of calls too.'

'About what?' Malloy threw the phone on the chair and ruffled his hair.

'About whoever decorated your flat with petrol.'

'Nah. How'd they pick that up so quick?'

'There's always somebody listening in to the police network. Or a cop called them direct.'

'Bastards,' Malloy said.

'Best turn your phone off again, Eddie.'

He picked it up. 'I'll just play these back first to check.'

By the time Cranfield's converted MPV pulled up outside, Houlihan and Malloy were dressed and had eaten breakfast. Houlihan parted the curtain and saw that Cranfield's chauffeur was Houlihan's boss, Sam Hooper. When he opened the door Hooper wheeled Cranfield in. Malloy stood up from the table and was introduced to a sullen Hooper. Houlihan hauled two of the chairs away from the kitchen table and Cranfield wheeled himself into the space. Hooper moved a chair as close to Cranfield as possible and sat down. On the opposite side of the table, Malloy playfully moved his chair closer to Houlihan's. Houlihan smiled. Hooper scowled.

Cranfield wrinkled his nose and looked around. 'Petrol,' said Houlihan. 'Fumes on Eddie's rucksack. It needs to stay in here so we can keep an eye on it.'

Malloy shrugged. 'Boss's orders.'

Cranfield said, 'They must have drowned the place.'

Malloy nodded. 'Smelled like they'd rolled a tanker up the drive and shoved a hose through the letterbox.'

'Are you all right?' Cranfield asked him.

'Pissed off. I could have done without it.'

'Did Houlihan tell you the press are on to it?'

Malloy nodded and held up his phone. 'I've over forty messages from them now. What's the line?'

'They want to know if you'll pull out of the RHT deal.'

Malloy pointed at himself. 'Me personally? Or Makalu?'

'Either. Both.'

Malloy laughed. 'Keelor would sooner give up his right arm for one of these,' he held up the prosthesis, 'than pull out. And if the press think I'm so scared then it can't be the racing press we're referring to. They know me well enough not to ask the question.'

Cranfield said, 'I knew that would be your answer. I wasn't sure where Keelor stood. He called me this morning demanding protection for you. Said if the Jockey Club couldn't keep his people safe he might need to think again.'

'He's bluffing,' Malloy said.

Hooper spoke. 'Your boss doesn't quite seem to grasp what my department does. He expects security to mean bodyguards for you.'

'Tell him, not me,' Malloy said coldly.

'How would you feel about a bodyguard?' Cranfield asked.

'It's too soon to be talking about that, Bobby. It'd be more effective to send a couple of your guys to interview Bonnaventure. I wouldn't mind seeing his reaction to that.'

Cranfield said, 'His reaction would be a writ and a call to the Press Association.'

'And maybe another call to his petrol man to pack it in since they've been sussed.'

Cranfield shook his head. 'I know your history with Bonnaventure, Eddie. You're going to need hard evidence or people will put it down to your feud from way back.'

'We'll see. I might just go back to my old ways and start a little investigation of my own.'

Cranfield laughed lightly. 'You'll be a bit rusty now at that stuff.'

Malloy sat back. 'I don't know. Good track record, remember? Your guys offered me a job once.'

'They did, you're right. You've come . . .' Bobby stopped himself and said, 'You've seen a few changes since those days.' And Houlihan knew that Cranfield had been going to say, 'You've come up in the world', or, 'You've come on a bit since then', but he'd stopped himself for fear of offending Houlihan.

Cranfield turned to Houlihan. 'Can we have a private word?'

'Sure,' said Houlihan, slightly surprised.

Cranfield said to Malloy, 'You don't mind, I hope?' as he wheeled himself back from the table.

'No problem,' Malloy replied and stood up. 'You sit there. I'll grab some fresh air.'

Cranfield raised his hand. 'Eddie, would you mind staying indoors?'

Malloy looked down at him. Cranfield said, 'Sorry, I'm not trying to boss you around but there are at least two reporters I know who live in Lambourn. I think it's best for now that no one knows you're here.'

Malloy pushed the chair slowly back under the table with his knee. 'Fair enough.' He returned to his bedroom. Hooper stayed at the table with Cranfield and Houlihan. Cranfield said, 'Frankie, how would you feel about keeping Malloy company for a while?'

'I'm the bodyguard you had in mind?'

'I'm not sure we can call it that.'

'I'm not sure we can either,' Houlihan replied.

'Apart from Eddie and how he'll take it, the press will have a field day. That's aside from the fact that if anything happened, Eddie Malloy's a lot tougher than I am. He's more likely to find me a hindrance than a help.'

'A case of modesty forbids, I think,' said Cranfield, smiling. 'And anyway, it's the deterrent factor that's important. These people will be less willing to take risks if there's a witness around.'

Houlihan looked at him for a few moments. 'Was this what you meant when you said on the phone that I had to start playing a bigger part in this?'

Cranfield nodded.

Hooper spoke. 'You've had it easy for long enough, Houlihan.' There was no lightness in his voice. Cranfield put out a hand to stop him saying anything else.

Houlihan ignored his words. Cranfield said, 'Obviously there's a potential danger in this. If your presence doesn't deter this fellow you could be putting yourself in the line of fire.'

Houlihan nodded and stayed silent. Cranfield said, 'Take some time to consider it. You couldn't stay here with him. I don't think Malloy would want to anyway. He needs to be in London. Wherever he goes, you'd have to be with him.'

'How long for?'

Cranfield shrugged. 'I don't know. We'd have to see if there were any more threats or if things cooled down.'

'I have some family issues back in Dublin. I may need the occasional day off.'

Cranfield looked up at Hooper and said, 'I'm sure we can organise that, can't we? Could Stonebanks fill in on the odd day?'

Houlihan said, 'Geoff's already picking up my other stuff. It wouldn't be fair.'

Hooper said, 'Stonebanks will do what he's told.'

'Then find yourself another bodyguard, Mr Hooper.'

Cranfield glared at Hooper and said, 'Leave this to me to sort out with Sam, Frankie. Will you do it? You'll get what time off you need for your family.'

Houlihan stood up. 'I'm not going to say yes or no without asking Eddie what he thinks.'

'You want to ask him yourself before I put it to him?' Cranfield said.

'T'would be best.'

'Fine.'

Houlihan went to the bedroom. There was a dull sound when he knocked on the door. Malloy had been leaning against it. He opened it. Houlihan went in and closed it behind him. Malloy looked at him and said, 'They want you to babysit me.'

Houlihan smiled. 'You heard?'

'No. Didn't need to. He flagged it well enough, don't you think?'

'I didn't twig.'

Malloy smiled.

Houlihan continued, 'Well, I'm hardly the bodyguard type, am I? You saw that at Kempton.'

Malloy laughed. 'I take it you told them to piss off?'

'I'm only allowed to say urinate off.'

Malloy smiled. 'So you said no?'

'I said I'd speak to you. It doesn't bother me. Remember, I was assigned to looking after Makalu in general some time back. It's just there hasn't been that much to do so far. What do you think?'

'I could use a friend. And I kind of lost the plot with Keelor on the phone last night and asked him what he was going to do about some protection. He called Cranfield. This is the result. I can hardly say no now, can I?'

'I suppose not.'

They looked at each other. 'Are you saying yes, then?' Houlihan asked.

'Only on the understanding that as soon as this guy pulls his next stunt you get yourself out of it. I don't mind playing along with Keelor and Cranfield but I'm not having you or anybody else putting their arse on the line for something that's down to me.'

'We'll worry about that when it happens.'

'No,' Malloy said sternly. 'We agree it now or no deal.'

Houlihan looked at him for a few moments. 'Do you really think I'd take this on then run away if something happens?'

Malloy's expression softened to one of apology. 'No, I don't expect you to. I just want you to.'

'I can't do it that way, Eddie, any more than you could do it if it were you.'

Malloy nodded. Neither spoke for a while then Houlihan held out his hand and said, 'Whole duck or no dinner?'

'Is that an Irish version of all for one and one for all?'

''Tis.'

Malloy shook his hand. 'Whole duck or no dinner it is, then.' They smiled and Houlihan turned towards the door. 'We'd better put them out of their misery.'

Malloy said, 'Just one thing before we do.' Houlihan turned again to look at his serious expression. Malloy said, 'Eh, you don't, er, hog the quilt or fart a lot in bed, do you?' Houlihan reddened, trying to figure out how to react. Malloy smiled slowly and raised a wagging finger. 'Had you going there, didn't I, Father?'

Houlihan smiled. Malloy said, 'Let's go and see the Half-assed Thickos.'

Later that day, Cranfield and Malloy drafted a statement for the press. Malloy cleared it with Keelor and issued it on behalf of Makalu. The gist was that nothing would make them pull out of the RHT deal. Keelor was quoted as saying that when the 'saboteur' was caught, not only would he face punishment through the legal system but that Makalu would sue him (they deliberately left out 'or her') for everything he had. Malloy hoped Bonnaventure would take special note of this.

THIRTEEN

Malloy decided that moving out of his flat might be interpreted as a weakening of resolve. He arranged to have it cleaned, redecorated and refurnished in a seventy-two-hour blitz. He also ordered a new safe – guaranteed fireproof and big enough to hold the rucksack. Makalu picked up the bill. He and Houlihan moved in the day before the planned opening of the new grandstand at Badbury.

In the early hours of that first morning back, when Malloy was pretty sure Houlihan was asleep, he got out the video tape he'd taken from the rucksack and went quietly to the living room. Closing the door softly behind him, he began opening the video case then realised that he had neither TV nor video to play it on. He banged his forehead with the heel of his hand.

He sat down to think, tapping the tape lightly on his thigh. He didn't want to keep this in the flat or in his car. With the grand opening of

Badbury coming up it was going to be a few days now before he could watch it. He'd hoped to do so before Keelor arrived so he could put the tape back in the rucksack where Keelor would expect to find it.

What was on it? What had Duncan filmed on Everest that Keelor was so desperate to get his hands on? Proof of his self-proclaimed heroics? Malloy doubted that. The more he'd got to know his boss the less he liked him. The public persona was far from the private one. Malloy stared at the tape. 'Fuck it!' he whispered harshly, cursing himself for his own stupidity. He couldn't risk having it copied in case the copier saw something. His choice was to put it back in Mark's rucksack and forget it, or to stash it somewhere till he could watch it. But what would Keelor do when he saw the tape was gone?

Malloy racked his brain. After a few minutes he got dressed and went out to the all-night super-market. He returned with a pack of blank video-tapes, unwrapped one, carefully unspooled the tape and spent the next half-hour scratching it in places along its length with a safety pin. He re-spooled the tape, closed the cassette, immersed it in a bowl of cold water, then put it in the freezer. Malloy set his watch alarm then dozed in the chair until six a.m., when he retrieved the tape from the freezer, put it in Mark Duncan's original tape box, and replaced it in the rucksack.

He then packed his sports bag, put the Duncan

tape in it and left a note for Houlihan: 'Gone swimming. Back soon.'

The evening before the grand opening, Houlihan and Malloy went running together in Hyde Park. The strong wind blew their words away as they tried to chat during the run. Malloy was keen to ensure Houlihan stayed in the background the next day. He'd have his own security on course, especially with royalty there. They talked it through as they walked, cooling down. Houlihan agreed. He knew there'd be plenty of press there and didn't want any of them picking up on his 'bodyguard' role.

They left London early the next day and reached the course as dawn broke. The guard on the gate, employed by contractors, refused to let them through until he'd called his boss to come and identify Malloy. Malloy waited patiently, pleased his security orders were being carried out.

Houlihan accompanied Malloy on a walk round the racecourse and into every public room. Malloy moved fast, commenting into a Dictaphone whenever he saw some detail that needed attention. Houlihan was impressed by his professionalism.

Malloy gave Houlihan a radio so he could monitor all that was being said on the racecourse's private network. When the staff started arriving, Houlihan, as planned, drifted away but kept the radio in his hand, and throughout the morning it relayed to him the story of raceday preparations from a side he'd never previously seen.

The racecard delivery's two boxes short. Get them couriered. *There's a burst pipe in the portaloo by the top entrance.* A plumber will be there in five minutes. *The stable manager's just been kicked by a horse that arrived last night. His leg might be broken.* Call an ambulance then get Jack to allocate the boxes. *One of the caterer's vans has broken down on the M5.* Their problem; tell them to get it sorted. *The royal security team want to do another check on the commentary box.* Get Ben to take them up there. *Mr Keelor rang, said to tell you he's on his way.* Oh joy of joys! *The princess has decided she wants her car to stop at the gate and not drive through the racecourse. She'll walk in.* If it's okay with Security it's okay with me. *Mr Bonnaventure's secretary rang to confirm he will be able to make it for lunch.* Tell her we'll book him a table in the Garden Restaurant. *Mr Bonnaventure's secretary says he'd like to have lunch in the Royal Box.* Tell Mr Bonnaventure's secretary there's no access for him to the Royal Box today for lunch or anything else. *Mr Bonnaventure's secretary says Mr Bonnaventure will be livid.* Ask Mr Bonnaventure's secretary what's new?

Houlihan smiled. As he moved around the racecourse, Malloy seemed to field most of the calls himself, calmly and quickly making decisions. Houlihan thought Malloy had something to learn about delegation or he'd burn himself out pretty quickly. But it made for entertaining listening.

Fifteen thousand people came to see the Princess open the new stand. Malloy would have been happy with half that number. Keelor, wearing a sky-blue suit that might have gone unnoticed in Miami but drew a few comments on a damp Dorset day, stood next to the Princess at the ceremony. If she moved a step to the side, he followed, like some adoring puppy, his constant flashing smile substituting for a tail. The ribbon safely cut and the applause fully milked by Keelor, the VIPs made their way to the Royal Box for lunch while the crowd dispersed to seek out burger stands, hot donuts, bars and bookies.

Ten minutes later Houlihan heard the head of security calling for Malloy. 'Mr Malloy, we have a gentleman outside the Royal Box who says he's here for lunch, a Mr Simon Bonnaventure. We can't find him on the guest list.'

'I'll be there in a minute. Please ask Mr Bonnaventure to wait.'

Malloy walked quickly from the weighing room to the new stand. He was pleased he'd anticipated things correctly. Security had used the exact words he'd told them to. He came out of the lift on the top floor and the first thing he heard was Bonnaventure's raised voice. 'Do you know who I am, Sergeant?' He was addressing one of the princess's plain-clothes men who replied calmly, 'I only know you're not on the guest list, sir, so you can't come in.' Malloy moved down the corridor. Twenty or more people from the other private boxes were watching the group. Bonnaventure was in the centre, ringed by two plain-clothes men, two of Malloy's security team and one uniformed policeman.

Malloy smiled as he said, 'Mr Bonnaventure, can I help you?'

Bonnaventure turned and Malloy saw exactly the same raging expression he recalled from ten years ago when he'd told this man he wouldn't ride his horse at Cheltenham. He'd heard enough stories since to know Bonnaventure's temper hadn't improved with age. Red-faced, Bonnaventure said, 'You know bloody well you can help me, Mr Malloy! My secretary rang this morning to make it clear I'd be here for lunch!'

'Indeed she did, but I'm afraid lunch is by invitation only.'

'I'm the bloody chairman of the BHB, man, I don't need an invitation to any racecourse!'

'You're free to visit the racecourse at any time. Lunch is by invitation to the Royal Box,' Malloy said, smiling pleasantly. 'And I'd be grateful if you'd keep your voice down. I'm sure you wouldn't want to unsettle Her Highness.'

Wide-eyed, Bonnaventure took a step away from the door and towards Malloy and glared at him from his three-inch height advantage. 'Don't you tell me to lower my voice! You're a fucking jumped-up ex-jockey who got lucky!'

Malloy smiled wider and said quietly, 'And you're an ex boy-band hustler who just got unlucky.'

Bonnaventure reached forward, stiff-armed, and pushed Malloy to the floor. He landed awkwardly on the prosthesis and it twisted out at right angles bringing gasps from onlookers. One woman screamed. The uniformed policeman put a forearm around Bonnaventure's neck and pulled him backwards, locking his wrist behind him. Houlihan arrived and, with the security men, helped Malloy up. The crowd gasped again as Malloy twisted his arm back into place.

'Take your hands off me!' Bonnaventure spluttered as the policeman seemed to tighten his grip. Malloy looked at him, then at the policeman, and said, 'My men here will help you eject Mr Bonnaventure from the racecourse.'

Bonnaventure howled. 'Malloy! You would not dare! Tell him to get his hands off me!'

The policeman said, 'I can charge this man with assault if you want me to.'

Malloy said, 'I'll think about it. In the meantime, get him off my racecourse.' He nodded to the two security men and they moved alongside Bonnaventure. As all three men hustled him towards the stairs he shouted, 'Malloy, you're finished! Do you hear me, you're finished!'

The Box door opened and Keelor stepped out. 'What's happening, Malloy? You got problems here?'

'No problems, Vaughn. None at all. Go back in and enjoy your lunch.'

Keelor looked at the detectives. 'You guys okay?'

'We're fine.'

Keelor looked at Houlihan. Malloy said, 'I'm sorry. Vaughn, this is Frankie Houlihan, Jockey Club Security Department.'

Keelor smiled and shook hands. 'I've heard a lot about you, Houlihan, good to meet you. Look after my boy here, will you?'

Houlihan was going to say he thought he could look after himself but wasn't sure how Keelor would take it. He said, 'I will. Nice to meet you.'

Keelor went back inside. Malloy dusted himself down with his good hand. One detective said to him, 'How's your arm, Mr Malloy?'

Malloy held the joint tenderly and frowned. 'Feels a bit rubbery actually.'

Houlihan, smiling wide, lowered his head, shaking it slowly in amusement.

Keelor travelled back to London with Malloy and Houlihan, and Malloy told him what had happened with Bonnaventure. Keelor said, 'And you really think he might be behind these attacks?'

'He's got the personal motive – he wants the Jockey Club dead and buried – and if the story I heard is true he's got the business motive too.'

Keelor said, 'You mentioned last time we spoke you thought he was setting up an offshore company to buy racecourses. I'll try and get that checked out and maybe we can just plan a little fightback against Mr Bonnaventure.'

'Let's make it a legal one,' Malloy said.

Keelor replied, 'We won't break any laws but he'll know he's been in with the professionals.'

When they reached the flat, Malloy said, 'Let's get you Mark's rucksack.' He led Keelor inside to his office and crouched to dial the combination on the new safe. Keelor watched. 'That's a hell of a size safe.'

Malloy twisted the handle and hauled the thick door open. 'Well I didn't want to take any more chances with Mark's rucksack.' He dragged the blue nylon sack out. A strap caught on one of the safe bolts. He freed it and handed the sack to Keelor, who screwed his nose up as he took it. 'Stinks of gasoline.'

'It's just the fumes still clinging. It didn't get wet.'

Keelor held it up and slowly turned it till his gaze rested on the stencilled words: *M. Duncan, Makalu on Everest '96.* Malloy and Houlihan watched him slowly shake his head. He lowered the sack, swung it gently. 'Feels like there'll be enough in there to bring a few tears to Gemma and the kids.' Smiling with what seemed sincere gratitude he shook Malloy's hand. 'Thanks, Eddie. I'm sure Gemma will want to call and thank you herself.'

Malloy shrugged. 'All I did was put it on the plane. The Sherpas are the ones deserving the thanks.'

'I'll make sure they're looked after. Don't worry.'

Malloy nodded, watching Keelor's eyes and

seeing what looked like jubilation, and he wondered if his boss was happier about the rucksack or the racecourse.

Keelor added, 'I'd love to buy you guys dinner but I've got to get back to the office. Can you get me to the airport, Eddie?' Malloy read that as an order dressed up as a question but he'd be happy to see Keelor out of the country. 'Sure.'

'Great. Let's go.'

Malloy reached towards the rucksack. 'Want me to carry this for you?'

Keelor turned it away. 'No. No, not at all. I'll be fine. Thanks.'

Malloy smiled to himself and thought of how he'd like to be there when Keelor ran that tape.

Next day's *Racing News* carried the story of Bonnaventure's ejection from the racecourse along with a picture of him being frogmarched away. He was quoted as saying it was all a complete misunderstanding and that he'd be speaking to his lawyers about what action he could take against the police for 'wrongful detainment'.

Reading it over breakfast, Malloy smiled. 'I waited ten years for yesterday.' He'd already told Houlihan the story of what had happened back at Cheltenham. 'And maybe this'll stop his cronies pitching bricks through my window.'

'Yesterday won't have made him any friendlier towards you.'

'But he's put himself right in the front line now.

He's not daft enough to try anything, not for a while anyway.'

'Was that why you set him up that way?'

Malloy feigned surprise, pointing at himself. 'Me! Set someone up? The guy's behaviour is so predictable. Some sort of confrontation was a certainty and I decided I might as well make the best of it. Maybe he wasn't high on the police's suspect list before, but if anything else happens he'll be right at the top after yesterday.'

Houlihan looked at Malloy, thinking he was maybe a little too smug too soon. He said, 'Well, as all the football managers say, let's not get complacent.'

'But I want to be complacent,' Malloy said, and Frankie could see that spark of mischief he'd recognised before in Malloy, who continued, 'And I want you to be complacent too. For a day. You could use a day's complacency as much as I could. Admit it.'

Houlihan smiled, shaking his head slowly. 'You're a mad man.'

Malloy stood up suddenly, leaned across the table. 'Come on. The work's done. The deal's sealed. The course is opened. The Princess has gone back to the palace. Bonnaventure's buggered. Frankie, what I'm saying to you is let's take the day off, have a nice long lunch somewhere, get drunk, get laid, piss around, be absolutely complacent, join the Half-assed Thickos. What do you say?'

Houlihan was laughing now. 'I say you're crazy, Malloy.'

'Come on, man! You're the fella for the Latin so *carpe diem*. Let's do it. I'll even teach you to swear with my easy-to-learn bad-language course. So fulfilling. I'll start you on the "buggers" and get you to the "bastards" before the main course arrives. Then we can curse in harmony and I won't feel awkward every time I want to swear in front of you.'

'Lead on. I know I'll regret it but since we're going to be flatmates for the foreseeable future we might as well celebrate now: we might not even be talking in a week's time.'

Malloy slapped him on the shoulder. 'Good man. I'll phone the River Café and book a table.'

By two thirty they were almost through their second bottle of wine. Malloy had eaten five starters and no main course, nibbling away as he drank. Houlihan, feeling quite drunk, had finished eating and was trying to sip water when Malloy wasn't watching him. Malloy had entertained him with tales from his days as a jockey and how poor he had been when trying to make it through the five years when he'd been warned off. Houlihan was happy to listen, knowing that if he himself drank much more he'd start blubbering about Kathy and love and his family troubles – how his life had been wrecked – and he didn't want to do that. He estimated the wine consumption at about sixty–forty as he watched Malloy top up his glass. Houlihan's own was still full.

Malloy commented, 'Two full glasses.' As Houlihan nodded he then continued, 'Want to go outside and finish these?'

Houlihan looked over his shoulder through the big windows. 'It's freezing.'

Malloy shrugged. 'We can put our jackets on. Come on, Frankie, fresh-air time.' As he was signalling for the bill, his mobile rang. The screen showed 'Number withheld'. Malloy answered it.

'Eddie?'

'Yes?'

'Nice piece in the paper today.'

'Who's this?'

'D'you think the stunt you pulled with Bonnaventure is an image-changer? I doubt it – you know, most people in racing still think you're an arrogant fucker.'

'Piss off,' Malloy snapped and ended the call. Houlihan raised an inquisitive eyebrow. Malloy said, 'Another dickhead on Bonnaventure's payroll.'

'What did he say?'

The phone rang again: 'Number withheld'. Malloy stabbed at the *yes* key in anger and raised the phone to his ear. 'Listen?' he started saying.

'You listen, brother killer!'

Malloy froze. Houlihan watched the colour drain from his face. The man said, 'Fratricide's the official term, I believe, though I think the tabloids will stick with brother killer. "Everest hero. Friend of royalty. Brother killer." Let's see you come up

152

with a nice quote then, Malloy; let's see you spin this one.' The caller hung up. Malloy lowered the phone in slow-motion as the waiter arrived with the credit-card slip. Malloy signed it almost in a trance and started towards the exit.

They walked the bank of the Thames, shoulder to shoulder, collars up against the January wind at their backs. Houlihan reckoned they'd gone about half a mile without speaking. His experience in counselling told him to wait and let Malloy tell him what had happened.

They walked on in silence for another minute. Houlihan could sense his friend composing himself. Malloy eventually said, 'Bonnaventure found out something about me. It looks like it might be in the papers tomorrow.' Houlihan recognised Malloy's professional voice, his slightly steely tone – a noticeable change from that of his earlier anecdotes – and Houlihan sensed he was having to tell it this way to get through it. He said, 'How bad is it?'

Malloy let out a sound somewhere between an involuntary guffaw and a desperate cry. 'Put it this way, there's never been a day in my life since it happened that I haven't thought about it.'

Malloy's distress was almost tangible. He continued, 'I was fourteen. My little brother, Sean, was eight. It was summer, a hot day, July twenty-fourth. I was heading out that morning across the fields to a new riding school that had been set up. Sean nagged to come with me; I told him to piss off.' He paused for a while but kept walking. Houlihan stayed silent. 'Mother made me take him. I walked my fastest, ran for a while because I was so annoyed with him. He ran behind me trying to catch up, crying all the time. I didn't wait. Didn't stop. I crossed the river on some rocks, ran up the far bank, didn't even look round, could hardly hear him he was so far back. About a mile further on I was nearly at the riding school. I turned round. Couldn't see him. I could see for more than a mile but there was no sign of him, no sound. And right then I knew something was wrong.'

Houlihan felt himself swallow involuntarily. Malloy went on. 'I ran back. You know that saying "your heart is bursting through your shirt"? That was what it felt like. I ran and ran and ran and felt I was never going anywhere, felt I was running on the spot, the panic rising. I was crying, falling over at the pure hopelessness of everything. Sean was in the river. In a deep calm pool about fifty yards below the crossing point. Face down. Dead.'

Houlihan reached out to touch his arm, to stop him walking. Malloy said, 'Need to keep moving, Frankie, need to keep moving.' Houlihan fell in alongside again. Malloy said, 'Every day since, I see Sean face-down in that pool, blue checked shirt, jeans, white trainers. I see the fucking bomb crater I put in everybody's lives. I've just about been able to handle it over the years but I won't get through it now. I won't get past this.'

Houlihan thought for a few moments then asked, 'Did this fella say he was giving it to the press?'

'No. But Bonnaventure will. After yesterday he's certain to.'

'This guy gave no threats to pull away from the RHT deal or anything?'

'Nothing.'

They walked on. Houlihan felt helpless. He said, 'Maybe he'll call back.'

'Even if he does, I can't make a deal, can I? I've barely managed to get through holding Sean's death against myself; what chance have I got with someone else holding it there too?' He stopped and turned to look at Houlihan. 'Couldn't function, Frankie, couldn't function.'

Houlihan looked at his friend's sorrowful, hopeless face. He reached and squeezed his arm. 'Let me think, Eddie. We'll come up with something.'

Malloy just shook his head. '"Brother killer", the guy called me. He said that's what the tabloids will run.'

'That's crazy, it was an accident. It could have happened any time, could have happened when you weren't there.'

Malloy was still shaking his head. 'Sean died because I neglected him. I was a hundred per cent responsible. It was me, Frankie, whichever way you dress it up!' He was getting angry. Houlihan decided to leave things for now.

They travelled home in a taxi. Malloy's mood

had sunk rapidly to a deep depression. Houlihan was worried. Inside the house, Houlihan tried to lighten the atmosphere and said, 'I'll make some tea, eh? Help sober us up.'

Malloy replied, 'I'm just going to go to bed for a bit, sleep everything off.'

Houlihan saw the haunted look on his face. He knew what Malloy really wanted was to pull the covers over his head and wish for the world, or at least the past, to go away. Houlihan looked at him. 'Eddie, we can work together on this. If you want to get through it you need to clear all the past stuff away and start seeing Sean's death for what it was, a terrible accident.'

Malloy looked at him with deep sadness and said, 'I'm tired, Frankie; very, very tired.'

FOURTEEN

Houlihan checked his watch: it was eight thirty. Malloy had been asleep, or at least lying down, for over four hours. Houlihan had sat in the house in silence, quietly checking on him every half hour, wary of what he might do when so deeply depressed. Houlihan had wrung out his mind trying to come up with a plan to help Malloy but he knew what grief and guilt had done to him in just a couple of years and could only wonder at the scars it had burned into Eddie Malloy after a quarter of a century.

He heard movement in the bedroom and rose quickly. Knocking lightly on the door he then opened it. Malloy was sitting in the gloom on the edge of the bed, elbows on knees. 'How're you feelin'?' asked Houlihan.

'Okay,' he answered quietly.

'Fancy some steak and onions? You must be hungry again by now.'

'That would be good. Thanks.'

'I'll make a start.'

Malloy lay down again. He placed his hands over his eyes, raised his knees so his feet were flat on the bed. The wine had brought on a dull headache, the short sleep a dry mouth. He tried to make himself focus on the problem. *Is it any different from those I've faced in the past? Any tougher? I've beaten death. Sent the old Grim Reaper away empty-handed a couple of times. I've been Champion Jockey, survived murder attempts . . . I've climbed Everest for fuck's sake! This is just a problem like all the others, Eddie, there's got to be a solution. Got to be.*

He sat up quickly, got off the bed and marched out of the room. The smell of frying onions hit him. He called through to Houlihan, 'Just going for a shower.'

'What?' the shout came back. Malloy walked to the kitchen door and looked in. 'I'm showering. Be five minutes.'

Under the warm jets, Malloy soaped himself and continued working on the problem. He steadily turned the temperature dial down until the water was very cold and he whooped as he tried to make himself stay under it for as long as possible, stepping out quickly just as Houlihan came running in, kicking his false arm which Malloy had left on the floor. Houlihan looked worried but recoiled instinctively when freezing drops struck his face as Malloy manically shook his head. 'Are you okay?' Houlihan asked.

'I'm f . . . freezing. Where's the friggin' towel?'

'I thought you were being murdered,' Houlihan said as he whipped the towel from the drying rail and handed it to him.

Malloy grabbed the towel and smiled at Houlihan. 'Many have tried. I'm indestructible.'

'Feeling better then?'

'I've got an idea.'

'Tell me about it over dinner.'

They sat across from each other at the table and cut into the steaks. Malloy sniffed the air. 'Place is going to stink of onions for weeks. Petrol, onions, what next?'

'Can't make an omelette without breaking eggs,' said Houlihan.

Malloy stopped eating and, pushing his knife under the steak, flipped it over then stirred the onions around looking quizzical. Houlihan smiled patiently and said, 'I know, I know, you can't find any omelette.'

Malloy looked across at him. 'Getting predictable already, aren't I?'

'Very. But it's good to see you're feeling better. Want to tell me about your idea?'

Malloy chewed quickly then swallowed. 'Mmm. It depends on one thing: this guy calling me back. If it's not in tomorrow's press then he'll call back for sure, cos he wants to trade what he's got for me pulling Makalu out of the deal.'

'I thought the deal was done?'

'It is, but there's a twelve month get-out clause on both sides. If we discover something at any of the courses which wasn't declared in the due diligence procedure, we have the option to pull out. If we don't meet our payments schedule to the Jockey Club or if anything happens which adversely affects the Makalu brand to what the lawyers have called "a catastrophic degree", then the Jockey Club have the right to take the courses over again.'

'So what's the plan?'

Malloy put down his fork and slid a fingernail between his front teeth, trying to free a piece of meat. He said, 'I offer to play along.'

'To kill the deal?'

Malloy nodded positively. 'I can string the guy out for months, find out who he is.'

Houlihan said, 'Then what?'

Malloy shrugged, forked another piece of steak. 'Persuade him it wouldn't be in his best interests to give it to the press.'

Houlihan saw a coldness in his eyes and said, 'And how far would you go to persuade him?'

Malloy started tapping his foot and, jaw set, looked at Houlihan. 'All the way if I needed to.'

Frankie put his cutlery down, rested his elbows on the table and leaned forward. Before he could speak, Malloy waved his knife in front of him and said, 'Don't go all holy on me, Frankie. I'm beyond redemption, believe me.'

Houlihan could see how psyched up he was and

decided not to try and dissuade him. Instead he said, 'How would this guy have found out about your brother?'

'I've been trying to work that out. My parents knew, but they're dead. You know because I've told you. I've only ever told one other person.'

'Your wife?'

He shook his head, still staring at Houlihan who hadn't seen him blink in the past minute, and said, 'Nope. Didn't have the balls to tell her.'

Houlihan waited, aware Malloy's foot was still tapping rapidly as he got noticeably more wound up. Eventually Malloy said, 'I told a psychiatrist. A guy I saw in New York in early '97, about eight or nine months after Everest.'

'Was that why you went to see him, to try and get it off your mind?'

'I went to see him to try and find out why I've been trying to kill myself all my fucking life! Right?' He slammed down his cutlery and knocked the chair over as he got up and went to the drinks cabinet. Wrenching it open he grabbed a bottle of Bushmills and a glass which he half-filled. Houlihan watched him, wondering how close to the edge he was, trying to use the experience he'd gained over years of helping people in conflict to decide what to do. He knew it was a pivotal moment, not just in his relationship with Malloy, but in Malloy's life.

Houlihan got up slowly. Malloy was staring into his glass; he hadn't yet drunk from it. Houlihan went towards him, took a pace closer than he normally would have and adopted his most serious look. Malloy looked up to see Houlihan's face less than a foot from his. Houlihan slowly raised a finger and pointed at him and said, 'You! Are going to need some ice in that.' Houlihan took the glass. Malloy rubbed his face with his good hand. His stiff body started to relax and he began giggling, although by the time Houlihan dropped the ice in his drink he wasn't sure if Malloy was laughing or crying.

They sat up all night: Malloy drinking whiskey to try and get to sleep; Houlihan supping coffee, fighting to stay alert enough to make the right decisions. He knew the value of being a good listener. He would prompt Malloy only when he judged it wouldn't upset him or stop him talking and there were long periods of silence as Malloy seemed to be trying to decide how deep he wanted to dredge his own mind. But as the hours trickled away, Houlihan, as skilfully as Malloy had ever handled a difficult horse, encouraged, sympathised and reassured until Malloy put down the whiskey glass and began talking with a degree of calmness and objectivity that made Houlihan believe he could safely start playing a more active part in the analysis.

'You've mentioned a few times this death-wish thing and you really seem to think there's something in it,' Houlihan said.

Malloy scratched his head. 'I asked myself a lot of questions after Everest. Why did I keep going back out of the tent looking for the others? Was it some sort of absolution I was hoping for, another chance to save a life when I didn't get back in time to save Sean's? Was it that I valued my own life so little that it didn't matter to me if I died up there?'

'Did you think about that at the time?'

'No. It never crossed my mind. But there were others who wouldn't help. They stayed in their tents. They claimed exhaustion. I was exhausted too but it never occurred to me not to keep going back.'

'And it never occurred to you that you were doing it for any reason other than you instinctively wanted to save lives?'

'No. No, that was it exactly. It was instinctive.'

'Then maybe the only fact you need to face is that you're a brave man and a good man.'

Malloy leaned forward, elbows on knees, shaking his head. 'It can't be that simple, Frankie. I don't believe it's that simple.'

'Only because you won't let yourself have the credit, because you keep punishing yourself for what happened to Sean. Because of that accident you don't believe you should be allowed to be happy, to feel at peace with yourself, ever.'

Malloy seemed to consider this, then said, 'So what made me want to become a jump jockey? Hardly the safest occupation, is it?'

Houlihan shrugged. 'No. But it's glamorous and thrilling and beats an awful lot of other jobs.'

'But it can kill you.'

'So can driving a bus.'

They looked at each other for a while then Malloy smiled tiredly. Houlihan said, 'If you really wanted to die you wouldn't have come back from Everest, would you? You survived a night in the death zone, without shelter, in a hellish storm. I'd say if you've got anything you've got a profound will to live. You might not always be conscious of it but it must be there.'

'So why is it that sometimes I am conscious of just not wanting to go on living? It must be a crazy subconscious that turns that around.'

Houlihan looked at him and asked, 'Have you ever tried to kill yourself?'

'No, but I've thought about it as an option. I've been driving along the motorway at ninety and it's occurred to me how easy it would be to just not turn the wheel on that curve and let the car run straight into the bridge parapet. I've been waiting on the platform as an express hammers towards the station and thought how simple life would suddenly become if I just took a step forward.'

Houlihan said, 'Not so much simple as just ended.'

'That's when the simplicity sets in,' said Malloy, smiling.

'Along with the rigor mortis.'

Malloy smiled wider. 'Like it,' he said.

Houlihan smiled too and said, 'How long have you had suicidal thoughts?'

'All my adult life. It's part of my character now. It was better for a few months after meeting Laura and getting married. That was the happiest I'd ever been.' He put his head back and sighed.

Houlihan said, 'And since then, how many times would you say you'd felt happy, or maybe reasonably contented?'

Still looking at the ceiling, Malloy replied, 'Well, I remember a couple of years ago, staying at a hotel in London and going for a walk one morning in March. It had been cold and grey and I was passing through one of these little squares they have dotted around, you know, with grass and flowers and a few trees, and the sun came through for a minute and I could feel the warmth of it and watched it shining on some buds on a bush, and I felt a little burst of joy. I remember how surprised I was by it and how good it felt for the few moments it lasted. Like a drug.'

'Nothing else? No other time?'

'Nope.'

'What about when you got this job and got back into racing? Didn't that make you happy?'

'It made me feel powerful and vengeful and . . . kind of righteous, I suppose. But no, it didn't make me feel happy.'

Houlihan didn't reply. The silence stretched beyond a minute then Malloy straightened and sat forward, looking at Houlihan, and asked, 'Well, Mr Counsellor, what's your diagnosis?'

'My diagnosis is depression.'

'Not me. I can laugh and joke with the best of them, Frankie.'

'So could Tony Hancock. I'm pretty sure you're suffering from depression and that the root of it is the guilt you're carrying over Sean's death.'

'Catch twenty-two, then, eh?'

'It doesn't have to be. You can shed the guilt.'

'Shed it? That easy, eh? Like a snake shedding skin or a truck shedding its load.'

'I'm not saying it would be easy but I know it can be done. I saw hundreds of men with depression when I was practising. Some took my advice and went to the doctor. Some didn't and said they'd handle it themselves.'

Malloy put his head back again and sighed. Houlihan said, 'You're a man that likes stats. Try this one. Five times as many women as men are diagnosed with depression but five times as many men as women commit suicide. Depression is an illness. It can be treated just like any other illness. The constant feeling of guilt you have is a classic symptom.'

'Not to mention wanting to jump in front of trains,' Malloy said, straightening and smiling wearily at Houlihan.

'Well, there could be a little clue there too,' Houlihan said.

Malloy leaned towards him and asked, 'So

what sort of treatment's been invented that suddenly removes guilt from a man who's killed his brother?'

'We don't need a treatment for that sort of guilt. You didn't kill your brother. You did what millions of snotty teenagers do when their siblings trail around after them; you got wound up and gave him the cold shoulder. It happens every day across the world. It's happening now in thousands of places. You were acting normally. Sean died in an accident. You weren't responsible.'

'I was supposed to be with him. He wouldn't have died if I had waited.'

'How do you know? He might have changed his mind if you'd waited and decided he didn't want to go with you after all, then he could have gone to the river on his own. He could have come with you to the riding stables and got kicked in the head by a horse. He could have fallen off a horse and broken his neck. Would that have been your fault then, for waiting for him, for taking him with you, for not running off without him? I'll bet if that had happened you'd be carrying exactly the same guilt now.'

Malloy looked up and Houlihan thought he saw a change in him. He continued, 'See, Eddie, there's no right thing and no wrong thing here. There's just a terrible accident. And you've allowed yourself to be another victim of that accident and it's time to stop. It's time to get healed and get on with your life. Your life. You've only got one and it's worth an awful lot more than you think. You deserve to live it as best you can and to get as much happiness from it as you can. A good doctor can help you do that. And I can help you do it.' Houlihan reached across the table to touch his arm. Malloy looked up at him sorrowfully. Houlihan said, 'Listen, Eddie. I will help you. I'll make things better for you. I guarantee it. I promise.'

Houlihan saw the look on Malloy's face that told him Malloy wanted to believe this but didn't. But Malloy clasped his hand and smiled wearily as he said, 'Good. Thanks.'

'I mean it!' Houlihan said.

'I know. I know you do.'

'Are you registered with a doctor here?' Houlihan asked.

Malloy nodded. 'A guy in St John's Wood.'

'How often have you seen him?'

'Once, when I registered. As an amputee I'm entitled to certain privileges but I need to be registered with a GP if I want to apply for disabled badges or allowances, stuff like that. Not that I have applied, but you never know what'll happen.'

'How would you feel about changing your doctor? I know a man who's brilliant on depression.'

Malloy shrugged. 'Sure.'

Houlihan checked his watch. 'It's just gone seven. I'll call him at nine.'

'Good.' Wearily, Malloy got to his feet and said, 'Fancy a walk to the newsagent to see if it's worth our while going to work today?. He yawned and stretched. 'Might wake us up a bit too.'

'If there'd been anything in the press your phone would have been ringing off the hook.'

Malloy nodded. 'True.'

'Whoever it was will call back. If Bonnaventure's behind it there's nothing financial in it for him to embarrass you in the papers.'

'Nothing but the old "eye for an eye".'

'But that doesn't get him those racecourses. Putting you out of the picture would just mean Keelor bringing someone else in and Bonnaventure's stuffed.'

Malloy thought for a few moments then nodded slowly. 'You might be right.' He got up from the table and stretched. 'Should be a fun time waiting for the next call then.'

Houlihan looked up at him. 'It'll be sooner rather than later.'

FIFTEEN

It was two days later. Houlihan and Malloy were on their way to Wincanton in Somerset when the 'Number Withheld' message appeared on Malloy's mobile-phone screen in its dashboard mount. They watched it together for a moment then Houlihan turned to Malloy and asked, 'Are you going to answer it?'

Malloy hit the *yes* button and said his own name confidently. The caller said, 'You on a loudspeaker?'

'Yes.'

'Anybody with you?'

'No.'

'That's good, nice straight answers this time. You've wised up a bit, Malloy.'

'Tell me what you want.'

'I want the Makalu deal on those Jockey Club courses to collapse. You're the guy who's going to find the holes in the contract.'

'There are no holes.'

'Make some.'

'It's watertight.'

'So was the *Titanic*.'

Malloy found himself smiling and shaking his head, glancing across at Houlihan then in his mirror before pulling off the road into a gate-sized gap at the entrance to a field.

Malloy said, 'It will take months.'

'You've got four weeks.'

'I can't do it in four weeks.'

'Too bad.'

Malloy sighed heavily. 'Look, I've got no choice here, but if you're going to make it impossible then I might as well hang up now. It can't be delivered in under three months.'

'Why?'

'The terms allowing either party an out are pretty narrow. It's going to take some very careful planning, even in three months. I need to manufacture something that will convince Keelor, not to mention a million pounds' worth of legal muscle, that the contract should be terminated.'

During the long pause that followed Houlihan and Malloy watched the phone screen intently, as though expecting the man's face to appear any second. Finally he spoke. 'I'll call you back.' He hung up.

Houlihan and Malloy looked at each other. 'Is there a Plan B?' Houlihan asked. They smiled.

There was no racing at Wincanton but they had gone there for two purposes: it was one of the courses Makalu had bought from the Jockey Club and Malloy was paying his second visit to brief staff; and Houlihan's friend, Dr Peter Harvey, lived a mile from the course. He had agreed to see Malloy, and Malloy had told Houlihan he would be frank with the doctor about how he'd been feeling and behaving but that he wouldn't mention his brother.

They parked beside the doctor's Range Rover in the drive and as they got out Houlihan said, 'Remember, you need to tell him about the guilt. You don't have to explain the source but you've got to mention it.'

'I know, Frankie,' Malloy said sharply. Then, 'Sorry, I didn't mean to snap at you.'

'It's okay,' Houlihan said as he saw the door open and Harvey come out smiling.

Houlihan waited in the kitchen by the warm Aga. He cradled Malloy's phone watching for the 'Number Withheld' message if it rang. Malloy had been in with the doctor for almost forty minutes and Houlihan was wondering how deep they were going into things. He trusted Peter Harvey to help him meet his promise to Malloy to make him better. He didn't doubt his own diagnosis but just wasn't sure what treatment the doctor would recommend.

Five minutes later he heard a door open then voices in the hall. Malloy came in first and Houlihan thought he looked like he'd been crying. Harvey followed him, saying, 'Can I offer you a hot drink? Or a cold one for that matter?'

Malloy looked uncertainly at Houlihan who smiled and said, 'Not for me, Peter. Unless Eddie wants one?'

'I'm okay,' Malloy said quietly.

Houlihan put a hand on his shoulder. 'Shall we hit the road then?'

'Sure.'

They thanked the doctor who said to Malloy, 'See you in four weeks at the most. Call any time before that if you want to.'

Malloy held out his hand, 'I will, Doctor. Thank you very much.'

'My pleasure.'

On the return journey Malloy said nothing for a long while, slumping slowly in the passenger seat as though drained. Houlihan asked nothing, having already decided he'd let him speak in his own time.

Passing Stonehenge in the dusk, Malloy finally spoke. 'People have been around for a long time.'

'Millions of years,' Houlihan replied.

'How many people do you think have ever lived?'

'I don't know. Hundreds of billions? I suppose somebody could work it out using average life-spans and stuff.'

Malloy was quiet for a few moments, then said, 'I wonder how many of them were as fucked up as me.'

'Plenty. Don't worry about that. Most of them got better too. What did Peter give you?'

'Prozac. "The miracle drug," he called it.'

173

'He's not the only doctor who believes that.'

'A long-standing, deep-seated depression. You were right.'

'Did he suggest a counsellor?'

'He told me research showed that Prozac alone doesn't work and neither does counselling alone, but both together do. So hello, counsellor.'

Houlihan looked across at him and pointed to himself. 'Me?'

'If you'll do it. Doctor Harvey recommended somebody but I said I'd stick with you for now.'

'What did he say to that?'

'He thought it was a good idea. You up for it?'

'Of course. No problem. Once you've outgrown me you can get a pro in.'

'You'll do for a while, Frankie.' Malloy settled back in his seat again and they drove on for a mile or so in silence before Houlihan asked, 'How do you feel?'

'Empty. Flushed out. Drained. I feel like someone's taken over responsibility for my life. In a nice way, if you know what I mean. Like I'm a kid again and my dad has said, "Don't worry, son, I'll handle everything. It'll be all right."'

'Good feeling.'

'It is. I feel clean. A bit like I used to when I came out of confession; when I was a lot younger that is.'

They smiled. Malloy continued, 'Doctor Harvey said the pills will take about three weeks to kick in and that I might get worse before I get better.'

Houlihan nodded. 'You'll see a big difference in yourself. The first steps to a long-term recovery.'

'It'll need to be a miracle drug, right enough,' Malloy said. 'I'll probably need a triple dose by the time I'm finished dealing with Bonnaventure and his mates.'

The blackmailer called that night. 'You've got sixty days exactly,' he told Malloy. 'If Makalu are out by then or we're certain they're on their way out you get to keep your skeleton in the cupboard, if you know what I mean.'

Malloy felt angry and humiliated and he promised himself he'd find this guy and see how brave he was face to face. The man went on: 'If it runs to sixty-one days you're all over the papers, Malloy. You won't hear from me in the next sixty days so don't count on any reminders and don't waste energy trying to track me down.'

'So if I don't hear from you how are you going to know I've delivered what you want?'

'We'll expect to see a formal announcement in the media.'

Malloy felt there was no point arguing. He had no intention of doing anything in the next sixty days except nailing this guy and Bonnaventure.

He hung up, then told Houlihan what the deadline was. He walked to the kitchen calling back to Houlihan, 'Want tea?'

Houlihan shouted, 'Is that what you're having?'

Malloy reappeared in the doorway. 'Yep.'

Houlihan nodded towards the clock. 'It's after ten. You're usually emptying a bottle rather than filling a kettle.'

Malloy smiled. 'Turned over a new leaf. I think caffeine will go better with Prozac, don't you?'

'Tea it is then.'

Soon after, as they sipped from yellow mugs, Houlihan watched Malloy. His eyes looked brighter. Houlihan could tell his brain was active and he knew the blackmailer had made the mistake of not knowing his adversary. Malloy thrived on challenge – that should have been pretty obvious to anyone just from reading his press cuttings. The bigger the risk or the more precious the prize, the better Malloy responded. He looked at Houlihan. 'I'll need your help. I've got to keep the business running while we're trying to trace this bastard.'

'I'm not doing anything else. What are you thinking?'

Malloy cradled the mug. 'The only place this guy could have got the information was from the psychiatrist I saw in New York. Either he bought it or stole it. One of us might need to go over there.'

Houlihan felt uneasy. 'We should stick together.'

'There's no point in us both being in the same place all the time. It's a waste of resources.'

'I'd rather be with you, Eddie, all things considered.'

Malloy got agitated. 'I'll be fine! I've got sixty days. They'll leave me alone till the deadline. Stop worrying, for God's sake!'

'You're assuming Bonnaventure's behind all this, everything that happened and—'

'Of course he is!' Malloy raised his hands in frustration then got up and began pacing. 'Who else would have done all this?'

'He might be behind the blackmail call but that's because he wants revenge for you getting him thrown out of Gloucester. What if all the previous threats weren't down to him?'

'Of course they were. They had to be.'

'What about Bert Jacobsen and RACE and all those people?'

'Stooges for Bonnaventure.'

'If you assume that you let your guard down. Let's just wait and see what we find in the next week or so, eh?'

Malloy stopped pacing and stood over Houlihan. 'Frankie, I've got a business to run. I can't hide here. And I've got a blackmailer to find.'

'*We've* got a blackmailer to find.'

Malloy threw up his hands. 'Then help me out, Frankie! I've got a shitload of work to do.'

Houlihan stayed calm. 'You shouldn't even be at work. You're ill. I'm not leaving you.'

'You sound like some ditsy woman for God's sake! No, scratch that last part – "for fuck's sake" was what I was going to say so I'm saying it!'

Houlihan got up now. 'So say it! Listen, you're not the only one that can make a decision here. I'm entitled to make a judgement too, and mine is that it's too bloody early to assume that Bonnaventure was behind the other attacks. That's my job. I might not be as good at it as you are at yours and maybe I'm not as brave as you are, or as . . . experienced, but—'

Malloy pointed a finger at him. 'You were going to say "not as old" then, weren't you?'

Houlihan smiled.

Malloy's expression was also softening. He said, 'You are cruel, Frankie Houlihan, you are a cruel man. Here's me, a manic depressive, worried about getting older, and you, my counsellor, taunting me. What kind of treatment is that?'

Houlihan laughed. 'That's right, I'd forgotten. I am your counsellor and I'm pulling rank. You're staying with me. Whatever work needs doing we can do together. If we need to go and see your trick cyclist in New York we go together.'

Malloy, a smile in his eyes as he tried to keep a straight face, said, 'That's it then, is it? An executive decision?'

'Exactly. All for one and one for all.'

'Whole duck or no dinner?'

'You got it.'

'Me and you all the way?'

'To the end.'

'Right!' Malloy left the room. Houlihan waited, smiling and shaking his head. But Malloy didn't come back. After almost five minutes Houlihan went into the hallway and listened out. Malloy called to him from his room. 'Oh Frankie!'

Houlihan went to the doorway. 'It's open,'

Malloy called out. Houlihan pushed it wide and slowly went in. Malloy was in bed, sitting up on the far side. He held open the covers, fluttered his eyelashes and said, 'Bedtime darling!'

Houlihan stared at him. Malloy burst into laughter. 'Not that keen to stick so close to me twenty-four-seven then?'

Houlihan laughed with relief. 'You're mad, Malloy.'

'I thought we'd already established that?'

'Goodnight.'

SIXTEEN

The next morning after breakfast, Houlihan produced a notebook and pen. 'Let's see if we can get a plan on paper.'

'It'll be a short one,' Malloy replied. 'I was lying awake thinking last night: Philip Maynard, the shrink, is the only person alive apart from me and you that knows about Sean.'

'What about the coroner in Cumbria?'

Malloy shook his head. 'We covered it up. My parents told the police that Sean went off on his own.'

Houlihan watched him, wanting to see how he'd handle talking about it in a factual way. Malloy stared into space then said, 'It was Dad's suggestion. It wasn't done for my sake. He said it was to protect the good name of the family. After the funeral, do you know he never spoke to me again in his life? I used to fantasise about getting my own back on him by going to the cops and telling everything.'

'How close did you come to doing that?'

'Very close. More than once. I remember flying down to town on my bike one day and I just managed to stop myself on the steps of the police station.'

'Do you think that was really to get back at your dad or was it just to be able to talk about it, maybe to try and get punished?'

Malloy shrugged. 'I suppose it could have been. I was fourteen. It seems like another lifetime, another person.'

Houlihan encouraged him and they talked about it for a while. Houlihan was learning more and more about the childhood that had shaped the man he was trying to help.

They concluded that, assuming Malloy's parents hadn't written it down somewhere and it had been found, Maynard, the psychiatrist, had to be the source.

Malloy said, 'If we assume that, then how did Bonnaventure get to know I'd seen a psychiatrist in the States? It's hardly something he'd find on my CV.'

'Who knew?'

Malloy pondered. 'Maynard, his staff.'

'Your friends?'

'Didn't really have any.'

'Did Keelor know?'

'Not from me he didn't.'

They were quiet for a moment, then Houlihan asked, 'Is it on your medical records?'

'I don't know. Could be.'

Houlihan called Dr Harvey who said he'd requested Malloy's records from his previous doctor but that they'd normally take a week or more to arrive. Malloy and Houlihan agreed they had nothing to lose by calling the psychiatrist.

They found his number on the Internet and Houlihan pulled the phone towards Malloy, who looked reluctant. Houlihan dialled it, listened to the long, American ring-tone, then handed him the phone.

'Philip Maynard please,' Malloy said.

There was a pause then the woman who'd answered asked, 'Who is calling please?'

'My name is Eddie Malloy. I was a client of Mr Maynard's in 1997.'

'Well I'm sorry to tell you, Mr Malloy, that Dr Maynard passed away more than two years ago.'

Malloy glanced across at Houlihan, then said, 'Oh, I'm sorry to hear that. Can I ask who's running the practice now?'

'Dr Bachmayer's the chief partner but he's on vacation. I'm sorry.'

'That's okay. Is there another partner I could talk to?'

'Mr Pearce might be available. Please hold.'

Malloy turned to Houlihan. 'Maynard died two years ago.' Houlihan shook his head slowly. Pearce came on the line and Malloy asked questions about how secure the files were.

Pearce said, 'Why do you ask?'

'Because someone's had access to mine.'

A slight pause, then, 'Not through us they haven't!' Pearce said vehemently and Malloy could almost smell the fear of litigation.

He replied, 'Look, I'm not interested in blaming anyone, I just need to know who it might have been.'

'Mr Malloy, our files are all password protected and the password is changed every three months. We employ the best security IT consultants money can buy. Our firewalls are provided by the same company who supplies NASA.'

'My file is on a PC?'

'All our records are scanned and stored. Common practice.' Pearce was trying to sound confident but could not hide his nervousness.

'Do you have a website?'

'Of course.'

'Where is it hosted?'

'Listen, Mr Malloy, I'm afraid I'm going to have to ask you to continue your inquiries on a more formal basis.'

Malloy prickled at that. 'Listen, I can get as formal as you want, Mr Pearce. I can instruct my legal guys to request access to all details of traffic on your site and in your office network. I think your security's been breached and that has put me in a very difficult situation.'

Another pause, then Pearce said, 'If you'd like to leave your details? I'm going to have to get back to you.'

*　　*　　*

Over the next forty-eight hours Malloy learned that his records had gone missing from his previous doctor who could offer Dr Harvey no explanation for the loss. Malloy also received a letter from the legal advisors to Maynard's psychiatric practice. It warned him that 'any impugning – private or public, intentional or not –' of their clients' security arrangements would bring 'multi-million-dollar writs'. He and Houlihan realised they'd need to settle for the assumption that the blackmailer had accessed his records; they did not have time to try and prove it and had to abandon the idea of tracking the blackmailer via the psychiatrist.

Malloy said to Houlihan, 'We keep talking about Plan B; I think it's time we made one.'

But nothing they could think of brought them any closer to discovering the blackmailer's identity. Houlihan called his police contacts to try and get his hands on mobile-phone data for the calls made to Malloy by the blackmailer, but nobody could help. Houlihan tracked Bonnaventure for three successive days to see who he met. He'd shoot video when he could and dictate descriptions quietly into a concealed microphone when he couldn't, and he and Malloy would go over them late each night. But they made no headway.

The first week of the blackmailer's eight had gone and they sat down to take stock. 'Any Plan C?' Malloy asked wearily.

'We'll be right through the alphabet soon,' Houlihan said.

Malloy rubbed his face with his good hand. 'I think I'd better warn Keelor. We're not going to get this guy, are we?'

'We've still got seven weeks.'

Malloy smiled. 'You didn't say that with much enthusiasm. Listen, we might as well bite the bullet. There's not even enough hours in the day for me to keep the business going, never mind find this guy. I might as well get myself ready for this stuff to hit the papers. I'll call Keelor tomorrow so at least he can start looking for a replacement. Then I'll bail out at the end of the month so Makalu aren't associated with me when the shit hits the fan.'

Houlihan looked at him for a few moments before speaking. He knew Malloy was right. He too felt tired and almost hopeless. And Malloy's acceptance of the situation cheered him in that it signified a change in priorities. They'd grown much closer since Malloy's visit to Dr Harvey. Malloy talked quite openly now about his brother and his family, and Houlihan felt optimistic about Malloy's long-term chances of recovery.

Houlihan had also been discussing his family lately. He'd convinced himself he had done it to make Malloy feel less sensitive about his own upbringing, to encourage him to open up, but he knew that he too had benefited from a sympathetic ear.

It had made him call home. He'd spoken to Margaret and Theresa in the past few days to learn that there was 'no change' in his mother's condition. He'd promised to go and see her soon. All in all, he felt better about himself than he had for a while and he realised, not for the first time, that although the unpredictability of his job brought occasional adrenaline-fuelled highs, he was happier when he was helping people. At times like this, returning to the priesthood didn't seem such a terrible idea.

He turned to Malloy. 'Fancy a run?'

Malloy shrugged and nodded. Houlihan said, 'Might shake out a few ideas.'

Malloy said, 'Yeah, like keeping going in a straight line for a couple of hundred miles.'

Houlihan smiled and got up to go and change. 'You'd need your swimming trunks, then, as well.'

They returned half an hour later. Houlihan always sweated more than Malloy and they had a silent understanding that he'd shower first. He came out towelling his hair and shouted his usual message, 'Shower's free!'

After he showered, Houlihan, fully at home now in Malloy's flat, went to the kitchen and began preparing dinner. A few minutes later, above the sizzle of frying steak, he heard the floorboards in the hall squeak and he left the kitchen to see Malloy walking towards the sitting room, drying his hair as he went, thick black bathrobe swinging mid-shin. 'You smell almost human again,' Houlihan said as he went past.

'You say the sweetest things,' Malloy replied

and Houlihan smiled as he returned to the kitchen.

Malloy made wet footprints on the wood as he walked across the sitting room. He hung the towel on his shoulders and turned to the mirror, fingers fixing his hair. He heard glass smash. The boom of it was followed almost immediately by another louder explosion, and the room was suddenly blindingly lit. A river of flame hit Malloy at knee height and his bathrobe ignited, engulfing him.

He screamed as Houlihan appeared in the hallway, bewildered as he ran towards Malloy, seeing his strange arms of fire trying to undo the bathrobe belt. Houlihan felt he was running in slow-motion. He knew he had to get Malloy on the floor, roll him over, smother the flames, but a couple of strides from the door he realised that the rug itself and the wooden floor were alight. He had to get him out of the room.

Malloy's screams were appalling. He fought with the belt. 'Get it off me! Get it off me!' But as Houlihan reached him he knew his flesh would probably be sticking to the burning material. The risks in trying to free him from the robe were probably greater than those from trying to extinguish the flames.

The heat from Malloy as Houlihan reached him seared his eyeballs and made him turn his head away as he grappled for a hold. Houlihan wasn't sure where on his body his hands gripped but he pulled Malloy towards him and down at the same time, feeling his fingers burning as he dragged him along the floor into the hall. There was little room to roll here. He considered falling on him and trying to smother the flames with his own body but the shower room was just three or four yards away and adrenaline suddenly pumped strength into him making Malloy feel as light as a doll.

Pulling him upright as he backed into the shower he hit the big stainless-steel tap lever with his elbow and thanked God as water fizzed out at high pressure, drowning the flames in seconds as Malloy's screams decreased to moans. Conscious of the fire raging in the sitting room, he dragged Malloy out more roughly than he wanted to and laid him slowly on the wet bathroom floor.

In the hall again, Houlihan saw the brightness had faded in the sitting room but the crackling noises were strong. Running to the door he pulled it shut then raced to the phone and called the ambulance and fire brigade.

He crouched over Malloy, whose face was now horribly blistered, eyelashes and eyebrows gone and what was left of his hair a soggy mess like a plastic wig that had been melted on. His eyes were closed, his breathing very shallow. Houlihan said, 'Eddie, I need to move you. Need to get you outside.'

Malloy's eyes were closed but he spoke. 'No, don't.' A croak, very weak.

'The place could go up, Eddie. The fire's still burning. I need to get you out.'

'No.' He shut his eyes again.

Houlihan didn't know what to do. There was

no telling what Malloy's skin was like under the sodden mass of charred cotton. If he tried to drag him, it might kill him. If it came to the worst he was sure he could lift him, get him across his shoulder, try and minimise the flesh damage that way. He looked out again along the hall. Smoke crept under the sitting room door and into the passageway. Houlihan knew it was smoke that invariably killed people in house fires.

He looked at Malloy and thought maybe they could hold out till the fire brigade arrived. He kneeled beside him. 'Eddie, I won't move you just now. I've called the fire brigade. We'll try and hold on till they get here.'

Malloy opened his eyes. They were filled with fear. He said, 'Frankie, help me.' His blistered, blackened wet hand came up, searching for Houlihan's.

Very gently, Houlihan took it and smiled at his friend. 'I will. You'll be fine. I promise.'

Malloy's eyes told Houlihan he was grateful. Houlihan kneeled above him, trying not to appear as anxious as he felt. He leaned forward to look again down the hall. Flames had eaten half the door. He tried to control the rising panic as he looked again at his friend. 'Won't be long now, Eddie.'

Malloy said, 'I guess I don't have a death wish after all.'

Houlihan smiled. 'Hate to say I told you so.'

SEVENTEEN

Houlihan sat nervously on the bench in the hospital. Malloy had been conscious when they'd sped along the corridor towards theatre with him. They'd patched up Houlihan's burns and now he'd been waiting more than two hours to find out how bad things were for Malloy. Houlihan tried to reassure himself that if he'd done Eddie any damage when hauling him around, it had been unavoidable. To have handled it any other way would have left him in a worse state.

So, Houlihan thought, absolve thyself in advance of any bad news. Elbows on knees, he hung his head over his bandaged hands, mind crumbling, exhaustion and desolation soaking into him as though his feet were in a well of it.

Sitting there trying to take in what had happened, Houlihan began feeling anxious about the well-being of his own family. Suddenly, it seemed to him that the world was a very unsafe place for everybody. If he had showered after Malloy instead of before, then he might have been the one in the operating theatre just now. And if these people were so serious, so violent, how could he protect those he loved? Whoever had done this must have been watching him and Malloy for some time. They must have known their habits. If it was the black-mailing team suddenly changing tactics then what did that mean for the Houlihan family? These crim-inals had found out all they needed to know about Malloy – what sort of suffering could they put the Houlihans through if they wanted to? He hurried outside intending to call his brother Thomas and warn him, ask him to alert the others, maybe con-sider moving away somewhere for a while. Scrolling through for the number he heard someone running from the direction of the car park. He turned to see a tall figure sprinting towards the ramp leading up to the entrance and as he came under the bright wall lights Houlihan recognised Ben Dillon, a *Racing News* reporter who lived in Lambourn. Anxious not to be seen, Houlihan turned his back to Dillon, bent over the railings and started coughing heavily into his hands. Dillon raced past and through the swing doors. Houlihan put the phone back in his pocket and moved away into the darkness.

Dillon was back out within five minutes. Walking now, he lit a cigarette and Houlihan saw the smoke from the flicked match arc towards him. When Dillon had gone, Houlihan returned to his telephone's address list and found Thomas's number. But the five minutes' cooling-off time he'd had had helped bring another perspective. He was still worried about his family but he realised Malloy was the primary target, and that it was pointless starting a panic in Dublin. He resolved to fly over and see to all of them together just as soon as Malloy was out of danger.

Houlihan went back inside to speak to the nurse on desk duty. 'The big thin fella, the one who was just in here,' he said. 'He's a reporter. He was asking me all sorts of questions about Mr Malloy. Did he ask you anything?'

'He asked about Mr Malloy, flashed his ID, but I blanked him,' she said in a matter-of-fact way.

'Persistent, isn't he?' Houlihan probed.

'I've seen a lot worse,' she said, picking up the phone. Houlihan took the hint that she was busy and left her alone. He went back to his seat wondering who had tipped Dillon off. The police had already been and gone. Houlihan had called Vaughn Keelor and Bobby Cranfield. Keelor had reacted with anger and threats against the perpetrator, Bobby with horror and sadness. Houlihan told them both they needed to arrange police protection for Malloy if he survived surgery. Keelor said he'd deal with it. No way would Keelor have spoken to the press and he didn't think Cranfield would have. So that left the police.

Just before midnight a nurse came and told Houlihan that Malloy had come through surgery well and was now resting in the Intensive Care ward. 'So he's going to be all right?' Houlihan asked anxiously.

'He's very ill. He's done well to get through surgery. We just need to wait and see now. We'll do everything we can for him, I promise.'

Houlihan smiled wearily. 'I know you will. I know.' He ran his hand through his hair. The nurse said, 'Do you want to stay till morning? I can probably find you a bed.'

'Thank you. I need to stay, but Mr Malloy is still in danger from the person who attacked him. I need to be outside the door of his ward or his room, wherever he is. Can you arrange that?'

'Have you told the police?'

Houlihan nodded. 'They said they'll send someone. If I could just stay with him until they do?'

She looked sympathetic but uncertain. 'Would you mind waiting here a minute, Mr . . .?'

'Houlihan.'

'Mr Houlihan. I need to speak to somebody.'

'Sure. I'll come and speak myself if you need me to.'

She smiled reassuringly. 'Let me try first.'

Houlihan watched her walk away then sat back down, rubbing his eyes, trying to make some sort of guess at how bad Malloy still was. He began to doubt the wisdom of deciding not to try and get the burning dressing gown off Malloy right away. Then he consoled himself with the thought that if he'd tried it may somehow have got itself entangled in the base of Malloy's prosthesis and made things worse. Not that he'd ever seen the joint close up while it was on Malloy's arm, but for the purposes of his own comfort just then he supposed it would have some loose or protruding parts.

The nurse returned. Houlihan stood up, trying to look hopeful. She smiled and said, 'We'll be able to put one of our own security guards on the door until the police arrive.'

Houlihan said, 'That's good. Thank you. Can you do it right away?'

She looked at her watch. 'He should just be stepping out of the lift now.'

Houlihan reached and laid a hand on her forearm. 'Thank you very much,' he said.

She touched his hand. 'You're welcome.'

He sat down again. 'I'll just wait here if you don't mind.'

'Of course. There's a coffee machine by the A and E waiting room which is along the corridor then right at the bottom.'

Houlihan nodded and raised a hand. 'Thanks.'

He bought two cups of coffee at once, sipping enough from each to make it easy to carry them back to the bench, which now seemed almost like home to him. He was hoping the caffeine would clear his mind, let him get some structured thought-processes going again. What had happened over the past few hours still felt like something in a movie, something that would turn out not to be true.

Who was after Malloy? Who wanted him dead? Was it Simon Bonnaventure? Could he really also be behind the blackmail attempt? If so, what had he recently discovered that had made him act so drastically with almost seven weeks still remaining till the deadline he'd set Malloy?

Had the humiliation of being thrown out of Badbury racecourse been eating away at him, driving him to want Malloy killed? No. Houlihan couldn't accept that.

Bad as the man's reputation was, there was a deep divide between being a bully and murdering someone; between threatening exposure about his dead brother and hiring a petrol-bomber.

But would Bonnaventure have gone as far as to want to give Malloy a real scare? Did the petrol-bomber know the flat was occupied? The lights had been on in the house. If he had been in the garden, why hadn't the security floodlights kicked in? Houlihan took out his notebook and jotted that down. Okay, assuming the bomber knew Malloy was in there, maybe knew they were both in there if he'd been watching the flat for a while, could he have seen enough of the room to know it was occupied at the time he threw the bomb? The window was high. Malloy had virtually just walked in there from the shower. Maybe the bomber hadn't noticed him entering and had thrown the bomb into what he believed was an empty room, just to scare Malloy? Even if Malloy was the intended target, he and Houlihan were similar in build, and both had dark hair. In that long dressing gown with his back to the window, it could easily have been Houlihan. The thought of this turned his stomach over and he gulped coffee.

And what now? If Malloy did recover would he be targeted again? How much could Keelor and the Jockey Club throw at this to try and find the attacker? How much probing could they do into Bonnaventure's activities without causing an almighty stink?

Houlihan searched through his call list to get Keelor's number. The big clock above him showed it was almost one a.m. – mid-evening in New York. He went outside and called Keelor.

'Eddie's out of theatre, still very ill. He's in intensive care.'

'Aw, Jesus!' Keelor said, and that grated on Houlihan. He'd been growing steadily used to hearing general cursing but he still hated to hear the Lord's name taken in vain. 'Have you spoken to the doctor who did the op?'

'No. The nurse was very helpful.'

'Nurses know shit. Get the guy at the sharp end. We need to find out what Eddie's chances are.'

'His chances would be helped by getting some proper protection here in case this fella comes back.'

'What about the cops? They're supposed to be

196

there. Two of them. I spoke to Cranfield, told him to arrange it. I'll pay. What kind of fuck-up operation are you guys running over there, Houlihan?'

'Listen, Mr Keelor, I don't know what Bobby arranged or what he thought was arranged. I'm not the Jockey Club and I don't care who pays for or organises security for Eddie. I'm staying here because I'm his friend. There's a hospital security guard on his door now but I don't know how long for. I'll be here all night and longer if I need to be, but I suggest you get in touch with the Metropolitan Police yourself or get one of your big shots to do it for you and make sure someone's here in the morning.'

'*You're* his friend?! Don't you think I am? How do you think I feel right now? I persuaded Eddie to take this job. He wasn't exactly beating my door down to sign up. I talked him into it and now he could be dead in the morning? How the hell do you think I feel, Mr Houlihan?'

Houlihan hesitated then said, 'Okay. I'm sorry.' Then immediately regretted apologising, feeling Keelor had railroaded him into it. 'Can you just sort something out with the police?' he said.

'Hold on . . . Okay, give me the details of the hospital again.'

Houlihan did. Keelor said, 'Call me if he gets any worse. I'll be on this number through the night. I have a meeting in the morning then I'll catch the noon flight to Heathrow. We should talk tomorrow.'

'Call me when you arrive,' Houlihan said and hung up. Keelor's attitude angered him. He saw enough traces of Bonnaventure in the American to make him wonder if all self-made men became that arrogant. And the sudden sympathy-seeking stuff about being Eddie's friend just didn't ring true with him. He gazed at the clear cold sky then rubbed his eyes, wondering if he was overreacting.

As he was about to go back in, Keelor rang him. 'There'll be two uniformed cops there very soon.'

'Good. Thanks.'

'If the security guard is on Eddie's door, where are you based?'

'I'm . . .' Houlihan had to think. 'I'm in D Wing, near the reception desk on the ground floor. I'm close to the entrance door in this wing.'

'Which floor is Eddie's room on?'

'The fourth.'

'Any other entrances in that wing? Any weak points?'

'I'd need to check. I'm in sight of the stairs and the lifts.'

'So you'd see anyone who tried to get to Eddie's floor?'

'I can't guarantee it, Mr Keelor, I don't know the layout of the hospital; but between me and hospital security, I'd say we've a very good chance of keeping Eddie safe until your policemen arrive.'

'Good. Call me if you have any problems at all.'

'I will.'

'And I'm sorry for losing it earlier. I really care for this guy. I think you know that.'

'It's okay. It's been a long night.'

Walking back in, Houlihan didn't feel quite so bad about Vaughn Keelor.

Three hours and five cups of coffee later the two police guards arrived. Houlihan checked with them that someone was booked to relieve them at the end of their shift then he thanked the nurse and left. Driving home to Lambourn, using the fingertips of his bandaged hands to steer and change gear, he prayed for the first time since he'd left the priesthood. Prayed quietly for Eddie Malloy.

EIGHTEEN

After less than four hours' sleep Houlihan rose and called the hospital to learn that Malloy's condition was still critical. The *Racing News* was on the mat. The front page said Malloy wasn't expected to make it. There was a picture of him, smiling, shaking hands with the chairman of Peterborough racecourse. Below this was a picture of the shattered window and blackened sitting room of his flat.

The paper reported that Simon Bonnaventure was out of the country and uncontactable and an alibi bell rang in Houlihan's head. The BHB issued a statement expressing shock and deep sympathy.

Bert Jacobsen's quote was, '*Nobody that I know of had any personal dislike of Mr Malloy. He was doing his job as he saw fit. Nobody deserves to be attacked for doing their job and my sympathy goes to Mr Malloy and his family. I very much hope he recovers.*'

Houlihan remembered Malloy telling him he had

an ex-wife, Laura, and a brother in Australia. He'd need to try and contact them.

There was a quote from Detective Sergeant Moran of the Metropolitan Police. "We're waiting to speak to Mr Malloy, should he recover, and we understand he was rescued from the burning room by a friend whom we hope to interview soon. Our forensic teams are gathering evidence from the residence of Mr Malloy.'

The *Racing News* reporter stated that the friend DS Moran referred to was believed to be an employee of the Jockey Club Security Department who'd been Malloy's bodyguard. Sam Hooper had refused to comment on this 'speculation'.

Houlihan called Bobby Cranfield. Bobby said, 'Frankie, I was just about to ring you. Where are you?'

'At home.'

'Are you all right?'

'I'm okay, but I think you've got a problem. How are the press getting hold of all this stuff so quickly? We must be leaking somewhere.'

'I'm not sure we are. Don't underestimate the connections some of these people have got in the emergency services.'

'Well, somebody should put a gag on them then. How did this guy Moran get to be a detective sergeant spouting stuff like that. He all but named me.'

'Frankie, I know.' Cranfield sounded exasperated. 'I've taken a dozen calls in ten minutes asking for confirmation. I'm working on a statement now. I rang the hospital but they won't tell me anything. What do you know about Eddie?'

'I was there half the night. He's very ill.'

'How ill? Critical?'

'Nobody used that word. Keelor organised protection round the clock so I'm a bit less worried on that front. He's flying over later today.'

'I know. That's another ball-ache. Keelor needs to find somebody else quick or this takeover's going to be affected.'

'Well forgive me, Bobby, if I don't shed a tear over that, eh? I think Eddie's condition might just be taking up a bit more of my consideration than Keelor moving on to the next piece of cannon fodder.'

'Frankie! You know I didn't mean to sound hard-hearted. I'm sorry.'

'Forget it.'

'Listen, the police want to come and interview you later today. Will you be at home all day?'

'Unless Eddie gets worse and I need to go back to the hospital.'

'Okay, I think it'll be this DS Moran who seems to be in charge of the case. I'll give him your number.'

'I'd rather you didn't. I don't want my number out there for somebody to sell to a reporter. Just tell Moran I'll be here. If anything changes I'll call you.'

'Frankie, I . . . okay.'

Houlihan knew Bobby was going to protest at his paranoia but had thought better of it.

Houlihan looked around him. He was back home again sooner than he'd planned to be. The place was tidy and warm; he'd left the heating on a timer for protection against sharp frosts. But he needed supplies: eggs, bread, coffee, milk. He managed to pull a twenty-pound note from his wallet and wedge it into a fold in the bandage covering the palm of his left hand. A three-minute walk in the rain took him to the local shop. Katrina, the assistant he knew best, was behind the counter. He held up his hands.

'What've you been up to?' she asked.

'Left the hot water on all night and was still half-asleep when I ran the tap to wash this morning. Big mistake.'

She grimaced then shivered, holding her hands to her face. 'Ow! How bad is it?'

'Well I'm glad it's not the golf season yet, put it that way. Would you mind picking a few things off the shelf for me?'

'No problem.'

She eased the filled carrier bags carefully over his wrists, her face a study in concentration as though she was defusing a bomb. Houlihan headed for home, forearms jutting ahead, bags swinging on them. He turned the corner and his heart sank as he saw a blue Peugeot estate parked outside his door. Behind the wheel was Ben Dillon, the Lambourn correspondent for the *Racing News*, the man who'd raced past him into the hospital the previous night. Houlihan clenched his fists, despite the pain, and drew his hands up inside his cuffs.

Dillon got out as he reached the door. 'Frankie, let me help you.' He reached for the bags.

'I'm okay, Ben, thanks.'

'You're obviously not okay.'

'I'm fine.'

'So why the bandages? Lost your gloves or something?'

'I had an accident?'

'It wouldn't have been the same accident Eddie Malloy was involved in?'

'No, it wouldn't.'

Tall and skinny, seeming twice the height of many Lambourn residents, Dillon stared down at Houlihan. Houlihan said, 'Can you get the door key? It's in my pocket.'

Dillon got it and opened the door. Houlihan put the bags down just inside it and turned to him. 'Thanks, Ben. See you.'

'Frankie, I know you were babysitting Malloy. I can write what others have told me or you can tell me your side.'

'There's nothing to tell.'

'Let me in for a coffee, then.'

Houlihan almost laughed. He stepped outside and looked above the door. Dillon followed his gaze then stared at him in puzzlement. Houlihan said, 'I thought somebody had put a café sign over my door while I was out.'

'Come on, Frankie, I've been up half the night. I'm cold and I'm hungry.'

'Ben, you only live up the road! Go home!'

'I help you out and you won't even give me a drink? I'll boil the kettle. I'll make you some.'

'I don't want any.'

'Fine. I'd better get back and get this story written. So I can just say, "Frankie Houlihan, hands freshly bandaged, hair singed, denied being the hero who dragged Eddie Malloy from his burning flat"?'

Houlihan sighed and opened the door wide. Dillon came in and sat at the kitchen table. 'Look, Ben, there's no story here. I singed my hair at my birthday party last week in Dublin, trying to blow out the candles on my cake. And I was still half-asleep this morning when I washed my hands. I forgot I'd left the water heater on all night and it was boiling when I turned the tap on.'

Dillon looked at him. 'Your birthday party?'

He nodded. 'In Dublin with my family. That's where I've been for the past few weeks.'

'How old were you on your birthday?'

'Thirty-two.'

'What's your star sign?'

Houlihan hesitated. 'Don't know. I don't go in for all that stuff.'

Dillon crossed his arms and leaned his lanky body back against the sink unit. 'I can easily check your birthday, Frankie.'

'Go ahead.'

He shook his head slowly. 'Don't try and make

a mug out of me. I've got a job to do, same as you have.'

'You said it. I'm just trying to do mine.'

'Likewise.'

They held each other's stare. After a while, Dillon broke away, spun round and turned on the hot-water tap. It ran for a few seconds then he stuck his hand under it and left it there. Houlihan reddened. Dillon turned it off and dried his hand on the bottom of his coat. 'Scalding this morning? Terrible insulation, Frankie. You ought to get your tank lagged.' He turned to leave.

'Ben!'

'Uh-huh?'

'I can't speak to you till the police have interviewed me.'

'When's that happening?'

'Later today.'

'Will you call me when they've gone?'

'Yes.'

'You won't call any other reporter first?'

'No.'

'We've got a deal then, Frankie. I expect you to keep your side of it.'

'I will.'

Houlihan rang Bobby and told him about Dillon. Bobby sighed heavily. 'That's all we need!' He was quiet for a few moments then said, 'Look, I know the chairman of the group that runs the *Racing News*. I'll get him to warn Dillon off.'

'I made a deal with him, Bobby.'

'Frankie, come on! You can't talk to the press about this. You know that!'

'I just said I'd call him when I'd spoken to the police. I don't have to tell him anything. But I don't want him thinking I've gone running to his chairman.'

'It doesn't matter what he thinks, for God's sake!'

'Bobby, I'll deal with it. Okay? I'll deal with it. Forget I said anything.'

'Okay. All right. I'll leave it to you. By the way, DS Moran will be there around seven.'

'Fine. Thanks.'

DS Moran turned out to be a she; Houlihan's height, probably not far off his age, maybe a bit older. When he opened the door to her he found himself staring into her eyes with embarrassing intensity and he flushed. She offered her hand as she introduced herself. He held both hands in the air to let her see the bandages. She said, 'That's the quickest surrender I've ever had.' They both smiled. Houlihan's thoughts and emotions suddenly seemed all over the place, like a faulty firework. She wasn't what anyone would call classically beautiful but he realised he'd immediately found her looks and sense of humour powerfully attractive.

She came in and took off her coat. 'Can I hang it here?' she asked, turning to the brass hooks on the back of the door.

'Sure.'

'Cold out there,' she said.

'D'you want a cup of tea?' he asked, trying not to look at her face.

'Yes please.'

He went to the sink, quite adept now at turning on the tap with his elbow. She came towards him. 'Should I do it?'

'I'm fine. I'm almost an expert now, and that's after just one day.' The water gushed out, splashing on his shirt-sleeve. She grabbed the kettle and thrust it under the flow. Water hit the edge of the spout and soaked his chin.

'Sorry,' she smiled, trying not to laugh.

He dried his face using the bandages on the backs of his hands, dabbing delicately. 'Sorry, Mr Houlihan.' And this time she looked genuinely sorry.

'It's okay. Call me Frankie.' He was surprised at how quickly his animosity towards the DS Moran quoted in that morning's paper had disappeared.

'Point me towards the tea bags and stuff and I'll finish doing this. Are you a teapot man or bag in a mug?'

'A bag in a mug's fine.' He tried to open the cupboard that held the tea and sugar but DS Moran chided him and told him to sit down. He eased a chair away from the table with his foot, wondering if this over-familiar woman was being herself or if this disarming friendliness was part of her professional modus operandi.

She chatted while the kettle boiled; about how she'd got lost trying to get there ('I'm sure I passed the same pile of horse droppings about ten times'), about trees looking scary in the dark. She kept up a stream of banter before she finally sat down with the mugs of tea and smiled at him.

She nodded towards his mug. 'Will you manage to drink it okay? With your hands, I mean?'

Houlihan got up and opened the cutlery drawer. Anticipating well, for once in his life, he'd bought some drinking straws earlier. Putting one in his mouth he returned to his chair trying not to look too childishly triumphant. She smiled. 'Forward planning or good luck?'

'Forward planning, of course. Not that I'd admit to anything else.' He sucked his tea reasonably quietly. She looked around the kitchen.

'Any biscuits?' she asked.

Some girl this, he thought. 'D'you think you're at your auntie's?'

'Sorry, I'm starving.'

'I could make you a sandwich.'

'Sausage sandwich?'

He shook his head. 'Banana.'

'Chips?'

'Banana. Or tuna.'

She wrinkled her nose, shook her head. He said, 'I actually do have some biscuits. Don't usually but I bought some today.'

'Chocolate ones or boring ones?'

'They were nearly two quid.'

'Can I see them?'

'Only if you can post the bail money.'

She smiled. He sucked. 'They're in the top cupboard on the right.'

She got the packet. 'Mmm, not opened either.' She ripped the wrapper top and took a round dark-chocolate one, which she ate with obvious enjoyment, nodding at him and sipping tea. He said, 'That's the quietest you've been since you got here, DS Moran. Have another.'

Oblivious to sarcasm, she said, 'I will. Thanks.'

She ate two more, finished her tea and finally took out a notebook. Houlihan said, 'No need to write out the dessert order, I can take it verbally.'

'I should think you could. Not hard to remember a banana, is it?'

She was smart and he realised he was beginning to enjoy this little joust. Kathy was never far from his mind and suddenly she seemed fully present and he felt an immediate stab of guilt. He still felt dedicated to his dead wife. He'd never expected to feel anything but deep love for her as long as he lived.

DS Moran seemed slightly puzzled as she watched the smile disappear so quickly from his eyes. She sat a little more upright in her chair and said, professional all of a sudden, 'Want to take me through what happened yesterday?'

Houlihan nodded, looked away as he felt his face flushing. 'Are you okay, Mr Houlihan?'

'Sudden pain in my right hand. Sorry,' he lied. 'It's okay now.'

'Are you sure?'

'Yes, fine. I'll tell you what happened.'

She listened without interruption, made notes and nodded at appropriate moments. She went through some standard police questions: Anyone loitering? Notice anybody tailing you? Did Eddie Malloy have any idea who might be after him? Did Mr Malloy discuss any other details of his life outside of work? Could the attack have been unrelated to the previous threats?

Her questions were sensible, and her reassessment of things after he answered each impressed him. She was serious throughout, much different from the biscuit-munching funny girl of earlier. Houlihan told her about Makalu, Bonnaventure and Malloy's history with him, and the story of what had happened outside the Royal Box. When it came to the blackmailer, Houlihan was conscious of the need to protect Malloy's secret.

'Somebody was trying to blackmail Eddie,' he said.

She stopped taking notes and looked up at him, her eyes prompting him to continue. Houlihan said, 'I can't tell you what the man was using, what the leverage was. It was something Eddie was involved in a long time ago, a family matter, nothing criminal.'

'Do you know what it is?'

He looked at her, trying to anticipate where she was going with this. 'I do. But it would be for Eddie to tell you, not me.'

She nodded slowly then said, 'What was the ransom?'

'The man wanted him to engineer Makalu out of the deal to buy the Jockey Club's racecourses.'

'You said that the deal was completed.'

'There's a get-out clause for either party.'

'Why would this man want Makalu out?'

Houlihan shrugged. 'So he or whoever he is working for could move in? Eddie heard some time ago that Bonnaventure had an interest in doing just that.'

She pondered this, then asked, 'Was there a deadline?'

'We had another seven weeks,' Houlihan said, only then realising how closely he now associated himself with Malloy. 'We were only one week into it.'

'Why do you say "we"?'

'We'd got pretty close, me and Eddie. We'd spent most of our waking hours together for the past month or so. I suppose I got quite protective of him.'

She looked away as though trying to think of another question, then asked, 'So Malloy had agreed to do something to activate the get-out clause?'

Houlihan moved uncomfortably. 'Well, he told the blackmailer he would, just to buy time, to see if we could find out who he was.'

'Is there any way the blackmailer could have known you two were just stringing him along?'

'No. We'd only discussed it between ourselves and made a few calls, ones we thought would be, er, relevant.' Houlihan was trying to think ahead. He didn't want to slip up and give away any clue about Malloy's dead brother.

'Who did you call?'

'I'm sorry. I can't say.'

She put down her pen and linked her fingers. 'Off the record, Frankie.'

He sat back. 'I wouldn't tell it in a confessional, DS Moran.'

She nodded, seeming to accept the finality of that. Houlihan said, 'Nothing we did on this would help you, believe me. It's just such a personal thing for Eddie.'

'Okay. I suppose the last person who'd want to kill Eddie would be the blackmailer. Eddie was his best chance of killing the Makalu deal.'

'Exactly. It has to be somebody else.'

She nodded, wrote another half page then looked up. 'If you were me, what's the next thing you'd do?'

'I'd probably go and see Bert Jacobsen and try and find out if there was a connection between the campaign he started up – RACE, he called it – and Bonnaventure. And I'd ask him for the list of people who responded to that ad he put in the *Racing News* not long after Malloy took over Gloucester racecourse.' He briefed her about the ad and RACE.

'Have you come across anyone else in racing

who had a grudge against Makalu, or Mr Malloy personally?'

'Can't say I have. But people moan about a lot of things. If you believe the press there's a fair groundswell of bad feeling against the company, but the reality is that it's such an incestuous business, racing, that most folk won't speak their minds for fear of finding Makalu as their new boss, or at least somewhere higher up the food chain than they are.'

'I think a chat with Bonnaventure is in order.'

Houlihan hesitated, not wanting to tell her how to do her job. 'It might be better to see what else you can build on before you see him.'

'Okay. So it looks like next stop Bert Jacobsen.'

Houlihan nodded. He checked his watch. He wanted to know how Malloy was. DS Moran suggested she ring the hospital, said they might give her more detailed information. The detail was that Malloy's condition had worsened and was giving cause for concern. DS Moran was sufficiently sensitive not to ask when she could come and interview him. She told Houlihan the news and he grimaced, ran his hand through his hair. 'I should have got to him quicker,' he said.

She watched him, then said, 'I'm sorry. It was thoughtless of me not to ask how you felt. It must have been a pretty awful experience.'

'He seemed to be in flames from head to foot. I feel I hesitated a bit too long before helping him.'

'I'd bet you didn't. When these things happen

it can feel like time's almost suspended. People involved in them always say to me how they felt that everything was happening in slow-motion. If you could replay it in real time you'd probably find you moved faster than you've ever done in your life. You're almost certainly the reason your friend's still alive.'

Houlihan thought of when they'd almost fallen out because Malloy had wanted them to split for a while to double their chances of catching the blackmailer. But he'd insisted they stayed together and that helped him feel better now. 'Thanks,' he said. 'You're probably right.'

Houlihan walked her to the door. She asked, 'How long will you be off work?'

'Don't know. I won't really be off at all, I suppose. I often work from home. Won't be able to drive safely for a few days but as long as I can punch in a phone number I should be able to keep occupied.'

'Would you like to come with me to interview Bert Jacobsen?'

She held his slightly surprised gaze but a tinge of red appeared on her cheekbones. He said, 'I don't think that would be a good idea. If I turn up with you it'll look like I'm riding shotgun for the law.'

She smiled. 'Riding shotgun for the law? You've been working from home too much, Mr Houlihan, watching those old cowboy movies in the afternoon.'

'You're probably right.'

She opened the door and stepped out and the wind blew her hair across her face. She pulled it back. 'Thanks for the biscuits.'

'Oh, hold on,' he said, and he went to the table and picked up the blue packet. He offered it to her. 'Take them home. It'll save you cooking for the next three nights.'

'Thanks but I'd feel guilty leaving none for your visitors.'

'I doubt I'll get any for a while. Take them.'

'You might get me. I'll probably need to come back.'

'Why?'

'You're a key witness. I'll have more questions.'

He met her gaze and tried to read it. All he could sense was that burning intensity he'd felt when he'd first opened the door to her. She said, 'I'll call you, make an appointment, if that's okay?'

He nodded. 'Okay.' He gave her his number.

'Goodnight, Mr Houlihan.'

'Goodnight, DS Moran.'

He closed the door and felt nervous about turning round to the empty house, for it wasn't empty. His conscience had brought Kathy in.

Houlihan went to bed early, his body clock still out after the previous night. He was very tired but couldn't sleep. The phone rang. He let it. The answerphone kicked in. He heard his own voice then that of Ben Dillon. The reporter did not sound pleased. Houlihan decided he'd call him soon. DS Moran came into his mind a few times before sleep but he always managed to push her back out.

Next morning, the hospital played hardball with him on the phone, refusing to give information. The nurse asked, 'Are you related to Mr Malloy?'

'No, but he has no next-of-kin that I know of. I'm his friend.'

'Sorry, I can't tell you anything. It's against regulations.'

Houlihan suddenly felt sick. Maybe Malloy had died. He said, 'Is his condition worse?'

'I'm sorry, I can't comment.'

'Listen, I was with him when it happened. I pulled him out.'

'Sorry.'

'Who are you giving information to, then?' he asked in frustration

'Close relatives. And the police.'

'Thank you.' He called DS Moran on the mobile number she'd left. She sounded surprised when she heard his voice. 'I need a favour,' he said.

'I'll help if I can. What is it?'

'I need to know how Eddie is. The hospital won't tell me. I know you called them last night but would you mind doing it again?'

'Sure. Give me a couple of minutes.'

Within five minutes she rang back. 'Mr Malloy's been moved to a private hospital.'

'Where?' Houlihan was confused.

'I don't know. The hospital doesn't know.'

'How can they not know if they were the ones that sent him?'

'They didn't. A Mr Vaughn Keelor did.'

'What? Keelor?'

'Do you know him?'

'I do. And there's no way Malloy was fit to be moved. No way. I'll call Keelor. Can I ring you back?'

'Of course.'

Houlihan knew Keelor should now be in the UK. He dialled his mobile number. 'Mr Keelor?'

'Mr Houlihan.'

'You moved Eddie.'

'That's right.'

'How? Why? He wasn't fit to be moved.'

'He's moved. Settled in. He's no worse than he was. What do you think I am? You think I'd risk his life?'

'Where is he?'

'You're the last person I'd tell, Mr Houlihan. Somebody's trying to kill Eddie. You're his friend. You were with him the other night. Do you really think it would be sensible for you to know where he is now?'

Houlihan hesitated, trying to take in all the implications. 'Maybe you're right,' he admitted quietly.

'I know I'm right. And I know Eddie's going to be okay. I'll make sure he is. I've got the top burns man in the States flying in on Thursday and I've got Fort fucking Knox around him, so don't you worry.'

'Is he conscious?'

Keelor sighed loudly. 'He's okay, Houlihan, stop worrying.'

'Will you keep me in touch with how he is?'

'You bet.'

Houlihan called DS Moran back and told her what had happened. She said, 'Sounds like Mr Keelor's got a lot of money.'

'He thinks he rules the world.'

'Is he going to be doing Mr Malloy's job, then, while he's ill?'

'I don't know. I doubt it. Got the world to run, hasn't he?'

'Somehow I don't think Mr Keelor is on your Christmas card list, Frankie.'

'Ahh, he just winds me up!'

'Don't let him. It's not worth it. Listen, I'd like to come back and speak to you this evening if possible.'

'Why?'

'Can I tell you when I get there?'

Houlihan hesitated, remembering how he'd felt when he'd first seen her, wanting to experience that again but afraid of where it might lead. 'What time?' he asked and immediately felt he was doing something he shouldn't.

'About the same as last night, if that's okay.'

'Okay,' he said. 'I'll see you then.'

'You don't sound over-enthusiastic.'

'I only have one enthusiastic day a month and that was yesterday,' he said flatly, enough to make her pause and wonder if he was being serious.

'How're your hands?'

'They'll be fine. More awkward than painful.'

'Awkward hands?'

'You know what I mean.'

'I do. Be careful shaving.'

That personal edge again. Disguised as light-hearted. Or was he being too sensitive about it? Maybe this was the way she spoke to everyone. Perhaps it was part of her technique. 'I will. Goodbye,' he said, and then thought, Goodbye Ms Confidence, Ms Modern Girl. Ms Trouble.

NINETEEN

Houlihan's hands were still sore and when the door-bell rang he was tempted to shout 'Come in!' rather than suffer the discomfort of turning the handle. But the thought of what Keelor had said about him being a possible target made him wonder how careful he should start being. He moved to the window and eased the curtain aside. It was Ben Dillon, the press-hound he didn't want to see. The doorbell rang again. 'Come in, Ben!'

Ben entered and closed the door quickly, blowing on his hands. 'Morning. Freezing out there. Been for your run yet? Hey, how did you know it was me?'

'Sixth sense, and no I haven't been for my run. Ever tried lacing up trainers with third-degree finger burns?'

'Third-degree burns, eh? Didn't realise it was that serious. Must have been some fire.'

Houlihan looked at him, knowing they'd both accepted the pretence was over.

'Should we have a coffee?' Dillon asked, raising his eyebrows.

'If you make it,' Houlihan said, knowing it was information, not coffee, Dillon was after.

'No problem.'

Five minutes later they sat at the table. Ben slurped his coffee while Houlihan sucked tea through a straw. Eventually Dillon said, 'Frankie, tell me what happened in Malloy's place.'

'I could tell you about every spark and lungful of smoke, but you couldn't publish it so just drink and warm your hands for a while.'

'Of course I can publish it. It'll be front page.'

'Ben, how much do you know about Jockey Club members?'

'Which ones?'

'In general. I mean, a few powerful people among them with friends in high places and all that stuff?'

'Sure. A few tossers too.'

'Well, one of the non-tossers was for speaking direct to your chairman yesterday. Your chairman, mind, not your editor, to get you off my back.'

He looked offended. 'So why didn't he?'

'Because I asked him not to. I told him I'd promised to speak to you myself and I wanted to stick to that.'

'So speak to me.'

'I am. I'm telling you you'll need to leave it for now.'

'Aw, Frankie, come on!'

'Ben, give me a break! Somebody tried to kill Eddie Malloy. They probably still want to. And now they know someone was with him, someone who may have seen them throwing the petrol bomb. All they need to do is read in the *Racing News* that it was me and there might be another bomb coming through that window behind you.'

'You'd get a police guard.'

'Big deal! Just so you can get a story? You're mad!'

Ben slumped back in his chair, opened pleading arms. 'Frankie, this could be my big break. All I ever get to write about is crocked horses or bent tipsters or so-called big gambles. I'm pig-sick of it!'

Houlihan laughed unintentionally at his tantrum. 'Find yourself a more fulfilling job. Or take up a gossip column on one of the dailies. Lambourn makes Sodom and Gomorrah look like Salt Lake City. Plenty of copy here.'

Ben sighed. 'And you know as well as I do that if I write any of it up, I'd need to pack my bags the same day. This one is just perfect: attempted murder, racecourse takeovers, big business. I will never, ever get anything like this again, I just know I won't! It's heaven sent. God even threw in a priest.'

'Ex-priest.'

He shrugged. 'Almost as good.'

Houlihan shook his head. 'Ben, the best I can do is sit down with you when this has all been resolved. I'll give you the full story then.'

'That's like . . . like Deep Throat telling Bob Woodward that once Nixon has resigned he'll tell him about Watergate. It's not a story any more, Frankie, it's history.'

'Better *it* being history than *you*, which is what you'll be if our man speaks to your chairman.'

'Oh, threats now, is it? Very nice!'

'No threats. The hard facts. I said I'd have a quiet word with you, try it that way.'

Dillon drank the remainder of the coffee and got up, still sulking, beetle-browed. 'I'll lose this one. I just know I will. Somebody else'll get it. Certainty. Absolute bloody certainty.'

He left without saying goodbye.

Houlihan stood at the window, staring out, thinking. That was Dillon dealt with for now. Malloy was somewhere safe. DS Moran was coming back that night. There was someone out there willing to kill Malloy and maybe Houlihan too. And here he was, grounded. Told to lie low for the sake of PR and politics.

He held up his bandaged hands; maybe he should go and see ma now, in this state, seek sympathy. He could tell her it was the stigmata, that he was still holy enough in God's eyes for Him to make him bleed. He managed to smile at the thought.

But this would probably be a good time to go back and see her. This limbo of waiting – for Malloy's fate, for his hands to heal – he might as well try and achieve something. The longer he delayed it, the harder it would be to do. He went to his PC and logged on to book a flight, ointment from his fingers glistening on the keys. Before closing the Internet link, he decided to check on some of his investments.

Half an hour later he looked at the ragged figures he'd jotted down. Kathy had left everything to him in her will and the insurance settlement had been much more than he'd expected. Insurance premiums had been one of her costliest expense items but they were tax-deductible. Kathy had been a top journalist, specialising in learning risk sports and writing of her experiences. One of her subjects had been horse racing – steeplechasing. It had found her a husband and cost her her life.

Maybe by Bobby Cranfield's standards Houlihan wouldn't be considered a rich man, but he had enough money to last him three lifetimes without having to work. A fortune he couldn't have dreamed of when he was a priest, but one, in the end, he had no real use for.

He didn't want to retire. His work was now all that kept him going. He needed no more than the comforts he had. The Jockey Club supplied his car; he was happy with the house. None of his family was in financial need. He already gave generously to several charities. He'd need to think of something else to do with it. No point in having it pile up over whatever years were left to him. No point at all.

DS Moran arrived at seven o'clock. Houlihan thought she looked slightly less exuberant than she had the previous night. There was just less of an edge to her. She took off her coat and sat down. He noticed her make-up. The lipstick looked fresh.

'How are the hands?' she asked.

'A bit raw, but they'll be fine. Any news?'

'On what?'

'On Eddie. On anything.'

'I need to find out where Eddie is. I'll have to interview him when he's well enough.'

'You'll need to speak to Keelor. He won't tell me.'

'I will.' She looked at him.

'Anything else?' he asked.

'How much time do you have? Can you go through a list with me? I've got all the respondents to Bert Jacobsen's ad.'

'You spoke to Jacobsen?'

'I saw him today. Added him to my bitter-and-twisted list. He showed no sympathy for Eddie Malloy so at least he's consistent.'

'Any chance he's our man?'

She took a folder from her leather bag. 'He was in hospital the night it happened. Heart palpitations due to the stress Malloy caused him, he says.'

'Did you check his story?'

She raised her eyebrows at Houlihan as she opened the folder. He held up a hand in apology and said, 'But he handed over the list?'

'Under pressure.'

'How many names?'

'Two hundred and thirty-three.'

'Quite a lot.'

'Mmm. But it shouldn't take long to go through. I'm sure you'll recognise some of them. Should I come to that side of the table?'

'I'll move to yours.' Houlihan wasn't sure why he said that. Maybe he was just trying to take away some of the control she seemed to want to build up. Not that his gesture had any real impact on that.

The list lay between them on the table. When she pointed a name out that might be of interest she'd sway slightly, almost leaning on him, then she'd look straight into his eyes with an intensity that made him uncomfortable. He considered moving his chair further away but couldn't decide if he was overreacting. Much as he hadn't wanted it, he knew that there had been an attraction between them last night and he almost loathed himself for allowing it.

Was DS Moran making some sort of play for him, or was his manic conscience magnifying everything she said and did? He had to give her the benefit of the doubt. He sat where he was and tried to cool down a bit.

More than half the names on the list were familiar to him and a few he knew quite well. 'Any potential petrol-bombers among them?' she asked.

'Tell me what one looks like and how he behaves on the run-up to it and I'll give you an answer.'

'Is that a "no" then, Frankie?' She sounded frustrated, Houlihan thought.

'That's a "don't know, it's almost impossible to tell", DS Moran.'

'You can call me Loretta.'

'DS Moran seems more appropriate, if you don't mind,' he said, knowing it sounded pointed.

She straightened up in the chair, crossed her legs, clasped her fingers. She shook her head once as though trying to dislodge something from her hair. Then she smiled at him. 'Tell me something, Mr Houlihan. What did I do between last night and tonight to become your public enemy number one?'

He hung his head and was silent for a while. 'Nothing. I'm sorry. I'm having a bad day. My hands ache. My brain's buzzing. I have too much money, too much time, not enough sense. And I need to go to Dublin.'

Slowly, he raised his eyes to look at her. Her fingers were on her chin. She shook her head slightly. Houlihan smiled. She started laughing. He joined in.

She said, 'Having too much money contributes to a bad day?'

'Ignore me. I'm rambling. My brain needs a rest.'

'And you need to go to Dublin?'

'I do. To see me ma.'

'Yer ma, is it now? And when would that be?'

'Saturday morning.' He smiled again at her pretty accurate Dublin accent. She said, 'Who's driving you to the airport?'

'I haven't arranged anything yet.'

'I'll take you, if you like.'

He looked warily at her. She smiled. 'It's all right, I'm not going to propose or anything.'

Houlihan reddened, then smiled. 'Can you be here for seven thirty?'

'No problem.'

'Congratulations, you've got the job.'

More relaxed now, having reached a truce, they ploughed on through the list without coming to any useful conclusions. DS Moran knew no one who featured on it. The ones Houlihan knew well-enough to make a character judgement about would normally not have been among his suspects, but, having said that, he'd also have judged that they wouldn't have responded to this ad.

'Would it be worthwhile interviewing all of them?' she asked.

'Depends who did the interviewing, the police or the Jockey Club.'

'I doubt we'd be able to find the resources,' she said. 'I could work my way through it but these people are all over the country. It could take months.'

'I think it would be far too politically sensitive for us to do it,' he said. 'I can ask the question but I think I know what the answer would be.'

She shrugged. 'Ask it. Let's see what they say.'

'What about Jacobsen? Did you speak to him about Bonnaventure? Did you raise the question of where he got the money for the ad in the paper?'

'I asked about the money. There's nothing to pin Bonnaventure to Jacobsen just now so I left that one out.'

'So who paid for the ad?'

'Sympathisers, according to Jacobsen, "People who were able to imagine what it must be like being made homeless."'

'Is there any way of checking his story on that? I don't suppose you get access to his bank-account details?'

'No chance. He'd need to be a pretty strong suspect for that sort of warrant and the reality is we've got nothing on him at all.'

Houlihan nodded, accepting what she'd said. 'I know. There's a motive of sorts, I suppose, and that's it.'

She moved forward, raised a hand as though to touch him, then lowered it hesitantly. 'Never mind,' she said. 'Something will come up.'

TWENTY

On Saturday DS Moran turned up at seven twenty, looking much more Loretta than Detective Sergeant: blue jeans and a black fleecy top, her hair in a shiny ponytail, tomboyish and feminine at the same time. The perfume was subtly there again but she wasn't wearing much make-up. 'Where's your bag?' she asked.

'I'm not taking one. I'm coming back tonight.'

She looked puzzled, seemed about to ask more questions then thought better of it.

A few minutes into the journey Houlihan began to regret accepting her offer. He realised they got on well but they knew little about each other. He felt it was only a matter of time before she'd be asking him how long he'd been in the job and what he did before that, etcetera. He never felt comfortable telling people about his past, trying to put a brave face on the fact that he'd left a vocation to God, broken vows, deserted his parishioners, shattered his family, skewered his mother's heart . . . for the sake of loving Kathy Spencer who was dead and buried within six months of their wedding.

All his friends and acquaintances and most people in racing knew of his situation. It was only new people in his life who required the biography. Although, now he thought about it, DS Moran was easily smart enough to have found out everything there was to know already and she certainly had the resources. He decided to take no chances, to ask her about herself, lead her well away from the subject of him.

She drove smoothly, tutting at bad driving. 'Got a blue light on this?' he asked.

'Sometimes wish I had. There are people driving cars who shouldn't even be allowed to walk along a pavement.'

They kept up this small-talk throughout the trip, though Frankie sensed she knew exactly what he was doing in keeping the conversation impersonal.

When they reached the airport, Houlihan struggled with the internal door-handle. Loretta leaned across and flipped it. He got out quickly. She stepped out and stood leaning on the door frame. 'Is someone picking you up tonight?'

'I can get a taxi.'

'To Lambourn? It'll cost more than the flight.'

'Something to spend my money on, then.'

She shook her head. 'I can pick you up, if you like. I'm going to see Vaughn Keelor today. I'll get him to take me to see your friend Malloy. I thought

I could give you an update if you want picking up.'

'Where are you seeing Keelor?'

'I hear he's got an office at Esher racecourse. Temporary, they tell me, but he's supposed to be there today.'

'And he's agreed to take you to meet Eddie?'

'Not yet, but I think he will.'

Houlihan looked at her smiling, confident face. 'Ask him if I can go and see Malloy. Maybe tomorrow. Would you?'

'Of course.'

'Thanks.'

'And the lift for later?' she asked.

Houlihan looked at her, trying to work her out. 'Haven't you got a life which this is disrupting?' he asked.

'Yes.'

'So why are you doing it?'

'I'm trying to make the best of my time and yours. It's my job.'

'You ought to get a more sensible one.'

'I might just do that, Mr Houlihan.'

A policeman came walking purposefully forward. The car was on a double-yellow line. She stood up straight. 'Chauffeur or not, Mr H?'

'Chauffeuse.'

She pulled a face. 'Well?'

'Okay. Thanks. My flight gets in at eight fifty.'

'I'll be here.'

* * *

Houlihan's brother, Thomas, was at Dublin airport, pacing outside the terminal doors in the rain, smoking. Houlihan thought he looked thinner, worried, a bit unkempt, but he smiled when he saw Houlihan and hugged him. 'Good to see you, Frankie. It seems more than a few weeks.'

'Is everything all right with you?' Houlihan asked as they walked to his car.

'Fine. I'm well. Thanks.'

'You look like you need a good feed and a haircut,' Houlihan said.

Thomas turned, smiling again. 'You sound just like Da. Getting to look a bit like him too as you get older.'

'No bad thing.'

Thomas went to the driver's side. Houlihan said, 'Can you open this door, Thomas, please? I hurt my hands.'

'Of course.' He hurried around the front. 'Let me see.' Houlihan held them open, blistered and discoloured as though they'd gone rotten.

'What happened, for God's sake?'

'Can I tell you on the way?'

By the end of the tale Houlihan could see Thomas was proud of him in the schoolboy way that younger brothers are. 'I didn't realise your job was so dangerous and exciting, Frankie.'

'It's not usually. A one-off. How's Ma?'

'Much the same. Margaret managed to talk her into seeing you. Everybody's nervous about it. Aren't you?'

'Me? Your hero of a big brother who's faced petrol bombs and infernos? I'm bloody terrified!'

They laughed and it came home again to Houlihan how much he'd missed most of the family. Ma deserved his resentment. It was her bitterness that had broken them all up.

He didn't even know what the others were doing with their lives now, what had happened to them in the past two years. On his last visit all the talk had been of Ma and the distant past, the days when they were all happy.

'How old are you now, Thomas?'

'Twenty-six. And never been kissed.'

'Yeah, I believe you.'

He chuckled. 'Honest. Free of all the shackles of your normal mid-twenties fella. No relationship. No job. No expensive addictions, apart from this rust-bucket we're sitting in, and as soon as I get my degree and Ma's better, I'm off.'

'Good man. Where to? Somewhere warm and dry?'

'Round the world.'

'Backpacking?'

'Cycling.' He smiled across, proud, looking again like a schoolboy, reminding Houlihan of their sister, Theresa. They were alike, all right, in their sensitivity, their lifetime hold on the child inside them. Yet Ma had never sent Thomas for any tests as she'd done with Theresa. He'd been the proper blue-eyed boy as far as Ma was concerned. Houlihan was the trophy priest, Thomas the one she doted on. Not that Houlihan resented that – he liked his brother, loved him, as did everyone who knew him.

'Cycling? Get away! You can't ride a bike; I remember every day for a full school holiday holding the saddle as you swayed and crashed along that path in the park. When did you finally learn to ride a bike?'

'July.'

Houlihan looked at him. Thomas laughed. 'Years ago, Frankie. I know I was a hopeless case when I was five but I managed it before I became a teenager.'

'And now you're going to cycle round the world?'

'I am. Got the route all planned. I'll show it to you later, if you like.'

'I'd love to see it. Might even come with you.'

He looked across. 'You're joking me?'

'Why not? Get a tandem. You do all the work. I'll be there, no problem.'

When they reached their mother's house (it had taken Houlihan much time and effort to stop thinking of it as home) the family were all there, sitting quietly in the living room in various awkward poses like animals on perches, all looking at Houlihan. He wasn't sure if he felt like their keeper or their prey.

Theresa was behind the door, waiting to break the ice by shouting 'Boo!' as he came through it.

She hugged him. He put his arms around her as best he could.

Margaret managed a strained smile. 'Hello, Frankie, how are you?'

'I'm not bad. You guys weren't supposed to be here. Wasn't that what we agreed?'

Margaret said, 'Mother changed her mind. Called me in a panic last night.'

'Told you to round them up? Get the wagons in a circle?'

Cornelius said, 'I've never been called a wagon before.' Most of them smiled at that.

Although they'd agreed only Theresa should be at home when Houlihan arrived, this gathering didn't surprise him. He knew his ma needed the grand gestures. He wasn't that put-out by it and something in him was glad to see them all together again. Every contact with the family made him realise how much he'd hardened himself against them when they'd turned on him. He wondered if any of the ice was melting with them.

Thomas was at his shoulder. He said, 'Frankie burned his hands saving a fella in a big fire. Somebody tried to murder him. Threw a petrol bomb into his house. Fella would have been dead if Frankie hadn't dragged him out. He's in intensive care. Police guard. Show them your hands, Frankie.'

Thoughts of the confidentiality clause he'd signed in his employment contract rose in Houlihan's mind and he swivelled his eyes accusingly towards his younger brother. 'Thomas . . . '

he turned to look round at the others '. . . if any of that gets out to the press I'll lose my job.' He was tempted to add that the killer might also come after him but he didn't want Thomas feeling guilty if something did happen to him.

Theresa reached gently for his hands, turning them upwards. 'Oh, Frankie, they look awful sore!'

The others left their seats to come and see. 'They do,' said Pat.

Margaret asked, 'What have they given you? What treatment?'

'Ointment and fresh air.'

'How are you managing on your own with hands like that?' she asked.

'I'm doing okay, thanks. They'll be back to normal in a few days.'

'Tell us what happened,' Cornelius said.

There was a loud cough from the bedroom, then a weary sigh. Margaret looked at Houlihan. He said, quietly, 'Not much wrong with her hearing or her sense of not being the centre of the universe.'

Margaret said, 'If you go in there with that attitude we'll all have been wasting our time.'

Houlihan nodded. 'Sorry. You're right.' She reached and touched his shoulder. He tried to get out of his jacket. Theresa helped. He took a final look round the others then turned to go into the hall. The bedroom door was open an inch. He took a few moments to compose himself then pushed it slowly. 'Ma, are you awake?' he asked quietly. She sighed again and he heard her turn, the bed creaking, duvet rustling. He went in.

The curtains were half-open, though little light came in from the grey morning and no lamps were on. There were fresh flowers on the dressing table. A chair stood by the bed, a hard kitchen chair, and Houlihan knew she wasn't having anything as intimate as him sitting on her bed. Nor was he to be comfortable where he did sit. He could see the corner of the seat pad that had been on the chair sticking out from under the bed. She'd removed it herself after the chair had been brought in.

He sat down. She lay on her side, her head away from him towards the window. 'Ma,' he said quietly. 'How are you?'

She didn't answer for a few seconds, then said, 'I'm sick.'

'I know. I've been keeping in touch with your progress.'

'There's been no progress! Don't be trying to dress things up in words.'

'It was just that I'd heard you were getting a little bit better. I wanted to come and see you, to see if I could help.'

There was a silence again for what seemed a long time. 'I won't look at you,' she said. 'I told them that.'

His turn to be quiet. She said, 'Did you hear me?'

'I did, Ma.'

'I don't want to see your face. You took the life out o' me, so you did.'

'It wasn't deliberate you know. I didn't do it to hurt you. It was the hardest thing I'll ever do in my life. It took me months and months to make the decision.'

'I don't want to hear anythin' about your soul-searchin', Francis Houlihan! You broke your vows to God for the sake of that girl, that stupid girl who should have had some respect for you and for God!'

'The decision was mine and mine alone. Kathy played no part. She'd not so much as said a word out of place in all the time I knew her before I decided. She didn't try to influence me in any way.'

'Shows you how much she deceived you then, doesn't it? She was a scheming bitch and that's the end of it.'

He felt the anger rise, tried to stay cool. All he managed to control was his voice level. 'Ma, Kathy was my wife. She's dead. I still love her more than anything in the world. Please don't talk about her like that . . .'

'She was a scheming bitch who knew exactly what she was doing. She got what was coming to her. Doesn't that tell you enough about how bad she was. God knew it well enough.'

'How would you feel if someone was sitting here talking about Da the way you're talking about Kathy?'

She turned quickly, propped herself on her

elbow, glared at him. 'Don't you ever compare your father with her! Don't ever!' She was shouting, bloodshot eyes staring, tears rising.

Houlihan almost recoiled at the sight of her. For the first time in his life he looked at his mother and did not recognise her. She looked like a stranger, a mad stranger: burning eyes, wet now; reddened cheeks; twists of grey hair sticking outwards and upwards. The Gorgon came to his mind. For the first time he realised he'd been wrong in condemning her, and the others for being taken in by her. This was a sick woman. Mentally ill, her hard-wired brain short-circuited by the news he'd brought her on that dull winter day.

She slumped back on the pillow, her stare now fixed on the ceiling, tears flowing freely, flooding her ears, spilling down her neck. He reached to touch them, to try and wipe them away with the back of his hand. She didn't flinch or make a sound, just stared vacantly upwards.

He heard the door creak. It was Margaret. He waved her in and got up. He touched his mother's cheek again. 'Sorry, Ma. I'm so sorry.'

Houlihan waited in dismayed silence with the others, listening through the wall to Margaret trying to comfort their ma. After a while Margaret came out looking strained and resigned. He looked at her and said very quietly, 'You were right. She's very sick. I'm sorry.'

Margaret clasped her fingers, looked down at

them. 'What next, then?' It was almost a whisper.

Houlihan felt he had to get out of there, to run. 'I don't know. I need to think. Can I call you?'

She nodded. 'Of course.' He went over and hugged her, felt her almost go weak then pull herself back together. He went around the others, touching their shoulders, offering a troubled smile which was meant to tell them that he now accepted they were all in this together, that he was with them.

Thomas took him back to the airport.

The ninety minutes spent waiting for his flight to be called gave Houlihan time to weigh up options; to run through a little honest analysis of where he was in his life. He knew he wasn't happy, hadn't been since Kathy died, and he accepted it was unlikely he would be again. The repercussions of his leaving the priesthood had caused too much collateral damage for him ever to be able to live comfortably with it.

Although the family thought that if he returned to his vocation Ma would regain her health, he doubted it. It seemed that his very existence was upsetting to her, that what had been done could never be undone. She'd probably think it a heresy for him to try and go back to the priesthood and a blessing if he was to be out of her life, and everyone else's, completely.

What else? His new friendship with Eddie Malloy had literally gone up in flames. Malloy had been on his mind almost as much as Kathy these past few days. Houlihan was increasingly uncertain he'd done the right thing in deciding not to try and get the burning gown off Malloy. Now there was the prospect of the bomber trying to reach Malloy and finish him off. Even if he recovered, even when he left hospital, if the attacker hadn't been caught then Malloy faced months, maybe years, of fear. And he'd probably need to face it without any realistic chance of defending himself.

Houlihan almost slumped forward in his seat at the thought of a badly crippled Malloy trying to make his way in the world. He had been so energetic, dedicated to fitness. And Houlihan realised that in the few weeks he'd known him, Malloy had also become the closest friend he'd ever had. At thirty-two that had been a new experience for Houlihan. He'd entered the seminary at seventeen and from then anything that had looked like developing into a relationship the priests considered too friendly had been nipped in the bud, and the boys told not to 'consort' with each other. And Houlihan had never realised he missed such a thing till he'd met Malloy. A shared sense of humour, interest in racing, Malloy's past antics in his own private investigations, their workouts, the Bushmills . . . Houlihan realised he missed Malloy a lot and that he felt guilty about that. He knew there was nothing sexual in his feelings, but still, his upbringing, his training, fonts of guilt for many things.

Houlihan sighed and wearily rubbed his face. They called his flight and he walked dejectedly towards the departure gate. He knew he had to do something to regain control of his life.

Loretta picked him up as arranged, opened the car door for him again. 'I think I owe you a cup of tea and another biscuit,' he said.

'Well pass the wine list!' she said.

He smiled. 'I know, it should be a five-course meal at least, prices of taxis being what they are and everything, but I don't want to embarrass you in a restaurant, dropping my cutlery everywhere and oozing on the bread rolls.'

'Oozing?'

'From my blisters.'

She made a face. 'Yeah. Let's make it the tea and biscuits, shall we?'

'Did you get to see Malloy?' he asked.

'Keelor wouldn't see me so I couldn't find out where he was.'

'Why wouldn't he see you?'

'I don't know. His secretary said he'd return my call when he could. When I insisted on having his direct number he was on voicemail. He just didn't return my calls. I need to pay him a visit.'

'I'll call him when we get back,' Houlihan said.

Each lost in their own thoughts, they hardly spoke till they reached the M4. Loretta settled the car at a steady speed then looked at Houlihan.

'How was the trip, anyway?'

'It was okay.'

'Miss Dublin?'

'She was okay too although she told me she's pulling out of the Miss Ireland competition. Fell down the stairs. Broke her eyelashes.'

'Very funny, Mr Houlihan.'

'Then why aren't you laughing?'

'If I start I'll never stop. I guess the question was too personal.'

'Maybe it was. Maybe if I start *I'll* never stop,' he said gloomily.

'And maybe that wouldn't be a bad thing.'

'Chauffeuse and therapist? I've struck lucky here, right enough.'

She glared across at him and he could tell she was angry at the sarcasm. He held a hand up in apology. 'I'm sorry, Loretta.' He sighed heavily and sunk lower in the seat. 'The trip was bad. And right now I don't miss Dublin. My ma's very ill. Has been since I told her I was leaving the priesthood.' He looked across at her. 'I've just kind of assumed that you know my history. Maybe you don't.'

'All I really know about you, Frankie, is that most of the time you're a really nice man. Your sudden sarcastic moments and the times you freeze me out for nothing, I'm still trying to work out.'

He said, 'Do you want to stop for a coffee?'

'At the services?'

'Yes.'

'Okay.'

* * *

245

Loretta carried the tray to the till. Houlihan, hands hurting, felt awkward trying to get cash from his pocket. She put the tray down and got her purse out. 'Thanks,' he said.

'You'll be a millionaire by the time they heal,' she joked.

When they sat down and she unloaded the tray, Houlihan saw that she'd remembered to pick up a straw for him. She put it in his cup. 'Thanks,' he said. He looked at her across the table and continued, 'Ready for a brief history of my life?'

'Will I need my notebook?'

'Only if you want to sell the film rights.'

She smiled. 'Shoot.'

Houlihan drew a deep breath 'I was raised in Dublin, second oldest of six in a staunchly Catholic family. At seventeen I went into Maynooth seminary; at twenty-two I was ordained. I moved to a parish in Gloucester, supposedly a short-term appointment, when I was twenty-six. I was still there three years later when I met Kathy Spencer at Cheltenham races. We fell in love. I left my vocation. When I told my mother I was quitting she lapsed into a deep depression. She's still in it. My family didn't speak to me, with the exception of our Theresa, for almost two years.' He hesitated. Loretta was watching him intently.

He went on. 'Kathy died six months after we married. Now the family thinks the easiest solution all-round is for me to go back to the priesthood. Then Ma will recover and all will be well with the world.' He looked at her. 'I get snotty with you sometimes because I'm still in love with Kathy and I . . . well, I kind of resent how you make me feel at times.'

'How do I make you feel?' She spoke quietly.

Houlihan moved uncomfortably, reached for his coffee. 'Guilty, I suppose.'

'About what?'

'About enjoying your company.'

'I enjoy yours. There doesn't have to be any more than that to it. There's nothing to feel guilty about. You're not being unfaithful.'

He nodded then averted his eyes, looking troubled. 'Anyway, that's it. I owed you that explanation. I'm sorry for being a prat.'

'You're forgiven. I'm sorry for your troubles. You've had a tough time.'

'I wasn't just looking for sympathy you know.'

'And I wasn't offering any. Relax, Frankie, will you?'

He sighed and sat up straight. 'Anyway, listen, I've had an idea that might help you get the man who threw the petrol bomb.'

She raised an inquisitive eyebrow. He continued, 'The press know somebody from the Jockey Club Security Department was with Malloy when it happened. The Lambourn reporter, Ben Dillon, knows it was me. We've got Ben to shut up for now but it won't last. Somebody'll break ranks with it so why don't we tell them it was me and that I saw who threw the bomb.'

Unblinking, she stared at him.

He said, 'Just say I could give a good description.'

'Set yourself up as a decoy?'

He nodded.

She shook her head. 'Bad idea.'

'Why?'

'Because you might get killed.'

'So might Malloy if we don't catch this fella.'

'Malloy's got a round-the-clock guard. Unless Mr Keelor wants to provide the same for you, you'd be far too exposed.'

He shrugged slightly and half-grinned in a way that said, I hear what you're saying but it won't change my mind. Loretta leaned across the table. 'Frankie, listen. Even with twenty-four-seven protection it would be a bad idea. You don't have a clue who this guy is. He could be a professional killer. Everybody lets their guard down at some point. That's why Eddie Malloy's in hospital.'

He gave the shrug again. She said, 'Anyway, if you did organise full protection the decoy stuff would be pointless. Either he'd find a way through it or he'd stay well clear. Nothing achieved.'

'Thanks for the advice, Loretta, but if you don't mind I'll mention it to my boss, get his thoughts.'

'Please yourself,' she said sharply. 'If he's got half a brain he'll tell you the same as I just did.'

Houlihan hadn't expected his proposal to raise so much tension between them but the atmosphere was chilly for the remainder of the journey. Loretta had made it obvious how strongly she felt about the idea. But Houlihan had decided on the flight back that he had to act to get some form of control back. He knew the risks. Knew Loretta was right in all she said. But he felt his life wasn't worth much any more. He'd tried to chide himself for gross self-sympathy but it hadn't changed the way he felt. Since leaving the priesthood he'd watched his life unravel strand by strand. Helplessly. That was the word he repeated to himself: Helplessly. And he could see nothing in the future that would stop the unravelling. So by doing this he could take charge. It might end in death but he would have driven it that way. His decision. It might save Malloy. If the worst happened, at least it would free Ma and the family and Houlihan would finally find peace.

When they reached the cottage, the tension seemed to ease slightly. Loretta busied herself making tea and Houlihan, watching her at the sink, opening the cupboards, getting more familiar with where he kept things, found it strange but not entirely disagreeable. He convinced himself that any relationship he developed with her would be platonic, and so long as she understood this he could let himself be more comfortable with her. He realised as he watched her that he wanted that, so he blurted out, 'Loretta, I want you to know just now that I don't want any sort of romantic relationship with you. Or with anyone else.'

She didn't flinch or stop her drinks preparation or even turn to look at him. She just said, 'Are you thinking aloud, Mr Houlihan, or is it just your ego grown too big?'

He blushed, suddenly glad her back was to him. He said, 'I'm sorry. That just came out. It was in my mind when I was watching you.'

She poured the boiling water into mugs. 'And what else was in your mind that led to that?'

'I don't know. I just feel I've not been very fair with you because I was, well, kind of afraid of you, I suppose.'

She brought the mugs to the table, went back for his straw then sat down and sipped coffee. 'Why?' She asked.

He looked at her eyes then, feeling awkward, stared down at his drink. 'It's stupid. It's me, my fault, not yours.'

'Afraid that we might end up in some sort of relationship?' She asked.

Frankie reddened. 'I'm sorry, I'm just trying to kind of help explain what I blurted out a few minutes ago.'

'You don't need to explain. You don't owe me anything. You be you and I'll be me. You don't owe anybody anything, Frankie.'

She held his gaze again and he realised that Loretta Moran instinctively knew a lot about him and his feelings.

He didn't explain anything. They sat for quite a long while in comfortable silence, sipping coffee. Eventually he said, 'You've ferried me around, at dawn and dusk, and I haven't even asked where you live. How far have you to travel home?'

'Guildford.'

'That's miles away.'

'Sixty-seven'

'Not a great route, it could take you an hour and a half.'

'I'm used to it.'

'You're welcome to stay in my spare room.'

'Sorry, I only stay in guest rooms. *Spare* rooms is for students and dossers and I was brought-up proper I was.'

'I have a guest room too.' Frankie said, smiling at her mock 'common' accent.

She pondered for a while then said, 'I suppose it would mean me making the breakfast?'

''Twould.'

'And having to go shopping early for a tooth-brush and clean knickers.'

'I have a guest toothbrush too. Only used twice.'

'Guest knickers?'

'What would you think of me if I had?'

'I'd think you'd been in the boy scouts.'

'No guest knickers.'

'Ah well, two out of three ain't bad. And it would be handy if I stayed because I want you to think very seriously about this decoy stuff. It's a crap idea, Frankie – for you that is. Maybe good for the police and the Jockey Club and Makalu but there's nothing in it for Frankie Houlihan. Sleep on it and see how you feel in the morning, please.'

'I won't change my mind, Loretta.'

'Never say never, Frankie.'

'You're full of advice tonight.' He smiled.

'Please think about what you're risking. I'm serious.'

'I thought about it a lot on the way back from Dublin. I don't need to think any more.'

They lay in silence in the dark, separated by a wall. As Houlihan had stated his case so plainly earlier he felt no guilt about Loretta sleeping under his roof. Kathy would understand. Thoughts of Kathy and Ma and the family, of a murderer on his tail, of the terribly scarred Eddie Malloy, all fought for space in his mind.

Loretta called out, 'Frankie?'

It made him hold his breath. 'Yes?'

'You know when I said earlier that you don't owe anybody anything?'

'I do.'

'That includes Eddie Malloy and your mother and your family. And Kathy.'

He felt thrown, touched by her perceptiveness and empathy, slightly and incomprehensibly angry at her speaking Kathy's name. 'I know,' he said.

'Goodnight,' she replied.

'Goodnight.'

TWENTY-ONE

Bobby Cranfield didn't like the decoy idea. Sam Hooper loved it. Keelor said he 'welcomed' it and volunteered to fund it so long as there remained a chance of the 'project' being successful. Loretta didn't have to translate this for Houlihan to know it meant that any protection would need to have enough gaps to let the attacker feel he had a chance of getting to Houlihan. Bobby Cranfield invited him to dinner and tried to talk him out of it. Houlihan wouldn't be swayed. Keelor didn't have time to meet him, but, through his connections, set up and paid for some 'survival' training for Houlihan.

He went to a place in Wiltshire. He'd been told it was a police training establishment but Houlihan concluded it was some sort of MI6 outfit, although the people there, and the police, of course denied it.

He learned how to 'prime' the entry points in his house and car when leaving them so that when he returned he could tell at a glance if a door or window had been opened. He was taught enough about the underside of a vehicle (and the best points for attaching explosives) to get a job as a car fitter. They gave him infrared glasses, short and long range, and an 'always on' micro-transmitter through which help could be summoned from a full-time 'support group' within minutes. That support group would be unarmed. The police had refused to get involved in anything other than the training. Keelor was paying a private company to 'support Houlihan at a distance.' The gaps, Houlihan realised, were going to be bigger than he'd thought, and he began regretting his impulsive behaviour in volunteering. The architect of his own doom, doubts flooded in now, bringing fear and self-recrimination.

While Houlihan was away, Ben Dillon, despite hearing Houlihan's recorded voice saying he was unable to return calls for a week, left frantic messages on his mobile pleading for an interview. Keelor brought in one of his American team, a man called Jack Keane, to hold the fort while he returned to New York on Makalu business. When Loretta turned up at Keelor's office he wasn't there, and Keane said he knew nothing of the whereabouts of Eddie Malloy. She drove straight to the hospital Malloy had been moved from and when she left there she called Houlihan. 'I found out where Malloy was taken to. Do you want to meet me there?'

*   *   *

Loretta was waiting on the granite steps outside the private hospital. Houlihan was surprised to find himself smiling as he approached her. She was smiling too. He was happier to see her again than he'd expected.

'Hi,' he said.

'Hi to you too. How're the hands?'

He held them out. 'Much better.'

She offered her right hand. 'Shake then. It's good to see you again.' They shook hands then went inside. Loretta badged the receptionist. 'I'm Detective Sergeant Moran from the Metropolitan Police. You have a patient, Mr Edward Malloy. I want to see him.'

The receptionist smiled falsely and said, 'Just one moment please, Detective Sergeant.' She tapped something on her keyboard. Loretta and Houlihan watched her eyes scan down the screen. She said, 'Mr Penrose should be able to help you. Would you mind just taking a seat for a moment?'

'Mr Penrose?' asked Loretta.

'Mr Penrose is a consultant. I've just paged him. He shouldn't keep you long.' The false smile again. Loretta and Houlihan moved away towards the window. The receptionist watched till she judged them out of hearing range and scowled as she said to two women working at desks behind her, 'Cow. Bet she's flashed more than that badge to get where she is.'

Mr Penrose arrived five minutes later, smiling pleasantly as he introduced himself and invited

Houlihan and Loretta into a small office. He didn't ask them to sit down. He turned to Houlihan. 'What can I do for you, Detective Sergeant?'

Houlihan pointed to Loretta. 'This is DS Moran,' he said.

Penrose made a half-turn to face her. 'I am sorry,' he said, not looking remotely as though he was.

Loretta looked sternly at him. 'We'd like to see Mr Edward Malloy.'

Penrose said, 'Not a name that rings a bell, I'm afraid.'

'It doesn't need to ring any bells. Is he here?'

'I'm sure you understand the importance of patient confidentiality, Detective Sergeant.'

'And I'm sure you understand the importance of not obstructing the police in an attempted murder investigation, Mr Penrose.'

Penrose looked at her for a few moments. Houlihan watched him weighing things up. Penrose said, 'We're a private hospital, as you know. Sometimes those commissioning us to look after patients attach certain conditions to that care. Who was it that led you to believe Mr Malloy is in this hospital?'

'One of the paramedics who picked Mr Malloy up at Guy's on February eleventh told a porter this was the delivery address.'

Penrose considered again. 'Paramedics are often under considerable pressure. They can get confused.'

Loretta sighed in exasperation. 'Look, Mr Penrose, you're doing a great job for your client here and I don't blame you for that. We know that Vaughn Keelor is probably paying you a lot of money. We know Eddie Malloy has a round-the-clock guard. We know and understand and even agree that it's very sensible to keep all this a secret. What we don't know is how ill he is and what the prognosis is. I need to speak to him as soon as possible to progress this inquiry. Now, which room is he in?'

Penrose stepped away and turned, took a few paces towards the desk in the middle of the office. He said, 'Mr Malloy is still very seriously ill. He drifts in and out of consciousness and when he is conscious he cannot speak. Apart from his burn injuries he's suffering from post-traumatic shock.'

'Can't talk, or won't?' asked Loretta.

'I'm still assessing that.'

Houlihan spoke. 'Is that likely to be permanent, the not speaking?'

'It's hard to say. It's almost certainly caused by the massive shock but we can't say what the long-term prognosis might be until we can better examine him. He is still far too physically debilitated for us to concentrate on anything other than the main injuries to his skin.'

'But he'll recover? There won't be a relapse now?' Houlihan asked.

'How much mobility he'll regain is questionable and his quality of life may never get very high on the graph, but he should continue to improve to the point where we can safely conclude he's no longer in danger of dying from his injuries.'

'So that's a yes, then?' Loretta asked, frustration obvious to Houlihan but not to Mr Penrose by the look on his face.

'A guarded yes,' he said.

'Would he be able to respond in some way to any questions I put to him. A simple "yes" or "no" code? Or could he write something?'

Houlihan watched Penrose's jaw muscles clench. 'Detective Sergeant, to question Mr Malloy about the incident that caused his injuries could do irreparable psychological or emotional damage. It certainly would right now and that may continue to be the case for months or even years ahead. It is likely to be many weeks before Mr Malloy is fit to see anyone at all, let alone someone who'll be asking him to revisit such a huge trauma. You have your job to do and, as you said, I have mine. Mr Malloy is not fit to see you or anyone else. When he is, I'll be delighted to have someone call you.'

Defiantly, Loretta turned to Houlihan. 'Do you want to look in on him, even though we can't talk to him?'

Houlihan thought about it and a flashback to the burning hair, singed eyebrows and charred skin as he'd tried to help him that day filled his mind. 'Maybe next time,' he said.

Houlihan and Loretta went to a coffee shop across from the hospital. Houlihan bought the drinks and two chocolate muffins. Loretta nibbled hers. 'What next?' she asked.

Houlihan shrugged. He'd felt almost redundant so far in this investigation. While Loretta was a professional, he considered himself an amateur. He wondered if that was one of the reasons behind his volunteering as a decoy. What was he trying to prove? 'I don't know.'

'Do you think Keelor will move Malloy now?' she asked.

'Depends. There can't be that many private hospitals specialising in third-degree burns. And if Penrose is telling the truth about Malloy being maybe months away from being able to tell us anything, does it matter where he gets treatment?'

'That's the question: Is he telling the truth?'

Houlihan shrugged again, stirred his coffee. He said, 'It's not going to be easy getting a second opinion.'

'You think we should take Malloy out of the picture as a witness?'

'It's hard for me to say, Loretta. I don't think he saw this fella, but he might have done. Maybe he saw something in the mirror before the bomb came through, but it's a long shot, isn't it? I think that all we can do is get the decoy story released and see what comes out of the woodwork. I'm going to Dublin on Thursday to tell the family what's happening. I don't want them to see it in the papers. And I also need to let them decide whether to tell Ma or not. I'll be back on Friday and Bobby's agreed to break the story then. I'm giving it to Ben Dillon. I promised him.'

She cradled the warm mug and looked at him. 'Why don't you give it a week? Maybe we can get a lead from the list of these people in RACE. We ought to go back through that.'

'Over two hundred names? Do you really think the attacker would have subscribed to Bert Jacobsen's scheme if he planned to murder someone?'

She narrowed her eyes and frowned. Houlihan raised a defensive hand. 'Loretta, I'm not trying to be smart, honest. I know the list is pretty much all we've got at the moment, but, honestly, come on?'

'It's a fair point but there's no way of knowing the state of mind of whoever did this. You're making the assumption he's cool and had it all worked out. Maybe it's just somebody who blew their top. We need to check it out properly.'

'What about Bonnaventure? He's got the motive and the money to pay for the job.'

'That's one of the things I wanted to ask Keelor about. He said he would try and find out. I need to see him.'

Back at home, Houlihan phoned Thomas, who answered sounding short of breath.

'Been out your bike training for that round-the-world ride?' Houlihan asked.

'Well, funnily enough I have. Just did thirty miles chain-ganging with the boys.'

'Chain-ganging?'

'Riding right behind each other. Minimises wind resistance and aggravates drivers.'

'For thirty miles? On a winter's night around Dublin? Are you mad?'

'Probably, but it's a good kind of mad. I feel great. Very alive.'

'If very knackered.'

'Pulse'll be back to normal in a minute.'

'Want to get a shower and I'll call you back in twenty minutes?'

'Shower's broke and we've no hot water anyway.'

Houlihan remembered that Thomas shared a flat with some students and all of them were eternally skint. He had money enough to help his brother, even allowing for the soaring property prices in Dublin, but he didn't know how to broach it with him. Since his return at Christmas he'd felt closer to Thomas than any of the others for some reason, even Theresa. Thomas had changed so much from the kid Houlihan remembered and he found himself wishing he'd spent more time with him when he was young. Thomas had always looked up to him, always had dreams. Houlihan liked people with dreams.

And Houlihan knew that part of Thomas's blooming had been getting away from the house, away from Ma. He hadn't much to live on but he thrived on the independence. Houlihan didn't want to risk damaging his growth or their relationship by offering to buy him a place of his own.

'So how's Ma been?' he asked.

'Ah, about the same really. Still in bed most days. Maybe she'll pick up a bit when spring comes.'

'I feel I should get back over and see her, though I don't know what way to approach things now. I think I did more damage than good last time.'

'She's over that, Frankie. I wouldn't dwell on it. There'd have been a bit of the drama queen about that episode, I'm sure.'

'I want to come back, Thomas. I feel I need to do something now to try and help her.'

'Have you a particular thing in mind? I'm not trying to be funny, Frankie, but maybe it would be helpful if we all met up again and tried to knock a few ideas around. It should be easier. We can just hear what everybody's got to say and try and come up with something?'

'You're just too sensible and well-balanced for your age, our Thomas. And diplomatic with it. I think it's a good idea.'

'Grand. That's great!'

'Would you speak to the others and give me a call? I can come over on Thursday if that suits.'

'I'm sure that'd be fine. I'll check with the others, though. Oh, how're your hands? Sorry, I should have asked.'

'They're fine now, no problems.'

'And did they catch the fella that threw the bomb?'

'Not yet. But they've got plans. That's one thing I want to talk to you all about.'

TWENTY-TWO

Thomas met him at the airport. They hugged, clapped each other's backs.

In the car, Thomas beamed. 'It's good to have you back again,' he said. 'It almost seems like you're back home and you just go away to work. You seem to be here every couple of weeks.'

'It feels good to be back. The city seems to be getting more familiar again, more comfortable; like it's beginning to fit me again.'

'And how do you feel about seeing the family so much?'

'How does the family feel about seeing me?'

Thomas smiled across at him as they trundled along in bad visibility caused by spray from the passing traffic. 'Well, Margaret's warming to the idea. Our Pat's a bit scared of you . . .'

'Scared! Why?'

'I think he was always in awe of you after your ordination, felt it distanced him. Maybe it was because Ma made us all call you Father Frankie.'

'You know I never wanted that.'

'No matter. No big deal.'

'And I never saw our Pat as being in awe of me. I thought there was some sort of resentment there and never knew why. No reason for awe, for goodness' sake!'

'I know, I know. It was just his way of handling everything. I think that as the oldest boy it maybe came as a relief when you decided to go to Maynooth. It lifted some sort of burden from him. He may have felt some obligation to do what you did for Ma's sake. But relief can sometimes cause a bit of guilt as well in those situations, and maybe you're right, Frankie, maybe there was a little bit of resentment caused by the guilt. I'm not saying it would be intentional, not from our Pat. I'm sure it wouldn't.'

Houlihan considered for a few seconds. 'Have you and Pat spoken about this?'

'Not in any detail. Only on the basis of how you were and how badly things had turned out for all of us as a family. No, it's just my own theory with Pat.'

Houlihan nodded. His little brother was a deep thinker, and, he was beginning to realise, a fairly shrewd judge of people. He said, 'Do you see much of Pat and the others? You know, when I'm not here?'

'Ah, often enough. We try to make an effort. We're all at Ma's at least once a week so we bump into each other there. I see more of Cornelius with

264

him being closer to me in age and us growing up together. We play snooker once a week and sometimes he asks me onto his pub quiz team. If he's really short of brains.'

Houlihan smiled. 'What is it, a weekly quiz?'

''Tis. In Rafferty's. Rafferty gives prizes of books or tickets to the theatre. Says his time on earth is dedicated to the eradication of philistinism in the Dublin male.'

Houlihan laughed.

Thomas said, 'It's not even as if the winners get to choose what book or play they've to see. Rafferty decides what's best for them and the following week they need to be able to give him a run-down of the plot of whatever they've had, and if they can't, sure they're barred until they can.'

'From the quiz?'

'From the bloody pub!'

'So he hasn't many customers left?'

'Aye, he has plenty. For smart as he is with the literature, he hasn't the brains to realise that Conor McQuillan sells a synopsis of all the plots for the price of a pint, and what Conor knows about literature you could write on a beer mat. He gets the answers from the Internet.'

'It sounds good fun.'

'It's a rare laugh, so it is! You should come down. We've one tomorrow night.'

'I might just do that.'

'Ah, good.'

They travelled in comfortable silence for a while

then Houlihan said, 'D'ye think our Pat would join us? We could enter a team of our own?'

Thomas smiled across at him. 'I think Pat would like that very much. The Houlihan brothers. Out on the town. Long time since that's been done.'

It had never been done. Houlihan had been in Maynooth before he was of legal age to drink. This would be a first. Whether Thomas realised that, Houlihan didn't know, but there was a contented smile on his face and he let it be at that.

As dinner at Margaret's house progressed, things got steadily easier and warmer among the Houlihans. This icebound family started to thaw, to reverse the drift apart that had affected all of them in the past couple of years. Talk, as it had done on Houlihan's previous visits, inevitably turned to the time when they'd been kids. Houlihan knew they couldn't keep harking back to the past forever but it was a useful crutch for all of them as the wounds healed; maybe an essential one.

All their childhoods had been happy ones. Da had been alive and well. Ma had been strict and tough at times but she'd managed to laugh often enough, although, when the boys heard the stories from Margaret and Theresa, most of the laughs had been in the company of women and at the expense of men.

They all agreed that the real change in Ma had come when Houlihan took an interest in becoming a priest. It transformed her hopes and prayers into fierce ambition, then even fiercer pride after his ordination. It changed everything for all of them.

But they ventured back onto happier ground with more memories relived, and Houlihan felt they could be forgiven these trips back over the years; they made everyone forget the rifts and the sorrow that had come afterwards. And sitting laughing at the table, comfortable with his brothers and sisters for the first time in years, Houlihan began wondering if volunteering as a decoy, the news he'd really come to break to them, had been a wise decision.

As they sipped coffee from Margaret's best cups, she brought everyone back to the present by asking Houlihan what he thought was the best move now with Ma. Houlihan had seen Margaret as wanting to take over the matriarchal mantle from Ma, to be the boss. But now he was beginning to realise she was just trying to be practical, to bring some sort of focus, to try and get a resolution. He wasn't so sure any more that she actually enjoyed the role.

Houlihan said, 'I don't know, Margaret, I really don't. You tell me she's still very much up and down with her health. I know how upset she got with me last time and I think it set her back a lot.'

Theresa nodded agreement, which surprised everyone. She'd always been his staunchest supporter but she was also the only one who saw Ma every day, saw what the real effect had been of his last visit. Her nod of confirmation had been a natural unconscious expression of her feelings and she was innocent enough to feel no embarrassment over it.

No one else commented on what he'd said. He went on, 'I really don't know what to do next. I'm happy to go and see her again. I'm even willing to bite my tongue if she starts slagging Kathy off, though it grieves me, I can tell you. I'll sit quietly and let her get it all out, all the bitterness that's built up over the years, if you think it'll do any good.'

Nobody responded. Then Cornelius spoke. 'Can I offer an idea?'

They all looked at him. He said, 'Frankie, why don't you ask Archbishop Mahoney to go and see her?'

Now they all stared at Cornelius. 'Why?' Margaret asked.

'Well it seems to me that Ma can't talk to Frankie nor listen to what he has to say because she thinks he committed such a terrible sin. If someone like the Archbishop were to tell her that Frankie's still a good man and has been forgiven for everything, then surely she'd start to see things different?'

Margaret shrugged slightly and raised her eyebrows as if considering the possibility. Thomas nodded, as though agreeing. Pat linked his fingers, looked at them, then looked at Houlihan with what seemed to be mild expectation. Theresa smiled widely and said, 'What a great idea, Cornelius!'

Houlihan bowed his head and wondered if he could make himself face this great man who'd been so kind and understanding when he'd come to say he was betraying him and the Church. This holy man who he'd never expected to have to face again. Would he be able to ask him now to come and try to help repair the damage he had done to his own mother?

The brothers met in Rafferty's for the quiz night. The place was packed. Cornelius had volunteered to turn up an hour before his brothers and secure a table and he looked very glad when Houlihan appeared. 'Thank God you've arrived, Frankie. Keepin' three seats for yous has been a bloody nightmare. One of yous can do it next time.'

Houlihan smiled. 'I will.'

Thomas and Pat came in within two minutes of each other and they all argued about who was to buy the first drink. Houlihan won and as he battled to the bar for the beer he found himself smiling, feeling a strange contentment, maybe even happiness. He'd never imagined he'd actually be happy again after Kathy died. He let the emotion flow through him.

It was being among family again, among Dubliners on a night out, in a place where the anticipation was almost tangible and there was laughing and joking. A bunch of silly men taking joy from the thought of a simple quiz night. There were few women. Those that were there seemed much less excited about winning a book or a night out at a play. It must be a man thing, thought

Houlihan. Maybe the competitive element. Perhaps just a chance for some good-natured ribbing. Whatever it was, it affected him, made him wonder why he spent so much time on his own, shutting out the possibility of anything other than arm's-length business relationships.

This smoky pub, noisy with the buzz of conversation, the bar area too warm, even on a winter's night, from the huge fire in the grate and the closeness of bodies; this air of expectation . . . he glanced back as he queued, at his brothers, heads together, talking, laughing, waiting for the Guinness. This, thought Houlihan, was life.

Houlihan flew back across the Irish Sea nursing a hangover. He couldn't recall who'd won the quiz, though he knew they certainly had not. Some of the microphone-brandishing Rafferty's ravings from the bar came back to him, as did the laughter among the brothers, the seemingly endless row of black pints, the vague recollection of getting into (but not out of) a taxi. And that was it.

Then he remembered with some embarrassment that he'd kept Thomas up for ages as he'd talked about Kathy and love and how important it was for his brother to find a woman so he could experience what Houlihan had experienced. He moaned softly at the thought and rubbed his eyes.

They'd stayed at Pat's and the others had been in bed when he'd left for this early flight. He'd managed to scribble a note telling them how great it had been and, despite the hangover, that feeling of warmth and belonging was still with him. He was glad of that. It took away a fair bit of the trepidation he felt at the thought of returning in just over a week for his appointment with Archbishop Mahoney.

As he drove home from the airport, Houlihan wondered how he could delay the decoy announcement another week. When Cornelius had raised the idea about the Archbishop, Houlihan had known he couldn't tell the family about his decision to be a decoy. It would have seemed selfish rather than courageous, even though he'd been planning to make out that it was no big deal really and that more than adequate protection would be in place.

He shifted uneasily in his seat as he also faced the increasing feeling that he'd been hasty in deciding to set himself up. Life wasn't as bad as it had seemed when he'd hatched the idea. The contentment, even happiness, of the last twenty-four hours in Dublin had made a big impact on him. And Cornelius's idea was growing on him too; maybe it would be the thing to turn Ma around. As he reached home he also realised that when he'd been with the family he hadn't thought about Kathy anywhere near as often as he normally did. The seed was there now. There may well be life after Kathy. It was a matter of how much he wanted to work at it. He felt he wanted to talk to Loretta, to hear her voice, and he searched for an excuse to ring her.

He showered, washed away the remnants of the hangover, made tea and toast, then called Loretta and asked if she still had the list of those who'd responded to Jacobsen's ad. She did.

'Do you want me to bring it over?' she asked.

'You've done enough running around. I'll meet you somewhere closer to home for you.'

'Okay, sixty-three Meadowville Park, seven tonight.'

'Where's that?'

'It's where I live. Can't get much closer to home than that, can you? I'll even make you a curry.'

'That's good. I'd like that. Can you give me directions?'

Meadowville Park was an exclusive, enclosed development in the countryside south of Guildford. As he drove through the grand pillared entrance he smiled, certain that Loretta had been winding him up. The roads were all block paved, the houses had names like Meadowlands and Larkrise; none that he could see had a number. Mercedes, BMW and Saab were well-represented in the driveways.

He stopped the car and looked around, expecting to see Loretta standing under one of the ornate lampposts, grinning. He waited five minutes but when curtains started twitching it was time to move on. Turning into a cul-de-sac he saw her car parked in a driveway straight ahead, the double gates open behind it. Edging closer, his headlights picked up a big number 63 on the small gate leading to the front door. He pulled in behind Loretta's car and as he got out she opened the front door of the house.

His first question was going to be, 'Is this really yours?' But he realised how chauvinistic he was being so he just said, 'Wow!' She smiled. He surprised himself by kissing her lightly on the cheek.

'Come in,' she said, stepping aside to let him into the hall. The lights were low and coal burned noisily in the big fireplace. 'Sit by the fire,' she instructed.

He could feel the heat as he approached, reminding him suddenly of the night of the fire. 'I'd rather not be toasted,' he said.

'Push it back a bit till you're comfortable.'

He eased the big armchair away then sat down. Loretta settled in the one opposite. She smiled. 'That's Dad's favourite chair,' she said. 'It reclines. Sunday afternoon, after a couple of whiskeys, you can't get him out of it.'

'He must be very proud of you. Having a place like this.'

'He bought it for me,' she said.

Houlihan raised a finger and smiled. 'Never explain, never complain.'

'Well I don't want you to think I'm into graft and corruption, or drug-dealing or something.'

'It never crossed my mind. What does your dad do?'

'Not much any more. He and mum had an ice-cream business. They sold it to one of the big conglomerates for an awful lot of money. *Mama Mia Ice Cream.*'

'Mama Mia! I used to love that when I was a kid! I still see it around.'

'They kept the brand name, that was the big attraction.'

'Mama Mia . . . Mama Mia. Got any?' he asked.

She shook her head. 'Sickened myself on it before I was ten. But I kept the sweet tooth, as you know by now.'

'So didn't your parents want you to go into the business?'

'Mum did. It was her family that started it back in the Forties in Italy and everyone, each generation, was expected to work in the business till they died.' She stood up suddenly, hands by her side as though to attention, and saluted. 'Glad to report, sir, that I was the first to escape!'

He smiled. 'How did she take it, your mum?'

She sat down again. 'Put it this way, I think she'd rather I'd told her I was pregnant to an alien.'

'How is she about it now?'

'Reconciled. So she says. But when you've tried all the old tricks, the horse's head in the bed etc., even Italian mothers need to admit defeat at some point. It got much better once they'd sold the business. Cruising the Caribbean and skiing in Aspen tends to take the edge off life's little daily difficulties.'

'I'm sure it does.'

She looked at him. 'Well at least we have something in common.'

'What's that?'

'Carrying the weight of parental expectation.'

Houlihan nodded, smiling. 'Yes, vanilla and the Vatican.'

'Vestments and investments.'

He chuckled. 'I think we best stop now.'

'Only because you can't think of another one! I'll get you a drink then, shall I? I've got some nice malt whiskey.'

'Thanks. I prefer blends, if you have any – Bells in particular.'

'Bells I have loads of. That's my dad's favourite. He'll be . . .' She got up without finishing it.

'He'll be what?'

'Nothing.'

'Pleased that I like it too?' he said as she walked towards the kitchen.

He could almost sense her reddening as he heard her open the fridge. She pretended she hadn't heard. 'Ice?' she called back.

'Yes please.'

'Are you hungry just now?' she asked, still out of his sight.

'Are you?'

'That means you are. Curry okay?'

'It's fine. Should be an interesting accompaniment to whiskey.'

She came back with the drinks. 'It should.'

* * *

They ate by the fire using lap trays. Afterwards Loretta offered to refill his whiskey glass. She had her hand out. He looked up at her. 'I'm driving.'

'Stay if you like. Plenty of room.'

He hesitated. She said, 'It's not like we're going to get through that list in ten minutes. It'll be midnight at least.'

He drained the glass and, smiling, gave it to her.

A short time later they sat side by side at the dining-room table, Jacobsen's list between them. 'How d'you want to do this?' Loretta asked.

Houlihan said, 'I think we probably need to be a bit more scientific than the first time we tried.'

'Well, you were all het-up back then, thinking I was trying to get you into bed. Now you know I'm not you can concentrate better.'

'So you were the totally cool professional?'

'Of course.'

Smiling, he shook his head slowly.

She smoothed out the list, sipped her drink and said, 'Come on then, Frankie boy, howsabout I call out the names and you give me a brief comment on each. We'll narrow it down through various short lists.'

'What's the criteria?'

'Simple. Could this be the killer or someone who'd hire a killer.'

'That's a tough brief, Loretta. If I gave you a list of a hundred people you know and asked you to do the same, how easy would you find it?'

'Depends on how well I knew them.'

'I don't know any of these people that well.'

She put down her pen and sat back. 'Frankie, we need to start somewhere. This was your idea.'

'I know. I know. I'd be more comfortable doing it first on the basis of how badly it will hit each person if Makalu becomes their employer or has any life-affecting influence.'

'And would you always know what the effect would be?'

'Let's try it and see. If I don't, we can always run this past a few others.'

'Fine.' She picked up her pen. 'Go. Lenny Caraldo.'

'Lenny's a photographer with quite a bit of influence. He covers all the northern courses, a few in the midlands, and he's making inroads with the southern tracks. Racecourse photographers pay no fees for admission or access to their subjects. They retain all the rights to their work and I understand Lenny even charges the racecourses if they want to use any of his shots in promotional literature. If Makalu took the view that they'd want a much more commercial approach on both access and future rights, it would hit Lenny pretty heavily.'

Loretta sat back again, put the pen to her lips and raised her eyebrows questioningly.

Houlihan shrugged, half-frowned apologetically. 'Better leave him in for now.'

She ticked his name and said, 'Did I say midnight? Make that dawn.'

Her estimate wasn't far out: it was after three

a.m. before they finished the process. In the end they were left with seventeen names they considered worth further investigation.

Houlihan lay in the very comfortable guest bed, yawning, tasting the whiskey residue in his mouth, worrying about drinking too frequently these days, but mostly reflecting on the strengthening partnership between him and Loretta. Working through that list tonight she'd probed in the right places when he was rambling on, helped break down some of his wilder speculations and had encouraged him to have confidence in his judgement. She'd done it all supportively and with wit. They worked very well together, almost naturally, as if they'd known each other for years.

Yet he hadn't done what he'd come to do, tell her he was thinking about pulling out as the decoy. He knew he'd just put the moment off. After the third whiskey he'd given himself the excuse that he shouldn't really talk about it in case she thought the doubts were alcohol-induced. He sighed. He'd do it in the morning.

They breakfasted on yogurt and strawberries. Loretta washed up the bowls. Houlihan stood by her side drying them. She said, 'You've been the quiet man this morning. Are you okay?'

He'd been reflecting happily on how pleasant it was to have breakfast again with a woman. Now she'd brought him back to the practicalities of their relationship and what he had come here to tell her.

Houlihan rubbed a spoon dry, polished it. He said, 'I have . . . I was . . . thinking again about this decoy business.'

'Uh-huh?'

'I think you were right when you counselled against it.' He felt her looking at him and he turned to face her. She crossed her arms and leaned against the sink, waiting for more. Houlihan said, 'I'm going to pull out.'

'Good. Good decision.'

He put the spoon in the drawer and laid the towel down. 'I just . . .'

She raised a hand to stop him. 'Never complain, never explain.'

He shrugged and looked awkward. 'This time I think I should.'

'Why?'

'You were the first person I told when I decided to do it so you ought to know why I've changed my mind.'

She considered this, then said, 'If it makes you feel better, go ahead. But you owe me nothing.'

He opened his hands. His face softened as the worry seemed to ease. 'I know, but I think it would help if I could talk to you.'

She gestured towards the chairs. They sat down. Houlihan told her everything, all the details, about Kathy and about his mother, his family. Loretta listened without interrupting. He explained how he'd felt much happier on his most recent visit. 'I think there's hope for all of us now,' he said. 'I didn't feel that way a few weeks ago. And I've been thinking about Eddie. I'd felt very guilty over what happened. It bothered me that I hadn't done more, especially that I'd decided not to try and get the burning gown off him. I think that might have been a mistake.'

Still she listened silently, knowing he wasn't seeking exoneration, he just wanted to talk it out. Houlihan said, 'But even if it was, there's no real saying what the difference would be. And whatever I do to help catch this man, it won't give me the chance to make that decision again. Eddie will be how he'll be. And I know he's well-guarded now. Keelor would never let anything happen to him.' He paused.

Loretta waited a few moments. Houlihan started speaking again. 'Of course, I'll still do everything I can to catch this fella. You know that.'

She nodded. He did too then lowered his eyes. She said quietly, 'I'm sorry for your troubles.' He nodded again, not looking at her. She said, 'Who do you need to tell next?'

'Bobby. I'll go and see him. Then Hooper. That should be good.' He smiled and looked up.

Loretta said, 'Don't worry about him. You're worth ten Hoopers.' She blushed at the implications of what she'd said, then got up quickly and finished putting the dishes away.

Fifteen minutes later, Loretta walked Houlihan to his car. She said, 'So you'll speak to Geoff Stonebanks about our list today?'

'I'll ring you as soon as I've spoken to him. He should be able to help chop one or two more off.'

'Is it worth asking him to look at the full list? He might be able to add some too.'

'Probably is. I'll let him see it.'

'Good.'

They stood looking at each other. Houlihan glanced around at all the big houses. 'I'd better go before the neighbours start talking.'

She smiled. 'You'd better.'

'Thanks for the meal and the whiskey, and the help with the list, and the sympathetic ear.'

She folded her arms. 'What about the bed for the night?'

He smiled. 'Thanks for that too. Very comfortable.'

He noticed the big number 63 on the gate and looked around again at the other houses. 'You're the only one with a house number,' he said.

She smiled. 'I only do it to annoy all the snobs with fancy names on theirs.'

'You really know how to lower the tone, don't you?'

'I'm an expert.'

'See you later.'

'See you.'

Houlihan looked in the mirror as he drove away and was childishly pleased to see her waving. Once out of sight, he pulled over and dialled Bobby Cranfield's number.

TWENTY-THREE

Cranfield seemed almost as relieved as Loretta had been when Houlihan told him he was dumping the decoy idea. He also offered to call Hooper and tell him the news. Houlihan declined. He knew he'd have to face his boss on it sooner or later.

The next morning, Hooper was on the phone when Houlihan arrived at his office and waved him away from his door in irritation. Houlihan spent ten minutes drinking coffee and chatting to Elaine on reception then Hooper shouted Houlihan's name from his office – not through being too lazy to get up but just to remind him and everyone else who was boss. Elaine's eyebrows must have risen a clear inch. Houlihan smiled at her. 'I didn't know you could do that,' he said.

As he walked along the corridor he braced himself, holding on to the thought that he didn't need this job. Didn't need any job. A privilege millions of downtrodden employees prayed for every time they handed over a lotto slip. He loved working in racing but not at all costs. Hooper wasn't going to treat him like something scraped off his shoe.

'How're you doing?' Houlihan asked as he closed the door behind him.

Hooper sat back in the big leather swivel chair, crossing his hands in his lap. 'I'll be doing better once you've outed yourself, Houlihan. When's it going to be?'

Houlihan settled in the chair facing Hooper. 'That's what I wanted to talk to you about, Sam.' He cleared his throat and saw Hooper's eyes darken as he read the sign of nervousness. Hooper said, 'Cold feet aren't welcome in my department. Don't tell me you're having second thoughts.'

'I've had second, third and fourth thoughts over the past few days. I'd like to say it's been a tough decision but it hasn't really. I'm sorry, Sam.'

Hooper sat forward quickly, frowning. 'What's the problem?'

'My circumstances have changed. I've got some serious family commitments.'

'That you didn't know about a couple of weeks ago? Come on, Houlihan!'

Houlihan shrugged. 'They took an unexpected turn.'

'Don't just shrug your shoulders and tell me that! We're supposed to be a professional organisation. We don't run on the whims of employees.'

'It wasn't a whim. I'm not going to get into a big argument with you, but it wasn't a whim.'

'Bollocks!'

Houlihan stared defiantly at Hooper who said, 'You're getting protection. You've had five grand's worth of training. The exposure on this is minimal for you. How come you're so scared now?'

'I'm not scared. It's not to do with me. Whatever happens, happens, but there are others I need to take into consideration now.'

Hooper sat back, shaking his head. He took a pen from his shirt pocket and twirled it between his fingers. He said, 'So what's her name?'

Houlihan looked baffled. 'Who?'

'The new woman?'

Houlihan reddened with anger and sat forward. 'There's no new woman and you are out of order!'

Hooper smiled falsely. 'It won't last, you know. Is she worth more than your friend Malloy? How are you going to feel if this guy catches up with him?'

Houlihan fought to control his anger. He could see Hooper was feeding on it. Slowly he sat back in the chair. Calmly he said, 'Tell me when you want to talk about getting on with the case.'

'We were getting on with the case till you crapped out.'

Houlihan said, 'I've got the list of people who responded to Bert Jacobsen's ad. They need to be interviewed.'

Hooper stared at him for a few seconds then said, 'Police job.'

'They haven't got the resources.'

Hooper sighed heavily. 'Oh dear! They're short

of resources. You're short of bottle. What *are* we going to do?' and he raised his hands theatrically.

Houlihan got up. 'I know what I'm going to do. I'll make a start on the interviews. When you've decided we can talk about this at an adult level, let me know.' He turned and opened the door.

Hooper called after him, 'That's it, do what you've always done when you can't hack it. Just run away.'

Houlihan slammed the door so hard he heard something fall to the floor in Hooper's office.

'Houlihan!' Houlihan ignored the call, then he heard the door open behind him. 'Houlihan!' He stopped and turned. Hooper was standing in the corridor.

Houlihan said, 'Hooper?'

His boss glared at him. '*Mr* Hooper to you!'

'You'll get Mr Hooper when I get Mr Houlihan,' he replied coolly and watched Hooper trying to compose himself as he sensed the activities of others out of sight in offices go quiet.

Hooper said, 'I need to see the list you mentioned. Come back in for a minute.'

Houlihan didn't move. Hooper finally and very grudgingly said, 'Would you come back into my office please?' Houlihan smiled and walked towards him.

Houlihan drove home, went for a run, showered, changed, and walked to Geoff Stonebanks' house.

He knocked and went in, in response to Stone-banks' shout, and found the big man on the phone, desk piled with papers, as messy as he'd ever seen it. Stonebanks' mobile rang and Houlihan shook his head as he watched him root around for it while still trying to continue his conversation on the landline. Houlihan spotted the mobile on the floor beneath the desk. He picked it up and answered it, taking a message.

Stonebanks finished his call and slowly put the phone down. He looked at Houlihan and said, 'Cavalry's always welcome. I didn't hear the bugles.'

'I fitted them with silencers,' Houlihan said.

'Ahh, that'll be the reason then.'

Houlihan smiled. Stonebanks said, 'Take a chair. If you can find one.'

Houlihan moved three box-files and a briefcase and sat down. 'Extra workload not causing you any problems then?' he asked.

'Not at all, young man.' He gestured at the mess surrounding him. 'Perfectly organised, as you can see.'

Still smiling but bothered at what his friend had been left with, Houlihan said, 'This isn't working, is it?'

Stonebanks stood up. Houlihan saw he'd put on more weight over the past few weeks. Stonebanks said, 'Now that depends on your point of view. I'm making all the calls I should be and writing up the stuff I need to. I'm just not getting anything important done. I've not been out for so long that a posse from the pensioners' home up the road broke my door down this morning to check I was okay.'

Houlihan got up. 'Let me make you a cup of coffee and see if we can sort things out.'

Over the hot drink they discussed Stonebanks' workload. Houlihan was feeling guilty. Hooper had forced Stonebanks to take on Houlihan's stuff and Houlihan felt he himself had been doing practically nothing. He could volunteer to take his caseload back but he knew Hooper wouldn't be dictated to. Stonebanks said he could handle things if someone could take over the bit he hated, all the admin.

Houlihan called Bobby Cranfield.

Cranfield said, 'I hear Hooper was his predictable self when you saw him?'

'He called you?'

'Of course. Had to bitch to somebody about it. Don't worry. You did the right thing. He'll calm down eventually.'

Houlihan told him about Geoff Stonebanks. 'He needs some help, Bobby. I know the work's too sensitive to get a temp in but we need to do something, he's swamped.'

'Give me half an hour. I'll call you back.'

While they waited Houlihan showed Stonebanks Jacobsen's list. Stonebanks mumbled his way through it with a series of 'Nos', 'Nevers', 'Doubt its', and 'Possibles'.

'Harry Shaw will be worth a visit,' he said. 'He

was real tough guy when he was riding and he's got a fair business to protect now.'

'Okay.' Shaw ran a big jockey's valet business in the midlands and south.

Stonebanks put a cross against a name. 'Lenny Caraldo. Met him once. Did not like him at all. Something about him.'

Very scientific and objective, Houlihan thought. But Caraldo was the first name he'd mentioned to Loretta when he saw the list, so Stonebanks' observation was interesting. 'Anyone else?'

'Not for now. Leave me a copy, will you, and I'll sound out a few others.'

Bobby Cranfield called back and spoke to Stonebanks. 'Ship all your stuff into the office as soon as you can, right down to the last paperclip and staple. You've got Belinda full-time to do all your stuff until Houlihan's back on the job.'

'Belinda! The dominatrix?'

'You wish,' Cranfield laughed. 'Let me know if you need anything else. But don't tell Hooper we're talking direct.'

'No problem. Thanks.'

Stonebanks put the phone down and turned to Houlihan looking slightly stunned. 'He got me Belinda.'

'So I heard. If she can't sort you out, nobody can.'

Houlihan walked home. The sky was darkening, the wind getting up, but he felt better now that

Geoff Stonebanks had some help. It was another thing crossed off his 'to do' list. The hardest task on that list was coming up the next day: his meeting with the Archbishop. Despite all the recent hassle, the meeting had never been far from his mind. It loomed large now, stirring dread. He looked at the grey clouds. Heavy storms were forecast for the weekend. Maybe, thought Houlihan hopefully, the plane would crash.

By the time he got into bed that night the meeting was coming at him like a train in a tunnel and he couldn't find a way to avoid it. Over a simple supper of soup he'd considered calling Loretta back. They'd spoken earlier about the list, Stonebanks' comments, and what had happened with Hooper. And here he was an hour later, wanting to tell her how afraid he was, feeling the need for some comfort from her, some strength for tomorrow from this woman who seemed to understand him so well. But it wouldn't have been right, for the sake of the case and for Kathy's memory. He left the phone in the cradle.

TWENTY-FOUR

The flight was punctual and smooth. Houlihan looked out at the blue sky above the winter clouds and wished he was flying away somewhere warm and free of meetings and mothers. He'd had no holiday since the honeymoon, when they'd gone halfway round the world in a cocoon of love. Not only had they loved each other but they'd been deeply in love in that way when nothing else matters. They'd spent many weeks travelling, staying in luxury hotels then in a tent in the North American wilderness.

He'd been a penniless ex-priest at the time but Kathy's success had meant they had no money worries. It had been the happiest time of his life by far, and one of the reasons he was disinclined to go abroad again now that Kathy wouldn't be there by his side.

Still, he wouldn't have minded one day in the sun away from the cold and damp.

* * *

Walking down Clonliffe Road his mind went back to the last time he was there, a year past in November. Archbishop Mahoney had greeted him warmly at the door. He recalled the smell of soap on the old man's skin and the terrible thought of being a Judas. The Archbishop had taken a great interest in his vocation since he'd been eighteen, encouraged him all the way. It was he who'd ordained him and had said to him that day, 'You will be one of the great priests.'

Houlihan stopped to look up at the cathedral then forced his feet off the pavement to cross the road and go through the gate and down the path to the big oak door with the black metal crucifix. As he raised his hand to the door-knocker, he took some strength from the memory of the Archbishop's kindness that day when finally, after telling him he was deserting the church, Houlihan had wept with guilt and sorrow and relief. The Archbishop had stroked his hair, comforting him as though he had been his child.

Like the last time, the old man opened the door himself and, if anything, his smile was even warmer. That gave Houlihan heart. 'Francis! You look wonderful. It must be that good English country air!' He put his arms around him and hugged him, patting his back gently. When he let him go and faced him again Houlihan replied, 'The Dublin air smells fresher, Your Grace.'

'Ah, you know the right things to say still, Francis. Come in. Maureen has the kettle on.'

He led him to a different room from the one they'd met in last time and Houlihan was grateful for that. They settled in comfortable chairs and the smells of cold stone and old varnish, of aged cavernous buildings that Houlihan's nostrils had collected on the walk through the passageways, settled pleasantly in his head.

Maureen brought the tea and left them alone. The Archbishop said, 'Before you tell me all your news, Francis, I'd like to say how terribly saddened I was to hear of the death of your wife. It must have been the hardest, hardest blow for you.'

'It was, Your Grace.'

'And how have you been since then?'

Houlihan shrugged, uncomfortable now. He so badly wanted to pour out all his thoughts and feelings, bring forth the demons, ask the advice of this man he loved and respected. He wanted to tell him of all the guilt and how he'd deprived himself of the solace of prayer and of mass. But he couldn't. He didn't deserve the comfort he'd get from telling, from the Archbishop listening.

'Things have been hard at times, Your Grace, but I've been all right in the main. That's not really why I've come today,' he added, probably a bit too hurriedly.

The Archbishop said, 'Maybe not, but I'm always here to listen when you decide you want to talk about it. I think I know you well enough to be sure you carry no resentment for God.'

'None, Your Grace, I just wish my conscience

would let me pray to him.' There it was, spoken, unplanned but out now. He had prayed for Eddie Malloy but deprived himself of the comfort of personal prayer.

The old man leaned forward, looking serious, putting down his cup of tea. 'You must pray if that's what you want to do. You've suffered terribly. Don't let your conscience deny you the friendship of God, Francis, please.'

Houlihan nodded. 'Maybe I could come back some time, Your Grace, when Ma is better?'

'You come back whenever you want to. But between now and then you must pray when you feel like praying.'

'Yes, Your Grace.' He wasn't at all sure that he could simply switch prayer back on and he regretted blurting out what he'd said a minute ago. He needed much more time to plan how to handle all the emotions that would come with a full-blown 'confession' to this great man.

Houlihan was waiting to be asked why he'd come, thinking the Archbishop might pick up on the mention of Ma, but he continued looking at him in earnest, caring silence. Houlihan said, 'Your Grace, I came to ask for your help with Ma.'

He nodded. 'Go on.'

Houlihan told him everything that had happened with her and the family since he'd seen her that November day and told her he was leaving the priesthood. He explained how she had been affected by what she saw as his great sin. The old man listened attentively, offering simple words of encouragement as he talked. Then Houlihan took a deep breath and said, 'Some of the family thought she might recover if you were to . . . if you could see her and, sort of, tell her, or kind of suggest to her that . . .'

'That it wasn't such a great sin after all?'

Houlihan gave the slightest of nods as he held the other man's gaze, trying to read what the next reaction might be. Houlihan said, 'It wasn't my idea, Your Grace. It was a terrible thing I did.'

'Not so terrible as to cripple your mother. There've been many worse things done in the world and for motives not half as worthy as yours. Would she be well enough to see me tomorrow?'

Houlihan was stunned by his agreement to do it and by the prospect of trying to arrange it for the next day. 'I, I don't know, Your Grace. I'd need to find out if she could get here.'

He raised a hand, waved it. 'No need for that. I'll go to her house.'

Houlihan smiled at the sudden craziness of it. 'That'd probably finish her off, Your Grace.'

The Archbishop smiled too. 'I think she'd survive a visit from a quiet old man like me.'

'I think she'd want to get the house decorated and send cards out to the rest of the street just to let them know. She was so proud of me you know, think what it would mean to her to have the Archbishop come to her home.'

He was still smiling warmly. 'She'd every right to be proud of you, Francis, still has. What you did you did for a great love and there is never much wrong with that, although if you meet any priests don't be telling them I said it or we'll have nobody left!'

Houlihan laughed nervously. 'Thank you, Your Grace.' He got up slowly. 'I'll take up no more of your time but may I call you later when I've seen our Margaret? To make the arrangements?'

He pushed himself out of the chair. 'Of course. I'm in bed by ten, so please call before that.'

'I will, Your Grace.'

As the Archbishop walked him out he said, 'I'll tell your mother how proud she should be of you, tell her some of the stories from the old days at Maynooth. I'll make sure she knows God has forgiven you.'

Houlihan felt elated and blurted something else he'd regret as soon as he was outside. 'Your Grace, has a priest who's left the ministry ever returned to his vocation?'

He could tell by the long pause how much the question had surprised the Archbishop but his step didn't falter as they came to the end of the passageway and reached the door. He stopped then and turned to him. 'It's not unknown by any means, Francis.' The question in his eyes was obvious, but he left it unsaid.

Houlihan felt his cheeks reddening. 'Thank you, Your Grace. I'll call you by eight o'clock at the latest.' The Archbishop smiled and patted Houlihan's shoulder as he opened the door.

When Houlihan told his sister Margaret that the Archbishop had agreed, her delight was tempered by the prospect of finding a way to make the visit seem unstaged. The family knew that if their mother suspected a set-up, especially one involving Frankie, all impact would be lost.

They decided that Margaret would go to Ma and tell her she'd been to mass in the cathedral on Sunday and that the Archbishop had been asking how the family was. Margaret had mentioned how ill Ma was and the Archbishop had said he must get out to see her. Margaret had forgotten all about it and then the Archbishop had called her at home that afternoon to say that he'd be in the area and wanted to drop in for half an hour. The only barrier was that Houlihan would need to get the Archbishop's agreement to stick to this tale if Ma asked. Houlihan was confident he would and that even he wasn't beyond telling a white lie in such a good cause.

Houlihan waited at Margaret's house while she went to Ma's. Margaret called him, sounding much less excited than when she'd left. 'She's quite ill again, Frankie,' she said dejectedly. 'When I told her she just said, "That'll be nice." She didn't take it in. If she's like that tomorrow she'll just think she's having a dream.'

Houlihan sighed. 'All we can do is warn the

Archbishop so he's not offended. Unless you want to just call it off?'

'No, no, I don't. It wouldn't be up to me anyway, or you. It would need to be a family decision.'

'Can we contact them all by eight?'

'I don't think there's any need to. Everyone was in agreement that this was a good idea and you've taken the time and had the courage to go and ask. Let's go ahead and see what comes of it.'

He hesitated.

'Frankie?' she prompted.

'Okay. I'll call Archbishop Mahoney.'

Houlihan flew home that evening. He saw no point in staying until after the visit. He'd done what he'd promised the family he'd do. If it went badly with the Archbishop, no number of family gatherings would come up with a cure for Ma, other than a revisit to their original proposal of him returning to his vocation.

And no one else but him was going to make that decision. He thought about it constantly on the plane, regretted asking that stupid question of the Archbishop. Why had he done that? Some attempt to redeem himself in his eyes? All it would have done was raise his expectations, and put pressure on Houlihan. He felt suddenly queasy at the thought that Archbishop Mahoney might mention it to Ma when he met her. Surely not?

TWENTY-FIVE

Houlihan was up early the next morning, anxious to find out how Malloy was. Loretta's mobile was engaged and he left a message. He was reading the *Racing News* when his mobile rang, startling him.

'Mr Houlihan, my name is Peter Burke. We haven't met. I work for the *Sun* and we plan to run a story tomorrow about you saving Eddie Malloy's life when the petrol bomb was thrown into his house. I'd just like a couple of quotes.'

Houlihan suddenly felt himself flushing warm. 'Mr Burke, I haven't a clue what you're talking about.' He was still uncomfortable telling lies.

'I'm talking about the bottle filled with petrol that was thrown through the window of twenty-three Ryman Terrace on February ninth when you and Eddie Malloy were inside. Mr Malloy had just come out of the shower and was drying himself when he went up in flames. You were in the house too as you had been shadowing Mr Malloy, who'd already been the subject of threats. Is this helping your memory any?'

'Give me your number. I'll need to call you back.'

'Houlihan, we're running the story tomorrow. It can be with or without your input. It's up to you.' He gave his number.

Houlihan rang Bobby Cranfield and Hooper. Neither answered. He left messages then tried Loretta again. She answered. 'How the hell's he got hold of that?' she asked.

'I don't know, but he's obviously got the full script.'

She was quiet for a few moments then asked, 'What are you going to do?'

'See if the police academy will take me back for a quick refresher course?'

She chuckled. He said, 'Seriously, I'm going to have to come up with some sort of plan. I'm waiting for Bobby to call, or Hooper. Can we meet later?'

'Sure. Want me to come over?'

'Might be best if I come to your place. If you don't mind?'

'Of course not. I'll make a few calls to our people. I just want to find out exactly who's had access to your file. I need to speak to my boss too, to see if protection's an option.'

'To see if it's an option? I'd've thought it was a given.'

'Not the way things are stretched these days, Frankie. Anyway, would you really want an armed detective beside you twenty-four hours a day?'

'No. I'd want at least three.'

She laughed again. 'Good to see it's not affecting your sense of humour.'

'I'm trying to use it up as fast as I can so there's less of it to leak through the bullet holes.' It was bravado but he liked to hear her laugh. Her calm acceptance of the news had cheered him too. It couldn't be that dangerous after all, could it?

'Call and let me know what time you'll be arriving.'

'I will.'

As he got into his car, Cranfield called. Houlihan filled him in.

'Oh dear,' he said, 'Dear, dear, dear. What does Hooper say?'

'He hasn't returned my call yet.'

'I'll try and get hold of him. Apart from the danger you're now in, we need to plan a response to the press.'

It was then that Houlihan remembered Ben Dillon, *Racing News* correspondent for Lambourn. 'Damn!' he said.

'What?' asked Bobby.

'Ben Dillon. He's going to think I've really stitched him up.'

'The least of your worries, old boy. Believe me.'

Houlihan was back home when Hooper finally called and he sounded far too worried on Houlihan's behalf. Houlihan thought that either he wanted to scare the hell out of him or he was trying to discourage a suspicion that had been slowly building in Houlihan's mind, that Hooper was the man who'd leaked the story. Houlihan had not only 'backed out' of a commitment as far as Hooper was concerned, he'd then made it plain in his office that, boss or not, Hooper wasn't going to make Houlihan do anything he didn't want to do.

Or was Keelor the culprit? The American was used to getting quick solutions to problems and he wanted Malloy's attacker caught. Keelor was ruthless enough to have done it too, Houlihan thought. It would all just be business to him. Houlihan had made a deal then tried to pull out. Had Keelor decided to haul him back into it?

Cranfield called back. 'Frankie, I'm sorry. I've spoken to the editor of the *Sun* to try and get this spiked but he's not having it and I'm afraid Murdoch's a bit out of my league. Your best bet might be to meet this reporter and try and convince him of the merits of not publishing.'

'I kind of think that if the editor wants it that's not an option.'

'It's all we've got. Want me to meet him with you and see if we can talk some sense into him?'

'Thanks, Bobby, but I don't think it'd do much good. I'd better call him.'

'Let me read you our planned statement to the press tomorrow, just so we're singing off the same hymn sheet.'

'You guys might be singing. Weeping and wailing's going to be more my line on this one,

I'm afraid.' There was an awkward silence. 'Feeble joke,' he said. 'Go on. I'm listening.'

Cranfield read, '"*The Jockey Club confirms that one of its security department operatives was at the home of Eddie Malloy when a burning missile was thrown through the window. In the interests of the welfare of the operative concerned, the Jockey Club will not be revealing the operative's identity. The Jockey Club confirms that the operative concerned showed considerable valour in rescuing Mr Malloy from the burning room and extinguishing the flames before calling an ambulance.*"'

Houlihan said, 'So what's the point of me calling this fella back if you're withholding my name?'

'Tell him he might get you killed but that if he goes ahead with the story you'll deny ever speaking to him.'

Houlihan thought for a moment. He had a lot of respect for Bobby. He said, 'That's not really my style, Bobby. It's probably best that I don't speak to him at all.'

He sighed. 'Fair enough, Frankie. It's your call. I'll keep trying to find somebody with some influence. In the end it's bloody irresponsible journalism.'

'Would it be worthwhile asking the police to speak to the *Sun*?'

'I'm not sure it's something they'd want to get involved with. Best bet on that front . . .'

He tailed off as though he'd started something he shouldn't have said. Houlihan pushed him. 'Is what?'

'Well, it would be an injunction, but I've had a chat with Sam about it and he's understandably reluctant to start throwing the Jockey Club's weight around in the courts.'

'I wonder if he'd be so reluctant if his was the name going in tomorrow's paper?'

'Fair question, Frankie. I'll put it to him.'

'Don't bother, Bobby. He'll find some way round it.'

'I need to speak to him anyway, about the relationship you two have. It doesn't seem what it once was.'

'And it won't be again. He won't forgive me for backing out of "volunteering" to be a decoy. Somehow I think that the way things have worked out just might not upset Mr Hooper too much. What you could ask him is who he thinks might have leaked this.'

A pause again, then, 'I should be rather careful about proceeding too far down that path, Frankie.'

'I'll say no more about it till we next meet.'

Houlihan boiled water for tea, reflecting on the conversation with Cranfield. He hadn't been as supportive as he'd expected. Houlihan wondered if Hooper was bullying him too? Houlihan considered Cranfield too nice a guy to be trying to live with sharks like Hooper. Socialising was Bobby's forte. Keeping the press sweet and wooing those involved at the top of racing politics. Operational dealings were not his strong point.

He sat down with a mug of tea, a pen and a notepad, and started jotting names and timelines, trying to make links. The firebomb had been over three weeks ago. He was pretty certain Bert Jacobsen hadn't thrown it. None of the suspects from his list had yet been spoken to and how many of those would be in a hurry to speak to him once this story broke? Ringing round them now to make appointments would smack of desperation.

Who had given this to the *Sun*? Had Malloy recovered enough to speak to anyone and been unaware of the consequences of naming Houlihan? Had someone on the short list found out they were due a call and tried to put pressure on him first?

And why had Hooper been so insistent he leave a copy of the list of names with him? That had been just forty-eight hours ago. What was Hooper's interest in this whole case? Houlihan was beginning to see this as a key question. Was his anxiety over it strictly to do with making an impression on a big 'customer' like Makalu? Did he see this as a chance to make a real name for himself at the Jockey Club, or in the racing world in general?

Houlihan doodled on the pad, pondering, and when his phone rang he jumped in fright.

'Frankie?'

He recognised Margaret's voice and only then looked at his watch. It was five twenty. 'Hello Margaret,' he said and found that nothing else came out.

'Are you okay?' she asked. Houlihan tried to

read her tone and judged it to be on the down side.

'I'm fine. Sorry, I was miles away when you called. How did it go?'

'Not too well, I'm afraid. She was completely overcome. She never said a single word to the Archbishop, just stared at him, her eyes wide open as though it were a dead man come back to life. She's still not opened her mouth and he's long gone.'

'What did the Archbishop say?'

'He said he was sorry to have affected her like that. He was quite embarrassed and promised to come back whenever we asked if we thought it'd do any good.'

'And what did he say to her?' This was what he had meant in his first question but he hadn't wanted to correct Margaret.

'He could not have been fairer to you, Frankie. He sang your praises and tried to explain how this sort of thing happened from time to time and that the church accepted it and that God would readily forgive you, same as he would any other sinner.'

That flinty little word, said with coldness to nail him at the end. But it seemed the Archbishop hadn't mentioned Houlihan's question to him about returning to the priesthood; although looking again at the mind map he'd drawn on the pad, thinking of Malloy's would-be killer scanning his soaraway *Sun* the next morning, the thought of an anonymous ministry in some tiny parish appealed more strongly than ever.

Houlihan said, 'How did the rest of them take it?'

She sighed. 'I'm sure you can guess. We'd held out a lot of hope on this, Frankie.'

'I did too. I tried my best for it.'

'Nobody's saying you didn't.' The hard edge that had crept into her voice with the word sinner hadn't eased.

'Listen, Margaret, I think it's been a pretty tense day over there, for everybody,' he said sympathetically.

'Well maybe you could have stayed, Frankie, and shared the load a wee bit.'

'Maybe I could have.' He wasn't sure now how to defuse this.

'But you thought you'd done your bit, eh? You went to see the Archbishop, you arranged the meeting, and that was your part done. Time to bail out.' She was getting herself into a proper temper and, given the repair work they'd all put into their relationships in the past weeks, Houlihan thought it best to try and stay calm.

'That wasn't the way I saw it and I'm sorry if that's how it came across to you. Think of how it would have been if it had worked out.'

'But it didn't bloody work out. It's probably set her back even further!'

Houlihan hesitated but couldn't let her pile all the blame on him. 'Margaret, whose idea was this?

Everybody thought it was a great one when it first came up. I wasn't that struck on it, but, you're right, that's probably because I was scared of it and didn't want to face the Archbishop. But be fair, if it's set Ma back don't load everything on me.'

She said nothing, though he could hear her breathing quite fast. 'You're right, Frankie. I'm sorry.' She started crying.

He said, 'Margaret, we'll think of something else, honest, don't be getting upset.'

'I need to go, Frankie.' She hung up.

Houlihan looked at the screen on his mobile: three minutes and seven seconds of bad news, of something else to add to his worry list, another problem to solve for everyone else's happiness. Except his. Slumping back in his chair he rubbed his eyes and found himself laughing as he tried to massage the tension from his face. It must have been nervousness combined with his inflated sense of the ridiculousness of his plight and the way things had spiralled so suddenly downwards.

But, he consoled himself, he had withstood the loss of Kathy and he'd loved her with the power of a thousand men. He'd sworn then that if he survived her death with his sanity intact, whatever happened to him in the future would be of no consequence. Measuring his possibly impending death against his loss of Kathy registered very low on his scale of misery. Even the death of his mother, he realised with some shame, wouldn't raise the needle much higher. But her loss would affect the others much more than him so that measurement didn't really hold up.

What a mess, he thought. What a bloody mess.

His phone rang again. It was Burke from the *Sun*. 'Last chance to tell your side, Houlihan.'

'Who's telling the other side?' he asked.

'I'm sure you know all about protecting sources.'

Houlihan suddenly had an idea that would make someone happy. He said, 'And I'm sure you know all about spoilers.' One way to wreck an exclusive was to give the story to someone else.

That got Burke although he tried to bluff. 'Too late for a spoiler. They'll all have been put to bed by now.'

'Except yours. Insomnia rules at the *Sun*, eh?'

'The story's ready, don't worry about that. We just wanted to give you a final chance.'

'Well, thanks for thinking of me.'

'Listen, I can offer you a fee.' Desperation there now.

'No thanks. Must rush, my friend at the *Mirror*'s got a deadline to meet.'

'Shit, don't call the *Mirror*, Houlihan!'

'Bye.' He laughed aloud again. He rang Ben Dillon. 'What time's your deadline?'

'Why?'

'Well, if you can still get it in tomorrow's paper I can give you the full story on Eddie Malloy. If you can't I'd rather save it.'

'I can get it in. Don't worry!' he said excitedly. 'Where are you?'

'At home.'

'Gimme ten minutes.'

Ben arrived soon after, letting himself in, the hefty push on his front door doubling as an introductory knock. He was jacketless. His thin white shirt looked as though he'd slept in it, the only symmetry among the wrinkles being his nipples, raised by the icy wind blasting him between his parking spot and the front door.

'Come in,' Houlihan said.

'Shit! Freezing out there!' Dillon shivered as he hurried towards the fire.

'Most people wear a coat in March.'

'I was dozing when you called. Didn't have time. Day off today. What've you got for me?'

'Will it make tomorrow's paper?'

'Not the first editions for up north but they're only ten per cent of the print run. We've got till half six.'

'Okay. D'you want to ask or d'you want me to just talk.'

'Talk. Please.' He came towards the table, pulling a Dictaphone from his trouser pocket. 'Happy for me to use this?'

'Whatever.'

Dillon sat down. Houlihan said, 'First thing. The *Sun* are running this story tomorrow.'

Dillon stiffened, stared at him. 'You're kidding?'

'I'm not. A guy called Peter Burke rang me. Heard of him?'

'Burke's their top news man!' Dramatic as ever, Dillon buried his head in his hands so Houlihan could barely make out what he said. 'Oh no, first time I've ever had the chance to call in and say "hold the front page" and it's going to be in three million copies of the *Sun*!'

'How many copies of the *News* tomorrow.'

'Seventy thousand tops. And it might well make the front page of the bloody *Sun*. Bollocks!' He looked up again. 'What did you tell Burke?'

'No comment.'

He sat bolt upright. 'Did you? Really?'

'Really and truly.'

Dillon smiled madly and reached across to grab Houlihan's arm and give it what was supposed to be a playful shake. 'Good man, Frankie! Good man. So I get the real exclusive?'

'You do. As promised.'

Dillon propped the Dictaphone up and started the tape then quickly switched it off again and grabbed Houlihan's notepad. 'Can I take some notes too?'

Houlihan snatched it back, conscious of his sketches. 'Use your own,' he said.

'I forgot to bring it, Frankie, gimme a break!'

Houlihan tore two pages from the pad and pushed it back. 'Can I borrow your pen?' Dillon asked.

Houlihan shook his head as he passed it to him. 'Call yourself a reporter?'

*   *   *

Half an hour later, Dillon phoned in his copy while Houlihan showered. Dillon was still sitting in the kitchen when Houlihan was ready to leave for Loretta's place. He got up as Houlihan came out of the bedroom, and Houlihan saw the reporter looking relaxed, with a 'job well done' kind of happiness about him that let him stretch to his full height. Normally he looked hunched and tense, constantly on the hunt while looking hunted himself.

Dillon smiled at him. 'Fancy a drink?'

'I do, Ben, but I've another appointment so I have.'

'Who with?' he asked, suspicion quickly returning him to his natural state of wariness.

'My psychoanalyst.'

Dillon moved forward, folding his arms so his hands went into his armpits. Brow creased in apparent concern he asked, 'Really? What are you seeing him for? The effects of the petrol bomb?'

'It's a her, not a him actually.'

'But why?'

Houlihan shrugged, 'Oh, I don't know, because women are more sympathetic I suppose.'

Hands quickly out now, spread wide in frustration, Dillon said, 'No, I mean why are you seeing her?'

'Well, it's because of this strange compulsion I have for concocting wild stories and feeding them to journalists.' He kept his face straight. Dillon leaned down, stared into his eyes, held his breath for a few seconds then said, 'You're kidding, right?'

Houlihan kept him waiting a while, then said, 'I'm kidding. And I'm late. Now please go.'

Dillon smiled, straightening up and smoothing his crumpled shirt. Houlihan picked up his jacket, car keys and wallet and opened the door for him. Dillon looked out. 'It's snowing,' he said, leaning forward.

'Which will slow me down even more. Move!' He nudged the reporter out with his knee and locked the door. Dillon stood hugging himself, mock shivering as the broad snowflakes settled around him. 'Scrooge wasn't this bad to Tiny Tim,' he said.

Houlihan got in the car, rolled down the window as he tried to think of something witty to say to that, but couldn't. 'Ben, you've got me there. See you later.'

As he pulled away, Ben shouted, 'Frankie, where are you really going?'

'East.'

All he heard as the window finally clicked closed was, 'East? That's a big—'

As Houlihan drove, the snow thickened to a hypnotic stream coming out of the darkness. It steadily layered the fast lane till it was unsafe to move into with any confidence, although that didn't stop the usual fools flying along as though it were noon on a midsummer's day. He called Loretta to say he'd be late.

Houlihan realised he hadn't seen her for a few days and that he was looking forward to her company again. Yet there was no guilt, no feeling of forsaking Kathy in any way. He tried to make sense of it. Loretta made him feel, well, worthwhile really, he supposed. She seemed to believe in him and trust him. Sometimes he felt she guided him and encouraged him, almost in the way his ma used to when he was younger.

Or maybe his ma never had. He wondered if that was just the way he'd have liked it to be. Was that what he wanted Loretta to be, some sort of surrogate mother? A woman he could turn to for comfort and reassurance when his world was crumbling? A woman he could be completely comfortable with and close to without any threat of sexual complications?

Was this what he wanted? At thirty-two years old? From a woman who was younger than he and whom any man who chose not to block it out could see was very attractive?

Bloody hell, he thought, what am I doing sieving all this stuff through my mind? He blamed the kaleidoscopic snow, then wondered if he did need a proper analyst after all.

As he reached the Guildford turn-off he remembered he had to call Bobby Cranfield. He didn't care how Hooper might feel when he opened the *Racing News* the next day but he had enough respect for Bobby to give him warning.

He pulled into a service station and parked, then called Cranfield and told him what he'd done. Houlihan could tell that Cranfield thought it was a wrong move, although he'd never be directly critical. Houlihan tried to explain. 'The *Sun* will name me anyway. I'd promised Ben the story and I didn't want him to think I'd stitched him up. A promise is a promise.'

'He's only a reporter, Frankie. Do you think his own scruples would match yours given similar circumstances?'

'Maybe, maybe not. But there's no damage done and it's made me feel better.'

'I hope you still feel that way tomorrow.'

'Probably the same way a rat in a corner feels when he's at least managed to bite one of his attackers. Burke will get a tough time from his editor. Dillon might get a promotion. I get to think about that and smile.'

He sighed. 'I'll tell Sam Hooper.'

'You might find Sam is nowhere near as upset about it as you think he'll be.'

'That's the second time you've hinted that Hooper might have another agenda, Houlihan. It's a dangerous road to go down.'

'I'm well down the dangerous road anyway, Bobby. Whoever was after Malloy will be sticking my picture from tomorrow's papers on his wall and aiming his gun at it. Don't expect me to lose too much sleep over hurting Hooper's feelings.'

Cranfield was quiet for a few moments, then said, 'You didn't say anything to Dillon about Hooper?'

'Not a word. And I'm not saying anything formally to you about him. But I may well call you pretty soon and ask you to take off your Jockey Club hat and join me for a drink.'

'We should talk sooner rather than later, Frankie.'

'We will.'

Cranfield said, 'You know when this breaks in the morning the media are going to be looking for a lot more, especially the fellows who've been left out, and that's most of them.'

'Well maybe you should just stick to your official line of not naming the "operative".'

'And we're going to look pretty stupid if that quote appears in the *Sun*, as though the left hand doesn't know what the right hand's doing.'

Houlihan let that one hang in the air. Bobby sighed again and said, 'The press are going to want to speak to you. They'll be digging back through your history. They'll doorstep your family.'

'Bobby, it's a small story in a small sport. It'll be dead in twenty-four hours.'

'Your naivety is almost touching, Frankie. It's racing, which the public believes is already full of skulduggery. There's a good-looking hero, an ex-priest, who risked his life for a friend who's made many enemies in the sport. In this case the hero also has his own background of . . .'

Frankie said, 'Of what? Personal tragedy? And they'll want to trawl through all that?'

'Frankie, I'm sorry. I was only trying to warn you exactly how this business works.'

'Well, if that's how it works it would have been

the same when the *Sun* published its piece. Me talking to Ben Dillon changes nothing.'

'Well, nothing except the obvious; that you're more than willing to speak personally to the press about it. Believe me, I'll start fielding calls when the first issues come off the presses later tonight. I'll have had no fewer than forty by tomorrow, you can bet on that.'

He was starting to convince Houlihan. Silently he tried to take in the possible repercussions. He said, 'What choices have we got, Bobby?'

Another deep sigh. 'We can say no further comment, no more interviews. Or we can arrange interviews and pictures for all who want them. The second way gets it over and done with quickly. The first way will have them digging under every stone for weeks. Camping out in your backyard and your family's, ferreting out friends, interrogating churchgoers from your old parish . . .'

'Okay, okay.' He thought for a while. 'Could we choose one or two of them and offer what they want, with pictures and everything, for a big donation to charity?'

'You could, but if you think women scorned match the "hell hath no fury" stuff, just watch what the papers who don't bid highest do to you.'

'So it's all of them?'

'It's your choice in the end.'

'Can I think about it and we'll talk in the morning?'

'Nice and early?'

'I'll be up for half six.'

There were a few moments of silence, then Bobby said quietly, 'Frankie, whatever happens, I don't want any damage done to our friendship. It means a lot to me.'

'It does to me too, Bobby.' Frustrated, Houlihan felt like asking Bobby why he did this job. He was a multi-millionaire who could have lived out his love-affair with racing in plenty of other hassle-free ways. He settled for telling him he was too nice a guy to be working in this business.

'Maybe we both are, Frankie. Goodnight.'

'Goodnight, Bobby.'

The conversation had shaken him. He thought he'd better let the family know in case they did start getting calls from reporters. He searched for Margaret's number in his mobile then stopped and thought for a while. Maybe he should call Pat. His conversation with Thomas in the car in Dublin came back to him, when Thomas had said Pat felt a bit overawed by Frankie and had never really thought they could have a relationship. A call to him might help repair things a little bit, might make him realise Houlihan respected him.

Pat was the oldest boy and Houlihan thought that if Margaret wasn't so bossy and Pat was more confident, he'd have become the natural head of the family after Da died and Ma took ill. Margaret would be annoyed if Houlihan called Pat rather than her but she'd hardly been full of sisterly love when they'd spoken earlier.

He found Pat's number and rang. Pat sounded surprised to hear his voice. Houlihan asked about Ma.

'She's still shell-shocked,' he replied and Houlihan thought he picked up a slight accusatory tone but decided that maybe he was just being ultra-sensitive because of everything that was going on.

He said, 'I'll get back over soon and we can all sit down again to try and work something else out.'

'Like what?' Pat asked coldly.

Houlihan guessed Pat had spent much of the day with Margaret, dissecting what they thought was left of Houlihan's character. And he suddenly felt very weary of this: the family, his job and where it had landed him, everything. The fight went out of him. He said, 'Pat, I don't know what. I really don't. And if you don't want me to come back then I won't. Speak to the others. Call me, or write, or send me a lawyer's letter or something.'

Pat didn't reply. Houlihan said, 'I need to tell you what might happen tomorrow and you'd best tell the others.' Still no response. He said, 'Pat, are you still there?'

'I'm listening.'

He told him everything and threw in most of the stuff Bobby had said. It was a lot for anyone to take in and he stopped twice to make sure his brother was still there, still listening.

Eventually, Pat spoke. 'Finished?' he asked.

'I am.'

'And why did you call *me*? To play the big-shot again? The man on the front pages?'

'Oh, Pat . . .' Houlihan said in deep frustration and regret. But he knew it was pointless telling him the real reason; Pat would have seen it as patronising rather than an attempt at bridge-building.

Pat said, 'You sat boasting to a reporter, knowing the press would be at our door in the morning? Ma's almost on her deathbed and all you can think of is your ego!'

'Pat, it's nothing like that. Come on, be fair for God's sake!'

'Don't you talk to me about fair, you pompous bastard! You've never had a thought for anyone but yourself! You're—'

Houlihan hung up and slumped over the steering wheel. Everything came together and flooded over him, all the tensions and fears, all the balancing he'd tried to do, all the wrong decisions he'd made, and he felt his eyes grow hot as tears came.

TWENTY-SIX

Candle-sized bulbs twinkled in Loretta's window and a big fire burned in the grate. The main lights were off and the fire's flames cast long shadows. Houlihan had kicked the snow from his shoes outside and left them in the hall. Loretta had a whiskey and ice poured and she brought it from the kitchen to where he sat by the fire, undoing a button on his shirt, already too hot.

He looked at the two inches of whiskey then up at her. She said, 'On the assumption you'll not be driving back in that.' She nodded to the view through the huge bow window where the world outside looked like it belonged in a plastic Christmas dome someone had just shaken.

He took the glass. 'Thanks. I wouldn't mind staying, if that's all right. It's been a bad day.'

'There are clean sheets on your bed already.' She sat down in the chair opposite him and stretched out. The fire's flames dappled her with shade and light; her hair shone, her smile was bright. Houlihan was still feeling emotionally tender from his call to Pat, but sitting here in the peaceful firelight, with someone who was fast becoming his closest friend since Kathy, felt so good it seemed almost worth everything that had happened.

He said, 'It seems a long time since I saw you.'

She nodded, looking at him, but said nothing. He gazed into the fire, so glad to be with her and away from all the troubles that he felt he was going to start saying things he'd maybe regret. He tried to calm himself and think of a change of subject. He said, 'Big logs. Chop them yourself?'

'I did, now you mention it.'

He waited for her to laugh, to acknowledge the joke. She didn't. 'You're kidding me?'

'I'm not. Keeps me fit. That and treading water for fifteen minutes every day.'

'In the swimming baths?'

She hesitated to see if he'd realise the silliness of his question then said, 'No, in the sink.'

Houlihan smiled. 'You could almost do it in your bath. It's big enough.'

They sipped their drinks. 'You run, don't you?' she asked.

'To keep fit? Yes. How did you know?'

'And you over-pronate.'

'I what?'

'Do you get twinges in your knee sometimes?'

'I do.'

'Over-pronation. Trust me. See a good podiatrist.'

'Loretta, how do you know all this?'

'I'm a detective, aren't I?'

'So they tell me.'

She said, 'I noticed your running shoes the first time I came to your place. There was excess wear on the outside of both heels and the inside edge of the midsole, which is caused by rolling from the outside of your heel to the inside as you run. It's called over-pronation and it almost always leads to some sort of joint pain.'

'And I can get it fixed?'

'Made-to-measure inserts from a good podiatrist. They'll add years to your running life.'

'And help me get away from assassins?'

She nodded. 'If you get the rocket model.'

'I'll have a pair please. Don't bother wrapping them.'

They were silent for a while, comfortably, as always. They looked at the fire. Houlihan said, 'I had an uncle who lived in a lighthouse way out in Mizzen Head . . .'

'On the Cork coast?' she asked.

'That's the place. Beautiful, wonderful, wild place, with clean air and big waves. We used to go there for our holidays when I was young. He had a big log-burning stove and I'd nag him to set it going even in the height of summer. I promised myself I'd have one of those when I grew up.'

'And did you?'

'I did. Kathy and I had one in the cottage we used to have in the woods.' He suddenly realised that this was the first time he'd mentioned Kathy's name to

Loretta without thinking. She smiled at him, nodding, encouraging him to go on. But he couldn't. He had separated her from Kathy completely in his mind. It wasn't right to talk to Loretta about his life with Kathy, his feelings for her. It wouldn't be fair to Kathy. She wouldn't have liked it.

He said, 'How have you been? Any luck with Keelor yet?'

She hesitated slightly and he thought he saw the tiniest touch of frustration in her eyes, as though she had been expecting him to finally open up to her. And his thoughts returned to that mother figure. He could have told a proper mother – but not his own – all about his feelings for Kathy and what her death had done to him. He could have stripped himself to the bone and cleaned himself out, flushed away all the grief and emotional backflow that had pervaded his body as well as his mind and made him physically sick, poisoned him, the toxicity levels growing by the day, slowing him, anchoring him, killing him.

'I need to go to the loo,' he said, and hurried out.

As they ate Dover sole and asparagus, Houlihan said, 'I feel I'm always talking about myself and my work and you always listen. And I feel grateful for that but I don't give you anything in return.'

She chewed and drank some wine. 'I don't want anything in return. I enjoy your company. I like to hear what's happening in your life. Especially as it might now be a very short one.' She cut viciously through an asparagus spear and raised her eyes mischievously and slowly to look at him.

'Thank you. What a delightful aperitif,' he said, laughing.

'Anything that gets you away from anal-retentiveness is bound to improve your appetite my dear.'

That hit him hard. There was no need to look in her eyes to try and find some 'excuse' for it, the way she'd said it, with that same edge he'd recognised in Margaret's voice earlier in the day. She watched him, coolly waiting for the response, and he knew it wouldn't be so much what he said as the way he said it that would matter. He felt childishly hurt and inclined to say, 'Oh, nobody's ever called me that before.' But he knew Loretta well enough by now to believe she wouldn't deliberately hurt him, and, when he thought about all the self-analysis and navel-gazing he habitually did, at least since Kathy had died and the family had turned against him, it wasn't even a matter of asking himself if there might be something in this. She was right.

He said, 'Tell me, am I the only over-pronating anal-retentive you know?'

She smiled wide and said, 'You are. A complete one-off.'

Towards midnight they sat on the rug by the dying embers of the fire. Loretta had dragged a tall lamp across and they were looking again at the short list of seventeen names. They'd already been through lengthy conjecture about who might have leaked the story, and concluded that whoever had fed the stuff to Burke had access to the detail. They decided Sam Hooper was favourite.

Loretta had run each name on the shortlist through a search for past convictions and had come up with an aggravated assault charge against one former trainer, Gus Grassick, now working in the horse-feed business. But there was also a conviction registered against Harry Shaw, whose name had now surfaced a couple of times. Shaw ran a successful and growing valet business servicing the needs of jockeys on race days. Twelve years ago, shortly after retiring from riding, he'd spent a year in prison for a serious assault on a motorist in a road-rage incident.

Loretta said, 'I think it would be worthwhile paying Shaw a visit, tomorrow if possible. Do you know where he's likely to be?'

Houlihan went to the hall and got his racing diary from his jacket. 'He operates in the midlands and the north. If he's working he'll either be at Worcester or Hexham.'

'You think he might not be working?'

'His son helps him run the business and they employ maybe a dozen valets. There'd be no need for him to work every day.'

'Can you find out in the morning?'

'Sure. I'll call Geoff. He'll find out.'

Until she'd mentioned it he'd had no plans whatsoever to show his face anywhere the next day. After Pat's diatribe he'd mentioned nothing to Loretta about Bobby's predictions on the press reaction.

There was a glint in her eyes and she leaned across and clinked her glass against his. 'To a quick result,' she said.

'You make it sound like a pregnancy test.'

'Not something I'm ever likely to be submitting.'

'Why, don't you like kids?'

'I love 'em. But I can't have any. It's a long story.'

Cross-legged, holding her gaze for what seemed a long time, he said, 'Do you want to talk about it?'

'Do you want me to talk about it?'

'Only if you want to.'

She sighed long and deep. 'I don't know if I do.'

Houlihan nodded and said quietly, 'You raised it. You might not want to talk about it but your subconscious obviously does.'

She stared at him, serious now, as though trying to read his mind. Finally she shook her head. 'No. You'll have me as crazy as you are.' Then she rose, like a genie floating, gradually uncrossing her legs as she pushed upwards. She smiled down at him.

He said, 'Very athletic. Think I can't do that?'

She put her hands on her hips and cocked her jaw as though to say, 'Just try it.'

Houlihan continued looking up at her, serious

now, ready for the challenge. He said, 'You think my dodgy knees and over-pronating feet mean I can't get up like that?'

'Don't forget your retentive anus.'

He put his drink on the rug, forced the edges of his stockinged feet against the floor and rose almost as gracefully as she had done. He smiled proudly, held out his arms, bowed low, and she reached forward, put a hand on his chest and pushed him over.

It was well after seven when Houlihan awoke the next morning. He was usually up by six thirty at the latest but he'd slept soundly and so now lay awake, enjoying the unusually relaxed feeling. He'd been a poor sleeper these past eighteen months.

He got up and wrapped a luxurious white bath towel around himself before leaving the room. He heard Loretta moving around in the kitchen and called out, 'Good morning.'

'Good morning to you.'

'Okay if I take a shower now?'

'Sure. You'd better make yourself extra pretty for your fans.'

'Pardon?'

'You're a superstar hero, Frankie boy, front page of the *Racing News* and page five of the *Sun.*'

'You get the *Sun* delivered?' he asked, incredulous.

'Don't be so snobbish. Good, concise reporting. Three million people can't be wrong.'

'Leaving fifty-three million who don't buy it.'

'Listen, if you want to debate the tabloids versus the broadsheets, don't stand around out there in a bath towel yelling at me, get in here and put your cards on the table.'

He smiled. 'Okay, I take the hint. On my way to the shower.'

'Scrambled eggs and bacon?'

'Yes please.'

'You've got ten minutes.'

The *Racing News* story painted him as the hero of the century and Dillon had overdone the 'he told mes', rubbing the noses of his rivals in the exclusive. Bobby's words came back to him. He'd promised to have his mobile switched on from six thirty. Damn, he'd do it after reading the papers.

The front-page picture upset him. The piece mentioned his time as a priest and the picture showed him solemn, black-suited, head partly bowed. Loretta picked up his mood. 'You don't like the picture.'

He kept staring at it. 'It was taken just after Kathy's funeral.'

'Bastards,' she said.

He nodded. 'It's probably the only one they had of me.'

'You're too charitable, Frankie, especially after you gave them the story.'

He turned to pages five and six which were also dedicated to the story, with panels inserted containing information about Makalu, the courses they owned, the political fallout from the takeovers, a picture of Eddie Malloy looking stern – or maybe even menacing depending on what you believed about Makalu's intentions. There was also a small copy of the ad Bert Jacobsen had placed.

He reached for the *Sun*. Loretta stretched across and held his wrist. She looked serious, worried. She said, 'I don't think you'll like the picture they've got either, Frankie.'

'Why?'

She hesitated. 'It's from your wedding.'

Loretta liked a joke but he already knew her well enough to realise she would never have joked about something like that. Slowly, he began turning the pages till he found it. Small, beneath a six-paragraph story, Kathy in her wedding dress, arm linked in his as they posed by the steeple-chase fence at Cheltenham where they'd first met. Since her death he'd never found the strength to look at any picture of Kathy. He stared at the black and white image, at her beautiful smile. He felt stunned. He held his breath and just looked at her, vaguely aware of Loretta quietly going out of the kitchen.

Houlihan didn't know how much time had passed before he got up, leaving the paper open and half his breakfast uneaten. He noticed most of Loretta's food was still on her plate. He wandered into the living room in a daze. Loretta was by the window, looking out as the daylight strengthened, helped by the reflection of the thick snow. She turned, then walked slowly towards him and opened her arms. Houlihan let her hold him in silence.

It was nine o'clock before he could face switching on his mobile. There were fifteen messages. Two from Bobby Cranfield, the rest from reporters. He called Bobby first.

'Houlihan, I've been expecting your call.' That was the closest Bobby would bring himself to a reprimand for having his phone switched off. 'It's been a tough morning,' he said. 'I'm so sorry about the pictures, they must have been very upsetting.'

There wasn't the slightest note of 'I told you so' in his voice. 'They were,' Houlihan said.

'Are you all right?'

'I'll be okay, thanks. What about you, I guess you've been up half the night?'

Cranfield tried to make light of it. 'I don't sleep more than a few hours anyway; it helped pass the time.'

'There's about a dozen messages on my mobile from the press. Most of them I've never heard of. What do I say when I call back?'

'Don't call them back. They won't expect you to. They'll just keep trying so switch your phone off. Can you get into the office?'

Houlihan looked out at the white landscape, suspected there'd be little racing on anyway so a trip to Worcester or Hexham to see Harry Shaw almost certainly wouldn't be necessary. 'Any meetings survive?' he asked.

'No. They're all off and prospects for tomorrow aren't bright.'

Loretta stood close by, watching him. He looked at her as he spoke to Bobby. 'I'd intended to join DS Moran today to do some interviews. I'd like to bring her into the office with me. We could be there for noon.'

'Fine. See you then. If you switch your mobile off is there another number I can get you on between now and when we meet?'

'Another number . . .?'

Using her fingers, Loretta signed her mobile number to him and he called it out. Bobby said, 'DS Moran's number?'

Houlihan felt himself blush. 'Er, that's right.'

'Good. Fine. See you here later.'

As soon as he ended the call his phone rang. He switched it off. 'Fancy a trip to London?' he asked.

'If you'll help me dig the car out.'

'With your wood-chopping muscles so finely honed? I'll supervise.' They both smiled.

Loretta drove but had trouble concentrating and kept commenting on the Christmas-card landscape. Deep snow in the south of England, especially in March, was a rare thing. Houlihan stared at the blank screen on his mobile, worrying in case any of the family were trying to get through. He knew he should make a call but he didn't want to talk to them – well, not to Pat or Margaret at least. He switched the phone on long enough to retrieve Thomas's number then remembered he'd probably be in class. He dialled anyway. It rang unanswered.

Houlihan thought that if things had kicked off with the press Thomas might be at his ma's house. He felt a prickle of sweat in his hairline. No choice but to make a call to Ma's and take his chances on who answered the phone, hoping hard it would be Theresa. It was.

'Frankie! The TV people have been here! You're a big hero. We've been trying to call you.'

'Theresa, I'm sorry, I've had to leave my phone switched off. How is Ma?'

'Ahh, she's just the same.' Each word was a tone below the previous one then Theresa picked up again quickly. 'I wish she was up and about to see all the excitement, so I do. You're famous, Frankie! I'm so proud of ye!'

He couldn't help smiling. At least someone was happy this morning. 'Is it snowing over there, Theresa?'

''Tis. One of the TV fellas slipped on the path.'

'It's a beautiful morning here. The snow's a foot deep.'

'Sounds grand, so it does. When are ye coming back over?'

'Soon, I'd think. Soon. Is our Thomas there, Theresa?'

'He is. Would ye like to speak to him?'

'I would.'

'I'll get him now. Frankie, will we be seein' ye on the news tonight?'

He wanted to tell her that that was the last thing he needed. 'Maybe. We'll see.'

Thomas came on. 'Frankie, how are ye?'

'Shell-shocked.'

'I should think so. Ye never told us it was such a big deal, all this! RTE's been here with cameras and lights and God knows what paraphernalia. They're wantin' to talk to Ma and to us all.'

His heart sank. 'And have any of you spoken to them?'

'Our Margaret said she was goin' out to tell them to go away as Ma was ill, but they ended up asking her questions and I think she kind of got caught up in it.'

Houlihan felt queasy. 'Are the TV people still there?'

'No. They said they've a team on the way to interview you so maybe we'll see you on the news?'

'Maybe,' he said, sick now. 'Is our Margaret still there?'

'She is. I'll put her on.'

'Frankie?' Stern, stressed, angry, all obvious to him in the way she said his name.

'I'm sorry,' he said quietly. There was silence for a while then she sighed and said, 'It's done now, I suppose.'

'Does Ma know?'

'Fortunately not. She's still in her own world.'

'What did the TV people ask you?'

333

'It's not just been them, Frankie. I've had to deal with all the Irish papers and a couple of correspondents from the English papers as well.'

There was pride in her voice now and an unmistakable edge of excitement, although Houlihan knew she'd never have admitted it. 'And they interviewed you on TV, did they?'

'Well, they said it was taped and would be on later.'

'What did they want to know?' He was dreading her answer.

'The usual stuff.' She was trying to make herself sound like a media regular now. 'You know, what you'd been like as a child, had you ever shown such courage before, how long had you been a priest, how did we all feel when you left your vocation to marry Kathy Spencer . . .' She let it tail off deliberately.

His next question felt like taking a turn at Russian roulette. 'What did you say to that?'

Silence. She was determined to squeeze the trigger very slowly, make him look at the chamber turning over to see if the bullet was there. She said, 'I told them it was a private family matter. I said I wouldn't comment.'

An involuntary prayer of thanks rose from his mind. He said, 'Thank you.'

There was a long pause, then she said, 'I did it for . . . for all of us.'

She'd been going to say for Ma, to keep him in his rightful place, and it lifted him greatly that she'd decided not to, that she'd chosen to include him again. Maybe the rebuilding work they'd all done in past weeks was still in place. He said quietly, 'How's Pat?'

'Quite bruised, I should think. He's had the worst of an argument with Thomas and Cornelius about what he said to you last night.'

'Would it be worth me having a word?'

She hesitated and he sensed Pat was close by her. 'Maybe it's best left till next time.'

'Okay. Give my love to Ma and to everyone, will you?'

'I will. When will we see you?'

'Best wait till all this dies down. I'll try and get over next week if I can.'

'All right.'

'I'll give you another number you can reach me at for the rest of the day. Please call if anyone else turns up asking questions.'

'Hold on. I'll get a pen.'

Loretta glanced across at him and smiled reassuringly, and once again he was glad she was there.

'Go on,' Margaret said, and he gave her the number.

'So this is another mobile phone you have?' she asked.

'It belongs to a friend.'

'Right. Well, let us know what's happening.'

'I will. Thanks, Margaret.'

There was another pause, then she said, 'Frankie, doesn't all this publicity mean that the fella who threw the petrol bomb might be coming after you?'

He glanced at Loretta. 'Nah, he's probably fled the country. He'll be long gone, I should think.'

'And what if he's not long gone? What if doesn't want to risk you standing witness against him?'

'I didn't see him. He knows that as well as I do. I was witness to nothing except a friend of mine going up in flames.'

Silence again. 'I'm sorry, Frankie. That must have been a very hard thing for you to see, and to have to deal with.'

'It's all right.' Another long pause. 'Margaret, I need to go.'

'Sure. Listen, 'twas a very brave thing you did, we're all proud of you. Take care of yourself.' She sounded on the edge of tears and had hung up by the time he said goodbye.

Slowly, he put Loretta's phone back in its holder on the dashboard. 'Are you okay?' she asked.

Houlihan nodded.

'And your family?'

'They're coping.'

They drove on through the slush, the white countryside behind them as they entered southwest London. Loretta said, 'Did you tell your sister I was your friend back there?'

'I did.'

'Mmmm. That's good to know. I wondered what I was.'

Not looking at her, he said, 'I'm not sure what I'd have done without you.'

TWENTY-SEVEN

Houlihan didn't go home for three days. One of the few benefits of having an office in the heart of London was that most of the media could get there easily. The next forty-eight hours were taken up with interviews, most with the press, two with a couple of the guys who'd done his training at the Police Academy. He'd taken Loretta's advice to have a couple of hours' refresher with them.

His first interview was to be with the BBC and Hooper had asked for a 'final debrief' an hour before it. Hooper greeted him with what passed for a smile, stood up, shook his hand across the desk. 'Would you like to close the door?' he said.

Houlihan turned to do so, saying, 'Isn't Bobby joining us?'

'We'll have a separate meeting once we've finished this one. Bobby will be there. So will Ken Ellroy, a detective inspector from the Met. But I just wanted to make sure we've got our ducks in a row before we go in there. Grab a seat.'

Houlihan sat.

'Tea? Coffee?' Hooper offered.

'No thanks.'

Hooper played with a paperclip, bending it. 'Frankie, you know that one question will come up time and again throughout these interviews you'll be doing?'

'What's that?'

'They'll want to know if you saw the man who threw the bomb.'

'Well, that's okay. It's an easy one to answer. I'll just say, "How do you know it was a man because I didn't see anyone."'

Hooper stared at him. 'I don't think that's the best approach. You want this man caught, don't you, and quickly?'

'Sure I do, but I changed my mind about being a decoy, remember?'

'Don't look at it as a decoy!' Hooper sat forward suddenly, dropping the paperclip.

'And what else would you call it?' Houlihan asked, trying to stay relaxed.

'Look at it as a tactical move in our joint strategy to nail this man quickly. It's to your advantage, for God's sake! He's got to make the assumption anyway – that you saw him – he needs to.'

'Well if he needs to there's no point in me saying I saw him.'

Hooper raised his eyebrows slightly and sat still. 'So you won't deny that you saw him?'

'Oh, I'll deny it all right.'

338

Hooper stood up. 'Stop playing games, Houlihan! This is serious. You're in trouble. We're trying to help you and you won't help yourself!'

Houlihan looked up at him and said quietly, 'Would you sit down, Sam. I think we need to talk on what you would call a more informal basis.'

Slowly, and with some hope creeping back into his eyes, Hooper sat. Houlihan moved his chair closer to the desk and leaned his elbows on it. He said, 'Stop treating me like some stage Irishman with half a brain, will you? "We're trying to help you and you won't help yourself." What kind of guff is that?'

Hooper looked taken aback. Houlihan continued. 'Listen, and try and fit yourself into my position. I should have thought a bit more about volunteering as a decoy before opening my mouth and I'm sorry if my change of mind embarrassed you and the department. But don't try and paint this as the same opportunity suddenly reappearing, because it's not.'

'Of course it is!'

Houlihan looked at Hooper and wondered why he was even bothering. He said, 'It isn't, and here's why. If we'd done it in the controlled fashion as first suggested, we could have limited a lot of the output and prepared everyone else who was going to be affected by it. Whoever leaked this story blew all that out of the water and the press are now as interested in my past as in what happened with Eddie Malloy. My family in Ireland have already had the media camped out on their door. My mother is very ill and this has increased the strain on everyone tenfold. Do you seriously believe that I'd jeopardise their safety in any way for the sake of the Jockey Club? Even if I did see the guy who threw the petrol bomb?'

For once Hooper was silent, although, judging by his look, far from repentant. More certain now than ever that he was the 'mole', Houlihan said, 'Sam, I suppose you'll be doing all you can to find out who leaked the story to the *Sun*?'

Hooper crossed his arms. 'There's nothing to say the leak was internal.'

Houlihan paused, waiting to see if Hooper would realise how defensively he'd said it, then raised his eyebrows in mock surprise. 'I never said it was.'

Hooper shifted uncomfortably and pinched his nose briefly.

Houlihan said, 'There were some telling details in there from the *Sun*, about Malloy having just come out of the shower, me being in the hallway when it happened. A few people might have known I was shadowing Malloy, but nobody without access to my report could have come up with the details printed in the *Sun*.'

Hooper opened his arms, palms upwards, trying to look relaxed now. 'Eddie Malloy could have talked.'

'Malloy wasn't able to, unless he's made a remarkable recovery in the past few days. Has he?'

'I don't know. I don't know how he is.'

Houlihan watched his face for any sign of embarrassment at such an admission. None showed. Shaking his head slowly, Houlihan said, 'I'd really like to know how Eddie is, even if nobody else is concerned. I think you'll find the press might also just show a little bit of interest. Keelor won't tell me and won't return calls to the police. Maybe you could use your influence with him?'

Hooper stared coldly at him. 'Leave me to decide on that. I suggest you go away somewhere quiet before you meet the press and think about the implications of what we've discussed here.'

Houlihan got up. 'That shouldn't take too long.'

In the meeting with Bobby and DI Ellroy, Hooper said unconvincingly that he 'fully supported' Houlihan's decision to make clear in the interviews that he had not seen the attacker and had seen no one stalking Malloy in all the time he'd spent with him. Hooper went so far as to recommend that he make a particular point of it to every journalist, even if the question wasn't asked. Houlihan concluded that he was trying to get Malloy's attacker to take the view 'methinks he doth protest too much'. Subtlety wasn't Hooper's strong suit.

At the conference, apart from the expected, 'Did you see who did it?' variants, sample questions were: 'How does it feel to be a hero?' 'Did your training as a priest make you feel obliged to save this man?' 'Did you stop to consider the danger to yourself?' 'You and Eddie Malloy are single men, how well did you know each other?' 'Have you seen Malloy since?' 'Do you plan to keep in touch?' 'Could the campaign against Makalu in racing have resulted in this?' 'Who do you think is responsible?' 'What do you think now of the campaign being run by Bert Jacobsen and others?' 'As a detective yourself, will you be involved in the hunt for the attacker?' 'How much danger do you consider yourself in?' 'How do you feel now about Makalu Holdings and their business practices?' 'What does your family think about all this?' 'How did your family feel when you left the priesthood?' 'Will this mean a promotion for you?'

The answer to the last, thought Houlihan, was a definite no.

It was late the next day when the feeding frenzy stopped and the sharks dispersed. Houlihan had stayed in London the previous night, feeling a twinge of regret as he waved Loretta off home. She came back the next day and sat in the office through the last of the press stuff. Then they went with Bobby Cranfield for a meal. Houlihan sat almost slumped at the table. Cranfield said, 'You look fried.'

Houlihan nodded. 'Fried, frazzled, wasted. Remind me, please, to call you for advice the next time I take the notion to do anything as stupid as talk to the press.'

Cranfield shrugged, moving slightly in his wheelchair. 'These things happen. I think we got away with it, don't you, Loretta?'

Houlihan liked him even more for including her. She said, 'You're the professional, Bobby, I'll take your word for it.'

'I think we're okay,' Cranfield said. 'At the expense of Eddie Malloy and Makalu Holdings. They are the story now, and will be till the press find out where Malloy is and how he's recovering. And there'll be plenty of them mixing it over Makalu.'

'Do you think they'll talk to Jacobsen and the others on his list?' Loretta asked.

'Certain to.'

'Which is more hassle for you,' Houlihan said.

Cranfield smiled and crossed his hands on his lap. 'At least Jacobsen and his merry band don't work for the Jockey Club. The main thing, Frankie, is that you've handled yourself exceptionally well under very trying circumstances. It looks like you're pretty much out of the woods.'

Comforting words to Houlihan's exhausted mind.

Houlihan spent the next four days staying at Loretta's house. TV and radio stations reported the issue as a straight piece of news and did almost nothing by way of follow-ups. The print media strung it out for a few days, chasing Keelor and Eddie Malloy. Keelor restricted himself to 'no comment'. The police could offer no update on Malloy's condition other than that they understood he was recovering slowly and intended to interview him when his doctors considered it appropriate. They couldn't give an indication as to when that might be. Nor was it reported anywhere that, in fact, the police did not know where Eddie Malloy was.

Loretta tried again to find out. She'd drawn a blank with Keelor who had shown no patience when she'd called, causing them to have a shouting match which ended in him hanging up on her. She resolved to confront Keelor once she and Houlihan had seen Harry Shaw. Houlihan had asked Elaine, the office secretary, to get him a copy of Shaw's itinerary, and the plan was to turn up unannounced after racing.

The list showed that Shaw would be at Doncaster on March 12th. The trip north, in driving rain and sleet, took them almost four hours. They hung around the darkening car park as the crowds filtered away then made their way to the weighing room where Shaw would be washing the muddy breeches.

But Shaw wasn't there. A valet who worked for him said he had decided to take a holiday in Lanzarote.

'When did he go?' Houlihan asked.

'This morning.'

'When is he due back?' Loretta asked.

The valet, hands in the big Belfast sink, shrugged. 'A couple of weeks, I think.'

'When did he decide to go?' Houlihan questioned him.

'He only mentioned it to me yesterday.'

'Busy time to suddenly be taking holidays,' Houlihan said.

'Damn right,' the valet said wearily.

Houlihan looked at Loretta then said to the valet, 'We'd best let you get on with it then.'

'Thanks.'

As they walked to the car park, Houlihan said, 'So much for surprising him.'

'Yeah. It stinks, though.'

'I know.'

'Who else would have had sight of that list Elaine sent you?'

'Anyone in the office really.'

'So somebody warns him and he leaves the country. Self-incriminating or what?'

'Maybe. I'm sure what he'll be saying is that he was sick of another British winter elbow-deep in muddy water.'

As they got into the car she said, 'Worth a closer look at Harry Shaw.'

They stopped for dinner and it was just before midnight when they got back to Loretta's place. This was Houlihan's ninth night in a row that would be spent here, and he was beginning to treat it like a second home. Loretta, subconsciously maybe, encouraged it. Throwing her coat over a chair she said, 'Will you fix the nightcaps? I'm just going to jump in the shower.'

He went into the kitchen and got the whiskey from the cupboard and two glasses. Then he stopped. This nightcap thing was becoming too much of a habit and one drink often led to two and he was just getting too used to it. He put one glass away again and filled the kettle. He was sipping cocoa at the table, staring at Loretta's lonely whiskey and ice, when she came in wearing her dressing gown, another sight he'd quickly accepted, and towelling her hair.

She stopped and stood as though transfixed. 'Frankie Houlihan! With cocoa! I'll report you to the authorities and they'll issue you with a wimp caution.'

He smiled a little.

'What's wrong?' she asked.

'I'm falling into bad habits.'

She sat down and picked up her drink. 'You're one of the most sensible drinkers I've met. What are you worried about?'

'I'm not worried. I just don't like drifting into things like this.'

'Like what?'

'Drinks and stuff.' He could feel himself squirming a little.

'What stuff?'

'Oh, I don't know. Coming back here every night, sort of slotting into a groove. I feel I'm almost taking you for granted.'

She held the drink, still hadn't touched it, had that serious look about her that made him uneasy. She said, 'I don't feel you take me for granted . . . and I don't think you really feel that either.'

Houlihan shrugged, wouldn't look at her, sipped his cocoa. She said, 'Do you like it here?'

He nodded. 'I do. And I'm really grateful to you for letting me stay.'

'But?'

He hated this. 'Well . . . it's beginning to not feel right.'

She turned the glass in her fingers and the ice clinked softly. She said, 'Have your feelings changed for me lately?'

'What do you mean?'

'I mean you said you enjoyed my company and we know we understand each other and we get on well. Has any of that changed for you?'

'Well, no. It hasn't.'

'Am I starting to bore you now? Too many wisecracks?'

'No, not at all. You've never bored me. And I like your wit. Most of the time.' He smiled at her.

'And you're comfortable in this house?'

'Yes. Of course.'

'And you're safe here. Do you feel safe?'

'Safer than my place, I suppose, the way things are just now.'

'So you're happy and comfortable and you still enjoy my company. So what is it, Houlihan? Is it getting just a bit too much like a proper relationship?'

He drank some cocoa to disguise swallowing the lump in his throat. 'Maybe.'

She looked at him and he tried to read what

was there. A mixture of frustration and pity with a touch of derision. He said, 'It's hard for me, Loretta.'

'You make it hard for yourself, Frankie. Very hard. Kathy's dead. She's gone. She's not coming back. You're keeping her alive in your head. Your conscience hears your alarm clock in the morning and it wakes Kathy up as well and keeps her right there beside you all day. And after a while you start to feel guilty about using up any of your emotions on anyone or anything else. And do you feel guilty because you still love her memory so much? Her memory? Or is it because you just can't get through your life without guilt of some kind? Which is it, Frankie?'

He looked at her for what seemed a long time and he felt empty and sick. 'Maybe I should just go home, Loretta.'

'Maybe you should. Lock yourself up there. Why don't you just climb into a barrel and pull the lid across and stay there for the rest of your life? Then you'll never have to risk meeting somebody you might actually feel something for. Why don't you do that? And eventually you'll fade away and die too and maybe you'll find that there never was a heaven and that Kathy was never waiting and that all you'd done was wasted most of your life.'

She left her drink on the table and got up. He heard her running upstairs and he sat shaking his bowed head and wondering how he'd managed to let it get this far.

He felt distressed, confused by her outburst, ashamed for some reason. Wasn't it right that there was a cut-off point between them? She'd made it sound like he was ill or something. He hated the thought that he'd hurt her. But he certainly didn't feel that he'd deceived her in any way. She was being unfair. He went upstairs and knocked on her room door.

'Come in,' she said quietly. She was sitting on the bed, looking sad. He stood at the open door, leaning on it, and said, 'I didn't mean to upset you.'

'I know.' She sounded tired.

'I want to be sure that I haven't, well, led you astray in any way. Led you astray is not the right expression. I—'

'Strung me along?'

'Maybe that's what I meant. I thought I'd made it really clear from the start that I wasn't looking for a romantic relationship with you. If I didn't—'

The fire came back into her eyes along with the frustration. 'Frankie, this is not about me or us! It's about you! Yes, you made it bloody clear from the outset what you didn't want. I accepted it then and I do now. I'm happy with it. It's your unhappiness that's getting to me. You are slowly torturing yourself to death with guilt over Kathy. Can't you see that?'

'You don't know everything that happened or maybe it would be easier to understand.'

She got off the bed, animated again now, and

came towards him. 'It's you who doesn't understand, Frankie. I don't need to know what happened, how it happened, what your part in it was. Whatever happened is done with; it's gone. You could live to be a thousand and double the guilt you feel every day of your life and then multiply it by a hundred billion and it would still not change a single thing. It wouldn't bring Kathy back. It wouldn't make you feel any better.'

Her face was close to his now and he could see how much she meant everything, how passionately she felt about it. And it overpowered him. He couldn't think of anything to say.

She said, 'Do you know what the really tragic, ironic thing about all of this is? If Kathy *can* see you now, if she is looking down from somewhere, she must be torturing herself about how you've turned out, how you've handled this. She loved you as much as you loved her. Do you think for a second she wouldn't want you to be happy? Do you think she really wants you to be miserable for the rest of your life? What kind of love would that be, Frankie? Look at it the other way around. What would you have wanted for her if you had died first?'

He looked at her. 'Do you think I haven't been through all that logic in my own head?' he asked quietly.

'I don't know. Have you?' As much aggression as passion now in her voice, her face.

'A million times.'

'And you always come to the conclusion that living in misery is the best answer?'

He could feel anger rising. 'I don't live in misery, Loretta.'

'You do a bloody good impression of it then, Frankie!'

'I'm still grieving, for God's sake!'

'Who for? Yourself?'

He stepped back, looked at her more coldly now. She hung her head for a few moments, clasped her hands. When she looked up, tears were on her cheeks. She said softly, 'I'm trying to help you, Frankie.'

He could find no warmth for her. 'Remind me not to be around when you're trying to hurt me.' He left the room and went to pack his things.

It was after three a.m. when he reached Lambourn. Between tiredness and the battering his emotions had taken his senses were not at their sharpest, but he parked half a mile short of the house and approached it as quietly as he could, although even careful footsteps sounded loud in the darkened streets of a sleeping village.

He had placed tiny pieces of putty, coloured to blend with the woodwork, across the seals on the back and front doors and on the downstairs windows. As he felt for them in the dark he was glad he'd decided to place them near the corners. They all still held the seal. No one had been in since he'd set them, at least not through these entrances.

He'd had special locks fitted to all the windows meaning they'd almost certainly have had to break the glass to gain entry.

He went inside and switched the lights on. It was as he'd left it. Some mail on the doormat and the sound of a dripping tap were the only differences. Maybe the tap had been dripping when he'd left and he just hadn't noticed. He turned it fully closed and there was silence. The house was cold. He went back for the car.

After less than four hours' sleep, Houlihan got up and got into his running gear then went out into the dreary dampness of a March morning, hoping the rhythm of a run would bring back some balance to his mind.

He usually ran the roads that the racehorses used going to and from the gallops as he enjoyed seeing them and nodding a greeting to their riders. But he didn't want to see anyone this morning so he jogged to the edge of the village and into the fields, squelching along muddy footpaths, trying to get to that steady pace that required two breaths out and two breaths in, each coinciding with a stride and building a tempo in his head that, with a little concentration, would start driving out all thoughts and worries till he reached an almost trance-like state.

He didn't quite get there, couldn't push Loretta and her words fully out of his mind. He'd spent the drive home last night nursing a steadily building resentment for her and her opinions, but he was surprised now at how bereft he felt having fallen out with her. The worse thing was he didn't know how to fix it, had no positive experience in how to mend bridges with women. With Kathy there'd been no need. With his mother he'd simply failed.

When he got home, Houlihan moped around the house, half-heartedly doing some cleaning, trying to get his thoughts in order. Loretta and he were supposed to make arrangements to go and interview Lenny Caraldo. He'd have to call her at some point. Or she'd have to call him. He also needed to ring home and see how the family were doing. He checked his watch: 10.20 a.m. No point in putting it off any longer.

He rang Margaret who told him his mother was no better. 'How are things with you now after all this kerfuffle in the papers?' she asked.

'I'm fine. It's all pretty much blown over now.'

'You sound a bit down, Frankie.'

'I'm tired, that's all. Didn't get home till the early hours and didn't sleep too good. But I'm all right.'

'Why don't you come over for a proper break? Stay a week or two?'

He sighed at the thought. No resolution over Ma, the conflict with Pat – it might make for a difficult time. But to stay in Lambourn with all the bad stuff that was going on was no more attractive. The mid-point was the Irish Sea and he wondered briefly about some fantasy island there. He realised he'd need to keep trying with Ma and the prospect of returning to the priesthood was beginning to take more than an ethereal shape in his mind. With all that was going on, he believed his emotions, at least, could begin to make a case for it.

Houlihan said, 'That might not be a bad idea, Margaret. Let me try and work something out and call you back.'

'Fine. You can stay here. You'd be welcome.'

'Thanks. Thank you. Give my love to Ma and to everyone.'

He put the phone down and sat awhile staring at the wall. He had to call Loretta. Her mobile was switched to voicemail. He left no message and tried her home number. It rang out. He called her mobile again. 'Loretta, it's Frankie. Please call when you can.'

TWENTY-EIGHT

Houlihan decided to try and track down Lenny Caraldo without alerting anyone he spoke to that Caraldo might be under suspicion of anything. He discovered pretty quickly that the photographer was in hospital recovering from being rolled on by a horse at Newbury. He'd been squatting by an open ditch, clicking the time-release shutter for his camera which was set up there, when a horse took a heavy fall, somersaulted through the rails and landed on him. Houlihan checked the online *Racing News* site and found the report from two weeks ago – something else he'd missed. There was a paragraph of an update from three days before saying Caraldo was making good progress.

He was in Newbury Hospital, a reasonable halfway point between Lambourn and Guildford, and Houlihan hoped Loretta would want him with her when she saw Caraldo.

* * *

Loretta called in mid-afternoon sounding very sub-dued. 'Are you all right?' she asked.

'Not at my brilliant best but I'm glad you called. I shouldn't have been so hasty last night in leaving.'

'I don't blame you. I'd have left me as well, the mood I got myself into. I went too far. I'm sorry.'

'It's okay.' He was going to say that her heart was in the right place but playing it in his mind it sounded patronising. She was quiet for a while then said, 'What do you want to do?'

'I just want us to get back on an even keel. I know I've got a lot of things to sort out in my head but I'm not ready yet to sort them. Not that I know how to but that doesn't matter too much just now. Am I just confusing things even more?'

'Yes.'

He smiled because he could hear the smile back in her voice and was pleased that she was confident enough in their understanding that she could say just that one word and know he'd take it as she meant it.

'Good,' he said. 'Now, I've found out where Lenny Caraldo is. He's in Newbury hospital.'

'He's the photographer, isn't he? Nothing too negative, I hope, or are the doctors awaiting developments?'

'Well I wonder how many times Lenny's heard those ones and burst his stitches laughing.'

'You never know. They might surprise him. Want to make an appointment or turn up at visiting time?'

They chose visiting time to make sure he wasn't alerted. But Caraldo couldn't talk to them. His broken jaw was wired together and his doctor said it would stay that way for at least another ten days.

In the hospital car park they sat in Houlihan's car for a while. Loretta said, 'Not exactly having the luck we need, are we? Two key people from the short list and we can't speak to either.'

Houlihan rubbed his eyes wearily. 'I know, and nowhere else to look for now.'

They were quiet for a while, then Loretta said, 'Let me get this right: the thinking behind any suspicion of Shaw and Caraldo is that Eddie Malloy could have done something to affect their business, right?'

'In theory.'

'He could have told Shaw his services were no longer required and started up his own Makalu valet business.'

'That's right, or he could have charged Shaw a sort of franchise fee. Same for Caraldo.'

'This doesn't stack up, Houlihan. I can't see Malloy messing around trying to screw a few quid out of people like Shaw and Caraldo, can you?'

'I think they'd have much bigger fish to fry until they've got all their acquisitions under their belt and the deal done on the betting rights, but after that, with Malloy in charge, he'd have started on the nitty-gritty.'

'So why did he start early with Bert Jacobsen?'

'I don't know, but I suspect it was because Malloy knew as soon as he took over Badbury racecourse that Jacobsen's house was going to have to go to accommodate the new grandstand. That was a big investment – millions. Knowing Malloy's straightness he'd have wanted to make it clear to Bert from day one instead of leading him on for a while.'

She nodded, looking thoughtful. Houlihan said, 'Maybe you ought to go and see Bert Jacobsen.'

'Maybe I should, but I think I'd much rather see Eddie.'

'Me too.'

'I've tried Keelor a dozen times. He's ignoring me and it's really beginning to piss me off.'

'I could call him. He might see me,' Houlihan offered.

'I think I'd rather pitch up at his place unannounced. What do you think?'

'Fine. When?'

'Do you know where he's staying?'

'I can find out, I think, in the morning,' he said.

'Will you call me and we'll go there tomorrow?'

'Sure.'

They sat quietly, awkward in silence for the first time. Then she said, 'I'd better get back home and get the Hoover out. I've got the dreaded parents at the weekend.'

'I thought they'd be skiing in Aspen?'

'In March? Far too cold for them. April or

May for Aspen. They're in the Bahamas, flying in Saturday morning.'

'Something special?'

She hesitated, then said, 'My birthday.'

He felt surprised. 'Oh good,' he said lamely. 'Big party?'

'Not really. Brother, sister, nephews, nieces, a few friends of the family.'

'That sounds nice.'

A few more silent moments, then, 'You'd be welcome if you wanted to come along.'

'Ohh, I?'

'I mean, I'm not inviting you to meet my parents or anything like that. Nobody would get the wrong idea, I'd make sure of that.'

Houlihan smiled slowly. It was the first time he'd seen her flustered. 'And how would you do that, then? Give me a badge saying "This is Frankie Houlihan and he's not Loretta's boyfriend or anything".'

Now she smiled. 'I'll think of something. Do you want to come?'

'Yes. I do.'

'I've booked some rooms in the hotel down the road. Would you be awfully offended if I asked you to stay there?'

'So long as I get to keep my badge on so the hotel staff know that there is no shame in being chucked out of your house.'

'If I think they'll be in any doubt, I'll give you a note as well.'

'It's a deal.' They shook hands and Loretta got out of Houlihan's car, to go back to her own.

As Houlihan drove out of the hospital car park the headlights came on suddenly in the moving vehicle behind him, which struck him as strange. It was very dark and curtains of rain in the strong wind made visibility poor. The driver had travelled through the car park with no lights on. Now the beam was high. It was a van or a big Jeep, and it stayed behind Houlihan as he drove cautiously through rain-lashed streets. Houlihan's normal route home would have been along some quiet back-roads. Not a good idea if this guy really was following him. He decided to head towards the M4, see what happened.

The vehicle followed.

Once on the motorway the weather seemed worse. Heavy spray didn't help and Houlihan stayed on the inside lane doing sixty. The vehicle was still there. He was pretty sure now it was a Jeep. Steadily, Houlihan reduced speed, encouraging the driver to overtake. At forty-five mph he realised he wasn't going to. The Jeep was still about fifty metres behind him.

Houlihan felt a ripple of queasiness. Malloy's burning form came to mind. So did his screams. Fear began taking hold.

He tried to think but his mind wouldn't function; it wanted to concentrate only on how much he might have to suffer. Houlihan had little experience to draw on. Before this case, nothing in his job so far had made him feel personally threatened. Playground fights had been his last experience of violence aimed directly at him.

He picked up speed again. Got back to sixty, checked the mirror. There it was. Houlihan needed to calm himself or risk doing something really stupid. He had to conquer the rising fear. He realised that this was a worse feeling than being suddenly confronted. He'd almost rather have had someone jump out at him, armed with whatever it was he had. Houlihan believed he'd never know how he'd react to something that extreme until it happened.

Maybe somebody else in his position would prefer it this way; the early realisation that a threat was building. The chance to do some planning while still relatively safe. And he knew this was a sensible attitude to take if he could get his mind under control. He did some deep breathing, forced himself to focus on it, the way he did when he ran.

He was currently in a relatively secure position. A locked car with no history of breaking down. Plenty of fuel. Fairly busy motorway. His mobile charging beside him. He could call the police. But what would he say? It would all sound so ridiculous.

He could ring Loretta instead. She'd understand, be more concerned. But what if it was a complete false alarm? How silly would he look then? He chided himself, knew that wasn't the way to think. The classic way to die of embarrassment.

There was one way to prove this once and for all. It was relatively low risk. He could stop on the hard shoulder. If the Jeep didn't want to lose him he'd have to stop too. If he pulled over suddenly the Jeep would need to stop in front of him, and by the time it'd come to a halt Houlihan could be away again and on the phone to Loretta. That was the way to do it.

Houlihan reset his odometer as he passed the next emergency phone. There'd be another phone exactly a mile away. He'd stop right beside it.

He kept his speed steady. The Jeep did too. Houlihan watched the tenths of a mile tick away on the odometer. At nine-tenths he steered onto the hard shoulder, started braking and put on his hazard lights. He sat almost rigid, eyes fixed on his rear-view mirror.

The Jeep went past. Houlihan watched for its brake lights coming on. They didn't. No discernible change in speed. Houlihan stared unblinking at the Jeep's tail-lights till they quickly disappeared in the spray. He put the reading light on and looked at his face in the mirror. His eyes were wide. He looked very pale in that dim light. He burst into relieved laughter and rubbed his face as though trying to get some pliability back into it.

A few more deep breaths and he switched off the hazards and got back onto the motorway, glad he hadn't called Loretta. He spent most of the remainder of the journey justifying all his thoughts and reactions to himself and by the time he took the final turn towards the village he was convinced that if someone had been following him he'd called all the shots right. It was good experience for any trouble ahead.

Just around a bend in the narrow road that brought him within sight of the lights at the edge of Lambourn he had to pull out quickly to pass a vehicle parked with no lights. He was lucky the heavy rain had stopped or he may not have seen it in time.

As he passed he saw it was a Jeep Cherokee, a very dark colour. Before the realisation dawned he glanced in his rear mirror and saw again those lights come on. His mind was still questioning this action replay from the hospital and trying to drop the pieces in place when the Jeep hit him from behind. The engine roar as he'd worked quickly up his gears was in his head as it bounced backwards into the headrest. Houlihan was dazed. Another hit. Houlihan held onto the wheel this time, saved his head another bang. More engine noise from behind, headlights in his mirror dazzling, seeming to light up the interior. He pressed the accelerator as the Jeep smashed into him again and his car lurched towards a ditch on the left. Houlihan wrestled it round, just kept it on the road, tried to concentrate on driving. His house was only five hundred metres away. He couldn't go there even if he could get there. Check the speedo. Fifty mph and climbing. Not good roads for fast driving. The impact was much smaller this time but the Jeep stayed on his bumper, pushing him, swerving, as though trying to get tangled up, get him off the road, stop him. Houlihan had one corner to turn to get into the village, a right turn. If he made it he could pull into the pub car park and run into the Red Lion. Tuesday night. There'd be two men and a dog in. Oh why couldn't it have been Friday or Saturday? Still, it was all he could think of. Doing over sixty now. No way could he make this turn. Still biting at his bumper with the big cattle bars, the Jeep wasn't going to let him. Two hundred metres from the turn he knew he had to go for it and take his chances: if the Jeep managed to force him out of the village, away from lights and people and safety, his chances of surviving this might be very slim. He prayed nothing would be coming the other way. He saw the road was clear, swung the wheel and felt a nudge that sent him spinning through the puddles in a terrifying waltz across the crown of the road, orange streetlights seeming to join with flashes of the Jeep's glaring headlights in some crazy disco effect. He sensed more than saw that the Jeep was beside him now; his car had turned 180 degrees and was still spinning fast. On the next turn he was ahead of the Jeep. Brake lights flaring, the big chassis bucking as the Jeep tried to stop dead, tried to make him crash into it in the next spin. And that was exactly what Houlihan's car was going to do but the Jeep braked too hard and now it spun too, sending spray across Houlihan's windscreen, watercolouring the effects of all the lights. Everything seemed in slow motion and Houlihan was beginning to assimilate things, get some sense of the way his car was behaving, the direction in which the spins were moving it. And he saw that in a maximum of two more turns it was very likely that he'd hit the lamppost on the corner, probably with the nearside wing. There'd be insufficient forward impact to do him any serious damage but he realised that the air bag would almost certainly inflate, dazing him badly at best but maybe knocking him unconscious. He pressed the cigar lighter till it clicked into its socket, then released the seatbelt clip with his left thumb, did it first time with a degree of calm and accuracy that made him smile briefly as he then let go of the steering wheel and ducked low across the passenger seat. He registered that his mobile was on the floor then heard the explosion at the same time as the sound of crunching metal. His head jerked back against the passenger seat upright and the airbag thumped him on the right hip. All the windows stayed intact. Through them he saw that the world had finally come to a halt. The airbag pinned him down. He didn't know where the Jeep was. The cigar lighter clicked and burned reassuringly red as he quickly pulled it out and rammed it into the fabric of the airbag, which was already deflating naturally. He could have punched the air with joy that his microsecond planning and action had worked out so sweetly. He sat up quickly. The engine was still running. Houlihan looked around. The Jeep was backed into a hedge, headlights still on, facing him at right-angles, wheels churning as it tried to come up out of the mud. Houlihan looked at the lamp-post he'd hit, askew but still upright, and not holding the car in any way. He found first gear and accelerated away towards the village, the lights of the Jeep finally, finally fading.

Safely inside the cottage he quickly locked the door behind him and pushed the bolt home too. Then he literally ran around the house checking locks. He didn't know where the Jeep driver was or if he was still coming after him and his compelling instinct was to try and make himself as secure as possible. Refuge in the Red Lion had been a brief thought again, but there were no locks he could use in there, nowhere he could find to hide if this guy was mad enough to come storming in after him.

Then he phoned 999. No point in messing about ringing Loretta or trying to find the number for Newbury police. For all he knew this Jeep could be coming through his front wall inside a minute. He had to fight with himself to keep a level of calm in his voice as he tried to explain to the 999 operator what had happened. She stopped the questions only when he said, 'Look, I think he may try and attack me again in the next few minutes and there's a strong chance he is armed.'

Houlihan turned off all the lights and went

upstairs, taking the mobile. From his bedroom window he could see the street and his crazily bashed-up car, which looked abandoned in the middle of the road rather than parked. He'd considered overshooting his house or stopping well short so his pursuer wouldn't know where he lived, but if the Jeep had come after him, two hundred metres or so on foot might have seen him finished off. Anyway, the driver had lain in wait. There had to be every chance he knew where Houlihan lived.

Watching from the direction he'd come, Houlihan could see for about 150 metres if he pushed his right cheek hard against the window. There was no one out there. He eased the lock off and raised the window six inches to listen for engine noise. Nothing. He rang Loretta on the mobile and told her quickly what had happened. She was totally calm and professional.

'Did you get a registration?' she asked.

'Er, I'm afraid I didn't. If he comes through the front window in it in the next few minutes I'll have pen and paper ready.'

'Okay. Point taken. Silly question.'

Still watching the street he said, 'Look, can you stay on the line here and also maybe contact the team that are on their way. I can talk you through what's happening and you can keep them up-to-date.'

'Good idea. Stay there.'

'Loretta!' he shouted.

'I'm here. You'll deafen me.'

'Sorry. Don't put me down.'

'I won't. Just be quiet while I try and set this up.'

'Okay.'

She made two calls. He heard everything she said but nothing from the other end. She came back on and said, 'We'll need to do it in a sort of four-way because of the radio system. You tell me, I tell Control, Control tells them. She thinks they're only a few minutes away from you.'

'Well, tell her to tell them that if they pass a Jeep in a ditch to have a look inside.'

'They can do that later, Houlihan, he might be on his way to you on foot.'

His stomach turned over. 'Gee thanks,' he said.

'You'll be all right. You've done well. The team will be there soon.'

'I know. Thanks.'

They were quiet for a few moments then she said, 'Do you plan to stay on in the cottage?'

Staring intently through the window he said, 'If the council will agree to a moat, drawbridge, portcullis – you know, the usual tried and trusted security methods.'

'I think you might have a few planning permission problems there.'

'Are yours any more understanding? I'll move in with you.'

'You can anyway. At least till this is over.'

He wasn't quite concentrating although he knew

she was trying to take his mind off what was happening. The suspense in waiting to see if the next vehicle along the road would have a dented front and a madman at the wheel, or a blue light on top, was becoming almost painful. He said, 'Will your guys use sirens?'

'Very unlikely.'

'Tell them they can. I don't mind. Honest.'

'They won't want to alert this man or risk panicking him if he's in a position to . . .'

'To what? Shoot me?'

'And they really won't want the public hearing the siren and coming out of their houses, er . . .'

'Into the line of fire?'

'Maybe I should shut up, eh?'

'Maybe you should,' he said.

'You'll laugh about this tomorrow.'

'I don't think so, Loretta.'

'Well, maybe not tomorrow, but sometime.'

He heard a tinny noise through the earpiece. Loretta asked him to hold. She came back on. 'Our boys have just turned into your street. Can you confirm there is no one on the premises but you?'

'Affirmative. I hope.'

'Frankie!' It was a reprimand.

'Sorry. All doors and windows are still locked and I've heard no sound of breaking and entering. I think it's safe to assume he's not in here anywhere.'

She reported that back.

Houlihan saw a steadily spinning reflection in

the wet streets and windows, which grew stronger and seemed to unscrew the tension tap in his body and let him start unwinding into what he was certain would end up with him a gibbering wreck. 'Loretta, I can see the blue light.'

He heard her sigh and finally drop the professionalism. 'Thank God,' she said, sounding for the first time as though she'd been as scared as he had.

TWENTY-NINE

Houlihan called Bobby Cranfield and told him what had happened. 'Armed police? At your place?' he asked.

'That's right.'

'Damn.'

'What's wrong?'

'The press often monitor police radio broadcasts. You might find somebody knocking on your door in the next few minutes.'

'I'll tell them it was a false alarm.'

'You can try. I'm not sure they'll believe you, and won't that fellow from the *Racing News*, the Lambourn correspondent, sniff this out anyway from all the commotion in the village?'

'Stonebanks told me Ben's in Ibiza. Not even his sense of smell stretches this far.'

'Mmmm. Well, Frankie, we'll just have to sit on it for now. I'll have a word with the police to keep it quiet from their end. If you get any calls from the press tell them it was an attempted break-in or something.'

'Fine. What about my car? It's pretty bashed up. Can you make arrangements to get it towed away tonight so nobody sees it in daylight?'

'I will. Leave that to me.'

'And will you tell Sam Hooper?'

'Yes, but he may want it from the horse's mouth.'

'Tell him the horse is very tired and a wee bit bruised.'

He chuckled. 'Okay. Try and get a good night's sleep. We'll talk tomorrow.'

'Bobby, one more thing.'

'What?'

'Do you know where Vaughn Keelor is based?'

'Why do you want to know?'

'He's not returning DS Moran's calls about the condition of Eddie Malloy. She wants to go along to his office.'

After a few moments' silence, Bobby said, 'I believe Mr Keelor is using one of the private boxes at Esher as his office.'

'Thanks. Last favour, please don't tell Sam Hooper we plan to go there.'

Cranfield sighed heavily. Houlihan said, 'Bobby, please?'

'Okay, Frankie, okay.'

One armed officer stayed downstairs till the next morning. Houlihan had a few snatches of sleep in between replays in his head of everything that had happened. He was unable to analyse it in any objective fashion but his overall conclusion was that a mixture of luck and the ability to keep cool and think under pressure had got him out of it. His belief that nobody knows what they'll do in a suddenly dangerous situation was borne out. Between saving Malloy and saving himself, he'd twice shown that he was able to cope, to function well, think quickly, and avoid panic. It helped his confidence a little bit – but not much, knowing that the man was still out there.

The police found nothing but the tracks gouged by the Jeep as it had freed itself from the hedge. They reckoned they might get some paint samples from where the Jeep had hit his car, but Houlihan knew the crime, at the moment, was nothing more than what cynics might have considered a nasty bout of road rage. The police wouldn't be pulling their forensic people off any murders for this.

Loretta arrived at ten o'clock and the policeman with the gun left. Houlihan was surprised at how glad he felt to see her. He felt he was among friends again. 'Thanks for coming over,' he said, kissing her on the cheek. She held on to his arms lightly and looked up at him. 'Are you all right?'

'I'm fine.'

'You don't look it.'

'Just a bit short of sleep. Want some coffee?' He was conscious of not following his inclination to pull away from her, of shaking off her grasp, delicate as it was. He didn't want another row. But she must have sensed it and she let go and said, 'Sit down. I'll make it. Have you eaten?'

'No.' He sat at the table, suddenly feeling weary.

'What do you want?'

'Well, we could have eggs, I think. The bread will be stale and the milk's probably off. I haven't been shopping for a while.'

She talked as she opened cupboards. 'No, that's what comes from living away from home for a few days. In the lap of luxury. Spoiled.' She turned to look at him. 'I could go to the shop if you like?'

'Nah, don't worry. I'm not that hungry. And I'm not inclined to stay here for the next few nights either.'

She filled the kettle. 'Coming back to my place?'

'And endanger you? I'd rather not.'

She stopped and turned to look at him as she fluttered her eyelashes and primped her hair. 'Why, that's the sweetest thing anyone's ever said to me.'

They laughed, the tension dissolving.

She sat down across from him. 'I've got no problem with you staying with me till this is finished.' She was serious now. 'I think it would reduce your risk a hell of a lot. Your attacker might find out, but he'd almost certainly also find out that I'm a police officer.'

'An unarmed one.'

She sat up straight, feigning annoyance. 'So that's it? If I had a gun you'd be rushing to pack your pyjamas right now?'

He smiled. 'Look, I really appreciate the offer. I do. Let me think about it.'

'Fine.' She made coffee and they discussed plans to try and see Keelor. They now knew he was based at Esher racecourse, the first the company had bought, but they didn't know his movements. Loretta rang the racecourse office. 'Hello, I need to send a fax to Mr Keelor, for his eyes only, around 2 p.m. today. Can you tell me if he'll be in his office to receive it? Good. What's the best number to send it to please?' She had to wait a minute then she jotted down the number. She looked at Houlihan. 'Ready?'

He looked at his watch. 'If we leave now we'll be about three hours early.'

'We're going somewhere else first to beat Keelor to it.'

'Where?'

'Back to see our Mr Penrose at the hospital.' She took the car keys from her pocket. 'I'll drive. You're pretty useless at driving in a straight line from what I've heard.'

Houlihan smiled and got up to follow her. In the car and moving, Loretta said, 'What's the betting Malloy's no longer in this hospital?'

Houlihan shrugged. 'What do you think?'

'I'd bet a million Keelor's had him moved. If not after we were there then definitely after the story broke.'

'The consultant said he wasn't fit to talk, never mind moving him.'

'Keelor already moved him once. He'll have done it again. Trust me.'

'So why don't we just go and see Keelor and ask him?'

'Because he won't tell. He knows exactly why I've been calling him,' she said.

'Penrose might not tell us either, but as soon as we walk out he'll pick up the phone to Keelor.'

Houlihan saw certainty in her face when she turned to him and said, 'No, he won't.

THIRTY

The hospital receptionist picked up what looked like an old-fashioned BBC microphone and said in a treacly voice, 'Would Mr Penrose kindly contact reception at his convenience. Thank you.'

'Would you like to take a seat?' she asked Loretta and Houlihan, and she opened both palms with a flourish indicating the soft furniture behind them.

'Thank you,' Loretta said coldly, then, as they walked to the chairs, 'Bet she used to be an air hostess. Did you see the way she did that? And behind you are the emergency exits, one each side of the aircraft.' She tried to mimic the receptionist's voice. Houlihan smiled. They sat down.

Penrose kept them waiting almost ten minutes, allowing Loretta's temper time to percolate. He came through the double doors and strode towards them. He was dressed in a brown suit, neatly pressed, and carried no medical paraphernalia. He managed a tight smile as he stopped beside them and folded his arms. 'Good afternoon. What can I do for you?' Loretta showed her badge. 'Remember us, Mr Penrose?'

'Yes, of course. What can I do for you?' Houlihan sensed a wariness in him.

Loretta said, 'Is Eddie Malloy still your patient?'

'Mr Malloy is still my patient.'

'Is he here?' she asked.

'Mr Malloy is still not fit to be interviewed.'

'That's not what I asked you.'

'I appreciate that, but it really is all that you need to know. With respect,' he swallowed a lump in his throat.

Loretta said, 'Mr Penrose, how many patients do you have here?'

He seemed relieved at the diversion and said, 'At the moment, seventy-seven.'

'Paying how much?'

'I don't see the relevance of that question.'

'Quite a lot of money no doubt. What, a thousand a night? Maybe more?'

Penrose simply shrugged. She said, 'I'll take that as a yes, and I guess that what these people are paying for are not just your skills, whatever they may be, but the nice plush address for their visitors and their get-well cards, the five-course meals from your Michelin chef, the widescreen TVs and perfumed Jacuzzis. Not to mention the dignified air, the peace and quiet.'

Penrose was smiling now, a nervous smile, with his top lip quivering slightly. He brought a hand to his mouth to disguise it and nodded. 'Possibly,' he said.

Loretta asked, 'Do you have a set visiting period or can people attend at any time?'

'Approved visitors coming to see patients who are healthy enough to receive them can come at any time, although most tend to come in the recognised hour beginning at seven o'clock.'

Loretta said, 'Well, in the recognised hour, when they're all sitting round their friends and loved ones, opening the Harrods mini-hampers and chatting quietly, I'm coming back here with a search warrant – and Mr Houlihan and I, along with four armed police officers, are going to be turning over mattresses, opening wardrobes, checking toilet cubicles, and questioning your visitors and your patients exhaustively in the search for Eddie Malloy.'

He stared at her, face reddening. She said, 'And if you think you can go away and ask the advice of Mr Keelor, then, when we arrive at seven, decide to tell us where Eddie Malloy is, that won't be acceptable. I will not be asking to see you again when we come back, Mr Penrose. It'll be too late for that. We'll come through those doors in a considerable hurry. I'll stop long enough to show you the warrant. I will not be talking.'

His hand was completely over his mouth now and a film of sweat had formed on his receding scalp-line. She let him cook for a few more moments then said, 'Is Eddie Malloy here?'

He shook his head.

'Was he ever here?'

'Yes.' He said it quietly behind his hand.

Loretta said, 'Pardon?'

He moved his hand. 'Mr Malloy was here.'

'When did he leave?'

'Ten days ago.'

'Discharged or transferred?'

'My understanding is that he was being taken to another hospital.'

'Did he walk out, or was he carried?'

'He left in a private ambulance.'

'What was his condition when you discharged him?'

'I didn't discharge him. He was not fit to be discharged. He was transferred at the request of his company.'

'To where?'

'I don't know. I honestly don't know.'

Loretta said, 'Sit down, Mr Penrose.' He almost slumped into the chair. She wore a look of mild disgust as she watched him before producing her notebook. She said, 'It's very important for your sake that you're completely truthful with me. Mr Malloy was the victim of an attempted murder. This case is extremely serious. Do you understand?'

Penrose licked his lips with the tip of his tongue and nodded. The sweat beads grew bigger. He was looking fixedly at Loretta. She said, 'If you're not one hundred per cent honest with me I need to warn you that a charge of perverting the course of justice may result.'

He nodded again. Loretta said, 'Do you know where Eddie Malloy was taken to when he left here?'

'No. I don't. I asked but they wouldn't tell me. I was concerned about him. They told me I'd still be retained and would be asked to come and see him soon at his new base.'

'And that's why you told us you were still treating him?'

'Yes. I didn't lie.'

'Okay. Who are *they*?'

'His company, Makalu Holdings.'

'And who was the person that you effectively signed Mr Malloy over to?'

Penrose hesitated slightly but knew he'd gone too far already. 'Mr Keelor,' he said.

'Do you have paperwork for this discharge or transfer, or whatever you want to call it?'

'Yes. It was all done properly, of course.'

'I'll want copies.'

'Fine. That's all right. I can get them now if you'd like.'

'One more question . . . was Eddie Malloy talking clearly and coherently when he left here, or at least capable of doing so?'

'He was suffering from amnesia.'

Loretta looked briefly at Frankie. 'Total amnesia?' she asked.

'Total. Although it's early days.'

'But he was talking?' asked Frankie.

Penrose nodded. 'The amnesia would have been the result of shock.'

'How was he in himself?' asked Frankie. 'How were the burns?'

'Responding to treatment, but still quite a way to go.'

'Fit to be interviewed?' asked Loretta.

'It's not just a question of a patient being able to talk or to listen; it's about the potential effect of some questions on his emotional and psychological recovery.'

'So is that a yes or no?'

'It's a no.'

Loretta nodded slowly, fixing her gaze on Penrose's eyes. She said, 'Tell me, was Eddie Malloy even here when we last called?'

Penrose looked away, then said, 'He left the same afternoon.'

She paused, staring at him. He wouldn't meet her gaze. She said, 'You called Keelor and told him we'd been here and Mr Malloy was on his way shortly afterwards?'

Penrose nodded. Loretta said, 'Listen to me.' Penrose looked at her. She said, 'If you call Keelor or anyone else to say we have been here I'll have you arrested and charged with perverting the course of justice. Do you understand?'

'Yes,' Penrose said quietly.

'I'll have you publicly frogmarched out of here by uniformed officers,' she said, and Houlihan heard an edge of cruelty in her tone.

Penrose replied, 'I will not call anyone.'

'Good. Now get me a copy of the transfer papers.'

They arrived at Esher racecourse at 11.50 and marched into the main office reception. Houlihan showed the woman behind the desk his Jockey Club Security Department ID card and said, 'Where is Mr Keelor's office, please?'

'Do you have an appointment?'

'I don't need one. This is a licensed premises under the jurisdiction of the Jockey Club.'

She frowned and tried to think what the best response was. She picked up the phone. 'I'll just tell Mr Keelor you're here.' Houlihan reached across and put his hand on the receiver. 'Please don't do that. We're on Jockey Club security business.' He managed to look at her quite coldly. She took her hand off the phone. To make sure she didn't call while they were on their way he said, 'Please escort us to Mr Keelor's office.' She began to look worried. Houlihan said, 'You'll be free to go once you've done that.'

The receptionist seemed relieved and quickly came out from behind the desk. 'This way,' she said.

They followed a few strides behind her and Loretta grabbed his arm and whispered, 'I love it when you're forceful!' He smiled. Not his usual way of operating, but he had to admit he'd admired the way Loretta had handled Penrose.

They followed their escort up two flights of stairs, then she pointed to a door without speaking and hurried away.

It was Loretta's turn now. She knocked on the door, and Houlihan stood behind her. Keelor called out 'Yes?' She turned the handle and they went in.

He looked across from his seat at a big desk, the glass doors behind him letting in plenty of daylight and showing the western end of the race-course as it fell away on a steady slope to the far side. Houlihan watched his face closely and thought he saw a glimmer of confusion before the cool-ness asserted itself and Keelor's eyes locked on him. 'Mr Houlihan.'

'Good morning, Mr Keelor.'

'I'm afraid I didn't have this one in my diary,' he said.

'I didn't either. But since DS Moran here seemed to be having trouble contacting you I thought I'd bring her along. Knowing how helpful you nor-mally are, you'll understand.'

Keelor nodded, weighing things up. He stood and walked across the room, held out his hand. Loretta took it. He said, 'Detective Sergeant, for-give me. Have you been trying to reach me?'

'You know I have. I've left numerous messages on your voicemail.'

He shook his head slowly. 'I must have a word with my secretary about being more selective. She screens all my messages you see. She must have erased them.'

Loretta said, 'She classes requests from the police about an attempted murder of one of your people alongside those from insurance salesmen then?'

He smiled. 'She's very protective of my time, Detective Sergeant. It's a valuable commodity.'

'Well, I'm going to have to ask you to invest some of it in helping us try and find Eddie Malloy's attacker. Would that be okay?' The heavy edge of sarcasm didn't seem to faze him.

'Sure. Come and sit down. Would you like some coffee? Tea?'

They declined as they sat down and faced Keelor across his desk. The American almost lolled in his chair, head back so that he slightly looked down his thin nose at them. Loretta took a notebook and pen from her handbag. Keelor said, 'Fire away.'

Loretta said, 'Where's Eddie Malloy?'

'In hospital.'

'Which one?'

'I'm not telling you.'

'Why not?'

'Because he's not fit to be interviewed.'

'I didn't say I wanted to interview him. I want to know where he is.'

'He's safe and under our protection.'

She paused. Houlihan could see from the corner of his eye that her head was perfectly still and he guessed she was having a staring match with the American. She said, 'Eddie Malloy is the prime witness in a case of attempted murder. If you don't tell me where he is, you may find yourself in court for obstructing the law.'

Keelor leaned forward and plucked a paperclip from his desktop tray and started twisting it. 'Malloy is under expert medical supervision to help him have the best quality of life possible in the long-term. He is also being guarded twenty-four-seven. The man who attacked him would, I'm sure, love to know exactly where Malloy is so he can have another crack. Ergo, the more people who know where he is, the more he is exposed to risk.'

'The information will be locked in police files, Mr Keelor.'

'It may well be, Miss Moran, but I'd guess you'll want to take yourself along to the hospital he's in just to check things out; or Mr Houlihan might, in his position as Jockey Club Security Department Investigator. Now, given the publicity this case has had, don't you think there's just a little chance that this guy you're so keen to nail will be tracking your movements?'

'Mr Houlihan won't go there. When Eddie Malloy is fit for interview, I'll attend.'

Keelor said, 'And do you think this guy doesn't know – well, put it this way – how closely you and Mr Houlihan have been working together on this case?'

Ridiculously and maddeningly, Houlihan felt himself blush and hoped that Keelor wouldn't look at him. He did, and smiled.

Loretta didn't miss a stride. 'The potential

danger is for us to evaluate, Mr Keelor, not you. If another detective needs to interview Mr Malloy to maximise security then that's what will happen. Now, where is he?'

Keelor sat up straight, placed his palms flat on the desk and sighed. 'Look, Miss Moran, I'll provide you with a letter from Malloy's consultant confirming he's not fit to be interviewed.'

'That's not what I asked you for. I want to know where he is right now. Are you going to tell me?'

'No. I'm not.'

Loretta put her notebook away and stood up. 'Then I suggest you consult a lawyer over the next twenty-four hours. Unless I have the information I want by this time tomorrow, a warrant will be issued for your arrest.'

He smiled and shook his head. 'Don't be foolish, miss.'

She put a card on his desk. 'My contact details. I believe you already have Mr Houlihan's number. A call to either of us will do. Goodbye.'

Houlihan followed her out.

Striding across the car park, Houlihan said, 'Was all that warrant stuff genuine?'

'I can get it. Might not be for tomorrow. Let's go and see Carter now, get things moving.' Carter was Loretta's boss.

They got in the car and headed back towards London. 'We need to think about this,' Houlihan said.

Loretta was obviously uptight. 'There's nothing to think about. He's obstructing the police.'

'Arresting Keelor would be news everywhere but the North Pole. Maybe even there. There's all sorts of implications, not least the damage to Makalu's share price. That guy is Makalu in the same way Richard Branson is Virgin.'

'I don't care if he's Colonel Sanders and Ronald Mcfucking Donald rolled into one. He's not above the law, Frankie!'

Houlihan raised his hands defensively. 'Whoa! I'm not saying he is. I'm just saying that you marching him away to be charged could wipe hundreds of millions off the value of his business, and—'

'Good incentive for him, then, isn't it?'

'Loretta, the vice-president of the United States is a personal friend of Keelor's. Keelor's lawyers won't be calling Carter, they'll be calling the Home Secretary.'

'So what are you trying to say, Frankie? That I'm a nobody? That my professional opinion won't count in this?'

'No, I'm not. I'm saying expect to find the bloody sky falling in on you in the next few hours. I'm on your side. Remember?'

Staring straight ahead, jaw clenched, she nodded sharply then reached across and surprised Houlihan by grasping his hand and squeezing it. He returned the squeeze reassuringly but the tension stayed in Loretta's face.

*   *   *

Averaging ten miles an hour in the traffic, Loretta had calmed down and was trying to figure things out. She shook her head. 'Keelor plays the Mr Cool act, and I'm telling you, Frankie, this thing doesn't sit right with me at all; it's just not hanging together. What's it been since Malloy was injured, a month? And he's still not capable of talking? Do you buy this amnesia stuff?'

'I don't know. I suppose it's possible.'

'I think it's bullshit. I think Keelor is just trying to keep us away. Why would he want to do that?'

'Maybe he's just trying to keep Eddie safe, like he says.'

'Nah, he's too manic about it, Frankie.'

'He's a manic sort of fella.'

Houlihan's mobile rang. He recognised Bobby Cranfield's voice and sensed from his tone what was coming next. 'Frankie, are you in London?'

'About three miles from the office. You want to see me.' It was a statement.

'Yes please.'

'Give me half an hour.'

'Okay. Is DS Moran with you?'

'She is.'

'I'll need to see you alone but I'd also be grateful if DS Moran could wait until after our meeting before she proceeds any further with this investigation.'

'You mean in case she gets that warrant Keelor rang you about?'

A long pause, then, 'Yes. We can't afford to

throw out the baby with the bath water here.'

'Some baby, Bobby.'

'You're right. And if we lose him we can probably say goodbye to the Jockey Club. For good.'

'I'll see you soon.'

Loretta turned to him. 'The lobbying's started, then?'

'Yep. He's asking me to keep you on the lead till we've talked. Metaphorically speaking.'

She smiled, shaking her head slowly. 'So Keelor called the Jockey Club rather than his fancy lawyers.'

'He'll want to use his contacts first.'

'No way, Frankie. He's not getting off the hook.'

'I agree. Just give me half an hour with Bobby before you meet Carter.'

'Why? It's pointless. It'll make no difference. We'll just be an extra half hour away from finding your friend.'

'I know, but . . .'

'Frankie! You owe the Jockey Club nothing, come on!'

'I know. But I owe Bobby Cranfield a lot.'

She sighed and turned to him, shaking her head slowly, but Houlihan could see she was conceding.

'Is that a yes, then?'

'I suppose so.'

In the Jockey Club offices, Houlihan trotted upstairs, nodded to Elaine on reception as the door swung closed behind him and hurried down the corridor to Bobby Cranfield's office. He stopped with his hand on the doorknob as he heard Hooper's raised voice from within.

'I'll make him see sense!'

'You'll make him angry, Sam, like you usually do. It'll be hard enough.'

'You're too easy on him. You can't treat your staff as equals you know.'

A pause, then Bobby, just about audible to Houlihan as he put his ear to the door, said, 'You mean tell them what you want and make them do it?'

'Exactly!'

'Fine, Sam. Get out. I'll debrief you after my meeting with Houlihan.'

Houlihan smiled and knocked on the door, keen to maximise Hooper's discomfort. As Bobby said 'Hold on', Houlihan opened the door and went in, his smile letting a red-faced Hooper know he'd overheard. Bobby sighed and said, 'I'll see you later, Sam.'

'Hi Sam,' Houlihan said as his boss marched past. Hooper didn't even look at him but slammed the door so hard the blast of air ruffled Houlihan's hair. Houlihan said to Bobby, 'In one of his better moods today then, eh?'

Bobby smiled wearily and spun the wheels on his chair to glide towards Houlihan and shake hands. 'Thanks for coming in at such short notice.'

'That's okay. We were on our way to Scotland Yard.'

'Take a seat.'

Houlihan did. Bobby said, 'Vaughn Keelor is very concerned.'

'About being arrested?'

'About having such a hot-headed officer as Loretta Moran trying to find Malloy's attacker.'

'That's his story.' Houlihan sat straighter.

'Come on, Frankie. I know you've got a good relationship with that woman but she's hardly the soul of discretion, is she?'

'She tried discretion with Keelor. We both did. It doesn't work. He knows where Malloy is, and DS Moran needs to speak to Eddie. Keelor won't let her see him.'

'For very good reasons. This man could be tracking her movements, waiting for her to lead him to Malloy.'

'Then she'll send another officer.'

Cranfield shook his head. 'Keelor is paranoid about Malloy's safety. He's not going to give in and he says Malloy's not fit to talk anyway.'

'Then get him to allow a police visit. If Eddie can't talk, he can't talk. The police will have what they want, they'll know they're not being obstructed and they can also approve whatever security arrangements Keelor's made. Makes sense to me. What do you think?'

'I think that Keelor is not used to having his judgement questioned. He was going completely apeshit on the phone.' Houlihan saw real concern in Cranfield's eyes. 'Listen, Frankie, he'll pull the deal for our courses. He's got a six-month get-out in the contract.'

'On what basis?'

'To cover any major external event. Anything outside his control that could materially affect the future profitability of the group.'

'Like being arrested? I'd have said that was well within his control.'

'A murder attempt on his top man in the UK wasn't, though.'

'Maybe not. Maybe not.'

Cranfield rubbed his eyes. 'Frankie, you know we were depending on this deal to stay alive, to keep the security department going.'

Houlihan nodded. 'To keep all of us in jobs.'

'More than that, Frankie, come on! The Jockey Club have been around for over two hundred years.'

'And they've gone from running racing to trying to hang on by their fingernails to some form of authority.'

'Of which you are a part, don't forget! It's as much your duty as mine to try and preserve this. If we go under, what happens to the integrity of British racing?'

Houlihan had never seen Cranfield so riled. He said, 'And how do you maintain this integrity when you're ready to knuckle under to Keelor's blackmail?'

'It's not blackmail. For Christ's sake! The man has a perfectly valid point.'

'And how long do you want your Security Department and the police to concede that point for? What if Keelor's making the same threat in three months or six months or a year?'

'That's ridiculous, Frankie. The heat's been on with the press. And don't forget who started that!' He paused to let Houlihan dwell on his 'guilt', then said, 'Vaughn Keelor will cool down given a couple of weeks and maybe Eddie will be able to be interviewed by that time too. Let's give him a fortnight, eh?'

'Is that what he asked for?'

'No, he didn't. I'm suggesting it.'

'And you think it will be acceptable to him?'

'I think if you can persuade DS Moran, I can persuade Keelor.'

Houlihan sighed. 'I don't think she'll have it.'

'Why? Because of a loss of face having threatened Keelor?'

'I think that might have some bearing.'

'Just proves my point then. She's a hothead, more interested in her self-image than in doing the job properly.'

'I'll tell her you said that, shall I, when I'm asking for the two-week concession?'

Cranfield opened his arms in exasperation. 'Frankie, help me out here, please!'

Houlihan got up. 'Let me think about it.'

Cranfield nodded slowly. He looked exhausted and that softened Houlihan, who said, 'Loretta's downstairs. I'll speak to her.'

'Thanks.'

Houlihan turned to go. Cranfield said, 'Frankie, forgive me, I should have asked how you were after your own scare the other night?'

'I'm okay, thanks. I'm going to stay away from Lambourn for a while.'

'Good decision. Where can I reach you?'

Houlihan hesitated long enough to realise he wasn't going to mention he was at Loretta's. What troubled him was the trigger for this hadn't been embarrassment, but doubt about whether he could trust Cranfield any more. He said, 'Best to get me on my mobile. I'll be going to Ireland pretty soon.'

'How is your mother?'

'Bearing up, I think. Bearing up.'

Houlihan went back downstairs much slower than he'd come up. He wasn't looking forward to telling Loretta what Cranfield had asked for.

THIRTY-ONE

She was asleep in the car, head back on the reclined seat, face peaceful. Houlihan stood for a while watching through the window, surprised by the tenderness he felt for her, trying in his mind to liken it to that for a slumbering child. He went to the passenger side, opened the door quietly and got in. He closed the door enough to dull the traffic noise then heard her say, 'Thanks. You can shut it properly.'

He looked across. Her head remained on the headrest, angled towards him, eyes open, smiling. 'Tired?' he asked.

'I often nap. I'm fine now.' She sat up, hit the button and the seat whirred back into the driving position. Houlihan said, 'You looked peaceful.'

'Unusual for me, ain't it?'

He smiled.

'Was my mouth open?'

'Only enough to let the saliva trickle out.'

'It wasn't!' She reached to feel her cheek.

'No, it wasn't. You looked . . . nice.'

'Lord, that silver tongue of yours will get you into trouble some day! What did your man have to say?'

'He thinks we're doing the right thing.'

'But?'

'He wants to give Keelor some time. He thinks all the press stuff spooked him and that he'll calm himself down and see sense.'

'And tell us where Malloy is?'

'Yes.'

'How much time?'

Houlihan looked at her. 'Two weeks,' he said quietly.

'No way! Absolutely no way, Frankie!' Her eyes were wide.

Houlihan smiled nervously and shrugged. 'I thought you'd say that.'

'Do you blame me? I threaten him with a warrant in twenty-four hours and end up sitting on my hands for a fortnight. No deal, Frankie boy!' She crossed her arms.

Houlihan giggled, although he hadn't meant to.

'What's so bloody funny?'

He raised his hands in a defensive gesture. 'Nothing, honest. You're making me nervous, that's all, and it looks like I giggle when I'm nervous. Sorry. It's like waiting for a volcano to blow, so I get nervous. Maybe I should shut up.'

She didn't reply, just stared through the windscreen, brows knitted. Houlihan told her about

Cranfield's fears of Keelor pulling out of buying the Jockey Club racecourses.

'That's blackmail,' she said.

'That's what I told him.'

They were quiet for a while then Loretta said, 'We need to find out more about Keelor.' She looked at Houlihan and continued, 'The more this unravels the more I feel it doesn't hang together. If you see what I mean. We've assumed all along from the previous threats to Malloy, the messages and stuff, that the real target was Makalu. Whoever did this wanted to stop the company operating in the UK and they tried to do it through intimidating Makalu's chief representative. Right?'

Houlihan nodded. Loretta went on. 'So, Eddie Malloy is in hospital and might never recover at all, never mind work for anyone again. There's no reason the attacker should need to go after Malloy again. But the objective wasn't achieved. Makalu are still operating. Not only that but their CEO and major shareholder is the man behind the desk, the new man in the firing line for this guy. Are we to believe that Vaughn Keelor, with a multi-billion-pound global empire to run, drops everything to be the hands-on man in London? To put himself at very serious risk of being the next victim?'

Houlihan shrugged and clasped his fingers. 'Remember, he's the Richard Branson of the USA. His brand is him. He's a tough guy who climbed Everest and survived when the rest of his party, including professional climbers, died. He's the leader *par excellence* as far as his customers are concerned, and his willingness to put himself in the firing line here rather than ask any of his people to do it will be playing big in America and around the world. Keelor might not want to be fronting things but he knows a PR opportunity when he sees one and he'll be more than aware of the potential damage to the Makalu brand if he cops out.'

'So where are the bodyguards? How did we manage to walk into his office unchallenged? That could have been somebody carrying enough petrol bombs to fry Keelor and the whole racecourse. How come it was so easy?'

Houlihan hesitated, thinking. 'Good point. Even if he wanted to be Mr Macho, his shareholders would insist on him having more protection than the President.'

'Can you get hold of the press cuttings since the story broke, here and abroad?'

'We can try.'

'I'd just like to know how he's painting this to the public.'

'We can do a web search on Google, that'll probably throw up ninety-nine per cent of the coverage.'

'Right.' She started the engine. 'Let's get back home and get cracking on it.'

Houlihan looked at her. 'What about the warrant?'

'Tell Cranfield we'll compromise and offer Keelor a week. But don't call him now. Let him sweat for a few hours.' Houlihan noticed her tone was now upbeat. He saw anticipation in her face as she eased out into the traffic.

'Why the change of mind? What about Malloy?'

'I don't think he's in any danger. I just want to figure out why Keelor is playing this like Malloy will be murdered if a single soul finds out where he is. You'd think Keelor would be happy to offer this guy a target, to give us and whatever security team he's got a chance of catching him.'

'I think I was meant to be that target. Hooper tried his best to persuade me to let on that I'd seen the attacker. Probably prompted by Keelor.'

'But you didn't go along with that.'

'And I still got involved in a game of dodgems on a dark night.'

'So who's planting stuff? Who's saying you know something? It would make sense if it was Keelor, but only if he had a system in place to get the guy when the guy came to get you. And I don't think you noticed the cavalry, did you? Not till we came along.'

'Maybe it happened quicker than Keelor expected.'

'No way. Too much at stake for him. And I don't care how you dress it up, Keelor's not stupid and the only sensible move for him since he took over from Eddie Malloy is to have enough security around him to nail a mouse in his kitchen. He might not want to advertise it, but it ought to be there. It ought to be there.' She set her jaw as she repeated it and Houlihan saw she was becoming more and more convinced that something stank.

He said, 'So we forget about Eddie for a while and concentrate on Keelor?'

'We do both. We'll try other ways to find out where Eddie is, forget going through Keelor, and then let's see what we come up against. That'll be interesting.'

Houlihan thought for a while then said, 'Why don't we go back to the hospital and see if they've got CCTV tapes from the day Malloy was transferred? We could get the registration number of the ambulance.'

She smiled and turned to him. 'Brilliant!'

He shrugged. 'My brain does work from time to time.'

'Want to turn around and go now?'

'Why not?'

They headed back towards St John's Wood. After ten minutes Houlihan said, 'Listen, Penrose might try and bluff us. Keelor could have talked to him since we left this morning.'

'He was too scared to call Keelor.'

'But Keelor may have called him. Why don't we wait till visiting time like we threatened and turn up with some uniformed guys. Railroad him. Make him think we're going to go through the place bed by bed. If there are any tapes he'll hand them over quick.'

'That brain of yours; once it starts it just keeps on going, doesn't it? Good idea. We've got more than three hours to spare. What do you want to do?'

Houlihan thought for a while then said, 'Can we find a cemetery?'

She glanced at him. 'Any cemetery?'

'Any one.'

'You watch the left, I'll watch the right.'

It was a small joy to Houlihan that she hadn't asked why.

In the dusk they couldn't make out the names on the gravestones as they wandered the paths, not talking. A sudden heavy shower sent them hurrying for shelter. 'In here!' Houlihan shouted.

'That's a crypt!'

'It's a dry crypt. Come on.' He held out his hand and she took it and followed him down some steps into the granite doorway. The rain came at them sideways and they huddled together, laughing, their hair and faces wet, dripping, just inches apart. Loretta said, 'You really know how to treat a girl.'

'I like cemeteries.'

'Well, you ought not to spend too much time in them while you're breathing. You'll be in one permanently, remember.'

'I feel at peace here.'

'Remind me never to go on holiday with you.'

Houlihan's arm was around her shoulder and he could feel the warmth of her, smell her perfume, see the rain run from the lock of hair plastered to her cheek. And he realised he was happy. Kathy came into his mind and he was sure she was smiling.

Their clothes were still damp when they sat down to eat in the restaurant of a hotel close to the hospital. Loretta had arranged to meet two uniformed officers outside the hospital at seven. During the meal, Houlihan told Loretta as much as he knew about Malloy's relationship with Keelor, how they'd been on Everest during the terrible storm that had killed so many.

He said, 'Malloy tried to tell me the whole story one night but he got really edgy and uncomfortable and didn't finish it.'

'Wasn't he left for dead and saved himself?'

'According to the news cuttings, he'd made it down to Camp Four from the summit in the storm and managed to reach his tent and get in his sleeping bag. He was exhausted. Some time later one of the guides crawled into the tent crying, saying five of his group had collapsed in the snow within a couple of hundred metres of their tents and that they were dying. The guide was completely done in and couldn't go back out. Malloy somehow found the strength and courage to drag himself from the depths of exhaustion, get his boots and crampons back on and go out to look for these climbers.

'He battled through winds of over one hundred mph in temperatures of forty below zero, snow and ice blinding him, cutting his face, and he found the party and saved three of them. He roped each of them and just dragged them back across the snow to their tents. When he went back for the others he collapsed beside them, hypothermic, totally wasted. Hours later, as the storm died away, a rescue party from further down the mountain found him and decided he was too close to death to save. They left him there.'

'Still alive and they left him there?' Loretta looked incredulous.

Houlihan nodded. 'That's what the reports say. Eddie never got far enough to tell me about it.'

'No wonder. Bastards. I thought they were a rescue party?'

'They said there were others lost who might have been able to be saved if they moved on from Eddie.'

'What about the other two people beside him?'

'They were dead.'

'So what happened?'

'Eddie lay there all night. Then he woke up, managed somehow to get to his feet, and walked into his tent. After a night in one of the worst storms imaginable, in what they call the death zone, even when it's calm.'

Loretta shook her head slowly. 'Something you would call a miracle then.'

Houlihan shrugged. 'Well the doctors couldn't explain it.'

'There must be a survival instinct so deep in some people . . . It must have been in his subconscious. What woke him?'

'Who knows?'

'A real tough guy. No wonder Keelor was impressed.'

Another surprise for Houlihan now was a twinge of jealousy at Loretta's praise of Malloy. He said, 'Well, he lost an arm to frostbite and part of his ear. And there was some damage to his face.' And immediately he hated himself for trying to make Malloy seem a lesser man in her eyes.

'A small price to pay,' she said.

'It was. It was. A real hero. A hell of a guy and we need to find him.' Houlihan felt a bit better for saying that and was relieved Loretta hadn't seen his spiteful comment for what it was.

'We will. He deserves some luck, I'd say. How many near-death experiences can a man have?'

'I think he had a few scrapes when he was a jockey too.'

'I look forward to meeting Mr Malloy.'

There. That stab of jealousy again. And he wondered if she had spotted his earlier insecurity and was playing on it. He excused himself before she read his feelings in his face and he stood in the men's room, staring at himself in the big, theatrically lit mirror. He told himself to stop this before it started because he didn't love Loretta Moran, and even if he ever did get to care for her this was a poisonous way to think. Eddie was his friend. So was Loretta. No more of this jealousy.

On the way back to the table, Houlihan remembered he owed Bobby Cranfield a call. Bobby had called twice asking about Loretta's reaction to his request for a two-week amnesty for Keelor. Houlihan rang back and said one week was on offer, no more. Cranfield said he'd let him know Keelor's response.

Houlihan went into the hospital alone as they'd planned, and asked for Penrose. As he watched the consultant approach down the stairs, people filtered past him on either side after being greeted by two smiling, uniformed receptionists, one on each side of the main door. Visiting time was just starting.

Penrose looked flustered. He steered Houlihan towards the small office they'd been in last time, speaking as he went. 'You know that Mr Malloy is not here. I told you that.'

Houlihan looked at the raised, scolding finger close to his face, then slowly up at Penrose who steadily lowered his hand. Houlihan said, 'We know he's not here. We want the CCTV tapes from the day Mr Malloy was moved from here.'

'The what?'

'The CCTV tapes.' Houlihan reached and opened the door then motioned Penrose to come to it. He nodded towards the cameras fixed to the coving above the reception desk. 'The tapes from those and the one from the car park.'

Penrose pushed the door closed and turned angrily. 'No! We have a number of people visiting our guests here—'

'Your guests? Your patients, you mean?'

'We call them guests, Mr . . .'

'Houlihan. We'll respect the privacy of anyone on the tapes, Mr Penrose.'

'No. You can't have them.'

Houlihan shrugged and began buttoning his coat. 'I asked DS Moran to give me a chance with you. I wanted to save you the disruption you were afraid of.'

Penrose folded his arms defiantly but looked no less worried. Houlihan pulled his phone from his coat pocket and dialled. Penrose watched. Houlihan spoke into it. 'DS Moran, you were right, I was wrong. You'd best do it your way.' He hung up and opened the door to leave. 'You may want to warn your, er, guests, Mr Penrose.'

Penrose followed him out into the marble-floored reception area. 'Where is she?' There was panic in his voice.

'She's here!' Loretta called as she reached the top of the steps and marched through the doors. She spun and spoke sharply to one of the uniformed officers. 'Close these doors. Nobody in, nobody out.'

The receptionists retreated towards Penrose, looking to him for guidance. 'You can't do this!' His voice was high-pitched. Houlihan watched Loretta approach him, staring intently at the consultant. A group of three waiting for the lift ignored the ping of its arrival and watched as the policemen swung the big entrance doors closed. Loretta stopped close to Penrose. 'The tapes. Where are they kept?'

'They come under the Data Protection Act, you're breaking the law!'

'They come under criminal evidence, Mr Penrose. You have five seconds to take me to where they are kept; then we start searching room by room, under every patient's bed if necessary.'

'Guests,' said Houlihan quietly, raising a finger.

Loretta looked at him, puzzled. Penrose glared at him, then defiantly back at Loretta. 'Okay,' she said and turned to one of the officers. 'Come with me.' She started running towards the door leading along a ground-floor corridor, her heels clicking sharply. The officer hurried after her.

The two receptionists seemed horrified. Penrose looked like he was about to cry with frustration. 'All right! All right!' he called out, and Loretta stopped and turned. Houlihan smiled as she strode back towards her victim.

Showered and in dry clothes, they sat by the fire in Loretta's house drinking tea. Houlihan noticed she had not mentioned alcohol and he remembered what he'd said last time when he'd talked about getting into bad habits. He knew she liked a drink at the end of the day and it seemed to him she was abstaining for his benefit.

She pressed play on the remote control and they watched the tape for the second time. It showed a dark-coloured vehicle, a cross between an MPV and a security truck, backed-up close to a fire escape in the car park of the hospital. The van had blacked-out windows and no markings. Nothing suggested it was medical transport. Two men got out of the front and opened the doors at the back to let two others out. All wore knee-length coats. No uniform could be seen under the coats. Two stayed guarding the back doors. The other pair went inside when the fire escape was opened for them. Within five minutes they came back out at the head and foot of a stretcher carried by two white-coated men. The person on the stretcher could not be recognised and was in view only long enough for the two men accompanying the patient to climb inside the vehicle and accept the stretcher as it was pushed in. The vehicle pulled away quickly, with, it seemed, little regard for the comfort of what was supposed to be a badly injured man.

Loretta rewound the tape. 'Now, did any of those guys look like angels of mercy to you?'

'Nope. Hired guns maybe, paramedics, no.'

As the tape whirred back, Loretta checked the time. 'What's keeping them, they should be able to run that registration check in a couple of minutes.'

'It's only been five minutes since you phoned it in.'

'Twice as long as they need then.' She stood up. 'You hungry?'

'No. Thanks.'

'You don't eat that much, do you?'

Houlihan sipped tea. 'I find the less I eat the more I enjoy what I'm eating.'

'Too much willpower for me! I'm for some peanut butter on toast.'

'There goes that old sweet tooth again.'

He called out to her as he heard the rustle of the bread wrapper, then the fridge door clunking shut. 'Do you think your techie fellas could blow that up, try and see the face on the stretcher?'

'They'll be able to do something but I wouldn't hold out too much hope for a positive ID from it. I think we've got more chance of getting something recognisable from the four heavies.'

The phone rang. Houlihan sprung up to answer it. Loretta appeared in the kitchen doorway. 'Whoa!' she cried. Houlihan stopped and turned to see her hurrying across the big rug. 'We're supposed to be protecting your whereabouts, remember?'

'Oops,' he said.

She picked up the receiver. 'DS Moran . . . Uh-huh . . . Are you sure? . . . Cloned or doesn't exist? . . . Okay. Thanks.' She hung up and turned to Houlihan, who looked concerned. 'The registration is false,' she said. 'Completely made up. Doesn't exist.'

'How did they do that?'

'Good question.'

'I mean, what are the chances of somebody making up a registration number that doesn't exist? How many vehicles are registered in the UK? The chances of getting a number that doesn't clash with one of them must be slim.'

'Must be.' Loretta looked thoughtful.

Houlihan's mobile rang. He sat back on the rug, below window level, before answering. It was Bobby Cranfield. Houlihan listened with a mixture of surprise and concern, asked a few questions as he looked at Loretta, shaking his head slowly as he did so. She frowned in an exaggerated way to show how impatient she was for him to get off the phone and explain properly. He ended the call and stood up facing her. 'Keelor has just appointed an ex Cabinet Minister as Malloy's successor.'

'Who?'

'Caro Brookes.'

Loretta looked amazed. 'Mrs Brookes of ban the cooks?'

'The very same.'

'Mrs Brookes of brook no nonsense?'

''Tis she.'

'What's the man thinking about? The cheese slid off her cracker years ago. That's why Thatcher sacked her.'

'Keelor's not daft, he'll have his reasons. She used to be president of the Racehorse Owners' Association, still owns one of the biggest studs in Newmarket.'

'Oh yeah? What's his name?' She pouted and fluttered her eyelashes.

'Very funny,' Houlihan said. 'And she'd put the fear of God into any man.'

'Well let's hope our petrol-bombing friend knows that.'

Houlihan nodded, stuck his hands in his pocket and walked towards the fire. 'Something else interesting. Keelor didn't think too much of your offer of a one-week stay of execution. He's gone back to the States.'

'When?' She looked suddenly alert.

'This evening. He'll be somewhere over the Atlantic as we speak.'

'Before or after we went to see Penrose?'

'I don't know.'

'This stinks,' she said, and picked up the phone to get the phone number of the hospital. Someone calling themselves Chief Administrator at the hospital told her that Mr Penrose was now on leave for three weeks and was not contactable. Loretta slammed the phone down and turned to Houlihan. He wasn't there. The sound of teaspoon on cup came to her from the kitchen and she found him carrying two mugs of tea to the kitchen table on which her peanut-butter sandwich waited.

He saw her vexed look and said, 'Come and have your supper.'

She smiled and her shoulders dropped as she walked over and flopped down in the chair, pulling the plate towards her. 'Thanks, Frankie,' she said, and drank some tea. 'Keelor's taking the piss. He's just going to mess me around, try and make me look stupid.'

'I think it's more than that,' Houlihan said.

'Nothing happens for weeks, then when we confront him the whole world changes in a few hours.'

She nodded. 'All to protect the whereabouts of Eddie Malloy.'

'A man who can no longer do any productive work for him. A man who Keelor gave a very hard time to when it suited him. Eddie told me of a couple of occasions when Keelor tried to bully him.'

'He'll have picked the wrong man for that by the sound of Malloy,' she said, biting into her sandwich and then wiping a squirt of peanut butter from her cheek.

'He did.'

She chewed and looked thoughtful. Houlihan said, 'It must be an offence to display false number-plates.'

'It is, but Keelor will claim he knew nothing about it and blame the people he employed to collect Malloy. Whoever they are. And they'll claim they did it because of Keelor's demand for water-tight security.'

'And I think we're agreed those guys were security men, not paramedics; so where is Keelor's big concern for Eddie's welfare, his recovery?' Houlihan suddenly felt angry. 'They slung him into that van and pulled away like there was butcher meat in the back. No drips attached to him, and he didn't move on the stretcher from what I could see so he was probably drugged for the journey. What is he, an intensive-care patient or a prisoner?'

Loretta said, 'Good question. And if he's a prisoner, why? What has Keelor got against him?'

Houlihan rubbed his face and looked at her. 'We need to find him.'

She nodded. 'We will. Keelor's blown his week's amnesty.'

Smiling wearily, Houlihan said, 'Now all we need's the extradition papers.'

'He'll be back. Don't worry about that.'

'So where do we go while we're waiting?'

'We start tracing high-level security companies whose employees all wear the same coats. We see what other CCTV footage we can pick up from around the hospital to get some idea of the route the van took, and we see just how far we can get with that. We get Keelor's phone records, office and mobile and wherever he was staying while he was here.'

'Some country-house hotel in Surrey; Bobby will know.'

'Well, we'll get their CCTV footage and any from Esher racecourse to see who called on Mr Keelor. We'll find Malloy, I promise.'

Houlihan nodded. At first he'd been reassured by Keelor's almost manic protection of Malloy's whereabouts but now he wondered what conditions his friend was being kept under and he felt a gloom descend. He'd let Eddie down. He thought of his mother, the family. He'd let them down too, had promised to return soon and try again to help, but all he'd brought them in the meantime had been hassle through giving that interview to Ben Dillon. Although he still blamed Hooper for engineering the piece in the *Sun* that had led to it. Elbows on the table, Houlihan rubbed his eyes and scratched his head.

'Are you okay?' Loretta asked.

Houlihan looked up. 'I think I need a drink.'

She smiled and got up. 'I think we both do after that soaking you got us in the cemetery. Bloody wind blowing a gale and lashing us in that crypt.'

'Bet you felt alive, though, didn't you?'

She thought for a few seconds. 'I did. I felt alive.'

'And it's not that often a person gets to feel alive these days, is it? Really alive?'

She paused again, looking caringly at him. He held her gaze. She spoke softly, 'You're right. It's not.'

'See, it's wild weather, unusual places.'

'Good company,' she added.

Houlihan nodded. 'I was happy there.'

'I was too. Maybe we could go back next time we know a storm's on its way.'

He shook his head. 'You should never go back. The freshness will have gone from it. We should find somewhere new.' He thought he saw her eyes moisten. She said nothing but her look seemed to ask him to think about what he'd just said. He did, and he felt an odd sadness at the absurdity of not practising what he was preaching.

THIRTY-TWO

The next morning they drove to Lambourn. They'd decided that Houlihan should stay at Loretta's place until Malloy had been found. He needed to pick up some more stuff, including his PC. They planned to return and start doing some web research on Keelor's press cuttings.

It was a bright morning, and as they got out of Loretta's car Houlihan's eyes went to the locations of the tiny putty seals on the front door and windows. The one on the door had been broken. His stomach lurched. He stopped on the pavement and said to Loretta, 'Somebody's been in.'

The place had been ransacked. Every floorboard had been ripped away, the contents of drawers lay scattered among the joists. Partition walls had been punched through, the bookcase toppled. The kitchen floor was wet where the contents of the freezer had been dumped and the freezer door left wide open. The downstairs carpets lay heaped in a corner. Houlihan's bedroom was partially flooded and they discovered a hole had been drilled in the water tank in the loft to drain it. All the panelling in the bathroom and toilet had been torn away. The cistern lid lay smashed on the floor. All windowsills had been crowbarred up, pillows and duvets were slashed. And Houlihan's PC was missing.

They picked their way through it all in virtual silence. From time to time, Loretta would reach out and put a hand on Houlihan's shoulder. They ended up back in the kitchen standing among soggy cornflakes, the almost-empty box lying on its side on the edge of the worktop. Loretta looked at the unopened tea and coffee containers and said, 'Well at least we know that whatever they were looking for was bigger than your tea and coffee jars, and smaller than a box of cornflakes.'

Houlihan stood, hands in pockets, shaking his head. 'Well it wasn't Eddie's address they wanted, that's for sure.'

'Eddie's out of their picture now, Frankie. It's what Eddie had and what he might have done with it they're after. The good news is it should make things just a bit clearer for us.'

Houlihan looked around him at the devastation and said quietly, 'Ah well, that's not so bad then, I suppose.'

Loretta smiled and took out her phone. 'I'll call in the fingerprint boys.'

'More in hope than confidence,' Houlihan muttered.

'Procedure, Frankie. Procedure.'

She finished the call. Houlihan said, 'I think we'd better get back to your house double-quick. They might know I'm staying with you.'

She suddenly looked worried. 'What about this place?'

'I'll call Geoff and see if he'll stay here till your guys arrive. It's not as if there's anything to protect.'

'Except any evidence.'

Houlihan started walking out. 'I'll call Geoff. Don't worry about here. Come on.'

She hurried out after him and they did the trip back in record time to find her house untouched. In the kitchen, Loretta said, 'Look, Frankie, we need . . .' He put his finger to his lips to silence her and signalled for her to follow him outside.

They went back through the gate and along the road. He said, 'In case your place has been bugged.'

She frowned, thinking about it. Houlihan said, 'Right, I'm moving out. I'll find somewhere this guy can't trace me to.'

'Frankie, I'm happy to take my chances. The place is well alarmed.'

'I know you are, but alarms won't do much good against this guy. Anyway, we wouldn't be able to get anything done, we'd be too afraid to leave the house. It's best if we work separately. Keep in touch by phone, although not the mobiles.'

She nodded. Houlihan said, 'Can you get the place swept for bugs?'

She began dialling on her mobile. Houlihan stopped her. She raised her eyes and said, 'Short memory, haven't I?'

'Where's the nearest payphone?'

'In the pub.'

'Do you want to go? I'll stay and watch the house.'

'Okay. But go inside.'

'I will.' He reached to touch her arm as she walked to the car.

By dusk the house had been declared bug free and Houlihan's place had been checked for evidence. Houlihan packed the few things he had at Loretta's and brought them downstairs. Loretta sat silently at the kitchen table. Houlihan sat down across from her and said, 'I think you should get out and about as much as possible in the next few days. If anyone's watching it'll let them see I'm not around any more and they'll probably start looking elsewhere for me.'

'I will,' she said quietly, and Houlihan could see she was subdued. He said, 'Look, I don't want you put at any risk and I don't want this house ripped apart like mine was. I like it here. When I come back I want to see it like I remember it. You know, with the fire burning in the grate, the toothpaste lidless in the bathroom, the curry stains on this table . . .'

She looked up, smiling now, and reached across to slap his arm playfully. 'Where will you go? Dublin?' she asked.

'No. I can't. I don't want these people anywhere near my family.'

'Of course.' She smacked her palm on her forehead. Houlihan said, 'A hire car should be here for me in an hour or so. I'll drive around for a bit to see if anyone's following then I'll find myself a hotel in London, see how it goes day by day.'

She seemed to brighten. 'So I'll be able to see you? To check on progress,' she added, and Houlihan noticed she blushed slightly.

'I hope so,' he said. 'I'll spend some more time in the office in Portman Square. He took a card from his pocket and gave it to her. My direct-line number is on there. If I need to speak to you I'll call your mobile and let it ring once, and if you can find a landline call me back at the direct number.'

She nodded. 'I'll do the same. I'll ring your mobile once and you can call me back here.'

'Fine.'

Silence then, till Loretta said, 'I take it you won't be able to come to the party after all, then?'

'I'd forgotten about that. Sorry. No, not unless we catch these people.'

She nodded. 'That's a shame.'

''Tis.'

Another awkward pause, then Houlihan said, 'I'll send you a present.'

'Good.'

'What would you like?'

She hesitated. 'I don't know, what about one of

those gift experiences, you know, a microlight flight, a parachute jump, a night in a crypt.'

They smiled together.

Houlihan checked his watch and said, 'Do you think it's worth me calling Keelor in America?'

'To say what – "Come back you absconding bastard"?'

'Well, maybe not those exact words. I just wondered how he'd react if I told him about my place being turned over. These people think Malloy's got something or had something they want badly. They didn't find it at his house so they think he might have given it to me.'

'So if it was that precious to them, why did they burn Malloy's house down before they had a chance to search the place for it?'

'I don't know. Maybe it's something they need to destroy.'

'So how do we know they didn't destroy it in the fire?'

He shrugged. 'We don't. But they've tried to get at me twice. They know I spent time with Eddie before they bombed him. I'd be the natural suspect to have had something passed to me.'

'So why didn't they come after you before you were outed in the press?'

Houlihan opened his arms in exasperation. 'I don't know, Loretta.'

'Frankie, take it easy, I'm only playing devil's advocate!'

'I know. I know you are. I just feel bloody

useless. I feel I've let Eddie down so many times. I just want to do something, try something, anything.'

'Well, call Keelor if you want to, it can't do any harm. But stop blaming yourself. You saved Eddie's life. Try remembering that.'

He nodded slowly. 'Maybe I said something at the press conference; unwittingly said something that told them the thing they're after wasn't burned. We should go back through the reports. Bobby Cranfield had a secretary transcribe everything that was said at the conference. I'll make a start on it in the morning at the office.'

'Good idea. I'll go and see our forensic guys and see if they turned up anything in the ashes that might give us a clue to what they might be looking for.'

'Yeah, set them your riddle: what's smaller than a cornflakes box, bigger than a coffee jar, and leads to houses being wrecked and people being burned?'

She reached and laid a hand on his forearm. 'It wasn't your fault, Frankie.'

He nodded wearily then took out his mobile. 'I'm calling Keelor.'

'What time is it in New York?'

'Quarter to two in the afternoon.'

'Do you think his secretary will put you through?'

Houlihan smiled. 'I have his direct number. He gave it to me himself the night Malloy was attacked.'

Houlihan found it on his phone list and pressed *yes*.

It rang out for almost a minute and Houlihan was about to hang up when it was answered: 'Vaughn Keelor.'

'Mr Keelor, it's Frankie Houlihan.'

Silence. 'Jockey Club Security Department,' Houlihan reminded him.

'Where'd you get my number, Houlihan?'

'You gave it to me. The night Malloy was hurt. You called me at the hospital.'

'You're right. I remember. What do you want?'

'It looks like whoever is after Malloy paid my house a visit last night and ripped it apart looking for something.'

A pause, then Keelor asked, 'For what?'

'I thought you might know that.'

'Why did you think that?' He sounded increasingly aggressive.

'Because of the way you're . . . protecting Malloy.'

'Why? Do you think Malloy has something these people might want?'

'I know he has,' Houlihan said, feeling a slight thrill, glancing at Loretta and smiling nervously as he waited out the silence on the other end.

'What? Did he give it to you?'

'Did he give what to me?'

'The fucking thing you're talking about!'

'Calm down, Mr Keelor.'

'Stop wasting my time, Houlihan. Did he give you something or didn't he?'

'He did.'

Silence again. Houlihan sensed that Keelor was holding his breath. The American spoke, calmer now, more measured. 'What was it?'

'That's confidential.'

'I'm hanging up. You're a time-waster.'

Houlihan glanced again at Loretta, who was staring at him, knitting her brows quizzically. He said, 'It was in a sealed, padded envelope, foolscap size.'

Another long pause, then Keelor said, 'What's your point here, Houlihan?'

'My point is that they got it when they turned my place over. My point is that Malloy's probably not under any threat any more. He no longer needs your protection. Tell me where he is and the police will look after him now. We'll get him the medical care he needs.'

'Bullshit. Tell me what was in the foolscap bag.'

'Let Eddie go. Then we've got a chance of catching these people. Then we'll all know what was in the bag.'

'Do you know or don't you?'

It was Houlihan's turn to hesitate. 'Yes.'

'Tell me.'

'I'll trade it for you telling me where Eddie is.'

'No deal you Irish bullshitter. Don't call me again.' He hung up.

Houlihan put his mobile on the table and let out a short nervous laugh. He filled in the gaps of the conversation for Loretta, then said, 'He's got a strong interest in whatever this thing is.'

'But he knows enough to know what it is already by the sound of things. He was just trying to find out if you knew too.'

'Maybe you're right,' Houlihan said.

'And I think he knows you never had it. You couldn't tell him what it was and when you told him the burglars had got it he didn't ask you if you were sure or where you had stashed it, or when Malloy had given it to you, did he?'

'No, he didn't.'

'He was just interested if you knew what was in it.'

Houlihan reflected on this. The doorbell rang, breaking the silence and startling them. Houlihan looked at his watch. 'That'll be the hire car.'

He got up. Loretta followed. 'Check at the window,' she said, easing back the curtain. They both looked out. 'Did you order a BMW?' she asked.

'I just asked for a decent car. That's what they suggested.'

She smiled, 'It's not a sin, you know!' She went to the door and called out, 'Who is it?'

'Hire car for Houlihan.'

'He'll be with you in five minutes.'

'No problem.'

She went to the curtain again and watched a short fat man walk towards the car and get in. Houlihan moved close beside her. 'Looks genuine,' she said.

'It does.'

She leaned back against the wall by the window, giving Houlihan the impression she wanted to stay close rather than go and sit down again. She said, 'So how come Keelor is so sure they didn't get what they were looking for at your house?'

Houlihan shrugged. 'Maybe Keelor's got it himself. Or Malloy's got it, and Keelor knows exactly where he is.'

'Or Keelor was the man who burgled your house.'

Houlihan stared at her for a few seconds, then said, 'Keelor was on a plane last night.'

'How do you know it happened last night?'

Houlihan looked thoughtful. She raised her eyebrows. 'You've been out of the place for two nights. It could have been done on Sunday night, or even yesterday morning or afternoon.'

'Why would Keelor do it?'

'Why was he so certain the bag you talked about wasn't there?'

'Maybe he already has it, like you said.'

'Then why this charade with Malloy?'

Houlihan rubbed his forehead slowly. 'I don't know. I don't know any more. Maybe it wasn't so smart of me to try to kid the man on.'

She reached to touch his arm again. 'Come on, Frankie, stop blaming yourself, especially for something that hasn't happened. You're tired. Why don't you sign for the car and stay one more night?'

He looked at her and thought of the comfort her friendship had brought him. He was tired and feeling emotional. The way they'd torn his cottage apart had got to him. He was worried about Malloy, about his responsibilities to his family, about the growing gaps of Kathy's presence in his mind, and he was worried for Loretta's safety.

Then she spoke what he was thinking: 'The last thing you need tonight is to go searching for a lonely hotel room in London.' Her hand remained on his forearm. She squeezed it gently and said, 'Stay.'

Slowly he pulled away and went outside to the car. Moments later he came back in, closed the door and took off his coat. Loretta smiled.

THIRTY-THREE

Houlihan lay awake. Something was nagging him and he couldn't pin down what it was. Gradually drowsiness overcame him, closing his mind down, and just as he was about to fall asleep it came to him. He raised his head quickly, rested on his elbow, waited for his mind to declare the thought a waking one and not a dream. Then he got up, put on his dressing gown and went to Loretta's room.

She did not answer the first knock. Houlihan knocked harder. He heard her bed creak then she called out, 'Frankie?'

'Can I come in?'

'What's wrong?'

He opened the door slowly. She sat up and switched on the lamp, hiding her breasts with the covers. Houlihan noticed her bare shoulders and how soft her skin looked. He stood by the bed watching the confusion in her eyes. He said, 'Something was bothering me. It kept me awake for a while, nagging at me. Then it came to me.'

She screwed her nose up, 'What is this? The midnight play or something? Just tell me!'

'When I called Keelor earlier the ringing tone was continuous. You know, like you hear when you watch American TV shows or films?' She nodded. Houlihan continued, 'When I rang Keelor from the hospital that night the ring tone wasn't like that. It was a British one.'

'So?'

'So he was supposed to be in his office in New York.'

'Which is where he must have been if . . .' She stopped and Houlihan noticed a spark come into her eyes. Suddenly she was fully awake. She said, 'He had his office number on call forward.'

'Correct.'

They looked at each other, silently taking in the implications. Houlihan said, 'Keelor was in the UK the night Malloy's house was bombed. He might have gone to the airport that day, but he never left London. He made a point of ringing me and giving me his New York number, insisting I call him back.'

'You think he was setting up an alibi with you?'

'Why else would he have done that? Why not just give me his mobile number?'

She thought about it and said, 'So you're saying that Keelor had something to do with the attack on Malloy's place? That's a big assumption, Frankie.'

'It is on its own, but add it to the fact that

Keelor had Eddie taken away from the hospital like a prisoner, and then the way he reacted to my call earlier. And why has he left the country so quickly? He knew he had a week's grace. Did he think we'd find something while we were trying to track Eddie down? It's going to be a hell of a lot harder getting anything from him in New York than Esher.'

'I'm warming to it. Give me a motive.'

Houlihan started pacing the perimeter of the bed. 'I don't know. It's got to be something to do with whatever they were looking for at my place.'

'Or whatever *Keelor* was looking for at your place, hence his confidence that nothing had been found there when you said it had been.'

'Maybe.'

'So maybe it was also Keelor in the Jeep that chased you that night.'

'Could well have been. Or one of his henchmen.'

'And do you think he was responsible for the other threats to Eddie?'

Houlihan was still pacing. Loretta watched him, then said, 'Houlihan, you're making me dizzy patrolling the bed like that.'

'Sorry. It helps me think better. On the other threats, we can't rule Keelor out. He could have been setting up this anti-Makalu stuff, I suppose, to strengthen his alibi when everything kicked off.'

'So he's taken Eddie on – big fanfare, both friends, heroes of Everest and all that stuff. He must have had a million chances to get what he wanted from Eddie without waiting till Eddie was so much in the public eye. He could have quietly engineered an accident while Malloy was still on the talk circuit and had no known association with him. Much safer, much neater.'

'I agree. The anti-Makalu campaign looked genuine enough from the start. There's no reason to suppose Bert Jacobsen wasn't the architect of that, which means Keelor just cashed in on it.'

She thought for a while, shifted in the bed and re-gathered the covers around her as Houlihan continued pacing. She said, 'So, between Malloy starting work for Keelor back in . . . when?'

'I think it was almost a year ago: February, March time.'

'So between then and now Malloy found something Keelor wanted badly enough to kill him for. And yet he didn't bother searching his house for it before bombing it. Could be a major stress-fracture in your hypothesis, Frankie.'

'Look at it this way, if what Keelor needs to find is damaging to him rather than precious, then destroying it in a fire is as good as finding it. Killing the man who knows where it is so he can't tell anyone else is a bonus. The petrol bomb was a good bet; two for the price of one.'

Loretta nodded slowly. 'Okay, okay. Let's assume you're right. So what was it? What did Malloy find? Did he give you any indication at all during the weeks you spent with him that he

431

thought Keelor was anything other than a straight, very successful businessman?'

'None at all. Not a jot. He said Keelor could be a bit of a bully at times, or try to be, and that he could be arrogant, but that was it.'

'If Malloy had found something in the company – major fraud, for instance – what would he have done?'

Houlihan shrugged, hands in the pockets of his dressing gown, still walking the three sides of the bed. 'I don't know. He might have given Keelor a chance to put it right.'

'Maybe he did. Maybe that was his big mistake.'

Houlihan stopped and sat on the bed, his back to Loretta, staring at the wall. After a while he said, 'If it was something in the accounts, he'd almost certainly have found it electronically, on a PC.'

'Right. And they took your PC when they raided your house.'

'But they didn't check the tea and coffee canisters where a floppy disk would have fitted easily.'

'Good point. Very good point.'

Houlihan turned his head, smiling at her in the lamplight. ''Twas you who spotted that first.'

She fluttered her eyelashes comically. 'You're too kind! So why did they take the PC?'

'I don't know. If Eddie knew something maybe he'd made a file or sent an email or something.'

'Or they thought it was concealed in the casing?'

'Could be. But they drained the water tank too,

remember, which suggests it was something less fragile than computer disks.'

'Or that it had been well-waterproofed.'

'True.'

'If you had to take a wild guess, what would you go for? What do you think Malloy might have been holding?'

Houlihan thought for a while. 'I really haven't got a clue. If Eddie had something he knew could endanger his life, I don't think there's any way he wouldn't have shown some strain, some sign of it.'

'Maybe he didn't know he had it, but Keelor did.'

'Then there must have been much easier ways for Keelor to get his hands on it than trying to kill Eddie.'

She sighed long and loud. 'We're going round in circles here, Frankie.'

'I know. I know we are. But it's two in the morning. If only there was something else we could be doing, somewhere we could be going to try and find more evidence . . . I think Eddie's in deep trouble and all we can do is sit here trying to work out the puzzle.'

'With only three bits of the jigsaw.'

He turned to her and the bed creaked. 'What did your guys recover from the fire at Malloy's?'

'Very little, and nothing that was usable. They found the bottom of the bottle used for the petrol but got nothing from it.'

'Could we get them back in?'

'To Malloy's?'

'Yes. With us tagging along?'

'I don't see why not. What are you hoping for?'

'I want to see if anyone else has been in there searching through the ashes. Can we get the same team that was there the first time so they'll know if the place isn't the way they left it?'

'We'll have pictures. We can have a look at them in the morning.'

'How early?'

'How early would you like? I can get my hands on the pictures any time.'

'Good. Get dressed then.' He stood up, smiling.

'What about my beauty sleep?'

'You can catch up double at the weekend.'

She glared at him in mock anger. 'Wrong answer, Frankie boy. Wrong answer.'

Houlihan drove. They sped into the city, slowing only for the speed cameras, and walked into Scotland Yard just after 3.15 a.m. Loretta scanned her security pass and the unmanned door clicked, letting them through to the lobby where they took the lift to the second floor. Two more doors beeped at the security pass and Houlihan followed Loretta as she strode into a large, well-lit, carpeted room. They stopped and stood still, both hearing the sounds of grunting. Houlihan thought it sounded sexual and he cursed himself for blushing as Loretta turned to look quizzically at him. She smiled and started walking quietly towards the desk. Houlihan stayed where he was.

Loretta reached the desk and looked over. The grunting stopped. 'Costello, what are you doing?' asked Loretta in the tones of a schoolteacher.

'Exercise,' said the fat man on the floor, elbows perched on an abs roller, white uniform shirt stained with sweat. He was still panting.

'Don't tell me you've got yourself a girlfriend?' she said, smiling.

'They're queuing round the block to shag me, Lola, you know that,' he said as he grunted again, trying to get to his feet. Houlihan reached the desk as Costello's sweating head came into view.

'A Lego block, you mean,' said Loretta, still smiling. 'I need to see the stuff we've got from the arson attack out at Hyde Park a few weeks back.'

Costello walked to a cooler in the corner and drew water into a plastic cup. He watched Houlihan over the rim as he drained it, then he refilled it and drank again and threw the cup in a bin. He nodded towards Houlihan. 'Who's your boyfriend?'

'Frankie Houlihan, Jockey Club Security Department.'

'Working late, Mr Houlihan?' Costello smiled.

Houlihan nodded, at a loss for words. Costello ambled back towards the desk. 'She's notorious for getting men up during the night. Isn't that right, Lola?'

Houlihan watched to see if Loretta would blush,

but she didn't, and he found he was annoyed. She said to Costello, 'Not something you'll ever experience personally, you can be sure of that.'

'I told you, I wouldn't be able to squeeze you in.' He hadn't stopped moving, twisting the combination on a walk-in safe as he talked. He came out with a bunch of keys and turned, heading along a corridor, calling as he went, 'You come and get this, Lola. I'm not getting my hands covered in shit and cinders at this time of the morning.'

Houlihan and Loretta sat at a table examining the smoke-stained remains of the bottle that had been found in the living room of Malloy's scorched flat. The circular base was intact, supporting an uneven mountain range of jagged peaks. Houlihan turned it upside down on the table and looked at the bottom, which was of very thick glass. The centre of it was inverted like some champagne bottles and Houlihan ran his finger round it, feeling the raised lines emanating from the centre like a thousand spokes from a hub. The spokes were overlaid in places with nine circular blobs of different sizes spreading out towards the rim. 'Very unusual design,' Houlihan said.

Loretta reached and her finger followed Houlihan's over the texture of spokes and blobs. 'It is,' she said.

He looked at her. 'Ever seen anything like it?'

She shook her head slowly. 'I don't spend much time turning bottles upside down.'

Houlihan handled it again, feeling the heft of it. 'There must be a cheaper way than this of making bottles. What do you think was in it?' He saw the mischievousness in her eyes and warned, 'Don't say petrol.'

She said, 'I don't know. Vodka? Could be a foreign brand.'

'I thought vodka was all foreign brands?'

'Probably is,' Loretta said. 'Stop being smart.'

Houlihan smiled, turned it upside-down again. 'Clear glass. A light spirit, maybe a soft drink. What would the chances be of tracking down the manufacturer?'

'Just from the design? I don't know. What would we do then? I mean, it's not serial-numbered or anything. We can't trace it to a retail source.'

'I'd like to know what was in it, where it could be bought in general? New York specifically? Airports only? We might find something.'

'You're right. We might. We can start first thing in the morning.'

Houlihan checked his watch. 'Not far away, a few hours.'

Loretta, hand going to her mouth, said, 'Don't remind me, you're making me yawn!'

'You need some fresh air. Let's go and have a look at Eddie's house.'

'It's still dark, Frankie.'

'You must have torches here, or some sort of emergency lights?'

'What about access? The place will be boarded up.'

'Call a twenty-four-hour joiner. We'll get it unboarded.' He got to his feet. 'Can we take these pictures?'

Loretta stood up slowly. 'Got the bit between your teeth now, Frankie.'

'I need to find Eddie,' he said.

She picked up the foolscap plastic file containing the pictures and linked her hand through Houlihan's arm as she led him back towards Costello's desk. '*We* need to find him, Frankie. *We*.'

He nodded as they walked, feeling a mixture of apprehension and excitement and a pleasant comfort at her touch.

They'd arranged to meet a joiner there and they saw his van parked, hazard lights flashing, as they approached. The man got out of the driver's side to meet them. Loretta introduced herself and Houlihan. The man said, 'So this is the right address?'

'Yes,' said Loretta.

He walked a few steps along the hedge-line to the gate opening and pointed at the house. A 'To Let' sign stood in the garden. The house's façade had been restored to its pre-fire condition; no boards, no shutters, just new windows and doors. Loretta and Houlihan looked at each other in silence. Houlihan took a torch from his pocket and turned the bezel as he walked up the path. A security light clicked on, flooding the garden, causing Houlihan and Loretta to shield their eyes. They continued to the big front window and Houlihan shone his torch into the living room. It looked as though there had never been a fire. The décor was as he remembered it, right down to the furnishings. Loretta was on tiptoe, her face close to his as they looked at each other again in silence then turned away. Loretta took out her notebook and jotted down the telephone number on the 'To Let' board.

In the car Loretta said, 'Where to now, Batman?'

'You tired?'

'I could do with a couple of hours' sleep.'

'It's nearly five o'clock. We could find a hotel, get our heads down for a while, get a shower.'

Half-smiling, she looked across at him. 'And put the same clothes back on again?'

He leaned towards her and sniffed. 'You don't smell.'

She shook her head, smile widening. Houlihan said, 'And even if you did, I wouldn't mind. Well, not for a day or so.'

Ignoring the comment, she said, 'Not the best value in the world, is it? A couple of hundred quid for two or three hours in a bed. We could be home by half six.'

'And we'd just need to turn around again to get back into Scotland Yard in time to start chasing this bottle and find out when Keelor wiped out all the evidence at Eddie's flat.'

'We've got a PC and a phone at my place, and more privacy.'

'If Keelor's boys haven't been there in the past few hours.'

'The techies left me a scanning device. We can check again for bugs.'

'Is your PC firewalled?'

''Tis,' she said, finding herself unintentionally mimicking him. He seemed not to notice as he stretched and yawned and sighed.

Loretta yawned. Houlihan said, 'Home, then?'

'Yippee!'

When they reached Loretta's place she ran the bug scanner, which came up clean. She said, 'Right, a shower for me, then bed.'

Houlihan said, 'I'll make a start on the Internet for this bottle, if that's okay?'

He saw frustration in her eyes as she looked at him and said, 'You're tired. Sleep till eight. Anything that's on there now will still be there at eight. Come on.'

Houlihan took off his jacket and went into the kitchen, talking as he walked. 'If we find out where Eddie is and get there two hours too late, I'd remember the two hours in bed.'

She sighed and followed him. 'And if you fall asleep at the wheel when you're speeding out there to find him, it'll be too late to remember the two hours you didn't have in bed.'

Houlihan smiled wearily as he filled the kettle.

'This could be a new parlour game.' He turned quickly from the sink and saw her looking annoyed. He said, 'I knew you were doing that.'

'What?'

'Clenching your jaw the way you do. Go to bed. I'll make a pot of coffee, keep me awake. Don't be worryin'.'

'I've been around you too long, Frankie. It's not worry with me now, it's guilt. I sleep, you work.'

He took a mug from a hook and smiled at her. 'Me Tarzan, you Jane.'

'You crazy,' she said, shaking her head.

'Go to bed. You can take over when you get up. I'll sleep then.'

She nodded. 'Okay. Goodnight.'

'Goodnight, Loretta. God bless.' She looked at him. That was the first time he'd ever said that to her. Houlihan realised this and shrugged, not feeling as uncomfortable with it as he thought he should. Further confirmation that things were changing for him.

He sat at the PC, coffee pot and steaming mug on a tray, small desk lamp lighting the keyboard, the Google search page springing onto the screen. He typed in 'glass bottle manufacturers' and hit return. Within a second he saw that 1067 sites had been found. He smiled and sipped coffee. For the first time in months he felt he was doing something positive.

In bed, showered and very pleasantly tired, Loretta had deliberately left the room door open. The study where Houlihan sat was at the end of the landing and the low whirr of the PC fan, the occasional click of the mouse or tap on the keys seemed to comfort her. Her last thought was that she liked having him there, liked him being awake as she slept, watching over her.

THIRTY-FOUR

Loretta woke just before nine to the sounds of a gale, and she rose and went to the window to see the tall conifers swaying and hear the wind whistle through the leafless branches of the older trees. She put on her dressing gown, brushed her hair, checked her face in the small magnifying mirror on her dresser then went to the study.

As she approached along the landing she could see Houlihan's elbows on the armrests of the tall leather office chair and his ankles crossed below it. He didn't turn as she came in and she found him asleep, hands linked on his lap, head tilted to the right. She watched him for a while, feeling a tenderness for him that seemed fitting. He had a beard shadow, which accentuated the strong line of his jaw. A forelock of hair hung over his brow and his nostrils flared slightly as he breathed. Loretta felt happy to see him looking peaceful. She couldn't really remember a time, even when he'd been smiling, that worry was absent from his face.

Quietly, she took the tray of coffee stuff and went downstairs. Fifteen minutes later she was back with the tray fully laden. She set it down noiselessly and took a piece of hot toast covered with marmalade. Holding it close under Houlihan's nose she watched him gradually shift in the chair then open his eyes. She smiled at him. 'Wakened by your taste buds,' she said and put the toast on a plate. 'Tea or coffee?'

Rubbing his eyes he sat up in the chair. 'Tea, please. How long have I been asleep?'

'Not long enough.' She poured tea. Houlihan leaned forward then stretched. 'I'll just grab a quick wash,' he said, getting up.

'Want me to bring this downstairs? We can eat at the table.'

'No, no, I'll be back in a minute. Get started again. Best, eh?'

She watched him walk to the bathroom, tucking his shirt in as he went.

Looking awake now but still unshaven, Houlihan chewed his third piece of toast. He said, 'You wouldn't believe how many people make clear glass bottles. You couldn't imagine how many examples and designs there are in the image banks of these companies.' He finished the toast, washed it down with a mouthful of tea then picked up a yellow notepad to show her. 'I've written down all the sites I've already checked so you don't duplicate.'

She nodded, picking up the remains of the bottle

and looking again at the bottom. 'Did you try a search for designers? Bottle designers?'

'I didn't. No. Might be an idea.'

'There can't be as many designers as manufacturers. Can there?'

'No. You're right.'

She stared again at the design on the bottom, ran her finger over the ridged spokes and the nine blobs. After a minute she got up and went to the window. She held the base high to catch daylight and said to Houlihan, 'Does that design mean anything to you now?'

He gazed at it, knitting his brow. 'No. Why?'

'If we imagined the spokes were rays of sunlight . . .'

Houlihan looked again and said, 'And the centre circle is the sun?'

'And the nine blobs that don't seem set in any particular symmetry . . .?'

'The planets,' Houlihan said, a smile developing. 'Genius!' he said.

Loretta lowered the glass. 'Amazing what a few hours' sleep can do. Do you remember any of those companies being called "Planets", or "Universe", or anything like that?'

Houlihan moved the tray and wheeled the chair close to the PC desk. '"Universe" is a good one,' he said, excited now. 'I like "Universe".'

He added it to a refined search and got 288 sites. Loretta stood beside him and in a commanding voice said, 'Up, Frankie boy. You've done enough. Take a break. Lie down for an hour.'

He was scrolling through the list of sites. 'You're kidding, Loretta.'

'Come on, give me a shot at it. You'll go blind.'

'Let me just try?'

She grabbed his ears. 'No!'

'Ow!' He raised his hands to cover hers.

She pulled. 'Up!'

He got to his feet slowly, following her rising hands. She turned him towards the door. 'Rest! Take a shower! Go for a walk!'

'Okay! Okay!'

'I'll yell if I find something,' she said as he walked reluctantly along the landing. He turned, backing away from her now, rubbing his left ear and pointing at her with his right hand. 'You're a crazy woman!'

'You'd better believe it!'

Smiling, shaking his head, feeling happy, Houlihan went to his room.

Despite hours spent going through all the permutations they could think of, they found nothing to associate the words 'universe', 'planets', 'solar system', 'galaxy' and other variations with the making, selling or design of glass.

Defeated, Houlihan closed down the PC, bringing silence to the room. He leaned forward, tired, head in hands. Loretta placed her hand on his shoulder and they were still and quiet for a while then Houlihan stood up and turned to her.

'You got the number from that "To Let" sign, didn't you?'

Loretta fetched her notebook and called the agent who told her the house had been repaired by the tenant, Makalu Ltd., and put back on the market, and that they'd already had inquiries.

'When was the work done?' Loretta asked.

'Very quickly, actually. Let me check . . . it was completed and the keys given to us on the fifteenth of February.'

'Thanks.'

She hung up and turned to Houlihan. 'What date was the fire?'

'The evening of the ninth.'

'Keelor had everything cleared out and repaired by the fifteenth.'

'When did your people finish with the place?'

'They were there most of the following day. I'd need to check if they went back after that.'

'Even if they didn't, shouldn't that have been classified a crime scene and protected?'

'It was. We did, we boarded it up, remember?'

'So Keelor's tampered with evidence?'

'Potentially. Looks like it.'

Houlihan shook his head and held his arms wide, appealing in frustration. Loretta said, 'I know. I know.'

Houlihan said, 'And he's in New York. The chances of even interviewing him, never mind arresting him, are a million to one.' His voice was tense.

Loretta said, 'I'll make coffee then we'll talk. Plan B.' She smiled and Houlihan knew she was trying to reassure him.

He nodded and tried to loosen up, release some of the tension. 'Thanks.'

They sat in the kitchen. Loretta had eaten two chocolate biscuits. Houlihan reached for one. Loretta said, 'You must need that cocoa kick. Too little sleep.'

'I'd better get used to it, I think,' Houlihan said.

'Can you find out where Keelor stayed? You mentioned some country-house hotel.'

'Bobby will know. He'll tell me. I just need to make sure he doesn't tell Hooper.'

'You still think Hooper's in Keelor's pocket?'

'There's some connection there. Might not be money, but he's beholden to Keelor somehow.'

Loretta took another biscuit. Houlihan said, 'Are you going to get the CCTV tapes from the hotel?'

She nodded, chewing. He said, 'Will you need a warrant?'

She swallowed, sipped coffee, said, 'Depends how cooperative they are.'

'What about the tapes at Esher? That's going to be harder. That's Makalu property. You won't get them without a warrant and that means the media will probably pick it up. We can't risk that. If Keelor thinks we're on to him and he is holding Eddie . . . We can't risk it.'

Loretta, nodding, looking thoughtful, finished the biscuit. 'Can you trust Bobby Cranfield to give you this hotel name without telling anyone else or asking awkward questions?'

Houlihan thought for a few moments. 'I can't guarantee what he'll do.'

'When do you think you'll want to tell your people we've got Keelor under investigation?'

'I'd rather not do it before we have some solid evidence. Otherwise I'll just have to wade through all the political bullshit. If Keelor goes down the money won't be paid for the racecourses, and the Jockey Club almost certainly collapses.'

'Taking your job with it.'

'I couldn't care less about the job, Loretta, I just want to find Eddie.'

'I know you do. I'm sorry, I didn't mean it to sound like that.'

He nodded, rubbed his face again, drank more coffee. He said, 'There can't be that many country-house hotels in Surrey. Let's get back on the Net and see what we can find.' He stood up.

'And just ring them?'

'Sure.' He headed back upstairs. Loretta grabbed another biscuit and followed then watched Houlihan type in a search for hotels. In the Country House category, twelve were listed. Houlihan printed the page and disconnected the PC to free the phone line.

Loretta said, 'How's your American accent? Think you could impersonate Keelor?'

He shook his head, smiling, 'I'm a useless mimic. Think you could do Keelor's secretary?'

'I don't know what she sounds like.'

'I doubt the hotel staff will either.'

She raised a finger. 'Good point.'

Houlihan stood up, offered her the chair as he slid the telephone across the desk. She sat down, hesitated for a minute, then said, 'There might just be a way of killing two birds with one stone here.' She picked up the phone and dialled the first hotel on the list.

'Hello, my name is Detective Sergeant Moran from the Metropolitan Police. I'm investigating a crime reported by one of your recent guests, Mr Vaughn Keelor, and I just want to ask the manager a few questions.'

On the seventh try she found Keelor's hotel and arranged to visit. Another call to a friend at Guildford Police HQ secured the promise of a fingerprinting kit, which she and Houlihan picked up on the way to the hotel.

The manager looked suitably serious when Loretta showed her badge, introduced Houlihan as Vaughn Keelor's personal assistant and explained that Mr Keelor had discovered when he reached the airport after checking out that his car boot had been very neatly drilled and an expensive set of golf clubs stolen. She told him that Mr Keelor had also lost a pair of solid gold cufflinks, although these had not been in his car. Had any staff member perhaps found them in his room after he had left? The manager was convinced that this would not be the case but hurried off to reception to check, before confirming nothing had been found.

Loretta nodded, making a note in her book. She said, 'Would you mind if Mr Keelor's PA takes a look around the room just to check that the cufflinks have not been overlooked by your cleaning staff?'

'Not at all. Our staff are very thorough, but Mr . . . er?'

'. . . Houlihan,' Loretta prompted.

'Mr Houlihan is most welcome to look round.' He turned to Houlihan. 'I'll have someone take you up, sir.'

Loretta added, 'While the search is going on I'd like to see the tapes covering Monday evening and Tuesday morning, please.'

'The tapes?'

'Car park CCTV?'

He looked relieved. 'Of course, yes, no problem. This way.'

The concierge was asked to take Houlihan to Keelor's room at which point Loretta said to the manager, 'On second thoughts, it would be best if I take the tapes back for more detailed examination. Would you mind getting them for me while I join Mr Houlihan in having a look through Mr Keelor's room?'

'Of course, yes.'

In Keelor's suite, Loretta thanked the concierge and he left. She produced the fingerprint kit from her bag. Houlihan said, in a raised whisper, 'They'll have cleaned the place!'

Loretta, smiling, matching his whisper, walked towards the bed. 'Why are you whispering?'

Houlihan chuckled nervously. She said, 'There's a good chance they won't have cleaned the bed-side lamp up close to the switch. She dusted the lamp and lifted the images then went to the cradle on the other side of the bed that held the remote control for the TV and audio system. She took prints from that too.

Houlihan asked, 'How will you know which are Keelor's?'

'We'll get a match from his office. Or from the car he hired.'

Houlihan smiled again, happier now they were doing something, progress was being made. 'Now would that be the same car that had the boot drilled and those expensive clubs taken?'

''Twould,' she said, trying to clean the white dust off with a Wet Wipe. 'This stuff is a bitch to get off.'

'Leave it. They can do it.'

She slid the handset back into the cradle and said, 'One more room.' She went to the bathroom. Houlihan followed, looked around the tiled cavern and said, 'I've seen houses smaller than this.'

Loretta dusted the handles on the mirrored cabinet and the underside of the loo seat. Houlihan said, 'Now, you're being very optimistic that a man living on his own would lift the seat to pee.'

'Maybe he wasn't on his own.'

'Why do you say that?'

She peeled off the tape with some prints and held it to the light. 'No reason, really. All men aren't as pure and clean living as you, you know.'

'That's true.'

She cleaned up quickly and they went downstairs, reassured the manager that his staff had indeed been thorough, and collected the tapes. 'I may want to see more tapes from earlier in Mr Keelor's stay, if you have them?'

The manager looked puzzled. Loretta said, 'Just to check that Mr Keelor was not being stalked. He's a very important man, as I think you know.'

The manager nodded. 'I'm sure the tapes will still be here. We keep them for one month and they're changed every day without fail.'

'That's good. I'll let you know if we need them. You've been extremely helpful.'

He smiled, looking relieved as he walked to the door with them. 'Please be sure to tell Mr Keelor that,' he said.

'We will,' Loretta replied.

The manager looked to Houlihan for confirmation. 'We most definitely will,' Houlihan said.

As they drove away, Houlihan looked admiringly at Loretta. 'You had him eating out of your hand, didn't you?'

'Acquiescence fuelled by worry,' she said. 'He was trying to help repair things with Keelor and he knows as well as I do that the number of car break-ins at these big hotels are way above the norm, especially the golf-course based ones. Thieves know the guests are rich or on big expenses and there's every chance they'll get a top set of golf clubs in the boot, at the very least.'

'So they don't all get reported?'

'Plenty do. They need the crime report for the insurance companies. But they never get publicised. The hotel acts all horrified that such an unusual thing could have happened, finds some way of mollifying the victims and persuades most of them that it was a complete one-off.'

'And there was me thinking the manager was just reacting to your natural charm,' Houlihan said.

'That too.' Loretta smiled.

They played the tapes as soon as they got back to Loretta's house and noted the registration plate on the silver Merc Keelor left in. A two-minute phone call and Loretta discovered the car was registered to an international car-hire company based at Heathrow Airport. She rang them and gave them the registration and the same spiel about Keelor having reported a theft. She said, 'I need to examine the car.'

'Hold on, please, let me track it down.'

Loretta tucked the phone under her chin and held. Houlihan watched her. The rep returned. 'Did you say Keelor – Mr Keelor – was the client?'

'That's right.'

'We have no record of a Keelor hiring that vehicle.'

Loretta read her the registration again and the rep said, 'That's the one I checked it on.'

Loretta said, 'And it came back to you two days ago?'

'That's right. It's here now. Hasn't been back out. Got valeted yesterday.'

Loretta raised her eyes in frustration at that news, then said, 'So who checked the car back in?'

'Well, some clients just leave them in the bay with keys in. They're in a hurry for flights, you know? They don't have to come and check the keys back in personally.'

'So how do you know the car is back? How do you know it's not been damaged?'

'We patrol the bays regularly. If it's damaged the client needs to claim on the insurance.'

'So who was that car checked out to and when?'

'My screen says it was an agency booking – Universe.'

Loretta suddenly stood up straight and shot a glance at Houlihan. 'Who? What agency?'

'Universe. You know, the millionaires' club and all that? They . . . oh, hold on . . . Keelor. You're right. It's here on the next screen. Universe, on behalf of their client, Mr Vaughn Keelor.'

Houlihan watched as Loretta did a little dance on her toes. She said, 'And when did Mr Keelor pick the car up?'

'The ninth. March the ninth.'

'And the car is there now?'

'That's right. In the bay.'

'Do me a favour, check for me – if it turns out the car wasn't valeted yesterday, don't let them touch it. I'm on my way.'

'It was done yesterday. No doubt. It says so here.'

'Check anyway. Please. I'll see you soon. Who should I ask for?'

'Marcia. I'm always here. I don't take lunch breaks. Nowhere to go except wander round the bays.'

'Mmm. See you shortly, Marcia.'

Loretta told Houlihan the story, reaching to clasp his shoulders, shake them in her excitement. He looked worried. 'What's up?'

'I was hoping we were wrong. For Eddie's sake,' he said, looking sadly into her eyes.

'Then where would we have been?' she asked, coming down quickly from her high. 'The betting is Universe arranged Keelor's shopping too and the bottle used to bomb Eddie's place was supplied by them.'

Frankie nodded. Loretta said, 'Houlihan, whatever Keelor's done to Eddie, he's done. We need to stop him doing any more.'

'I know,' he said, very subdued.

'Well, move your arse!' she said, grabbing his sleeve and turning towards the door.

THIRTY-FIVE

Marcia smiled at Loretta as she looked at the picture on the badge. 'You're way prettier than the picture,' she said. 'What're you doing being a cop?'

Houlihan watched in amusement as Loretta blushed at the compliment and stumbled over her answer to the girl's question as she took the badge back. 'Thanks. I often ask myself that,' she said.

Marcia leaned on her elbows on the high counter and said, 'What's it like being a cop? Must be cool sometimes. Think I could make it?'

'I'm sure you could. Go for it. Can I see Mr Keelor's car?'

Marcia scooped the keys from a rack on the wall, talking as she did so. 'You got a number I could have, a contact? What's the money like? Do you get a travelcard and stuff?'

Loretta took the keys. 'Can I tell you about it when I've seen this car?'

'Sure you can. I'll call Kenny to take you over

there but he'll be a while. He always is. Can never find him when you want him.'

Loretta raised her hand. 'No need. What bay is it in?'

'N-Seventeen. I'd take you there myself, you know, but I can't leave the desk.'

'No worries. We'll find it.'

Marcia looked at Houlihan who smiled. Marcia said to Loretta, 'That your man?'

Loretta, smiling, shook her head and said, 'See you soon, Marcia. Did you check on the valeting?'

'Sure did. Yesterday right enough, and those boys are good. No fingerprints left I would think.'

'Thanks. Best if you don't mention this to anyone else at the moment. *Sub judice*, you know?'

That silenced Marcia and she just nodded.

Loretta picked up prints from around the boot catch and the underside of the boot lid. Also from the sun visor and glove-box handle. Crossing the tarmac on the way back with the keys, Loretta said to Houlihan, 'It might be worth taking a chance with Marcia. She's a pretty talkative girl. Maybe she can confirm that it was Keelor himself who picked up the car, show us his signature, time of arrival, that sort of stuff.'

Houlihan shook his head. 'Not worth risking. I wouldn't. She's too talkative. If she mentions it to her boss and he calls Keelor . . . maybe a courtesy call or something, you know. Not worth taking the chance till we've got more evidence.'

'You're right. I'll steer it away from Keelor.'

By the time they reached the desk, Marcia had recovered her curiosity. 'Find anything?' she asked.

Loretta raised a hushing finger to her lips and Marcia ducked her head, hunched her shoulders and squeezed her eyes shut. 'Sorry, I forgot.'

'No problem. Between you and me we got something. Might help us, we'll see.'

'Cool. Will you let me know if you catch the guy?'

'Sure, but I need a favour from you.'

'Say it.'

'This car thief might actually work from here, you know, checking out your clients as they arrive, watching what sort of stuff they stow in the car. If he does, it's really important he doesn't get the slightest hint that we might be on to him or we could lose him.'

Marcia nodded solemnly. Loretta lowered her voice. 'So can I ask you not to mention this to anyone for now. Not to any of the staff, not even your boss.'

Marcia waved away the chance of that, 'Ahh, he's never here anyway.'

'Good. We'll do a formal report for him when it's all finished and I'll let you see it first.'

Marcia beamed. Loretta took out her notebook. 'You said it was some agency that booked the car for Mr Keelor? We'd better let them know where we are with this. What did you say they were called?'

'Universe. All snotty cows that work for them. You'd think they were the millionaires, and they're just reps same as I am.'

'Do they book much through you?'

'A couple a week, I suppose. They're a pain, always reminding you about the Universe hamper.' She mimicked an American accent, 'Now don't forget to put the Universe hamper in the passenger side front and remember to connect the cooler!' She made a sour face. 'Connect the cooler; can't they just say plug it in?'

'So what's the Universe hamper?' Loretta asked, trying to sound casual.

Marcia said, 'It's a – well, wait a minute, I'll show you.' Six steps took her behind a partition.

Loretta turned to Houlihan. 'What's the betting on the bottle?' she whispered.

'No offers,' Houlihan said.

Marcia came back carrying a wicker basket big enough to hold two footballs. The phone rang. She put the basket on a chair and answered it, took a number and promised to call back. She smiled at Loretta as she put the phone down and picked the basket up again. With some effort she raised it to the counter and slid it towards them. 'Have a look in there,' she said.

Loretta undid the gold-coloured catch and raised the lid. The basket weave hid a standard plastic cool box. An expensive card covered the contents. It said, 'Take a cool break from your drive with the compliments of Universe'. The logo on the bottom centre of the card was the planets design from the bottle bottom. Loretta moved the card. There were various packages and tins but all she focused on was the clear glass bottle of water. Slowly she pulled it out and raised it above her head. The roof lights shimmered and fragmented through the thick glass bottom, making the sun and its planets look almost alive.

Conscious of Marcia watching her, Loretta replaced the bottle and took out some of the other stuff, all Universe branded: a half-bottle of champagne, a small tin of caviar, sealed cheeses. 'Fancy stuff,' Loretta said. 'And they all get one of these, the Universe clients?'

'Sure do. Millionaires. Different world, know what I mean?'

Loretta nodded. 'So Mr Keelor's might have been stolen as well as his golf clubs?'

'Maybe he used it all,' suggested Marcia, trying to make an early start to her police career.

'You're right, maybe he did. But I'd really like to take this hamper just to get pictures of it and all the stuff. Is it okay if I do that?'

Marcia looked doubtful. 'Somebody got sacked last year when one of those went missing.'

'Don't worry, I'll give you a receipt and I'll bring it back tomorrow. In full.'

Still uncertain, Marcia said, 'Let me just check we've got enough left.' She went behind the partition again and returned to say, 'Three left. Can you definitely bring it back tomorrow?'

Loretta raised her hand. 'I promise.'

'Okay.'

'Let me write you a receipt. Have you got some paper?'

Marcia put a compliments slip on the counter. 'Will this do?'

'That's fine, but I was just thinking, there's no point in taking this unless we're absolutely certain one went into Mr Keelor's car.'

'It went in all right. Kenny will have put it in. He's slow but the boy is thorough.'

Loretta nodded, smiling. 'I know you'll be right but could you get Kenny here so he can finally confirm. Don't want to be humping this halfway across London then back again for nothing.'

Marcia reached for the phone but her big-eyed look told Loretta she knew this was going to be a waste of time.

A few minutes later Kenny wandered through the main terminal doors and across to the desk. He confirmed he'd put the hamper in Keelor's car and remembered when he took Keelor to the car that Keelor had got him to move the hamper into the boot.

Houlihan put the hamper in the boot of Loretta's car and they headed for Scotland Yard. Houlihan said, 'Ever get a sense of doom? That heavy feeling in your belly?'

'Sometimes.'

'I think Eddie may be dead already.'

She hesitated before answering. 'We're closer to finding him now, Frankie. We almost know for certain that Keelor's involved in the attack somehow.'

Houlihan turned to her. 'We might, but even a crap lawyer would get this thrown out. All Keelor has to say is that someone stole the hamper from the car. Someone, the same person with the grudge against Makalu, stole the hamper and used the bottle.'

Loretta shrugged. 'Maybe. But given that Keelor was supposed to be in New York when the attack happened, how would this hamper thief have known he was here?'

Houlihan nodded slowly. 'Good point.'

Loretta said, 'And what about the Jeep that rammed you? If Keelor was driving, did that car come through Universe too? If it did we can trace it and get a paint match from the damage done to your car. And what else do you think Keelor might have organised through Universe? If it's the type of agency I think it is, all Keelor would need to do is make a phone call, say what he wanted and leave it to them.'

Houlihan thought for a few moments then said, 'You think they might have organised the security company that collected Eddie from the hospital?'

She smiled. 'It would have been ideal for Keelor, wouldn't it? No direct connection with his name, no research to do looking for the right people, and I'll bet you a pound to a packet of crisps that one of the big selling points for Universe is confidentiality. It'll be a nightmare trying to get information from them.'

Houlihan said, 'I wonder if Bobby Cranfield uses them?'

Loretta reached across and touched his arm. 'Good one! Maybe he does, or maybe he could register with them! Would he do that?'

Houlihan took out his phone, called Cranfield and agreed a meeting at Cranfield's house that evening. When he ended the call his phone immediately rang.

'Frankie?'

'Yes?'

'It's Margaret.'

'Margaret, I didn't recognise your voice. Is everything okay?'

'I need to see you. Mother's okay, but I need to see you.'

'Are you all right? Is everyone else?'

'We're as all right as we're going to be, Frankie. Nobody's had an accident, nobody's sick, but something's happened and we need to talk face to face.'

'Just me and you?' he asked, growing anxious now.

'Just me and you.' She sounded very tired.

'Is it about Ma?'

'It is.'

He stifled a sigh of frustration. 'Can it wait, Margaret?'

'Not any longer. We've been trying to find a

way round it these past few days but we can't. We need your help. You promised you'd help. You said you'd come back over.'

That old guilt-pitch again, inbred in her, thought Houlihan. He didn't want an argument in front of Loretta. He said, 'It's not safe for me to come over just now, can—'

'Oh, not safe for you! You, you, you! For years you put everybody else first and since you left the priesthood it's you, you, you!'

Houlihan drew breath as he saw Loretta had heard the outburst. Fighting for control, he kept his voice even as he said, 'It's not safe for you, for the family. Somebody may be following me. He's already tried to kill one man and he's had one go at me. So it's not me, me, me. Right now I couldn't care less about me but I do care about you and Ma and Theresa and Thomas and Cornelius and Pat.'

There was a pause, then Margaret said quietly, 'I'm sorry. It's been an awful strain these past few days. I'm sorry.'

Houlihan softened. 'It's okay. I was going to ask if you could come to London? I'll pay for the flight.'

Houlihan sensed that her hesitation was based on the threat he'd mentioned. He said, 'You'll be all right, Margaret. We can meet at a hotel. Nobody will know you're with me. We'll enter and leave separately and I'll book a room where we can meet.'

'It's not just that, Frankie, I'm worried about you too.'

'I'll be fine. Don't worry.'

'You say that, but?'

'Listen, I know how to handle these things. I just don't want to lead anyone to the family. I'll be all right.'

'Can I come over tomorrow then?'

'Of course. Book your flight and let me know what time you get in. I'll be at the hotel at Heathrow, waiting for you.'

She sounded relieved. 'Good. Fine. I'll call you soon. Bye.'

Houlihan looked at the silent phone and said without any enthusiasm, 'Look forward to it.'

Loretta looked across at him. 'You okay?' she asked in a concerned tone.

'Yep. Fine and dandy,' he said with a sigh. 'Fine and dandy.'

She asked him no questions. He appreciated that.

THIRTY-SIX

Loretta sweet-talked the technicians at Scotland Yard and got a quick result on the prints from the hotel room and the Mercedes; there was a matching set which she logged as Vaughn Keelor's with a question mark.

They photographed the contents of the hamper, taking several shots of the bottle, then left and returned to Loretta's house where Houlihan found the Universe site on the Internet. 'No applications,' he called downstairs to Loretta who was making coffee. 'By invitation only.'

'Yeah, don't call us, we'll call you,' she replied. 'No big shock there. Good marketing point for them.'

Houlihan clicked through various pages covering press information and testimonials. He heard Loretta coming along the landing and smelled the coffee as she entered the small room. Not turning round he quoted, 'We can get you anything from an ivory thimble to a trip into space. One call does it all and discretion is our watchword.'

'I bet it is,' said Loretta, setting down the tray.

'What are the chances of subpoenaing their records on Keelor?'

'Where are they based?'

'Malaysia.'

'About the same chance as I have of making Chief Constable.'

Houlihan smiled, leaned back trying to relax. Loretta said, 'Drink your coffee.' He picked up the mug. 'Have a biscuit,' she said.

He shook his head slowly, smiling. 'Mrs Biscuit,' he said. 'You'll turn into a biscuit.'

She nodded, munching happily. He said, 'So we find out if Bobby's a member of Universe, then what?'

'Then we ask him to book something through them, like a very discreet security company with the wherewithal to collect a patient from hospital.'

'And we hope it's the same one Keelor got.'

'There can't be many doing that sort of work.'

'So we raise the false number-plate stuff with them and threaten prosecution?'

'Maybe. Depends how certain we are that we've got the same people, and it depends what they're willing to do to stay out of trouble with the police.'

'But it also all depends on Bobby joining in.'

'Will he?' she asked.

'I don't know. We'll need to tell him pretty much all we know then ask him to help us bring Keelor down, and the racecourse deal with it.'

'To finish off his beloved Jockey Club.'

Houlihan nodded. 'Canvassing turkeys to vote for Christmas.'

'He might as well get the Jockey Club on the right side of it before the story breaks. Sell that to him.'

'I'll try. The really hard part is going to be keeping it from Hooper. If he hears, Keelor hears.'

'Then you need to persuade Mr Cranfield that he'd be taking a monumental risk speaking to anyone at all. Tell him that if Hooper screws up the investigation the Jockey Club becomes complicit rather than coming out with some glory for exposing Keelor.'

Houlihan looked at her. 'You are coming with me tonight?'

'Sure.' She bit again into the chocolate biscuit.

'Then it'll be a joint effort.'

Although it was very late when they arrived, Bobby Cranfield greeted them with his customary warmth and Houlihan couldn't decide whether the wariness he observed in Cranfield's face was real or just something he himself saw through tired and apprehensive eyes. Houlihan felt strung out. He was nervous about Cranfield's reaction to the Keelor story, concerned about Cranfield suspecting any form of relationship between him and Loretta, and he was worried about the next day's meeting with Margaret. He was already pretty certain what she'd ask for.

But what weighed most heavily on him was the aching dread about Eddie's fate. As Cranfield preceded them along the cavernous hall in his wheelchair, exchanging the usual pleasantries as he went, Houlihan was finding it increasingly hard to focus his mind on anything positive.

Chair on electric, tray in his lap, Cranfield cruised across the room bringing soft drinks to his guests, seated together on the sofa. Watching him, Houlihan admired the fact that Cranfield did not ask any of his house staff to serve guests. Houlihan knew it was important to him to be as independent as possible, especially in the eyes of others.

Cranfield whirred back to the kitchen with the tray then returned and parked the chair at a comfortable distance. He raised his glass of orange juice. 'Cheers. Soft drinks for hard times. I know you're not a lover of small talk, Frankie, and I suspect you aren't either, DS Moran. And I think you may have some news that will not have me cheering from the rooftops, so let's hear it, eh?'

Loretta looked at Houlihan. He cleared his throat, sat forward, elbows on knees, and said, 'Bobby, before I can tell you anything I need to ask for complete confidentiality.' Houlihan watched the other man's eyes, knowing that excellent mind would be processing the combinations of scenarios that such a promise, given blindly, might cost. He knew his friend would need to weigh his trust in Houlihan's professionalism and integrity against any potential damage to the Jockey Club. Houlihan knew that if Cranfield felt he needed to ask more questions before giving his promise of secrecy then that was proof that Cranfield's trust in Houlihan's judgement had faltered.

They looked straight at each other. Cranfield said quietly, 'Okay. You have my word.'

Houlihan nodded solemnly, trying not to show his relief. He told Cranfield everything they'd discovered about Keelor. Cranfield's face remained impassive throughout but Houlihan knew he was good at hiding his feelings. When Houlihan stopped talking Cranfield said 'Phew!' and rubbed his hands together. 'A pretty strong circumstantial case then?' he asked Loretta.

Loretta nodded. 'It is wholly circumstantial. We need something more solid.'

'And then what?' asked Cranfield.

'Then, if the DPP agrees the evidence is strong enough, we issue a warrant for his arrest.'

Cranfield said, 'Apart from burying the Jockey Club that would start a hell of a bear run on Makalu shares. Keelor is Makalu. An attempted-murder charge would wipe a billion pounds off the company. A conviction might finish it off completely.'

Houlihan said, 'And that's without the exposure of whatever it is Keelor is trying to cover up, trying to find.'

'It would need to be bad to beat throwing a petrol bomb at your Chief Operating Officer. That's straight out of the Saddam book on management discipline.' Cranfield smiled as he said it then saw

Houlihan's pained look and realised how poorly he'd put it. 'I'm so sorry, Frankie, I didn't mean that to sound so insensitive towards Eddie. It was stupid of me.'

Houlihan waved it away. He knew Cranfield had just being trying to lighten the generally gloomy atmosphere. 'It's okay, Bobby.'

Cranfield said, 'Have you any idea at all what Keelor is after? Did Malloy give you the smallest clue? Think back. It might well have been something inadvertent he said.'

'I've racked my brains, gone over what I could recall of conversations. There was nothing, or if there was I missed it. And if he was worried about it he never showed it. I spent a fair bit of time with Eddie, driving, sitting with him in his office, walking around racecourses, eating meals, swimming, running, going to the gym, he never—'

Houlihan stopped suddenly, saw Loretta turn to look at him.

'What is it?' Cranfield asked.

Houlihan shook his head. 'Nothing. Sorry. I completely lost my train of thought.'

Cranfield said, 'You were saying about how much time you'd spent with Malloy and that you hadn't noticed anything.'

'That's right. But now I think of it he didn't seem in the least worried about the threats, at least the early ones. Maybe there was something and he just wasn't bothered about it. I don't know.'

None of them spoke for a few moments then Cranfield said, 'So what do you want me to do, enrol with these Universe people and see what I can find out?'

Houlihan and Loretta looked at him. Houlihan felt slightly embarrassed that Cranfield had read their motives so easily. Cranfield shrugged and said, 'Well you didn't come out here for nothing and you were taking a risk telling me what you know. There had to be a trade-off. And anyway, it's nothing less than I'd expect of you both. You seem to be working very well as a team, and, putting aside all the other considerations, you're doing a pretty good job. Hold on just a minute.' And he wheeled himself out of the room. Houlihan and Loretta looked at each other. She made a face and giggled quietly and Houlihan knew nerves had set that off.

A few minutes later, Cranfield returned. 'They send me flyers from time to time, these Universe people. I thought I might have kept one but I can't find it. I'll call them tomorrow. I guess the objective is to find the security company that moved Malloy?'

Loretta nodded. 'That seems the most sensible thing to try.'

'I agree,' Cranfield said.

Houlihan looked at his watch. Cranfield picked up the gesture and its meaning. He said, 'It's after nine, Frankie. Even if I could enrol tonight they're not going to be able to sort anything out until tomorrow morning. I promise I'll do it first thing.'

'Thanks, Bobby. I appreciate it.'

'Not at all. Now you two look as though you haven't eaten a decent meal in weeks. Will you stay and share some extremely succulent venison and a bottle of wine?'

Houlihan and Loretta looked at each other and agreed with their eyes, the way, Houlihan realised, only close couples do. He felt suddenly tired and emotional and he'd noticed that it was at times like this that he was very glad she was around.

Loretta said nothing to him as they waved goodbye to Cranfield and walked to the car. She sensed his tiredness, head slightly down, hands in pockets, carrying his ever-growing burden. And Loretta wished he would let her take some of it from him. But he didn't know how to share it. She saw his life as a mould he'd been poured into: stirred, manipulated, exploited. It was still happening, with his family problems and all the old guilt festering away inside him. Her only consolation was that the mould hadn't quite set yet. There was still a chance that she could help him turn out all right.

In the meantime she knew what was important: silent companionship when he needed it, like now; the occasional one-liner to make him smile and the rare physical contact; the light touch on the arm, the hand left resting on the shoulder for a second too long, the 'accidental' brushing together as they walked. She knew these lifted him but he wouldn't admit it. She valued them, these tiny stitches that kept them linked.

She started the car and headed down the drive. It was time to talk. 'What was it that came to you in there?' she asked.

'The gym, where Eddie swam. He had a locker there. He paid extra for exclusive use.'

'You think whatever Keelor's looking for might be in there?'

'Unless Keelor's already been to see.'

'Did he know about the locker?'

Houlihan shrugged. 'Don't see why he should have done.'

'Can you get access to the locker?'

'Doubt it. I'm sure you could.'

'What time do they open in the morning?'

'Seven.'

'I'll be there for seven. You have a lie-in before you go to the airport to meet your sister. You sound exhausted.'

'You've been running around as much as I have,' he said.

'But I haven't been carrying so many worries.' She glanced across and saw his tired smile as he raised his hand to wave away her comment in the way she could just picture him doing as a priest. She said, 'I always make a point of going to my worry drawer before going out and picking just the odd one or two to take with me.'

He turned to her. 'Where do you keep them, in your handbag?'

'That's right. It means I can never find them anyway so I just forget them till I get home.'

'I prefer to have mine with me at all times. Keep an eye on them. Stop them breeding.'

'Get them neutered. Best investment I ever made.'

'Yeah, but it's pinning them down long enough, that's the hard part.'

'Gimme a shout next time. I'll lend a hand.'

'Thanks.'

Loretta felt better after that exchange. She knew it had helped him, and they settled back to silence as she drove the dark, quiet roads heading southwest and home.

THIRTY-SEVEN

Loretta's radio alarm woke her at five a.m. and she quickly switched it off to avoid disturbing Houlihan. Before leaving for London she ate a chocolate biscuit and drank half a cup of coffee, standing in the kitchen listening to the rain squalls in the morning darkness.

By the time she returned Houlihan was up and dressed but sitting quietly in his room, preparing himself mentally and emotionally for his meeting with Margaret. He heard a door slam downstairs then Loretta calling his name. There was an edge in her voice that made him rise quickly and hurry to the landing. She was smiling wide, looking up at him and waving something in her right hand. 'A video,' she said. 'That was all that was in Eddie's locker. Coming down for the matinee?'

It was in a yellow case of thick vinyl. The words '*Everest '96 – 3*' had been written on the case with a broad-tipped black marker pen. Loretta pushed the cassette into the video player and they both sat on the rug close to the TV.

The tape was of Vaughn Keelor's Makalu expedition to Everest, and during the hour that followed Houlihan and Loretta got to know the members of the expedition quite well. The cameraman/director was a thirty-four-year-old Texan called Mark Duncan. His face appeared rarely on the film but his was the voice most often heard as he cajoled others in the party to repeat certain moves or to hold halfway up an ice climb so he could get above them for a different viewpoint. It became clear to Houlihan and Loretta from the shots Duncan was getting and the way the others on film treated him that he was a very skilled and experienced climber.

Duncan had a winning personality too and, using a combination of compliments, witticisms and pleas, he almost always seemed to get what he wanted from the others, although their good-natured agreement faded noticeably the higher they got. Everyone on the film agreed that altitude made people much more sensitive, selfish and irritable.

Tom Hutchison, thirty-five, from Seattle, was the guide, although Vaughn Keelor made it clear that he himself was to be seen as joint leader at the very least. Hutchison gave a morning briefing each day and Keelor would always be standing beside him, ensuring he was on film, nodding wisely at Hutchison's advice and instructions, adding gung-ho comments and generally acting as a cheerleader. Keelor would talk to each member of the party regularly, in a fatherly manner, consoling those suffering from the effects of altitude – piercing headaches, harsh and dry coughs, skin sores. Everyone except Keelor seemed to be feeling the physical effects.

But a certain incident showed Keelor to be as vulnerable as the rest. Mark Duncan filmed him bent double in the tent, coughing so hard he was crying. Keelor gasped to Hutchison, the only other occupant, 'This is breaking my fucking ribs!' When he recovered and realised he was on film, Keelor turned savagely on Duncan. 'What the fuck are you doing? Have you been filming that? Cut it and keep the camera off me for all that shit!' Duncan didn't reply but he kept the camera running long enough in close-up to catch the malice in Keelor's still-wet eyes.

At that point, Houlihan and Loretta looked at each other. Houlihan said, 'You know the story here? Keelor's the only one that survives this. Assuming that what we're watching is the summit party, the other five don't make it back.'

Loretta felt the hairs on her neck and arms prickle as she turned back to the screen. As the six members moved steadily towards the final camp, Camp Four on the South Col, Loretta paid special attention to every word the soon-to-be-dead people uttered. She felt a deepening sadness at the enthusiasm of Wayne Bachelor, a sixteen-year-old sports-sales trainee who worked in one of Makalu's outdoor gear shops. She cringed each time Keelor put his arm around the boy and said, 'This is the kid that'll get the world record and he'll get it for Makalu. Youngest person to summit: Wayne Bachelor!' And the boy would lean smiling towards the camera and say, 'It's for you too, Mom!'

The only woman was Clare McArthur, thirty-seven, from Milwaukee. Keelor paid her little attention and Houlihan and Loretta drew the conclusion that she was the token black person for Keelor's publicity machine. The film showed McArthur to be superbly fit and an excellent climber. Her stamina reserves were easily the deepest in the party and she suffered fewer ailments than the others. A consultant sports scientist to Makalu, she impressed Loretta with her quiet independence and natural dignity. There was an element among the others of playing up to Keelor, the boss. McArthur never did that. She didn't speak unless she had something to contribute, she was always ready first each morning and she was happy to lead climbs and fix ropes. She seemed closest to Ngawang Dorje Sherpa, their Sirdar.

Ngawang Dorje was twenty-eight and had summited Everest twice. On film, Mark Duncan had skilfully caught a touching piece on a ledge the Sherpa and McArthur had shaped with their ice axes. The couple sat waiting for the remaining climbers coming up the ropes and Ngawang Dorje told Clare McArthur of his dreams of starting his own trekking company in Kathmandu with, eventually, his own small plane to fly clients into Lukla. McArthur offered encouragement and empathy, spurring the excited Sherpa on to talk of making it a family business so his wife and sons could be with him all the time, and, as he was at his most animated, Mark Duncan closed in on the young man's weathered face till it filled the screen and all of his dreams could be seen in his eyes and his spectacularly white-toothed smile.

Loretta wept silently. She looked at Houlihan. He would not turn to meet her gaze and she saw tears run down the side of his face.

From that moment Houlihan and Loretta were captivated. They followed the progress of the doomed climbers in silence until they made final camp at the South Col. Houlihan checked his watch. 'What time are you meeting your sister?' Loretta asked.

'Her flight is due in at ten past twelve. I should be okay.'

'There can't be much left in this,' Loretta said, and they turned again to the screen to see sweeping shots of the icy wasteland that was the South Col, the flattish wind-scoured shoulder at 25,938 feet from which the 27,890 foot peak of Lhotse rose to the right and the 29,035 foot pinnacle of Everest to the left. This was the point from which the final summit attempt would be launched. The panning camera passed more than twenty tents, not dwelling on them or on the climbers in their thick down suits. The next shot was of a frozen corpse, face down, bright blue jacket shredded at the edges by the incessant wind, the madly flapping remnants reminding Houlihan of the fringes on buckskin jackets.

The camera panned to show the litter of discarded oxygen bottles then opened out again to take in once more all the tents, their fabric constantly reshaped in dents and furrows and waves by the wind.

The next shot was of Keelor's excited group discussing the final arrangements for the summit attempt. Keelor was geeing everyone up. 'We go in the early hours of tomorrow. Everything's right. The forecast is perfect. We all go. Seven of us can make it. The whole party. No failures. Right? No failures!' There were cheers from all except guide Tom Hutchison who got up slowly and said, 'I want to speak to the other teams before we make a definite commitment.'

'Let them worry about their problems, Tom, we ain't got any,' said Keelor.

Hutchison's smile was laboured as he said 'Be back soon', and ducked out of the tent.

The next shot was of Hutchison leaving one of the tents of the other teams and walking towards camera. He said, 'I'm just about to tell Vaughn Keelor that we ought to postpone the summit attempt, so walk this way if you want to see some fireworks.' He smiled nervously then Mark Duncan called him back and asked him to go back in the tent and come out and do it again, urging him to shout so his words could be heard more clearly above the wind.

The next scene was in Keelor's tent with just him, Hutchison and the cameraman. Keelor stared coldly at the guide as Hutchison spoke. 'Vaughn, we should leave this another twenty-four hours. Every other team is going for it in the morning. They'll be waiting in line at the Hillary Step like they do for the Christmas sales.'

Keelor said, 'And we'll be at the front.'

Hutchison shook his head. 'Vaughn, trust me, there are going to be far too many people up there tomorrow and more than half of them are clients. Slow, inexperienced, vulnerable. A big accident waiting to happen. If we hold off another day we'll have the hill pretty much to ourselves.'

Keelor walked towards him. 'Listen, Tom, the reason they're all going for it is the weather forecast. It's perfect for tomorrow. It might not be perfect for Thursday or Friday, or for weeks afterwards.'

'The weather should hold another few days.'

'Should? Should! How many times have you seen it change completely, from one minute to the next, never mind one day to the next. Come on, Tom, you're being too cautious.'

'You can't be too cautious on the South Col, Vaughn. That's why I'm still alive and a lot of the guys we both know are dead.'

Keelor seemed to soften. He put an arm around Hutchison's shoulder and said, 'Okay, Tom, let's have a sensible look at the pros and cons. What do you say?'

Hutchison shrugged. 'Fine.'

Keelor turned to Mark Duncan. 'Kill that,' he said, pointing at the camera. The camera was quickly lowered and the sound of switches being clicked was heard as though Duncan was switching the camera off. But he left it running, held at waist height, catching Keelor and Hutchison in head and shoulder shots.

Keelor turned the guide towards him and put a hand on each shoulder. His conciliatory tone had gone. He said, 'Listen, Tom, we go tonight. The kid has four days to break the youngest summiter record. In five days' time he's a day too old. There's no way I'm risking that.'

'So you'll risk his life instead?' Hutchison asked.

'There's no risk, nothing he wasn't up for. It's a bigger risk sitting here on our asses neglecting a perfect day, waiting for a fucking storm instead. How much sense does that make?' He was shouting.

Hutchison's temper was also rising. 'Tell me, big shot, how many times have you climbed Everest? What makes you the best authority?'

'That's a dumb question, Hutch. I've been on plenty of mountains. We're only nine hundred metres from the top, the weather's good, we're all fit enough, we've got a world record on. It doesn't matter what way you look at it or how many times you've been on top, those are the facts. You don't have to be Reinhold fucking Messner to interpret them! Everything says go and we're going!' He still had his hands on the guide's shoulders. With a sharp upward sweep Hutchison knocked them away and said, 'It doesn't matter how good the weather is, there'll be teams that will reach the Hillary Step before us. One man at a time on the ropes there and that means queues, and queues mean people get frustrated and start taking risks. It means they ignore turnaround times and find themselves trying to get down in the dark. It means—'

'We'll leave before midnight and be the first at the Step.'

'And you'll get caught on the way down with everyone else coming up. One man on the rope still applies, and it'll be a hell of a fight trying to persuade people out to beat the clock on the way up to stand aside and let you guys down.'

Keelor tilted his head back as though thinking about it. All the camera could see was the U-shape of his jaw. Then he looked again at the guide and said, 'I'm paying you one hundred thousand dollars to get us up this mountain.'

Hutchison blew up at this. 'You're paying me one hundred thousand dollars to keep you alive, for Christ's sake, and that's what I'm trying to do! And it's not just you. I've got a responsibility for everyone on this trip and I'm telling you we don't go tonight!'

Keelor considered him and said coldly, 'You stay here. Ngawang will take over guiding. You've lost your nerve.'

Hutchison made a grab at Keelor's jacket but his gloved hands couldn't get a grip on the shiny fabric. He shouted at Keelor, 'You've lost your fucking brain, man!' and he pushed Keelor hard. Keelor stumbled backwards and fell, panting in the thin air as he tried to get back up. He seemed to be using his rucksack for leverage as he pushed up off his knees but when he turned again to Hutchison he had his ice axe in his right hand. 'You bastard!' he cried, and raised the silver axe. Mark Duncan's voice was heard, 'Hey! Hey, Keelor! I'm still shooting. You're on film. Put it down, man!'

Keelor looked down at the camera, his chin tilting upwards again as Duncan raised the camera to shoulder height. Keelor looked murderous and Loretta reached to clasp Houlihan's hand, raising her other hand to cover her mouth. Then Keelor somehow forced a slow smile. 'I knew you were shooting, Mark. You didn't think I was serious, did you?' Keelor laughed. 'I was playing up for the camera.' He lowered the ice axe and came towards the camera, smiling, and said, 'I'll be looking forward to seeing it on the out-takes show.'

Keelor's body obscured Hutchison but the guide's voice came over. 'Let's hope it's not part of the posthumous tributes.'

Keelor's smile faded as he looked straight at Mark Duncan. 'Time to turn the camera off now, Mark.'

'Too late,' Duncan said.

'Did you switch it off the first time I told you?'

'Nope.'

The flare of anger in the billionaire's face was familiar now to Houlihan and Loretta. Keelor said, 'Give me the tape.'

'Nope. Whatever else you do in this tent goes on tape.'

'The tape's mine. I commissioned you. Remember?'

'Keep your money. I'll keep the tape.'

Keelor stared, almost dead-eyed now. Houlihan and Loretta knew he still held the ice axe and they wondered if they were about to see a murder on tape. Suddenly, Keelor's face disappeared from screen as he cried out and Loretta gasped and jumped in fright. Duncan zapped the zoom out quickly to show Keelor struggling on the floor of the tent as Hutchison tried to pull the axe away from him. The guide was on top, trying to straddle the cursing, writhing Keelor and Duncan dropped quickly close to ground level as Hutchison's gloved fist pounded Keelor's face. Keelor tried to fight but a long powerful hook from the guide caught him on the left temple and he lay still.

Duncan moved around to catch Hutchison's wild-eyed face as he sat on Keelor, panting loudly. Gradually a degree of composure came back to the guide's face and he shook his head slowly as he got to his feet holding Keelor's ice axe. He looked at Duncan and said, 'We'd best go tell the others before this fucking wacko wakes up.'

Duncan's camera panned slowly round the faces in the big tent as Hutchison told the story. Wayne, the sixteen-year-old, watched Hutchison as he spoke, the youngster's face pale and unblinking, listening as though hypnotised by horror. Hutchison ended by saying, 'Keelor will be up and around soon and he'll no doubt be painting you a different picture. He's already accused me of losing my nerve so he might spin you that story.' He turned to the Sirdar. 'Ngawang, he'll probably promise you the moon to get him up there. He won't be paying me I don't think, so there'll be some big numbers getting talked.' As hard as he tried to look solemn, that lit a spark in Ngawang's eyes.

Hutchison looked at the boy. 'Wayne, I know you want to do this for your mom as much as anything else but it ain't worth it for a record that might last a few months, maybe a year. Getting you home safe will be what your mom wants. You're sixteen. The mountain'll be here for a long time. You'll have more chances than anyone to come back and do it.' Wayne's hypnotised stare didn't change.

Clare McArthur's calm face came on screen. Hutchison said, 'Clare, I got nothing to teach you. You could outclimb me in your sleep. None of you are in any greater danger than you thought you'd be when we set out. The danger here is all those guys out there as desperate as you are to get to the top. And the other danger is Keelor's judgement. It's my duty to give you my assessment and I'm repeating it to you now, on film,' he turned to nod towards Mark Duncan. 'Wait twenty-four hours. Let all those guys race each other tomorrow. Everest will still be here.'

The next scene showed a party of four setting off from camp in the dark. Mark Duncan was voicing over. 'Didn't expect to be shooting in the dark so I didn't bring any big lights. It's one thirty a.m., May tenth. That's Hutch at the front, then Keelor, Ngawang and Wayne. Keelor offered Ngawang fifty thousand dollars to get them up there and that's a hell of a lot of money for anybody, never mind a Sherpa who wouldn't earn that in a lifetime. Clare and I took Hutch's advice and decided to wait but when Wayne said he was going, under serious pressure from Keelor, Clare said she'd tag along to keep an eye on the boy. But Hutch said he felt that was his responsibility. So Clare and I are waiting here and saying prayers. Our guys are first away but looking around me here (the camera panned, catching little more than vague shapes of tents) I can see and hear many of the other teams putting the final touches to their preparation. Over the next two hours or so, more than sixty climbers will head up that ridge. Statistics show that for every seven people who summit, one dies. Those odds say that nine or ten of these guys might never get off this mountain.'

The story unfolded in scenes featuring Clare on the radio to Tom Hutchison. Within three hours of leaving camp, Keelor was showing signs of exhaustion and was having to take a dozen breaths after each step and half-hour rests every fifty metres or so. Keelor had refused to turn round and all the other teams had passed them well below the Hillary Step. The enforced rests were so frequent the remainder of the party were getting very cold and serious frostbite was becoming a real danger.

Ngawang offered to short-rope Keelor, attach a six-foot length of rope between them and literally haul Keelor up the mountain. Keelor agreed but the radio conversations between Hutchison and Clare showed a growing anxiety on the part of the guide about the situation. At one point he said he'd give Keelor another hour and if his condition was worse by then, Hutchison would turn the party round, leaving Keelor if he refused to come.

At 11.20, almost ten hours after leaving camp eight hundred metres below, Tom Hutchison radioed in to say they had reached the Hillary Step and that the queue there wasn't as bad as he'd feared. He estimated they'd be up the forty-foot wall via the ropes within an hour, keeping them within a safe turnaround time.

His next call was a tired but joyful report that all four of them had reached the summit at 1.43 and that at two p.m. they would leave to start the descent. The guide's next call, just after three p.m., was less happy. Keelor's effort in getting to the top had resulted in a switch-off of his willpower. The 'target reached' message to his brain had caused a physical collapse and he was unable to move. Tom Hutchison reported that he had sent Ngawang down with Wayne and he was staying with Keelor to try and revive him.

An hour later Hutchison called to say he had short-roped Keelor to the top of the Hillary Step to find Ngawang and Wayne waiting there. The fixed ropes allowing ascent and descent had been cut to free a client from another party who had flipped over on the way down and entangled the rope around his neck. Tired, cold and frustrated climbers and Sherpas were trying to re-fix ropes of their own and the situation had become chaotic. The guide's anxiety was ratcheted up another notch by what he could see in the sky and he asked Clare to look south and please tell him that the clouds that looked like they'd come 'from a tyre-dump fire' weren't heading his way. Clare left the tent and the wind was already high enough to drown any words from the radio as Duncan's camera moved from a close-up of her worried face to a shot of menacingly dark, billowing clouds headed towards them at speed from deep in the Himalayan valleys.

Duncan filmed the storm coming in until the fury of blinding snow reduced visibility to inches and the wind howled in the microphone so loud that Loretta had to hit the mute button on the TV.

The final scene was inside the tent, wind flailing the walls, all talking obviously impossible as Clare sat writing urgently on a notepad which she then held up to the camera. It said: '8 p.m. Terrible storm. 30 below. People dying. We're going out to try and help.'

The remainder of the tape was blank. Loretta turned to Houlihan with tears in her eyes. 'What happened to them?'

'They died. They never got back.'

'How?'

'I don't know. Malloy only told me his story, or part of it. I don't know the story of Keelor's party.'

'You know a lot more about it now. He caused the deaths of all of them by ignoring Tom Hutchison's advice.'

Houlihan nodded slowly. 'Now we know why Keelor was so desperate to get his hands on the tape.' They both sat in silence, heads bowed, for what seemed a long time.

Loretta rose and ejected the tape from the video. Snapping the case shut on it she said, 'I'll take this into the office and get copies made then I'll go back and see Marcia, try and get her to trawl through for a Jeep that Keelor might have hired through Universe.' She looked at her watch. 'You'd better get moving, Frankie, or you'll be late.'

Feeling dazed by what he'd just sat through, Houlihan went slowly upstairs and put on his navy blue suit, his tie and shoes, combed his hair, all in a robotic fashion, his mind working on the possibilities of Eddie still being alive. He knew that if Keelor thought Eddie had hidden the tape somewhere it might be found – or had given it to someone – there was no way Keelor could kill him until he'd talked. Unless Malloy had already died from his injuries.

THIRTY-EIGHT

Houlihan checked into the room he'd booked in the airport hotel under the name of Foster, and he paid cash. He sat waiting for Margaret, watching the planes come and go, still undecided on how to handle the request he knew she was bringing.

The knock at the door startled him. He hurried towards it, moving quietly. He stood by the wall on the hinged side of the door and asked who it was.

'Frankie, it's Margaret.' Her voice sounded strained but he recognised it all right and opened the door.

She looked pale and worried although she tried to smile. Houlihan felt a sudden and surprising tenderness and protectiveness towards her, his 'big sister', the woman who was usually all business and efficient at looking after herself. He opened his arms and she moved towards him, hugging him so tightly it moved him quite deeply. They had never been a physically affectionate family; hugs

493

and kisses had been actively discouraged all their lives by Ma, who considered it 'sissy'. Only Theresa had ever ignored Ma on that, one of the traits that Ma decided marked her as 'backward'.

Houlihan held his sister to him. She had been a constant in his life as much as his parents had been, and the parts she had played in that life reeled rapidly through his mind now. Comforting her made him feel like a priest again and he realised it was a feeling he'd missed: doing something for others, meaning something to people.

He eased his hold on her as he felt hers slacken and he took a step back to look at her face. 'Are ye all right, our Margaret?' he asked in his purest Dublin accent, smiling warmly at her. She nodded but there were tears on her cheeks. Houlihan went to the bathroom and brought her some tissues, then clicked the switch on the kettle to reheat the water he'd boiled earlier.

He sat on the bed beside his sister as she dried her eyes. 'How is everybody?' he asked.

'They're fine. Theresa sends her love.'

He nodded. 'Give her mine when you get back. Tell her I'll be over soon.'

She turned to him, eyes red, worry still in every feature. 'What's this awful thing with this man who's after you?'

'That'll be sorted out soon. He's left the country now so there's no danger any more.'

'Where is he, do you know?'

Houlihan realised she was fretting that he might

be in Ireland. 'Don't be worrying now, he's in America and won't be moving till we go and get him.'

'You and the police?'

'That's right. Now, I'll make us a cup of tea.'

Houlihan fixed the cups and worked around the small tray of sachets wondering whether to start talking now in an effort to try and make himself sound more casual than he felt. Maybe Margaret would start. She didn't, but she moved from the bed to a chair by the coffee table and she gathered her coat around her and opened her handbag and fiddled with stuff inside it before closing it and sitting straighter, lifting her head, preparing herself as Houlihan brought the drinks.

He sat in the chair at the opposite end of the table as Margaret stirred sugar into her tea. When she'd finally picked up the cup and sipped, Houlihan looked at her and said quietly, 'Well, who told Ma?'

Margaret reddened slightly. 'Who told her what?'

'About the suggestion I return to the priesthood.'

She looked at him, unblinking, for what seemed a long time. Houlihan held her gaze although he hoped the look on his face was a kind and understanding one; that was what he was trying for.

Finally, Margaret said, 'Pat.'

Houlihan nodded. He'd known the answer and now awaited the next certain thing, the assurances of how unintentional it had been. Margaret said, 'He didn't mean to do it, Frankie. He feels absolutely terrible about it. He was visiting her. He thought she was asleep. He was thinking aloud, he says, nothing more. But she was still awake.'

Houlihan choked back the words 'surprise, surprise' and just nodded again and said, 'And she liked the idea.' It was a statement.

Margaret said, 'Frankie, it did more for her than any amount of medicine. You'd need to see her now to appreciate the difference it's made.'

'Not bed-bound any more then?'

'She's been getting up most days, getting dressed, sitting by the window like she used to.'

'Watching for me,' Houlihan said. 'So it's a little bit more than her thinking it's just a suggestion?'

'She took it that you were coming back. That you were returning to your vocation.'

Houlihan looked at her for a few seconds, then said, 'And nobody thought to tell her I had said no to it?'

She paused now as she looked at him. 'We didn't have the heart. We decided to cross that bridge when we need to.'

'But first you'd come and tell me so I'd be sure of the consequences of sticking to my decision.' There was no effort in keeping his voice calm for he felt no anger. There had been an inevitability about it all from the day Cornelius had raised the idea. He had known that they would run out of patience after all the other things had been tried; he'd been certain that Margaret or Pat or, at a real pinch, even Cornelius would decide the time had come to play the ace card. And this was it. Margaret was just the messenger. They must have reckoned, thought Houlihan, that as he and Pat had some history of not getting on, then Pat had the least to lose in being the Judas.

Margaret's head was down. Houlihan said, 'When is she expecting me to do this?'

'We told her you had a big job to finish.'

'And she pressed you for some idea of a date.'

Margaret hesitated once more, then said quietly, 'She did. We said before summer was out.'

'So what were her conditions?'

Margaret looked puzzled. Houlihan said, 'I'm a sinner. She wouldn't have me come back without conditions.'

'She wants you to have the Archbishop hear your confession and give you absolution.'

Houlihan leaned forward, elbows on knees, and nodded slowly. 'And if I don't come back will Pat confess that it was all built on clay, that I never promised anything of the sort and that I indeed never said I'd do it? Will you be telling her that or will I be the villain of the piece again when she relapses?' He felt no anger or animosity towards her or the others, he just wanted them to know he was no fool, that he had seen all this coming. 'Well?' he asked softly.

'We'll tell her. We'll take the blame. I promise you that.'

Houlihan left the hotel, walked to the main terminal building and went to the coffee shop where he was to meet Loretta. She was waiting, drinking cappuccino, smiling at him as he approached. He sat down and his phone rang. It was Bobby Cranfield.

'Frankie, can you talk?'

'Sure. Yes.'

'Sounds noisy there?'

'I'm at Heathrow with Loretta.'

'Any developments?'

Houlihan glanced at Loretta, unsure about mentioning the video. He said, 'Best not to talk too much on mobiles, Bobby. Are you at home?'

'Yes.'

'Give me two minutes, I'll call you back.'

Houlihan said to Loretta, 'Everything okay?'

She nodded, sipping then putting the mug down. Houlihan thought she looked bright-eyed and positive, a big contrast to Margaret's downcast, anxious face. She said, 'Keelor hired a black Jeep Cherokee through Universe the day you were rammed. It came back with accident damage to the front offside wing and the back nearside taillight. We've got a guy on the way here to take some paint samples.'

'Your guys took some samples from my car that night, didn't they?'

'Way ahead of you, Frankie boy, the lab boys are digging them out as we speak.'

He smiled. 'I need to ring Bobby back. I won't be a minute.'

'May be best not to mention the video for now.'

'I thought that too,' he said, and left her.

He put a pound in the callbox and dialled Bobby Cranfield's number. Cranfield answered on the second ring and asked him if he really thought his mobile might be being monitored.

'I wouldn't like to bet it's not, and you might just want to bear in mind that yours could be too. Loretta had her place swept for bugs; I'm sure she can arrange the same for your house or the offices at Portman Square.'

'I think that would cause too much of a stir, Frankie, but I'll follow your advice to be careful in communications. What were you going to tell me?'

'Just that the pieces seem to be falling into place. We've picked up some more stuff that drops Keelor even further in it. How about you?'

'Well, interestingly, I contacted Universe first thing this morning to enrol and I asked them to find me a security company who could do the type of work you suggested. They've come back with just two names. I didn't want to call either without speaking to you.'

'Well, thanks. And thanks for moving so quickly. I appreciate it. Can you let me speak to Loretta and give you a call back within the next hour or so?'

'Certainly. I'll be at home.'

'Thanks, Bobby.'

'You're welcome. Frankie, do you have enough on Keelor to kill this deal for our courses?'

Houlihan hesitated, then said quietly, 'Yes, I'm pretty sure we do. Sorry.'

'That's all right. It just means some shrewd strategic planning and at least I can make a start on it now.'

'I'll call you back soon.'

Houlihan returned to Loretta's table to find a mug of cappuccino waiting for him and Loretta drinking from a full mug. 'Your second?' he asked.

'Third.' She smiled.

'You'll never sleep tonight.'

'I think I will, you know.'

He smiled. 'Thanks for getting me one.' He sipped some, wiped the froth from his lips and told her what Cranfield had said.

'What do you think?' she asked.

'I think we should get Bobby to call Universe back and refine his requirements; spin a tale about ultra-secrecy in moving a private patient, stressing that the vehicle may be under surveillance at the pick-up point and should, effectively, be untraceable from any video footage of it arriving or leaving.'

'In other words, make sure it's fitted with false plates.'

'Correct.'

'And who's the patient?'

'Me.'

'And which hospital are you being picked up from?'

'Same one as Eddie.'

Loretta raised her eyebrows. Houlihan said, 'You

can pull that with whatshisname . . . He's terrified of you.'

'Penrose?' She shook her head. 'Not worth it. Too much resentment there. He might be forced into agreeing but there'd be too big a chance he'd try and contact Keelor.'

'Fair point. Okay, what then?'

'It doesn't have to be a hospital, these people won't care. What about Bobby Cranfield's house? Would he let us set it up from there. You as the patient, me as your escort?'

'He might. I'll ask.'

'Why don't we get them to involve both companies on the same day? Tell them that one is to pick up then meet the other at a specified place to transfer the patient into that vehicle to complete the journey. Same rules to apply to both as far as non-traceability goes. If one vehicle turns up with the same number plates they used to move Malloy, we pull them in.'

'And what if they alert Keelor?'

'They can't, they don't know he was their client.'

'True, but they might try and bounce it back to Universe,' said Houlihan.

'I kinda think they'll take the easy option if we offer it.'

'Which is, tell us where you took Eddie Malloy.'

'Correct.'

Houlihan thought about it, sipping coffee, nodding, then smiled and said, 'Let's do it.'

* * *

As they'd come in separate cars each drove back to Loretta's place. Houlihan spent the journey thinking about the ends of roads. In the next couple of days, with a bit more luck they could well find Eddie, or discover what had happened to him. With all the evidence they had they looked pretty sure to nail Keelor too; they could do it by releasing the tape if nothing else.

And what did that leave him with? A job with a company that looked doomed. A loyalty to Bobby Cranfield and no one else in the Jockey Club. Even if the Jockey Club survived and the Hoopers among the employees were weeded out, did he really want to be in racing for the rest of his life, or even the next few years? It was riven with politics and in-fighting. Greed was slowly strangling the sport. He wasn't enjoying racing the way he had when he'd just been a fan.

So where to next? He glanced at the car in front, at Loretta's head bobbing from side to side. He smiled, knowing how loud she liked to play her music when he wasn't in the car. He suffered a pang at the thought that he might not see her again after all this was over. But he felt that at least he could return to being with Kathy every day, in his head, the way it had been until all this started.

All this. The phrase resounded in his mind and he recognised it as his euphemism for 'When Loretta walked into my life'. And he knew he'd fought hard to prevent any relationship developing.

He couldn't make it stack up. He had reached the age of thirty with no commitment of any kind to anything but his parishioners and God. He'd served that long with nothing other than the mildest temptation on rare occasions. And what was he facing now? Was his mind, his chemistry, his emotional shortcomings, whatever, asking him to accept; to believe that after all those years of needing no one, after meeting and falling so deeply and completely in love with Kathy Spencer, that another such woman had come along?

No. He couldn't. To follow that road, to trust in it, would lead to nothing but more sadness. The very fact that it had presented itself, that Loretta had turned up within such a comparatively short time of Kathy's death, devalued everything about love in his eyes. How could something he'd thought so precious – unique – suddenly prove not to be so?

If he unshackled his feelings, allowed himself to be himself, let the relationship take proper root and grow, then what would be the outcome? How long would it last? How many more Kathys and Lorettas would there be before his life was over? Three? Five? Ten? The thought pained him. He gripped the wheel, angry now, for he felt cheated. The woman he'd given up everything for, the love he'd made the sacrifice to experience, was won much more cheaply than he'd thought. Every new Kathy would devalue the first one, mock his stupidity and immaturity, damn him further in the eyes of his family, and mean, ultimately, that his mother had been right.

What a sad thing love is, thought Houlihan.

So, was he to make his ma happy again? Was he to bail out his siblings and let them get back to their lives, free from worry or responsibility for Ma? Was he to go back to being a quiet observer of everyone else's lives? A comforter of others? A non-participant?

Decision-time was coming closer.

THIRTY-NINE

Cranfield agreed to let his house be used as the base. He called Universe and told them he needed the pick-up to be made the following afternoon. He stressed that complete confidentiality was crucial and said that he would ask the representative of the security company to produce on arrival a piece of headed paper from the company with their Chief Executive's name written on it in black letters more than one inch high. He asked Universe to call him back confirming this would be done and giving him the name of the Chief Executive.

The next day, Cranfield, Loretta and Houlihan were in the snooker room watching the vehicle approach along the drive. Houlihan wore a white dressing gown. Cranfield, using binoculars, called out the registration plate. Loretta checked it and said, 'That's the one. That's it!' Houlihan left quickly to get dressed.

Cranfield went outside and waited as the vehicle pulled up. Loretta, watching from the window, thought it was the same vehicle as well as the same number-plates; a hybrid of MPV and security truck, dark brown, no markings, blacked-out windows.

A man dressed in a black suit, white shirt and black tie got out of the passenger side, smiling and reaching inside his jacket pocket as he walked towards Bobby Cranfield. 'Mr Cranfield, my name is James Willoghby, I believe you have a patient for transfer?' Cranfield opened the offered envelope to find a letterhead with the security company's name, address and contact details. Written on it in large black letters was the name John Penman. Cranfield said, 'Would you excuse me a minute?' and went inside.

Cranfield called Penman, told him his men had arrived for the pick-up and asked him to hold on. Loretta took the phone and said, 'Mr Penman, my name is Detective Sergeant Loretta Moran of the Metropolitan Police.'

Ten minutes later, Willoghby was in Loretta's car giving directions to where Malloy had been taken. Houlihan was in the back seat, feeling more optimistic than he had for weeks. Willoghby had been nervously talkative and told them that he remembered the pick-up from the hospital well as he'd been struck by the severity of the scarring on the patient's face and his complete silence throughout the journey. The driver had also got them lost twice and Willoghby had written down the directions he'd received by phone and was fairly sure he recalled them sufficiently well to go straight back there.

Malloy had been taken to a house in Sussex close to Gatwick Airport. This worried Houlihan a little as he wondered if Keelor had subsequently flown Malloy out of the country. Willoghby described the house: 'Big country place, a bit like Mr Cranfield's, you know, the long driveway, a few acres of trees, gardens, outbuildings. Well-kept. I remember seeing a fine film of polish on the big brass door-ring. Must be quite a few staff, though I didn't see many.'

'Who did you hand the patient over to?' asked Houlihan.

'Can't recall his name. American guy, well-dressed, maybe late fifties, sixty. Grey suit. Open-necked shirt. Then two younger guys came and took the patient into the house.'

'Still on the stretcher?' asked Houlihan.

'Definitely. There was no way he was walking anywhere.'

'Any gates at the entrance?' Loretta asked.

'Yeah. They were open when we arrived. But closed when we drove back out. We had to call them on the intercom to let us out.'

Houlihan and Loretta's glances met in the rear-view mirror.

Half an hour later, Loretta drove them through a series of sharp bends on a country road. Willoghby sat forward. 'It comes up soon, on the left, I'm sure. Driveway comes off this road at an angle of forty-five degrees. Take it easy.'

Loretta slowed to fifty mph. A few minutes later, Willoghby shouted, 'That's it! You've passed it!'

Loretta braked quickly but smoothly, reversed, turned the car up the driveway and accelerated, wheels spinning. Houlihan said, 'Loretta, we were going to suss the place out first, remember?'

'Executive decision, Houlihan. I didn't expect the gates to be open and they might not be again. Notice any CCTV?'

'I might have done if it wasn't for your dust.'

They caught glimpses of the house through the trees, a four-storey building of red sandstone, the weak sun glinting on the many windows at the front. Coming into the clearing where the house lay they saw two cars parked. Loretta pulled in alongside them, then turned to Willoghby. 'You'd best wait here.' She wrote a number in her notebook and tore out the page. 'Here, if we're not back out in ten minutes call that number and tell them DS Moran needs assistance. You can guide them in.' Nodding slowly, Willoghby took the page and reached for his mobile phone.

As Loretta and Houlihan got out, the door of the house opened and a man in a grey suit came towards them. Loretta put her head back inside the car and asked Willoghby if this was the man they'd handed Malloy over to.

'Yes. Definitely.'

The man stopped a few yards from the car, hands in pocket, short grey hair, tanned and fit-looking, around sixty, Loretta thought. He looked stern.

'This is private property.' American accent.

Loretta produced her badge and held it in front of him longer than she needed to. His expression didn't change. 'Who owns this private property?' she asked.

'A very private man. What do you want?'

'I want to see Eddie Malloy.'

'Who? No such person here.'

'So where is he? What did you do with him?'

'I've never heard of him, miss. You've come to the wrong place.'

'I've got a witness in the car who brought Mr Malloy here on March fifth and signed him over to your care.'

Hands still in pockets, the man ducked down. Willoghby stared at him. The man looked at Loretta again. 'Don't recognise him.'

'You've got a very short memory, Mr . . .?'

'Kidd.'

'Mr Kidd, if Eddie Malloy isn't here you won't mind if we search the house?'

'I won't mind at all if you have a search warrant.'

'I haven't got a warrant but if you want to just pass on the warrant then I won't add obstructing the police to suspicion of abduction when I arrest you.'

Kidd looked at her for a few moments, showing for the first time signs of uncertainty. 'I need to make a call.'

'Good. I'll come with you so I can speak to Keelor when you're done.'

Houlihan started walking towards the house. Kidd, looking alarmed, turned and called after him, 'Where are you going?'

'Inside.'

'You haven't got a warrant!'

Houlihan spoke without turning round. 'I don't need one. I'm not a policeman.'

They found Malloy in a room on the ground floor at the back of the house. He lay in bed with a drip attached to his arm. When Houlihan saw the burns damage to his friend's face he had to stop himself from recoiling in horror. Malloy lay staring blankly at the ceiling. When he blinked, Houlihan noticed that the only unscarred parts of his face were his eyelids.

Watched by Loretta and Kidd, he bent over and spoke quietly to his friend. 'Eddie. Eddie, it's Frankie. Frankie Houlihan. Come to take you home.'

Kidd claimed to be Malloy's doctor and the only one living in the house apart from Malloy and a maid who owned the other car parked outside. He denied that there had ever been guards of any kind keeping Malloy there. 'The poor guy'll be lucky to ever walk more than a hundred metres again in his life. He doesn't need a guard.'

Kidd claimed he'd just been treating Malloy for his injuries and trying to help him recover from the huge shock, which had caused amnesia. He admitted that Keelor was in charge and that they spoke daily. His orders were to call Keelor at any time, day or night, as soon as Malloy recovered his memory. Loretta arrested Kidd and called for support to have him taken away.

An ambulance arrived and Houlihan and Loretta walked beside the stretcher as Malloy was carried from the house. Malloy closed his eyes against the daylight, his grimace kaleidoscoping his facial scars. Houlihan was longing to lay a hand on his friend, offer him the comfort of touch, but he thought he might hurt him. Leaning over slightly he said to Malloy, 'We'll get you through, Eddie, you'll get your memory back.'

Malloy glanced up at him as they stopped at the entrance to the ambulance. Malloy said, 'Frankie, there hasn't been a day gone by since the fire without me wishing I had lost it.'

Frankie felt like smiling with relief but the sadness in his friend's eyes stopped him.

They took Malloy straight to hospital in London. During the journey, Malloy told them what had happened when he'd regained consciousness. He'd woken to find Keelor at his bedside, angry and anxious. The American started grilling him immediately.

'Remember that rucksack I brought to your house?' he asked Frankie. His friend nodded. 'There was a video tape in it, from Everest.'

'I know,' said Frankie. 'Loretta found it in your

locker.' He nodded towards Loretta. She smiled, still trying to balance her first impressions of Eddie with the picture she had built in her mind. One thing she did know; there was a charisma about him despite the terrible scarring. She was fascinated by his eyes, strangely symmetrical in that damaged face, the clear whites making the blue irises all the more vivid.

Malloy looked at her. 'What was on it?' he asked.

'Keelor, ignoring the advice of his guide. He bullied everybody. Tom Hutchison told him it was dangerous to go for the summit. Keelor overruled him. He got everybody killed.'

Eddie looked up at the ceiling for what seemed a long time. Frankie said, 'It was Keelor that threw the petrol bomb. Remember you dropped him at the airport that night? He never flew.'

Eddie looked puzzled. 'I put another video tape in the sack, there's no way Keelor could have known so quickly it was a fake. I mean, where could he have played it in the airport?'

'What was on the tape?' asked Frankie.

'It was blank. I bought a pack of five and doctored one, unspooled it, scratched the tape then ducked it in water, stuck it in the freezer for a couple of hours then put it in the sack. I thought there was a chance Keelor would think it had got damaged on the mountain.'

'Do you know American tapes are different from British ones?' Houlihan asked.

'Looked the same to me,' said Malloy.

'We work on what they call the PAL system; the American system is called NTSC. The system type is usually marked on the tape.'

Malloy shook his head slowly and almost smiled. 'So much for me being smart.'

'We all make mistakes,' said Loretta.

Malloy nodded. 'How do you know it was Keelor who threw the petrol bomb?'

'It's long odds-on, as you guys would say,' Loretta replied. 'We've got plenty of evidence but it's all circumstantial.'

Slowly, Malloy closed his eyes. Houlihan looked across at Loretta then down at Malloy. 'You tired, mate?'

Malloy nodded. 'We'll leave it now, then,' said Frankie. 'We can talk again tomorrow.'

Houlihan paid for a private room for Malloy in hospital, and Loretta arranged an all-night guard. They left hospital and went straight to Scotland Yard. Loretta filed her report and formally charged Kidd, ensuring he would remain in custody and out of touch with Keelor.

On the journey home they agreed that once Keelor knew they had the tape his legal team would do all they could to ensure it was kept from the public for years, if not forever. It contained nothing that could be considered as evidence that Keelor had done anything illegal, and they would claim it would be used only as a character assassination vehicle by his business enemies.

'But we've got to let Keelor know we've got the tape,' said Houlihan. 'And that we've got Eddie.'

'You think that'll keep him safe? It would be in Keelor's interests to see Eddie still being pursued. He'd argue that it's nothing to do with him, that it's the person with the grudge against him and Makalu, the person who's been trying to get this tape from Eddie so it can be used to embarrass Keelor.'

Houlihan sighed heavily and rubbed his eyes. 'So you're saying that despite everything we've got, we're no further forward?'

'What we need to find out is how did Mark Duncan and Tom Hutchison really die?'

They were at Malloy's bedside just after nine the next morning. They'd spent ten minutes with the doctor who had told them that Malloy's post-trauma treatment had obviously been excellent. He predicted that the combination of skin grafts, physiotherapy, and, possibly, psychotherapy might see Malloy regaining a very reasonable quality of life in the long-term. Houlihan left it at telling Malloy that the doctor thought he would eventually get back to full health.

Malloy smiled at the news. 'I've been fractured, fried and fucking frozen and I'm still here.' Houlihan chuckled; Loretta laughed.

Houlihan explained how difficult they thought it would be to nail Keelor through the legal system and he asked Malloy if there had ever been an inquiry about the death of Keelor's party on Everest.

'Not as far as I know.'

'So there was only ever Keelor's version of the truth?' asked Loretta.

'That's right. It was pretty straightforward; the storm killed them all. Keelor said he and Hutchison were the only ones to make it back to camp and that when he woke up in the morning, Hutchison was dead. Keelor claimed he'd stayed with Wayne – the kid – sheltered him with his body, and that when the kid died he had helped Hutchison get back to camp.'

'Bastard!' said Loretta and they both saw the anger in her eyes. 'Going by the tape he would have had a big interest in Mark Duncan's death. How did he say Mark died?'

'He said a Sherpa told him he'd seen Mark walk over the Kangshung face in the storm. That stacks up; it was on that side that Mark's rucksack was found.'

'Yes, but did he fall or was he pushed?' said Loretta. 'Keelor knew he had that tape. He probably wanted him dead more than anybody else. Is there any way his body could be recovered?'

'It's not impossible,' said Malloy. 'If you could get a big-enough party of Sherpas, they might take it on.'

Loretta looked at Houlihan. 'What do you think?'

'It would be a nightmare. We'd need his family's

permission. What if they wanted him left there? It's not as though we can just pitch up and say we think Keelor killed him.'

Malloy said, 'It's the time element too. It would be a bitch to organise. I think there's a better way to nail this guy.'

Houlihan and Loretta listened intently as Malloy explained his idea.

FORTY

Six days later, and fifteen months after his last triumphant visit, Eddie Malloy was back in the Makalu conference centre in San Francisco. He sat in a wheelchair at the front of the auditorium alongside two other disabled pressmen. His accreditation badge featured the name Collins. Houlihan sat one row behind him wearing a badge in the name of Crispin. Loretta's badge was in the name of Caspar. She stood at the top of the stairs, close to media control. She'd been the one who'd hovered around reception until she got sight of the guest list, then chosen three under the C heading.

As the lights went down, Loretta reached nervously inside her handbag where another badge was stashed. The badge said 'Carolyn Harding, Makalu Staff'. She had stolen it from a jacket in the ladies room. From her vantage point Loretta estimated there were close to seven hundred people in the theatre. Most of them applauded heartily when

Vaughn Keelor finally walked on stage. Loretta put on her staff badge.

When the introductory music died away, Keelor picked up the microphone. 'You lucky people!' A wave of chuckles. 'You know it's easier to get a ticket for the Super Bowl than it is to get in here. Welcome to the nineteenth annual Makalu press bash!' Another burst of music. More applause. For fifteen minutes Keelor talked about what Makalu had accomplished in the past year. As he began talking about the UK racing division, he did not notice below him Eddie Malloy being wheeled away by Frankie Houlihan. Malloy remembered the access points to the stage from his previous visit and Houlihan rolled him on from the wings. Keelor didn't see them until they were almost beside him in the spotlight and neither Malloy nor Houlihan would ever forget the look on Keelor's face as he recognised them.

At this point, Loretta made her move towards the Media Controller whom she'd already 'briefed'. Smiling widely she handed him the tape and said, 'This is our cue.'

So shocked was Keelor that he did not resist as Malloy reached and took the microphone from his hand. 'Ladies and gentlemen of the press, I'm Eddie Malloy. Until recently I headed up the UK racing operation Mr Keelor was talking about. I met Keelor on Everest in '96. He likes to tell the heroic tale of that expedition – you remember, the one that cost five of Keelor's party, including

Wayne Bachelor, a young kid, their lives?' At the use of his boss's surname only, the buzz in the room died quickly as the reporters' natural instinct kicked in and they sensed a story. Malloy continued, 'Well, you've heard him tell it, you've read his book, now see the movie.'

The lights went down. Loretta smiled her sexiest smile again at the Media Controller and, as he'd promised her, he ran the tape.

Keelor's global Makalu business imploded in a matter of days. He went into hiding. The families of those who had died in his party launched multimillion-dollar lawsuits. The attorney general announced that the FBI would be investigating the deaths during the expedition, and, three months later, Tom Hutchison's body was recovered from the crevasse Keelor had buried it in. The postmortem discovered that the guide had died from suffocation. A piece of down bearing both Hutchison's and Keelor's DNA, and originating from the lining of Keelor's right glove, was found in the guide's lungs. Vaughn Keelor was charged with murder and sentenced to life imprisonment. The body of Mark Duncan was never found.

With the collapse of the Makalu deal, the Jockey Club again took over the running of their thirteen racecourses, awaiting the resurrection of the deal with the underbidder to Keelor.

Frankie Houlihan took a six-month leave of absence from his security job to spend time helping

Eddie Malloy return to some form of normal life. He walks with Malloy (and Loretta, when she can make it) and every day they go a little bit further. Malloy has plans to get back into the mountains and to teach his friend to climb.

Houlihan visits his mother once a month. He has promised her that once his friend Malloy is well again he will speak to the Archbishop and take advice on returning to the priesthood. He hasn't yet been able to make himself promise to actually go back to his vocation but his family are happy again.

Houlihan knows deep down that the reason he can't make that promise is Loretta Moran. Loretta knows this too but they don't talk about it. They just keep seeing each other, using Eddie Malloy's rehab as an excuse. Loretta is there often to help out, and a deeply selfish part of her hopes Eddie will never get better.

She has always sworn it would never be this way for her, and, sometimes, as they share yet another platonic meal or an outing, she says to Frankie Houlihan, 'I wish I could quit you.'

And Houlihan always says, 'Sometimes I wish I could quit me too.'